A TIMELESS Romance ANTHOLOGY

Road Trip Collection

Copyright © 2016 by Mirror Press, LLC
Print edition
All rights reserved

No part of this book may be reproduced in any form whatsoever without prior written permission of the publisher, except in the case of brief passages embodied in critical reviews and articles. This is a work of fiction. The characters, names, incidents, places, and dialogue are products of the authors' imaginations and are not to be construed as real.

Interior Design by Heather Justesen
Edited by Julie Ogborn and Lisa Shepherd

Cover design by Mirror Press, LLC
Cover Photo Credit: Shutterstock #305638093
Cover Photo Copyright: EpicStockMedia

Published by Mirror Press, LLC
http://timelessromanceanthologies.blogspot.com

ISBN-10: 1-947152-06-8
ISBN-13: 978-1-947152-06-9

Road Trip Collection

Jolene Betty Perry

Sarah M. Eden

Raneè S. Clark

Annette Lyon

Heather B. Moore

Aubrey Mace

More Timeless Romance Anthologies

Winter Collection
Spring Vacation Collection
Summer Wedding Collection
Autumn Collection
European Collection
Love Letter Collection
Old West Collection
Summer in New York Collection
Silver Bells Collection
All Regency Collection
Annette Lyon Collection
Sarah M. Eden British Isles Collection
Under the Mistletoe Collection
Mail Order Bride Collection
Blind Date Collection
Valentine's Day Collection
Happily Ever After Collection

Table of Contents

What Falling Feels Like   1
by Jolene Betty Perry

Antiques Road Trip   62
by Sarah M. Eden

Wouldn't It Be Nice   116
by Raneè S. Clark

Head Over Heels   172
by Annette Lyon

Two Dozen Roses   228
by Heather B. Moore

Try, Try Again   284
by Aubrey Mace

What Falling Feels Like

By Jolene Betty Perry

To Afton, the real owner of Camp Fancy.

Chapter One

Kendell

These are not the shoulders that Tyler Brady had back in high school. The way his T-shirt stretches over the muscles of his chest and shoulders is the first indication. And it's not even a normal T-shirt. It's one of those with the baseball sleeves and buttons at the neck. This means that he put a little more effort into dressing than grabbing the first clean thing out of the dryer. Even his jeans are dark washed and sit low on his hips. My best friend's little brother is now bigger than me. I'm standing on his porch, and all I can think is that six in the morning is far too early for this kind of shock.

"Kendell?" he asks with his new, husky voice.

Okay, fine. Tyler had that voice back in high school. But, when he was so skinny I felt like I could haul him over my shoulder, his voice didn't vibrate in my stomach like it does now.

"Hmm?" I drag my eyes back to his face.

"You okay?"

"Yep." I'm totally not okay. I tuck a stray, frizzy curl behind my ear. Really, I could have at least showered this morning before coming to pick Tyler up for our trip. It's just that five thirty came so fast. Curse Ivy for not preparing me for her little brother's transformation.

"My furniture pieces are in the garage," Tyler says. "You're ready for me to load them in your truck, right?"

His brown eyes have these little gold flecks in them. Did they always? "Yeah. Load. Fine."

He chuckles. "You never were much of a morning person."

"Nope." I try to laugh back, but laughing is harder after a pathetically failed marriage—especially when you're twenty-two, everyone warned you, and the marriage doesn't even make it a year.

"Um . . ." His brows do this pinching thing that used to bump his glasses up. The glasses are gone, of course.

I have to stop staring.

"Sorry," I say. "It's early, and I haven't seen you in ages."

"Oh, right." He gives me a quick half hug—just long enough for my hand to touch that nice shoulder of his and for whatever cologne he's wearing to jump-start my imagination, sending it to places it has no business going right now.

I turn around on his porch, still in a daze, really wishing that I'd at least put on non-stained sweatpants or done *anything* to make me not look like a complete bum.

Ivy is so getting a call . . . once it's not so early that she has every right to kill me for waking her up.

When I pulled in, I angled my shiny, new blue truck so that Tyler could get his furniture into the bed without bumping into my newest creation—a 1978 Coachmen trailer that has been restored to Camp Fancy glory: The systems. The electrical. The paint. From the curtains and knobs on the inside, to the new tires on the outside—this baby is prettier now than when she was born. I call her Trina, and in about fifteen hundred miles, she'll be dropped off at her new home.

I pat the cool metal on the front. "You are just beautiful," I say.

"Um . . ." Tyler stops, holding a large desk in front of him.

What Falling Feels Like

But before he can comment on how personal I just got with Trina, I climb into the bed of the truck. "I can help from here."

"Great," he says before using those perfect arms of his to lift the desk high enough for me to help.

I run my hand over the smooth wood as Tyler heads back to his open garage door. His home seems out of place on this Bellevue street of large, suburban homes—like a modern house dropped into the middle of a long line of cloned houses. I mean, it's very *Seattle*—all grey, steel cables for railings, and stained cedar planks—the perfect blend of modern and rustic, just like the desk beneath my hands. The wood on the desk is old, I know that much, but I'm not sure where he got the metal for the legs. By the looks of the rivets, he salvaged the legs from some kind of old equipment.

"Ready?" he asks, standing next to the truck again with two chairs.

No . . . No, I'm not ready. My brain won't keep up with the action. "Yeah."

I tuck the desk as close to the cab of the truck as I can before reaching back and helping him with the two chairs. This early in the morning and this late in the fall, we only have street lamps for light.

"This is a nice truck," he says.

"Yeah. I pretty much sold my soul for the start-up of Camp Fancy."

A brow quirks up as he asks, "Camp Fancy?"

"You know." I point back to the Coachmen. "I restore campers and trailers. Sell them."

"Right." His eyes hold mine for a second. I still can't wrap my head around this being skinny, gawky *Tyler Brady*. "Ivy said."

I almost open my mouth again to ask him what else Ivy has told him about me lately but stop just shy of mortal embarrassment.

As he walks back toward his garage, it hits me that the last time I actually saw and spoke to him was *four years ago*. I was one year out of high school then. He was a senior, and his prom date had just backed out on him.

Guilt clamps down on my heart. If I remember right, I sort of laughed when he begged me to take her place and then said that he had to be joking . . . But I was prom queen my senior year. To go back the next year as geeky Tyler Brady's date felt too horrible to consider. So I totally deserve the sinking feeling in my gut right now—it's a feeling I should have had back then.

Why did I ever care what people at my old high school would have thought if I'd gone with the brother of my best friend? With *my* friend?

As Tyler makes it back to my truck, heat spreads up my neck and across my cheeks.

"You don't seem . . . well," he says. His dark, shaggy hair isn't shaggy anymore but neatly trimmed and pushed back off a face I barely recognize.

I'm just in a weird, messy place this morning, and I need to snap out of it.

I wave him away. "Fine. So totally fine." I reach down and help him slide over the coolest counter-height table I've ever seen—more of what has to be his signature style of reclaimed pieces combined to make a new whole.

Three more loads and a few minutes wrapping a tarp and rope around his furniture, and I'm in the truck.

"Thanks again," Tyler says as he climbs in the passenger's seat.

"No problem." I turn on the truck, and the engine roars to life. His cologne has wafted through the cab, making my stomach flutter again. This is going to be the longest two days . . .

"It's just that the dealership Ivy's husband works at, in Albuquerque, had the exact truck I wanted, and then the furniture delivery coincided with your Fancy Camper thing . . ." Tyler adjusts his seatbelt over his shoulder and then smooths his hand across the belt that rests on his very nice chest.

Must. Stop. Staring. "I'm glad it worked out," I tell him, even though I'm not at all sure I'm glad.

There are a few beats of silence as I start out of his neighborhood. I steal a glance back at his very cool house. I'd love to see the inside.

"So, it's been a while . . . since I've seen you," he says.

"Just before your prom." I swallow.

He glances out the window and shifts in his seat slightly. "I remember."

"I . . ." I start to say but don't know how to finish. There's no good way to try and explain to this new version of Tyler what was going through my head at that point in time, just a week or two before I left for Europe.

"So, Ken-doll, how you been?"

Ah. The nickname. Tyler never used to use that. "You can ask me anything but that."

Tyler's mouth twitches into a frown.

But I just . . . How can I sit next to this now insanely handsome man, knowing I could have dated him?

I've gained so much weight since my divorce that I'm now down to one pair of jeans that fit, and I can't talk about Anton without crying. I'm afraid to talk about anything since high school, and talking *about* high school will just be a horrible reminder of what a follower, puppy dog Tyler used to be and how much nicer I could have been to him.

"Sorry." I flip on my turn signal at the roundabout and manage to jolt the camper by not giving myself enough space on the corner. I'm a better driver than this.

What on earth are we going to do to pass the time?

"You know what?" I say. "I wanna know what you've been

up to, I just . . ." I blink, and his eyes are still on me: Curious. Inquisitive. Maybe even a little guarded.

"That doesn't really seem fair, Ken-doll." His voice is teasing, but there's enough of a bite in his tone that I shrink in my seat.

Instead of looking at him, I stare back out at the road. We're about to hit the freeway, so I have an excuse not to look at him. I'm driving. And then I wonder, *How much did Ivy tell her brother?* But I probably don't want to know.

"I want to know what makes a girl leave her home and her family and hook up with a crazy Italian," he says.

Kill me now.

Chapter Two

Tyler

Kendell Adams looks so . . . different. And it's not that she's finally shed the stick figure shape that made her look as if she'd blow away in a fierce wind. Or that her blonde, messy hair makes her as gorgeous as it ever did. But she's so . . . guarded and quiet. She's made eye contact maybe twice. I never thought I'd see her *broken*.

It's petty and stupid, but I know I've been unusually successful for my age. And yes, after she so thoroughly rebuffed me, I wanted her to see what she missed out on. I followed Ivy and Kendell like a lame little brother when I was in high school. But there were times, when everyone else was gone, that Kendell treated me like an equal. And then, for her to not understand how much I needed her for my prom . . . The sting of rejection is as familiar as the memory.

Yes, high school politics are stupid. No, in the grand scheme of my life, skipping prom didn't matter. But I missed both valedictorian and salutatorian by a sliver of a hair, and then my date backed out of prom.

Kendell should have known me well enough to know that I needed her. And now, I don't know what to make of her. She ran away, turned her back on everyone, and married some ego-filled artist. I still don't get it. I don't get her.

She coughs. "Oh, you know . . . I'd always wanted to travel." She flits her small hand up flippantly, like she just woke up one morning and decided to go to Europe, but that can't be the whole story.

"I remember that about you." Pathetically, I remember everything about her. I remember how she used to eat three pieces of café pizza on pizza days because they'd serve the rectangle pieces like we had in elementary. I remember that she doesn't like to drink caffeine. And I remember how she bites the inside of her cheek when she's terrified. In fact, she's doing it now. Probably because I'm being a jerk.

Kendell sighs. "I don't think that anything I remember about you would do me any good in getting to know you now."

As she gestures up the length of my body, an unwanted rush of warmth floods through my body. She just admitted to noticing me.

"You were really good at shop," she says. "I had no idea you'd make a career out of it."

"Me either," I tell her. "After you . . . *left* . . . Ivy moved to Albuquerque, and I followed for a while. I ended up at this furniture store—Rustic Creations—and looked at what people paid thousands for and knew I could do that."

"So you did."

"So I did."

"That's . . ." She swallows. "It's really impressive. Your pieces are great."

I rub my hands over my face. This isn't what I wanted from her. I wanted her to push back when I asked about her ex and her impromptu running away to Europe. I wanted her to show me the same attitude that finally convinced me she wasn't a good person for me to be heartbroken over after high school. But she's just . . . She's no longer the type of girl who would punch my bony shoulder with her knuckle and laugh about it.

Swallowing again, I start to wonder how much was taken from her. Instead of asking her anything else, I slump in my seat and look at the passing landscape as we move farther and farther from Seattle.

There's something about sitting next to my old high school crush that's taken away a bit of my ability to feel like my new self. I've spent a stupid amount of time today checking my email and listening to messages I've already heard, just to show her how busy and important I've become.

Kendell has checked her phone too—about twice a minute—but she never actually touches anything on it, so I have no idea . . . I have no idea about anything. The brown landscape of eastern Washington is numbing my brain.

"Do you think your sister is awake yet?" Kendell suddenly asks.

"Um . . . I have no idea."

"So . . ." Her gaze flits sideways to me so fast that I almost miss it. "So you two don't talk much?"

"What is *much*?"

"Uh . . . Never mind." She shakes her head and then tucks hair behind her ears, almost like she's one of the shy girls from high school instead of the Great Kendell Adams. "Stupid question," she mumbles.

Oh-kay. I want to call her on being weird. On being different from what I remember. But I'm worried she'll crack if I poke too hard. Ask too much. Tease her.

"Let's stop," she says.

I scan the rolling hills around us. "Where?"

"There's a spot just up here. I've driven this direction a lot since I started Camp Fancy." Her voice sounds stilted, and her knuckles are white on the steering wheel.

"Want me to drive for a bit when we get going again?"

She readjusts in her seat about four times and finally says, "Yeah. Sure."

This is the oddest situation I've been in for a very long time.

Chapter Three

Kendell

I should probably be locked up in an asylum. Tyler, I'm sure, thinks I've completely lost my marbles.

Maybe I have. I've been checking my phone repeatedly for any indication that Ivy is awake, even though I can't actually talk to her while sitting next to her brother. The second I stop next to the gas pumps, I grab my phone and jump out of the car, texting Ivy first thing.

You owe me a phone call. Like, now.

Just before I try to slip my credit card into the pump, Tyler reaches around me with his new manly arms and runs his card instead. "You can get the next."

I just stare . . . because, apparently, I'm now mute around maybe the only guy I have never put on pretenses for. Tyler leans against the bed of the truck while it fills up, and then my phone rings.

"Oh! Shoot!" I jerk it from my pocket so fast that it flies into the air. I catch it only by slamming my hand and phone against the side of my new car. Flinching, I say a silent prayer that I didn't scratch the blue paint.

Tyler just stares at me, one eye open slightly larger than the other in a *she's-turned-completely–nuts* kind of way.

Clearing my throat, I step back and clutch my phone. "I'll be back."

Silence.

I accept the call, and Ivy's voice immediately pipes in. "So, how's it going?"

"I am so furious with you right now," I say through my teeth as I jog toward the small gas station. The people in there can think I'm as insane as they want to think, but I can't have this conversation within earshot of Tyler.

"What?" Ivy laughs. "What are you talking about?"

"You said that your brother was doing well, but you didn't tell me he's now . . . he's now . . ."

"Actually not bad looking? Less dorky?"

"Yes!" I shout, and the woman next to me scowls before turning away.

"I totally have, Ken. You just don't listen."

"What?"

"I told you that he'd gotten stronger from all the building. I told you he was successful."

"*Successful* and *lives in the nicest house on a really nice street* are two totally different things."

"Are you finally interested in him?"

"What? *Finally?* What are you talking about?"

"When you slept over, you two used to sit up and play video games long after I went to sleep."

"We did?" No, wait. I do sort of remember that. But he was just . . . dorky little Tyler.

"You know what? You two enjoy the drive. He's met some pretty cool people. Built furniture for names you'd recognize."

I want to crawl into a hole because I'm being the worst, most superficial version of myself right now. All that I can think is that a girl with my status in high school should be in his position and that he should be in mine. How have I not matured past that yet?

What Falling Feels Like

"I have a sneaking suspicion that I'm not at all good enough for your brother."

"Ken?" Tyler calls from the front door. "You ready?"

"Gotta go," I say just before hanging up. I plaster on something that feels like it's maybe a smile, but again, my brain isn't working right. "Ready. Yes."

"I'm going to get you a coffee, okay?"

"Sure. I like—"

"Decaf and three of those fake Irish cream plastic thingies?" he asks. "If that's still in effect, I remember."

Tears well up in my eyes. Anton never knew these simple things about me. Ever. And I *married* him. I could be the dumbest woman on the planet. If Tyler is half as nice as he used to be, he's definitely out of my league.

"Bathroom," I croak. "I'll be out in a sec."

After a couple long minutes of staring into the mirror, I decide that walking into the bathroom was a mistake. I'm a worse disaster than I thought. My hair is wild and messy with curls and not in the cute way but in the frizzy, bed-head way. There are also circles under my eyes, and my face is in serious need of a facial. I admit now that I didn't even bother with makeup this morning because it was *just Tyler* and that my stained white shirt, which says SOMETHING INTERESTING HERE, really needs to be thrown out.

Why did I think it was okay to leave the house looking like this, unless I was sick? The old me never would have allowed this to happen. So, there are some things about the old me that I don't love, but really . . . I could use a little bit of her right now.

I turn on the faucet and run my hands under the warm water.

Using the dampness of my hands, I try and scrunch my hair to help my curls look less like frizz, and more like curls.

My mouth dips into a frown. My hair is now wet, frizzy, *and* the blonde curls are half straight. Maybe a ponytail would hide the mess. I slip my hands into my worn pockets and come up empty.

"Could this be any worse?"

"Best not to ask that, dear," someone says from inside one of the stalls.

"Um. Thanks?"

I can't look at myself in the mirror any longer. Shoving out of the bathroom, I'm resigned to feeling like a puddle of regret. When I step outside, the sun hits me, and I wince, cupping my hands over my eyes. Then I spot my truck and the Camp Fancy trailer off to the side of the parking lot.

How long has Tyler been waiting?

I just need to get through the next few days. Hopefully Tyler won't stick around his sister's house so I can enjoy my visit. And Tyler, fortunately, will be driving his new truck home instead of riding with me.

"Two days, Kendell. Two days," I climb up to the passenger's seat, Tyler's yummy smell wafting around me again.

"Is your hair wet?" he asks, an incredulous tone in his voice.

"Long story," I say and leave it at that.

Chapter Four

Tyler

Thirty minutes after leaving the gas station, Kendell's fingers haven't stopped flying over her phone.

"Everything okay over there?" I ask.

Her body doesn't move, and her eyes don't lift from her phone. "Texting your sister."

"And, how is she?"

"What?"

"How is she?" I ask again.

"We haven't gotten to that part yet."

Girls baffle me.

She's back to typing, her feet now on the seat. Her shoes are on the floor, of course. Kendell always rode that way.

"It couldn't have been that big a deal," she grumbles.

"Can I help with something?"

I'm dying of boredom here. We've barely spoken. I figured that it would be like old times with Kendell—only I did, admittedly, want to rub in some of my success.

She types into her phone for a second more and then sets it on the console between us. Face down.

"I wanted to apologize for something," she says.

"What?" Today or years ago, or . . .

"Your prom," she says.

All the air in the cab of the truck thickens. "What?"

"It was really just . . . I should have gone with you. My stupid ego, the one that got me into so much trouble, stopped me. I'm sorry."

This isn't like Kendell either, but maybe in a good way. I feel the fuzzy edges of excitement around my ribs—like I used to whenever Kendell was around.

Not a good idea.

"Oh," is all I manage.

"It's that . . . I was stupid and selfish, and even your sister thinks so, and I was mad at her for it, but she was right. I half knew it back then, but I didn't want to think about how I let you down. And I definitely know it now."

"That was high school, Ken."

"And that's what I thought at the time. But we were friends, right?"

My mouth dries out. How many hours of my life have I spent thinking about Kendell Adams?

"Yeah," I answer. "I mean, sort of."

"More than sort of," she says. "You're a night owl like me."

I chuckle a little. "Still am."

"We should have started this venture at noon instead of 5:00 a.m., huh?"

"Maybe, yeah," I agree.

"Okay. So, sorry."

"It's okay, Ken," I say, and in a weird way, it is. Even just her acknowledging that she didn't make the best decision helps me to forgive her.

She rubs her face and then curls up on the seat.

"What happened after that?" I ask. "Why did you just take off?"

"Kind of a long story involving my parents," she says.

Wasn't expecting that. Wonder if I'll get the full story.

"I'm going to try and get some sleep."

Guess not.

I take another long drink of my soda since I'm definitely going to need the caffeine.

A raindrop hits the windshield, and then another one. *Bummer.* This time of year, up in the mountains, rain turns into ice, turns into snow. So our stellar driving conditions may have just taken a turn for the worse.

An hour of Pandora and a sleeping Kendell has my brain as fuzzed as the noise of the tires on the pavement.

Kendell's phone rings, and she snaps awake.

Ring is not exactly the right term. It sounds more like some kind of foghorn.

"Hey, Mom," she mumbles. "Bad weather?" Kendell blinks a few times, taking in the rain and slush slapping onto the windshield.

"Just the last seventy miles or so," I say quietly.

Kendell nods once. "Yeah, Mom. It's not so bad . . . We might stop early . . . It's going fine . . . Yes . . ." Kendell's body shifts, and she glances my direction twice before looking out the passenger's side window. "We *all* change, Mom . . . I know . . ."

Are they talking about me? Instead of sitting as still and silent as I'd like, I let out a sigh and fiddle with temperature dials, all the while trying to pick up snips of their conversation.

"I'm fine, Mom . . . No, I haven't talked to Anton. Why would I?" Kendell rubs her forehead. "Um . . . You seriously want to have this conversation now? Of course I'm not going to be a hermit for the rest of my life. I'm not a hermit now. I'm in Idaho, on my way to New Mexico."

I can just make out Kendell's mom's voice but not her words.

"Mom, seriously, can we not talk about this?" Her voice gets tight enough at the end of the sentence that my ribs squeeze together in concern. "Please?" she whispers.

It takes everything in me not to turn and face her, but I still see her swipe at her eyes. So I hold out my hand, and Kendell immediately sets the phone in it.

"Hey, Mrs. Adams!" I laugh, trying to play like this is all some great game. "Sorry that I stole your daughter's phone, but it's not like you can really have a serious conversation when she's in the car with someone, right?" I laugh a little again.

"Oh, hi Tyler!" she yelps. "How are you? I hear that things for you are just going so fantastic! And, I got remarried, so I'm Mrs. Delaney now!"

Kendell sits up taller, flips down the visor, and checks herself in the mirror. *So very Kendell*. But the way her mouth dips down makes me wonder what she sees that I don't.

"I forgot. Congratulations."

"Thank you!" Kendell's mom says, sounding more like the old version of Kendell than Kendell does now.

"The guy who gave me my first break selling furniture pieces asked me for a few more, and the timing just worked out. It was so nice of your daughter to let me tag along on her delivery."

I glance over at Kendell as she flips the visor shut and sits sideways to face me.

Thank you, she mouths.

No prob, I mouth back.

"You two drive safe, okay? I know funds are tight for Kendell right now. So, if you need a hotel, tell her she can use my credit card, okay?"

All I've seen of Kendell is the trailer she had to have put a bit of money into, and the truck, though she did say something earlier about selling her soul for it. At the time, her comment felt like a fun little joke.

"I got it covered, Mrs. *Delaney*, don't worry."

"Always a gentleman, Tyler."

"Great chatting. I'm going to focus on the road now so your daughter can get some more rest."

"Okay then. You tell her to text me when you two are settled for the night."

"Will do," I say and hang up before she can ask to talk to Kendell again. Obviously, Kendell isn't really in the mood to chat with her mom.

"Isn't it amazing how one person, even with seemingly good intentions, can make you feel about this big?" Kendell pinches her fingers together. "And she doesn't even mean to."

"I'm sorry."

Kendell shakes her head. "I think she's still mad."

"About what?"

The way that Kendell's arms wrap around her middle says that she doesn't want to answer.

"Sorry," I say.

"My dad had been lecturing me about responsibility and starting a life for myself," she begins to explain. "And then I went to his office one day, and he and the other manager he worked with . . . They jumped apart, and he tried to make it seem like no big deal or like they were *just talking*. But you can tell when something else is going on, you know?"

Wow. "I knew your parents divorced," I say, "but I didn't know why."

"And so, I wanted to do the stupidest, most irresponsible thing I could do under the guise of adventure and growing up and all that. But I really just bought a ticket, got an international plan on my phone, and left."

"That's so . . . brave," I finish. And it was. I can't imagine moving to a new place without a lot of research and planning.

"Or it's just . . ." she trails off. Her knees tuck closer to her chest again, and she bites on her thumbnail. "It obviously didn't lead to anything good, you know? So that's a big, lovely *I told you so* for Mom."

I can see Kendell's mom saying that. Maybe Kendell's mom is what happens when someone like Kendell doesn't mature after high school.

"Well, you just keep handing that phone over to me then, okay?" I tease.

But Kendell scowls and then says, "I can handle it, but thanks."

And that's the strength of the girl I remember.

Instead of continuing to ask Kendell about her life or her mom, I just drive. There's a lot more going on there than I can help with on a two-day drive. And she clearly doesn't want my help anyway.

Chapter Five

Kendell

I can't believe that Mom would be pulling a *now-that-you-have-a-nice-eligible-boy-in-the–car*, on me, and then add, *you should pull out whatever you used to nab that Anton.*

I need to scream. And, yes, I'm grateful to Tyler for distracting Mom.

Mom and I both know that I'd be in about half as much debt and heartbreak if I'd handled more things with Anton than I did. He always just said, "Let me take care of this." And, pretty soon, all I did was smile and sleep with him and cook his meals . . . I'm not sure how that happened. Without falling into working on campers, I'm not sure how I'd have survived this last year.

Another hour or two or three passes in near silence, except for the sound of the tires on the road and the slush on the windshield. As the fading light turns to black, I see a construction sign out of the corner of my eye. We hit a bump, and the truck lurches forward, the trailer making a jolting sound behind us.

"Whoa," Tyler says. "Not my fault! I swear!"

"It's fine."

As he flips on the blinker to change lanes, the signal does that frantic blinking thing that lights do when there's an electrical problem somewhere.

"Crap," I say, letting out a sigh. "You need to pull over. The problem is probably on the trailer."

He peers outside. "In this? Can't it wait?"

"I really can't have anyone accidentally running into the rear of this trailer seeing as it has already been paid for."

"Fair enough." Tyler peers through the rain again. "It's not a real rest stop, but I just saw a sign for a scenic outlook."

I reach into the backseat and grasp my small tool kit. "That'll have to work."

The rain is now part slush and part snow. But I don't want Tyler to think that I'm completely incompetent. I taught myself how to rewire the campers, so I know I can fix this. I readjust my headlamp and crouch lower. At home, I just sit on the floor to work on the low taillights, but with the slush under my feet, that won't work. My legs begin to shake with the strain.

I shiver again as the water soaks through my thin coat. When I was packing for this trip, making sure that I had my winter coat on top hadn't seemed important. Now that I'm in the mountains between Boise and Salt Lake, or wherever we are, it seems pretty obvious: the winter coat that I brought just for this part of the drive should be *accessible* during this part of the drive.

"Here." Tyler sets his coat on my shoulders.

The warmth immediately helps the shaking in my hands still, and I pull the housing for the light out of the back of the trailer, releasing a breath when I see the detached wire. A simple fix.

Tyler has already unplugged the trailer from the truck, so I don't have to worry about being electrocuted. I reach in and start twisting the wires together again.

Tyler leans forward, shining his headlamp into the small space as well.

What Falling Feels Like

Like an idiot, I take another long breath in, soaking up as much of him as I can get. Another round of shivers racks through me, and I jerk a little, undoing some of my work.

"Why don't we just drive and fix this tomorrow?" Tyler suggests.

"I almost have it."

"You're freezing, Ken. It's dark."

"I said I almost have it." I reach in again and start twisting. And then I slide the housing back into place and start to screw it in from the outside. I'm shaking, shivering so hard that my hand slips. And then it slips again.

Tyler crouches next to me. "I don't know electricity, but I can handle this part, okay?"

But I keep working, determined to show Tyler that I'm not as helpless as I seem.

"Ken. Please."

"Almost got it." A few more twists and the housing tightens back up.

"Okay. I'm driving," Tyler says. "Climb in. You need to warm up."

I try to stand, but my legs have frozen stiff. Tyler hoists me back to a standing position. He rests his arm on my lower back as he walks with me to my side of the truck, but I shrug away from him. I can do things on my own.

"I said I'm fine."

"*Fine.*" He takes a step back, and starts for his side.

My fingers grasp at the handle, slipping twice. I can barely even feel the handle. Am I holding it hard enough? I jerk again, and the door flips open, sending me flying backwards. I grab the door just before my feet nearly slide out from underneath me. Tyler leans across the cab, reaching his hand toward me.

Reluctantly, I let him help as I step up into the truck.

"You're freezing. I know that you wanted to get farther than we're going to get tonight, but we need to stop so that you can warm up."

I want to disagree, to tell him that I'm fine, but I can't stop my teeth from chattering. My socks are soaked through, so I pull off my shoes. But just touching the tread makes my hands ache because they're so sensitive from the cold. My feet burn enough that I know they're freezing too.

"Why do you have to be so stubborn, Ken," I mumble to myself to break the silence.

Tyler chuckles next to me. "Because you wouldn't be Kendell if you weren't."

No, I think. *That was the old me.* But maybe he's bringing out some of the old Kendell, some of the parts I've missed.

Chapter Six

Tyler

As we dash into the lobby of the small hotel together, Kendell is shaking so violently that I'm wondering if I should take her to a hospital.

"Ken?" I ask. "Do we need to worry about hypothermia or anything?"

Her teeth chatter as she says, "Shower."

"We have four rooms left," the guy at the front desk says. "But please say that you only need one."

"What? Why?" I ask.

"The weather," he says flatly, like I should have caught on. "I expect we'll get a few more last-minute guests stopping in tonight."

Yeah. He's probably right. "One room is fine."

"Separate beds, then?" he asks.

"Please."

Though, with how Kendell is shivering, part of my Boy Scout training is coming back to me. The idea that climbing naked into a sleeping bag together fights off hypothermia is . . . Is far too distracting a thought. I do not have time for that right now.

As soon as our room cards are handed over, I wrap Kendell against me. She needs to get warm again.

The second we're in our room I start the shower on hot, in the hope that bringing the whole room to a warmer temperature will help.

"I'm okay," she chatters, reaching for her bag.

Instead of letting her take it, I bring the small duffel into the bathroom and set it on the wide counter. "Just take some help, Ken. You look miserable."

"Cotton," she says, her voice shaking. "Freezing 'cause I wore cotton."

Now she's in the bathroom, and I'm in the bathroom, and fog is covering the mirror. She looks so . . . fragile.

"Okay. Get warm. Take your time," I say as I back out of the room, her eyes fixed on me.

This is nothing like what I expected from Kendell when Ivy first mentioned the idea of us riding together. I watched her fix that light, which would have taken me about five times longer with triple or quadruple the cursing. But she didn't hesitate and knew what she was doing.

And then, on the phone with her mom, she was a mess. Though, it's not like I've ever loved anyone enough to get married or been heartbroken enough to get a divorce. So maybe that changes someone in ways I don't understand.

I want to understand.

After forty-five minutes, Kendell is still in the bathroom.

I knock twice just to ask if she's still okay, so she probably thinks I'm a pervert or a weirdo or both.

Unfortunately, the TV isn't providing enough of a distraction from how worried I am.

In a burst of steam, Kendell steps out of the bathroom in

leggings and a sweatshirt. All of her straightness from high school has turned into smooth, perfect curves.

"I know I'm too fat for these," she says, "but I'm freezing, and they're comfortable."

I'm so baffled by her comment that it takes me a moment to recover. "I'm sorry, what?"

"Never mind. Crazy that I'm still cold, right?"

"Never, ever think you're fat, Ken. Look at you. You're perfect." My cheeks start to burn as soon as the words are out. "I'm sorry. I'm just . . . Look at you. I can't figure out how you could say that."

"Oh, whatever." She rolls her eyes. "Sometimes people eat instead of dealing with their broken hearts."

I know broken hearts. I will never forget how I felt when Ivy called to tell me that Kendell got married. I knew at some point I'd tell Kendell how I felt about her, but I didn't even know she was involved with anyone when I learned that she'd gotten *married*. My chance had been stolen and now . . . Now she's a mix of my friend, and someone I don't yet know or understand.

"You got quiet," she says as she rips apart the blankets on her bed and starts to make a nest around herself.

"Just remembering something," I tell her, flipping through the channels again.

"*Something* . . . That's very mysterious of you to say." Her shoulders convulse in another shiver.

"Was just remembering when you got married and how surprised I was."

"You and me both." She rolls her eyes. "Falling that hard and fast is a high I'll never forget, but I will also never forget how much it hurt."

She's still shivering.

"Kendell." I stand and take the two steps to her bed before sitting down. "I'm worried that you're still cold. You shouldn't still be shivering."

"You going to offer to be a good Boy Scout now?" she teases with a laugh.

How? How could she even know that this is where my mind had already gone?

"Relax. I'm teasing." She shakes her head. "I just remember that when you were in Scouts, you made a joke once . . . Never mind."

Instead of being smart and asking first, I move her nest over slightly and sit down, pulling her against me. "Just be good and snuggle in for a few, okay?"

Kendell's still for a minute or two, but then her body softens against mine, her head resting more fully on my chest. I never want to move.

Blinking in the flickering lights of the TV, I start to shift when my whole body suddenly aches.

Kendell lets out a soft moan and rolls away from me, her head leaving my chest. She grabs a few blankets, bringing them up to her chin, and then her body stills again.

3:00 a.m.

I slide off the bed. My shoulders are stiff. My hips are stiff. My chest feels cold where Kendell's head was just resting. But I'd pick stiffness over going to the empty bed next to hers. Still, it feels weird to slide in next to her again.

After changing from my jeans into sweatpants, I lie in my bed and stare at the ceiling. I leave the TV on, and the light flickering on the ceiling helps to numb my brain, but not enough for my thoughts to stop racing.

In my twenty-two years, I've only told four girls I loved them. One is my mom. Another is my sister. But one is the girl sleeping in the bed next to mine, though she wasn't awake at the time. The fourth girl was someone I dated right after I learned that Kendell was married. I jumped into that relationship headfirst, but there came a point where we both just knew we weren't going to continue to be a thing. I couldn't have asked for an easier breakup. But, sometimes, a guy just misses having *somebody* after knowing what it's like.

And now, the impossible, the unreachable, is maybe within my reach. But I don't know . . . Maybe we've both changed too much. Or maybe we haven't changed enough. Maybe I need to turn off the TV and go to sleep.

Chapter Seven

Kendell

So, I'm pretty sure I fell asleep on Tyler last night, but he's in his own bed and still sacked out. He probably needed his space.

Today, I get a do-over. Yesterday, I was a mess, but today, I can be a new, confident me.

I may be recently divorced and heart-broken, but couldn't that also mean I now have the experience of someone five to ten years older? And I run my own company. Okay, fine. I just started running my own company, but it's still an accomplishment.

So, maybe today, instead of talking about personal stuff, I'll talk about Camp Fancy.

After thirty minutes in the bathroom, I feel a shade more like my old self, and it's fantastic. My long blonde hair is the good kind of straight-messy. And, for the first time in a month, I put on makeup. I grin at myself in the mirror, not with a small smile or a polite smile or the smile I stick on for my mom so that she won't worry, but with a real smile.

I step back out into the room. The TV is on, and Tyler is spread eagle on the bed with his chin resting on his hands, just like he always used to do.

In this second, I remember we're not strangers.

What Falling Feels Like

Yesterday, I was worried about all the wrong things. I didn't want to look like a failure in front of him. I didn't want to let him see me cry—because of what? Because he suddenly looks different on the outside? He's probably the same old Tyler, with a few years of experience. I'm the one whose insides have been mashed up. I always look forward to talking to his sister, and there was a time when Tyler was involved in most of our conversations just because he was around.

Getting ready this morning almost feels like a waste of time, but honestly, I'm in a much better headspace, so it wasn't really a waste. How many more good days could I have had over the past six months with a few extra minutes in the morning? My attention goes back to the TV.

"Still into car shows, huh?"

"Oh!" Tyler says as he scrambles into a sitting position. His eyes don't leave me for a second. This is the old Tyler I remember.

"Bathroom's all yours. I'll go check us out."

"No." Tyler jumps up. "I've got it."

I shake my head. "This is my trip more than yours. I'll pay for the room."

Tyler's mouth dips into a frown. "But your mother said—"

This is when I'd normally crumple. When the reminders would become too much for me to deal with.

"My mom's worried about my financial situation because I was stupid and didn't make my ex get his own credit card. But I'm fine. It's fine. I'll check out with mine."

Tyler's gaze darts around like it used to whenever I said something to make him uncomfortable. "Sorry."

He's definitely still the old Tyler. My smile widens.

After an hour or so on the road, we pass a sign for fresh fruit and antiques, and I immediately scan ahead for more signs. And then I see another sign that says, *ESTATE SALE*. I'm practically salivating. I've found the most incredible things at small roadside antique places. So often, they don't even know what they have.

1 MILE—ANTIQUES AND FRESH APPLES

Now I'm drooling for more than one reason. But . . . But we're already behind.

"I'm . . ." I start to say but stop myself.

Tyler's staring out the window, and when we pass the *half-mile to the exit* sign, he lets out a sigh.

"I was thinking . . ."

"Can we stop?" he asks.

"Yes!" I say and immediately turn on my signal.

Tyler clears his throat. "It's that I sometimes find great old wood or metal pieces . . ."

"And sometimes there are campers," I say as I pull in to the gravel parking lot.

"Huh."

Tyler's out of the truck the second I stop, and I pause for a moment watching him move straight for the big pieces just outside the open barn doors.

As a little man with white hair and a leather apron steps out, Tyler smiles and gestures toward a few metal rods. I continue to watch, feeling a bit like a stalker or something.

An old trailer sits off to the side, one of the big, silver Airstream ones. The tires are smooth and worn, and the door sits a little crooked, but these things go for big bucks. A sign on the broken door says, *MAKE OFFER*.

Huh.

I start an online search on my phone and then step into the musty space while Google does its work. I sneeze so hard that my forehead hurts. So, it's more than musty. A little gross. A few cabinet drawers hang broken. The fridge has been ripped out, which is fine, I'd rip it out anyway and put something new in.

"Ken?" Tyler's voice echoes inside the trailer.

"Yeah." I turn to face him, clutching my phone in my hands.

His gaze scans the decrepit space before landing on my face. "You okay?"

"I . . ." I begin to say but then flip the phone over and hold it out for him to see the large price tags on the restored trailers. "Look."

"What?" He grabs my phone and stares at the asking prices for the *smaller* versions of what we're now standing in. "Whoa."

"Right?" I ask, rubbing my now sweaty palms down my thighs. "What should I offer?"

"We could feel him out?" Tyler suggests. "See what price he had in mind?"

"He'll start high."

"He's used to bargaining," Tyler agrees. "Let's do it. You can pick it up on your way back."

Right. I already have a trailer attached to my truck now. Suddenly, I want to drop it off and run back here. But then I'll miss my week with Ivy, which I can't do.

"Yeah," I say.

"So, I already bought a few pieces of metal—just stuff I wanna use for chair and table legs—but I'm not sure that the back of your truck has room. If I wrap the poles up well, is it okay to set them inside the trailer?"

"Yeah. Whatever," I say, feeling too excited about this little treasure we're standing in now to give a crap what happens to the little trailer in the lot. Well, that's not entirely true. I do love Trina, and the owner is expecting it to be immaculate. But this one . . . If I could sell this thing, I might be able to make a noticeable dent in my debts.

I follow Tyler out of the Airstream, shoving my phone into my pocket, and trying to look bored.

"You interested?" the white-haired man asks before I even get back to the barn.

I shrug. "I don't know. It's really beat up."

He points to my camper. "Looks like you know what you're doing."

Glancing behind me, I try to keep my face even. "Sometimes."

"Don't think I don't know what I have here." His brows go up. "I'm online. I've seen what these go for."

"Everyone's online," Tyler says and gives him a friendly smile. "What price did you have in mind?"

I hold my breath, waiting to hear a figure way above my budget.

"I won't take less than five thousand."

"Five," I repeat back. Is he seriously going to let that thing go for five thousand?

He sighs.

"I'll have to cut my trip short to pick it up," I say. "And the fridge was *ripped* out."

"Not to mention the broken cabinets," Tyler pipes in.

Even at five thousand, that camper is a deal.

"You two seem like a nice couple," the man says as he rubs his wrinkled forehead.

I start to correct him, but Tyler tucks me into his side. "Just getting started out, you know?"

The man lets out a small sigh. "I remember those days well. Okay. Fine. Four thousand, but that's final."

I grab his hand and pump his arm. "Thank you. I'll be back in a week to pick it up. I can wire you the money now."

He shakes his head. "That price is good for four days."

I glance up at Tyler, who gives me an apologetic frown.

"Four days, then," I say.

The man hands me his card, tapping his email address. "You can send the money here."

So much for my long trip to see Ivy. But I want to hug Tyler for helping me seal this deal.

"You'll have your money this afternoon."

Now, I just need to pull off my best restoration yet.

Chapter Eight

Tyler

Kendell unlocks the door to her trailer, pulls open the door, and I'm stunned for a moment. I mean, the outside looked great, and my tastes are much simpler than this, but . . . "Wow."

"You have your stuff wrapped up and ready?" she asks, leaning half out of the camper.

I peer in around her. "I'm incredibly impressed."

"Oh?" She steps back. "Come on in."

I step up, which puts us chest to chest in the small doorway, and I'm stuck for a moment—not because I *can't* get past her but because I don't want to leave this spot.

She stares at my chest then says, "Um."

"Sorry." I take the next step into her trailer. All the cabinets have been painted bright white, and she's added small black knobs. The countertop has to be new Formica laminate, which is probably the only thing you could use in here. Tile or solid surface countertops would be too heavy. Everything is a perfect mix of old and new: the table is finished in an almost rustic wood, the curtains, the cushions, the carpet, the new fridge . . .

"You're very quiet, so I'm kind of panicking, even though it's already sold," Kendell says.

Turning to face her, I shake my head. "No. I mean . . . This is . . ." *Words—I have to remember how to use words.* "This is really impressive."

"I do everything myself," she says, smiling now. "Benefit of having a dad who manages a Home Depot." She laughs lightly.

"And he used to always be tinkering with old furniture in the garage."

"He still does that." Kendell smiles a little. "So, yeah. I mean, the Formica and contact adhesive took a while to get used to, but I practiced on a few small tables first, and . . ." She pauses. "The wiring took the longest to learn, but I have that down now too."

"That's . . ." I begin to reply and then swallow. My fingers twitch as I think of how much I want to touch her, to have her in my space again. "Really impressive," I finish.

Her brows pull together. "Okay, then." She steps back down and picks up my wrapped pieces of rusted metal, which I'll use in my next project.

We set my stuff on the floor, and then I come back down the steps, stopping next to her. Again, I feel stuck. Stuck by wanting to be near her, by wanting to say the perfect thing, but feeling like I'm a shade away from something spectacular with her, which is both fantastic and terrifying. "In my head, I sort of made fun of Camp Fancy."

Her eyes drop to the ground, and then she shrugs. "Yeah, well."

"But I'm completely blown away." I wince, realizing how she might take this. "Not surprised, though. I don't want you to take 'blown away' the wrong way."

"I can follow *Tyler-speak*," she teases.

I stare at her lips as she talks, feeling like I'm sixteen again: Next to the girl I'm sure I can't have. Telling myself that I probably shouldn't want her.

As she steps around me, I reach out and grasp her arm lightly. *Soft skin.*

"Something wrong?" she asks.

"I'm . . ." *Think of words. Think of words. Think of words.* "I'm glad we stopped. Thanks."

"Ha!" She steps back and tosses me the keys. "Me too. Your turn to drive."

After lunch, Kendell changes into shorts. Short ones. That show off her tanned legs.

"So," Kendell says as she turns in her seat. It takes every ounce of my self-control not to stare. "Your sister said that you were quite entangled with a girl a while back."

"I was," I say slowly. "Does this work both ways? I give you insight into my life, and then you'll give me insight into yours?"

"I got married in a stupid move to a guy who then used me as his ticket to come to America. I thought I knew what falling in love felt like, but really, I learned what falling into being completely used felt like." She swallows, her lip quivering, but then she sucks in a breath. "So, that's my story. What's yours?"

There are a hundred more things I want to know about her and Anton. But, with the thought of her quivering lip, I let those things go. Then I tell her about meeting Tori, about how we hit it off, and about how we were practically living together for a while.

"And then, something in me knew we weren't right," I say. "So I avoided home for a while . . . avoided her for a while. Then she came to me with the easy out: We just weren't right for each other."

"Wow." Kendell sits back. "Kind of weird, isn't it?"

"What's weird?"

"That you can get along with someone well enough to really be together, and then just . . ."

"Know it's not right?" I offer.

What Falling Feels Like

"Yeah." She stares out the window for a moment. "What prompted the sudden jump into dating a girl seriously when you'd kept to yourself for so long? Hazards of growing up?"

I'm doing it. I'm going to tell her. I'm going to say it. A snort escapes.

"What was *that* about?" She mock punches in me in the arm.

"More personal than I'd like," I say as an excuse to save face.

"Riiiight," she draws out, clearly not believing me. "I just told you that I was stupid enough to fall for a guy who used me horribly and made me broke, and now we're too personal?"

But I know this tone: she's only half teasing. "First off," I say as I reach out, grab her hand, and give it a light squeeze, "you're not stupid, Ken."

In a flash, her lips tremble again, almost like she's trying not to cry. And I can't believe how fast she gets brought back to this crappy place. I want to destroy that man for doing this to her.

"And second . . ." I say, trying to control my voice. *I'm doing it. I'm just . . . doing it.* "The girl I thought I loved got married, and I realized that I'd missed my chance."

When she doesn't move—like, at all—I think to myself, *Stupid. Stupid. Stupid.*

"You didn't even know me," she says softly.

"What?" I lean forward and glance toward her. "How can you say that?"

"You looked at me like . . . But I was spoiled and selfish then, and you didn't see that. You loved what you thought you knew about me."

"I knew how you liked your coffee," I say. "I knew that you mumbled in the morning, that you were quick to judge and quick to anger. I knew that you'd stay up all night if anyone would stay up with you, and sometimes that person got to be me. So don't say that I didn't know you."

She lets out a harrumph and then says, "You have terrible taste in girls."

"No." I tighten my grip on her hand because I've already come this far, so I might as well embarrass myself thoroughly. "We both had a lot of growing up to do."

"And now?" she asks.

I let go of her hand again and attempt to laugh. "We probably still do."

Kendell turns to face forward, kicks off her shoes, and reclines the chair. "Can you find some music or something?"

Anything would be better than continuing a conversation I don't yet know how to decipher.

Chapter Nine

Kendell

Did Tyler really think he was in love with me back then? I mean . . . I understand him sort of wanting to be with a girl who he liked spending time with, one who (not to be snobby) was a few rungs higher on the social ladder and a few years older, but to *love* her?

My heart gives an extra ka-thump. Neither of us talks, but it's the relaxing kind of silence, not the horridly awkward kind. What would have happened if I'd gone to prom with Tyler? And if we'd hit it off in a new way? How much grief would that have saved me? I'm not sure, and there's no way to tell. That's all years behind us now.

"My turn to get gas," he says as he flicks on the turn signal.

"Nope." I bite my nail. "It's mine."

There's a short pause. "Okay."

We arrive at the gas pumps, but neither of us gets out.

"I didn't create weirdness between us, did I?" he asks.

I turn to face him, and instead of seeing Tyler Brady, Ivy's little brother, I see . . . someone new, full of possibilities. "No," I tell him. Then my lips tug themselves into another involuntary smile. "I'm good. Great. Better. I don't know."

"Okay, now that we have that cleared up." He smirks before

tilting his head toward the small gas station. "I'm gonna get us a snack."

Butterflies flutter about in my insides as I swipe my card and then lean against the truck. The weather is warmer this far south, and the sun beats down on my face. I lean back against the truck and let my eyes fall closed. Tyler. Possibility. My new trailer. Maybe there are still really great things to look forward to. Things I might not screw up.

"Just me," Tyler says, and then the warmth from him touches my shoulder. I peek his direction, and he's leaning back with his eyes closed, just like me. His profile hardened as he grew up—in a good way. He has a nice jaw and the same straight nose as his sister.

"I'm glad we're doing this together," I say.

"Me too."

Before thinking, I lean forward and press my lips to the corner of his mouth. As a test, maybe, to see where we are now . . . where he is.

His eyes shoot open, and we both lean there, against my truck, as the gas nozzle clicks off. We stare at each other, but our eyes aren't still. It's as if we're both looking, searching for some sign from the other.

Tyler comes my way. Just an inch. Just enough that I know he's okay with whatever's happening between us. I lean my forehead against his and our noses touch. We breathe for a moment, and I soak up the smell, warmth, and closeness of him— this guy I've trusted probably longer than I've trusted myself.

His face tilts just slightly, bringing our lips together. Small bits of stubble tickle my face, sending my heart racing. I thread my arms around his neck, tugging him to me, and lose myself in the depth of his kiss. His strong arms hold my body tightly to his, and the feeling of being wanted rushes through me.

He pulls back too soon, looks at me for a moment, and my

hands slide back off his neck. He kisses my cheek before turning to put the nozzle back onto the pump. He screws the cap back on the gas tank and then faces me again.

I take his face in my hands, feeling the strength of his jaw, the bits of beard trying to come through. "I sort of wanted to touch you like this when I picked you up," I admit.

He turns his head quickly and plants a kiss on my palm. "Me too."

My thumbs trace along his jaw, feeling his stubble, but then I stop because his eyes are so penetrating. So *Tyler*.

He leans forward and whispers, "I'm going to kiss you again."

This impulse isn't fed from the rush of the moment like when I first grabbed him, or from anything but him wanting our lips together again. This time, the kiss is soft, exploring, sending a thrill swirling through my body to my toes.

I feel wanted by Tyler, and it has been far too long since I felt wanted by anyone.

When we pull up to Ivy's house, hours later, it's dark, late, and I reluctantly unthread my fingers from Tyler's.

Ivy rushes out of the small stucco house, her little pregnant belly sticking out in front of her. I grab her stomach first, and then she grabs me in a hug. "You!" she squeals. "It's been way too long!"

"Way," I agree as I hug her back.

We step away from each other, and I still just have to stare at her stomach. *Amazing.*

Then Tyler steps around me and hugs his sister long and tight. They talk quietly to each other, and I try not to listen.

"Come on inside, you two," Ivy says.

Tyler touches my arm, and electricity shoots through me. "I can get the bags. I'll meet you inside."

"Tyler can crash on the couch downstairs, and I have the guest room all set up for you," Ivy says as she loops her arm through mine. "That work?"

"Perfectly." I release a breath and lean into the girl that feels more like my family than even my parents do. "I can't wait to meet this baby."

"You and me both! Trevor is still at work. He was finishing up a sale."

"It's okay. I have a couple days," I say.

She opens the front door. "No! I need a week!"

When I face her in the full light, it hits me how much she and Tyler look alike. Same light brown hair. Same gold flecks in their eyes. Same oval face.

"I have a trailer I need to pick up. It could make me some serious cash. I can't walk away from it."

Ivy frowns. "I'm not thrilled, but I get it."

As Tyler steps through the door, I lose my breath for a moment. He smiles in return. My heart flips, and I wonder if his does the same.

"Okay." Ivy points between us. "What's going on?"

"What?" we both ask at the same time.

"You two. You're like . . ." Her finger goes back and forth. "*You know*."

My phone begins to ring, but I ignore it. "There may have been a kiss," I say.

"Or two," Tyler adds, grinning at me, and I want to kiss that smile.

"Make the phone stop!" Ivy laughs. "Seriously!"

I don't recognize the number, but my work phone is also my cell. "You've got Kendell Adams," I say.

"I'm hurt," the caller says, and his accent sends a spike of cold dread down my spine. "What happened to *Russo*?"

"Anton, this is bad timing."

"Kenny . . ." he purrs, and my heart trips. I want to smack my heart. "Just a moment."

I swallow. His voice, its familiarity—these affect me every time I hear him speak, making me remember how I fell apart when he left.

"Please say that you still have a moment for us. Huh?" he asks, the Italian part of him drops and smoothes out every word.

I blink back tears, but I don't fully understand where they came from or whether they're tears of frustration, loss, anger . . . My emotions are too mixed up where Anton Russo is concerned.

"Go down to the guest bedroom," Ivy says and points to the stairs. "We'll be down in a few. It'll give you some privacy, okay?"

I nod and quickly glance toward Tyler, which is a mistake. He's frowning, his eyes on fire with anger. But I can't deal with the jealousy thing. Not right now.

"Is that Ivy I hear?" Anton asks, his voice actually lifting as he talks, despite having Ivy call him every choice name under the sun—to his face.

"Don't forget who you are now!" Ivy calls down from behind me. "He doesn't deserve anything from you!"

I wave to acknowledge that I heard her but continue down the steps to the basement.

"I just wanna see you, Kenny. That's all. I miss you."

"It's more than that," I say, tears rolling down my face. *Why? Why can't I be over this?*

"No. Just you. I *miss* you. Am I not allowed to miss my wife?"

"I'm not your wife."

"Now you're just trying to be mean. I'm not trying to be mean. I call you to make nice."

I used to love how he'd mix up his English like this. But now

I realize that we never spoke any of the same languages. "What do you want?"

"I want us to try again, to spend time together. I think we were—What's the word?—*hasty*."

He knows the word. He also knows I used to think that his lack of English vocabulary was charming. My hands shake so hard that I have to sit down on the corner of the bed. Tears have run down my neck and are starting to soak the top of my shirt.

"Come on, my bella girl. Listen to me. Please. Remember the coast? That little place where we made love, and you—"

But I don't need to hear the rest of his words because it's as if I'm back there: the tiny villa on the beach. At the time, it was the epitome of perfection. Now, that time we spent together feels like the biggest lie in my existence.

I can't think, can't answer. But he keeps talking, taking my silence as an invitation for him to continue. Even as I drop the phone, his voice fills the room—that quiet, pleading voice he uses when he wants something. He's maybe being deported, or needs me to lie to help him get a job. I don't want to know.

Finally, I reach down and end the call. I'm weak from driving, weak from feeling, weak from having my relationship with Anton tossed back in my face like this at the worst possible time. I mean, what are the odds of him calling now, just as I think I'm getting my feet back underneath me again?

Chapter Ten

Tyler

I want to break something. Anything. I slam another cupboard in search of a glass.

"Whoa there," Ivy says and grabs my arm. "You okay?"

"She's so different. And it's all his fault." My teeth grit together.

"No." Ivy shakes her head. "Some of it is his fault. Some of it is hers."

I groan.

"Stop being dramatic," Ivy says. "So, what happened?"

"I told her how devastated I was when she got married."

"And?"

"And we've just gotten to know each other again," I say, though I hope that we're leading up to something bigger.

"And you kissed?" she asks.

I'm nodding when I'm not even sure if I mean to be.

"Come here," Ivy says and starts down the stairs.

Half of me wants to be as far away from that phone conversation as I can be, and the other half wishes I could listen in. As we walk down the stairs, all I can hear is soft whimpers from behind the guest bedroom door. My fists tighten in response.

But Ivy grabs my hands. "Your anger is not what she needs."

"I know," I say and rake my hands through my hair.

"Don't get me wrong, little brother. I'd love to see you two together. But, do you hear her in there? She's not ready yet. Kendell forgot how amazing and special she is, and you shouldn't carry that for her. She needs to remember that on her own."

"I hate that you're right." I drag my hands through my hair again. "I don't want you to be right."

"But I am."

I lean forward until my head bangs against the wall. "I finally . . . I mean . . ."

Ivy grabs me in a sideways half hug. "I know."

"I'm going to go home, then. I have my truck. I'll leave her a note and take off early in the morning, before anyone's up. Maybe tonight."

"You need to talk to her first," Ivy says. "Tell her what you're thinking."

I shake my head. "No. That won't work. Any hesitation from her will ruin the very few bits of resolve I have when it comes to walking away from her right now."

"Well, then whatever you write to her had better be amazing."

I give my sister a salute and wonder how much of my soul I can spare to put on a piece of paper.

Then Kendell steps out of the room, swiping at her eyes. "Can we just watch a really stupid movie? Can we just do that?"

Ivy hugs Kendell and promises to bring down some snacks. So I flip on the downstairs TV, having no idea what to say.

"I finally just hung up," she says softly. "I mean, he wants something—he always wants something—but at least I didn't stay on long enough to know what it is. That's usually the part that hurts the worst: the being let down again because he doesn't call for me, he calls for himself."

I almost kill the remote by pressing the buttons too hard. "Ghostbusters?" I offer.

A corner of Kendell's mouth kicks up, but her eyes are still red and splotchy. I don't know what my role is. Without the phone call, I'd have tucked my arm around her, sat on the couch, and hoped she would lean on me the whole time. But now . . .?

Kendell sits, and I realize my mistake right away. I should have sat down first. Do I sit close to her? Give her space?

"You look lost," she says, her voice still scratchy from crying.

"Yeah," I admit. "I'm lost."

She pats the cushion next to her.

I sit. And, within three seconds, Kendell rests her head on my shoulder and her hand on my thigh. I'm once again in a position that I never want to change.

Ivy comes down and tilts her head sideways to look at Kendell.

"I'm fine," Kendell says, waving her away with a halfhearted smile. "Just watching."

My sister sets down a snack tray of fruits and veggies—*typical*—and sits next to Kendell's feet. "I'm gonna give you a foot rub tonight. Then you can do me tomorrow. And the next day. And the next day."

"Deal," Kendell mumbles, pressing her face into my shoulder.

I want this situation to be better, her to be better. But I don't have the power to do that.

Chapter Eleven

Kendell

My whole body hurts when I wake up. Opening my eyes, I discover that I'm still in my clothes from the day before, the TV is off, the room is empty, and, instead of resting against Tyler, I'm resting against one of Ivy's massive couch pillows.

I set my hand down to push myself up to a sitting position, and paper crackles under the pressure. A note?

Kendell—
I don't know how to say this to you. I'm hoping that by writing it out, the words will come. You are amazing, and I know I could love you, I mean, really love you. I want to try it out. Try us out. I can't remember ever wanting anything this badly. But I can't shake the feeling that you have things to do on your own first. I can't be the rebound guy—not with you.
So I left early this morning. I'll pick up your trailer and drop it off at your house. Enjoy your time with Ivy. I'm not going anywhere, Ken. My heart is full of you. I just want to make sure that yours is full of me or, at least, ready for someone new. I can't break twice over the same girl.

Call me when you're ready, or just drop by anytime. You know how I like to work nights.

Love, Tyler

I both hate and love his note at the same time. He's right, of course. I hate that he's right. I'm not worthy of him yet. I'm not ready, but I want to be. "Waiting sucks," I say aloud.

"You okay?" Ivy asks as she knocks on the wall by the stairs and then steps into the open room.

I hold up the note. "Your brother went home."

"I know. He didn't mean to wake me up, but he did. Are you okay?"

"That's a dumb question."

"That's always a dumb question. I mean, when we feel the need to ask that question, it generally means that the other person isn't okay, right?" She laughs a little. Then she sits next to me, and I lean my head on her shoulder. "Tyler's loved you for a long time, Ken. He's probably terrified right now."

"I know how he feels."

"Good. Then you keep pushing yourself to work harder to be the girl you were before your divorce."

"She doesn't exist anymore."

"Don't say that," Ivy whispers.

"No." I raise my head. "That's a good thing. I'm smarter now. More careful. Tyler's right. I need to get past this point where I feel like I'm going to cry if anything I perceive as a weakness is pointed out."

"And . . ." Ivy prompts as she folds her arms. "And you have to love yourself enough to give the right kind of love to someone else."

"Oh my gosh." I laugh. "You sound like Dr. Phil."

Ivy laughs with me. "I know! I'm sorry!"

"So, what do I do now?" I ask her. I want a list or answers or . . .

"You shower because, wow," Ivy says as she widens her eyes at me. "And then you spend the next week helping me get the nursery together."

"That sounds . . . great," I finish. And it does. I want to be outside of myself for a while. I don't want to think about me or feel things about myself. I want to be excited for her and for the new addition to her small family.

"Good," Ivy says as her smile turns mischievous. "Because all I've done so far is paint."

Chapter Twelve

Tyler

After making this long trip *with* Kendell, driving the same road back without her is a bit torturous, quiet, and not the kind of quiet that can be filled with the radio.

The hotel I crash in is nicer than the one where we stayed, but there's nothing cozy or restful about its wallpapered walls and tidy desk. I know it's because Kendell isn't here. But I try not to think about missing her. Over and over.

My second day on the road seems to be creeping by even slower than the first. But it's early yet. Since our last trip was a short first day and a long second day, I know that I have to be close now to the antiques stand.

When I pull into the parking lot under the estate sale sign, I already know that I'm going to pick up a few more things for myself. I have my new truck now and more room than I'll need.

"Back so soon?" the white-haired man asks. "I figured you two lovebirds would have taken the full four days." Then he winks.

I shrug. "She's spending some time with my sister while I'm picking up the trailer."

He gestures with his hand. "Well, come on then. I checked the tires for you after you left. They won't last much longer, but they're full now."

Once I'm in my truck again, he guides me back so that I can secure Kendell's new trailer. When I jump out to help with its attachments, he already has me half hooked up.

"I hope this helps with your new life together," he says.

Guilt pinpricks in my chest. "We're not . . ."

He chuckles. "Oh, no? I saw the way that woman looks at you. You two will be just fine."

What way had Kendell looked at me? "What?"

He laughs again. "You two will work it out."

This guy seems to think that he is some sort of a fortune-teller or magician. Or, maybe he's just creepier than I gave him credit for.

I thank him, shake his hand, and get back into the truck with Kendell's trailer hooked up and ready to go. Then the man knocks on my window. I pause before rolling it down.

"Don't think that I don't know what that trailer is worth," he says. "Consider the discount an early wedding present."

It's my turn to laugh. Kendell isn't likely to jump into that again anytime soon—no matter who it's with. I start to tell him as much, but then my throat thickens, and I get that feeling I get whenever I match a piece of wood up with the right metal for a project: When everything just *clicks*. When I know it's right. When I know it'll turn out to be just as I imagined, but maybe better.

"Thank you. Really," I tell him.

The man gives me a wave and starts back toward the open door of the barn. Then he turns and calls, "Come back for more rusty metal parts anytime!"

As I hit the road by myself, Kendell's trailer in tow, I am more filled with hope than I think I've ever been about anything.

Chapter Thirteen

Kendell

Four weeks it took me to renovate the Airstream, but now it's spectacular. All I can think of as I stand here, in the newfound glory of its renovation, is that I want to show it to Tyler, that I *need* him to see it.

Every day I tell myself, *Wait one more day before talking to him again.* And then I last another day. As much as I know that Ivy was right, the problem with Ivy's reasoning—that I need to learn to stand on my own two feet—is that I can't very well erase the knowledge that this amazing guy, this longtime friend, who builds beautiful things with his hands . . . wants *me.*

Five weeks. Tyler left me that note five weeks ago. It's still in my pocket. He doesn't know this. If I start something with him, it needs to be right, but the thought that I've waited too long has begun to plague me over the last week or two.

Instead of thinking too hard or planning what I'll say, I pull my phone from my pocket, sit on the newly covered mini couch, and call him.

As the phone rings, I imagine hearing his hopeful voice on the other end. I imagine the relief in his voice that I called. But, as the ringing continues, I wonder if, after five weeks of silence on my part, if he still even wants this. Wants *us*. Maybe I've been imagining a reunion that will never happen.

"Hey. You've reached Tyler Brady. Leave a message."

What—? I didn't plan for this. Crap. What do I say?

"Um . . ." I say, and then I hang up, staring down at the phone in disappointment.

Then, suddenly, the phone rings. I jerk in surprise, and the phone flies across the trailer.

So grown-up, Kendell.

I leap across the newly scrubbed floor, fall on my stomach and pick up my phone with a raspy, "Hello?"

The deep chuckle I hear in response spreads another one of those fantastically massive smiles across my face.

"Hey, Kendell," Tyler says. "I just missed you. I see you're working late."

"Is it late?"

"About 1:00 a.m., yeah." He chuckles again, his deep voice vibrating through me, even over the phone.

"I miss you," I say simply, still grinning, still catching my breath. "And I finished the Airstream. And I thought between those two things . . ."

"How about I pick us up dinner? We can celebrate in your new fancy camper?"

Perfect. This is perfect. "I would absolutely love that."

"You know, choices are limited at one in the morning."

"Anything is great."

Even just two months ago, I would have panicked at the thought of meeting up with someone for dinner. But that's two more months of me actually moving forward with five weeks of hopefulness that felt more exciting than scary.

I'm so ready for this.

I don't want to leave my new, perfect trailer, so I open the garage door and hope that Tyler will just walk in. From the printed cushions to the perfect, old teapot, this place is ready.

I'm too exhausted to photograph the Airstream tonight, and I'll need outside lighting anyway. But the pictures need to go up soon, and then I'll get to cross my fingers and hope that it sells fast. Leaning my head against the wall, I let out a long, slow breath.

I'm not sure if I'll ever know whether I'm perfectly ready for Tyler, but I do know that Anton has called me about fifty times, and I haven't answered once.

"Wow," Tyler says, his voice echoing in the small space.

My eyes fly open, and I sit up so fast that I knock two pillows onto the floor. All the things I wanted to tell Tyler leave my brain. I jump up, throw my arms around him, and revel in the feeling of his arms around me.

"I missed you, Ken," he whispers.

"I missed you too." I swallow. "I needed . . . You were right, and I . . ."

"Not important." He kisses my temple before letting me go. "I have food, and this is . . . I remember." He points. "The broken doors were there, and this is a new fridge." He runs his hand over the stainless.

"It's *all* I've done this past month . . . besides think."

"More than a month," Tyler says as he shakes his head. "Almost six weeks. Thirty-nine days, to be exact."

"I'm not perfect," I tell him.

"I'm not perfect either."

"And I'm not the Kendell you knew from high school."

Hearing this, he cups my face in his hands. "I know."

"But, I could love you too," I whisper. "And, more than anything, I can't miss out on the chance of that."

Tyler leans in until his lips touch mine. Soft. Careful. Then he slides his hands down my arms before he breaks our kiss and pulls me into a hug.

"You ready to eat?" he whispers.

I'm mostly ready to sit in this trailer and make out with him all night. But, instead of saying this to him, I ask, "What did you bring?"

"I have a friend who works at Claim Jumper."

I grab the bag from the table. "You didn't."

"I did."

"You remembered?"

His brow quirks up. "Pretzel bites with cheese sauce?"

Emotion wells up in my chest, lodging a small ball in my throat. "Yeah."

"I told you," he says, kissing my cheek. "I know you, Ken." His smile is full and genuine.

I realize then that whatever happens for us next is going to be because we're finally on equal ground, in every sense of the word. So I grab Tyler in a hug and hold on like my life depends on him. "We're going to be great," I whisper.

His arms tighten around me as he says, "I know."

This is what falling feels like.

About Jolene Perry

Jolene Perry grew up in Alaska, and graduated from Southern Utah University with a degree in Political Science. She started writing when she taught herself to play the guitar, and when songs weren't long enough to tell the story, she began writing novels. After living in Washington, Utah, and Las Vegas, she now resides in Alaska with her husband, and two children. She is represented by Jane Dystel and writes fiction for young adults as Jolene Perry.

Jolene Betty Perry is also the author of the *Almost a Fairytale* series, *The Next Door Boys* series, the Christmas novella, *Pretty Near Perfect*, as well as the stand-alone contemporary romances, *The Weight of Love* and *After All*. Her modern-day cowboy story, *Chasing Kisses*, can be found in the Anthology, *Curl Up With A Cowboy*.

Twitter: @JRV_Perr
Facebook: Jolene Perry
Website: https://jolenebperry.com

Antiques Road Trip

by Sarah M. Eden

Chapter One

Kelsey Kirkpatrick had dreamed of Jane Austen's England her entire life. She'd watched every movie and TV adaptation of Austen's books before she was even old enough to understand the story lines or appreciate the romance. She'd examined the horses, studied the carriages, and memorized the clothes. First, she had read all of Austen's books as a tween. Then, during high school, she began researching the time period, devouring every bit of information she could get her hands on. Later, she'd majored in history in college, focusing on early nineteenth-century England, and she now worked as a high school history teacher.

She was a nerd and proud of it. That nerdiness had brought her eagerly to the geekiest of all reality-television programs: *Antiques Road Trip*, a public-television venture meant to teach about history and culture and customs. The contestants would dress and behave and interact as nineteenth-century Britons while undertaking a journey in an authentic carriage along a road that the producers had created to mirror those of nineteenth-century England.

Horses, carriage, clothes, culture—it was her dream come true.

The grand prize was an all-expenses-paid, literary-themed tour of the British Isles—something she'd wanted to do since high school—and $100,000, enough money for her to go to graduate school, so she could teach at a university, another lifelong dream.

She stood now in the studio building, eying the other seven contestants. If only she could tell at a glance who among them might have her same background. Her knowledge of history was her edge, and she was depending on it, since she didn't have any experience with competitions or being on television.

"Everyone face this way," the production assistant called out. She had been introduced to the contestants earlier, sometimes called by her full title, sometimes just called the PA. It was clear that, other than the director, she was the boss. "The show's host will come through this door and give you instructions. We need quiet from everyone while that happens."

A moment later the scene played out exactly as she had said it would. The host, who looked like he'd come directly from a magazine shoot, entered with a self-assured swagger. That was the kind of confidence she needed to exude. Self-assurance played well on screen; she'd read that online while getting ready for the competition.

"Eight of you have taken up the challenge of a road trip. But, what you don't know is . . ." The host paused, looking them all over. "You will be making that road trip in 1815."

They did actually know that. She'd been amazed at how many things over the day had been portrayed as surprises, while the cameras were rolling, that weren't surprises at all. The host then talked about contestants beginning their challenge with no idea about history and the stringent rules they were about to live by, when, in reality, all eight of them had been sent information about exactly that. No one was going into this entirely blind.

Their host knew his part well, though. He made his announcements in the smug tone of someone who felt certain his words were tying peoples' stomachs in knots. "In a moment, you will be escorted to a changing room and given clothes to wear, clothes exactly like those worn in the era of Jane Austen. All modern conveniences will be locked up until the end of your trip.

You will be divided into two teams, and each team will be assigned a carriage and driver. A series of nineteenth-century inspired dirt roads and English roadside inns have been constructed throughout the area. Your task will be to navigate those roads, live according to the rules and expectations of 1815, successfully complete challenges given to you, and reach your final destination in time for the grand ball three days from now."

Kelsey's broad grin would probably make her look like an imbecile on camera, but she couldn't help herself. She loved everything about this. Everything.

"Once you pass through these doors," the host continued, "you will be given your character, your historical wardrobe, supplies for your trip, and a booklet on nineteenth-century etiquette and rules. Study it closely, because you are expected to live by what the booklet says for the next three days."

He paused, looking them over slowly, dramatically, before taking up his instructions again. "Contestants will be awarded points throughout the competition. Succeed at your challenges and stay in character, because, in the end, only one person will be declared King or Queen of the Road. Good luck."

He stepped aside, and one by one the participants filed out. He watched them with an unnecessarily heavy look. It wasn't as if they were gladiators, heading into the arena. They were stepping back into history. They were experiencing the most magical moment Kelsey could imagine.

As she made her way out, Kelsey bumped into someone very tall and very solid and, as it turned out, unmistakably handsome. She'd noticed him earlier in the day, but from a distance.

"Sorry." His quiet, unassuming voice caught her by surprise. Instead of the broad smile and self-assured expression she would have expected, he kept his gaze a little lowered, the corners of his mouth pulling down with uncertainty. "Ladies first."

"Getting into character already?" She referred to his gallant gesture, but also wondered if his shy demeanor was only an act.

He shook his head. "We haven't been assigned characters yet."

That was true. But, did it mean he was being genuine or not? There was really no way to tell. This was, no doubt, part of the challenge: not knowing anything about the other contestants.

The room they stepped into had curtained dressing rooms running along either side with a name card pinned to each one. She spotted her name at the far end of the row. *Her* name. This was really happening.

The cameras were being repositioned, not filming at the moment. So Kelsey turned to her neighbor.

"I'm Kelsey."

"Devon," was his simple response. He looked nervous. Either he was even more unsuited to the limelight than she was, or he was a terribly good actor, determined to not seem like a threat.

"What convinced you to sign up for this show?" she asked.

"My sister. She wanted to do it, but her health's not good. So I signed up in her place."

"Either you really love your sister, or you're a total pushover."

His smile made a brief appearance, and it seemed genuine. *He* seemed genuine. She hoped that would prove to be true. Why, she couldn't say for certain.

The production assistant got everyone's attention again. "When you're given your cue, find your name and step inside your dressing area. Inside, you'll find your costume for the day. Wardrobe will be available to help you—these clothes weren't meant to be taken on and off without assistance."

Kelsey knew that already. She'd rolled her eyes through far too many poorly researched novels, in which fine ladies managed to get in and out of their fancy gowns and dresses in the blink of an eye, often unassisted.

"Once you are dressed," the PA continued, "you will be given your character assignment. Then report to the camera at the far end of this room and follow the instructions you are given."

The contestants all nodded their understanding.

"Okay, get to it," the PA said.

Kelsey slipped inside her dressing room. Her clothes were hung up in layers. A linen chemise, faux-bone stays, white stockings, a pale green day dress, a cream-colored tucker, brown leather ankle boots, cream gloves, and a straw bonnet with a thick green ribbon that perfectly matched the dress. She almost couldn't hold back her giddiness. How often she'd dreamed of living in this era that she loved so much, even for just a little while. She didn't want to take up permanent residence there—she was far too fond of modern conveniences for that—but to have just a taste of it . . . It was magical.

She quickly undressed and slipped on the chemise. It was just as soft as she'd imagined. The stays were front-tying, allowing her to secure those on her own. Then she pulled on the tucker, pinning it to her chemise. The stockings had elastic tops. Not exactly historically accurate but far more convenient than tying them with ribbons and hoping they would stay up. Lastly, she laced up her boots. That was as much as she could do without help.

She peeked her head out of the dressing room and asked for assistance. One of the wardrobe ladies hurried over and stepped inside.

"You've done this before," she said. "No one else is this far yet—or managed to do it on their own."

"History is my favorite thing in the world," Kelsey said.

"Then you must be in heaven."

She was. She *so* was.

After a moment, the day dress was on and fastened. Pins were placed to give it the perfect fit and shape. The tucker was adjusted. The skirt was smoothed.

"Have a seat on the stool," the wardrobe assistant said. "I'll let hair and makeup know you're ready."

She was even getting her hair done! This was going to be the best week ever. She didn't sit immediately but took a moment to look at herself in the mirror: her historically-accurate-costumed self.

This was a moment out of a dream. She was certain her heart would never settle back into a calm rhythm again.

She stared at her reflection as the hair and makeup women did their part. Makeup was necessary for the cameras. In that aspect, historical accuracy would have to be set aside.

Twenty minutes later, she was the first contestant to emerge from her dressing room, ready to begin the competition. That, she decided, was a good sign.

Remembering her instructions, Kelsey crossed to the far side of the room, where a stationary camera waited.

The PA smiled as she approached. "This"—she held up a small drawstring reticule made of cream fabric with tiny flowers—"contains your character assignment for the next few days as well as a pamphlet with information about the rules and expectations of the time period and a few instructions about your journey. Keep the bag with you throughout the journey."

Kelsey nodded her understanding, even as her heart leapt again. *A reticule!*

"When you get your cue," the PA continued, "open the bag, pull out your character card, and read your assignment out loud."

Kelsey slipped the drawstrings of the bag over her wrist, as it was meant to be carried, and waited. The cameraman made some adjustments. The director gave more instructions. Kelsey was repositioned. Hair and makeup came over and tidied up a few things.

"In 3 . . . 2 . . ." The PA pointed to Kelsey.

She opened her reticule and pulled out a thick piece of stationery. She took a breath to calm her nerves. "Miss Kelsey Grames," she read. They were keeping their first names, at least.

That would simplify things. "Youngest daughter of Mr. Grames, a vicar in a small parish. You are traveling to the Grand Ball in the company of your brother, Mr. Gregory Grames, along with your fiancé—" *Fiancé?* "Lord Devon Bartlett," *Devon!* She continued reading, "second son of the Marquess of Habersham, and his sister, Lady Amanda Bartlett. The Marquess's family feels that Lord Devon has chosen a bride who is too far beneath him in station, thus you are tasked with proving your worth to them." *Oh, lovely.* "This will be best accomplished by proper behavior, decorum, and the reassurance that comes from a determined spirit."

So, she was meant to be just the right balance of feisty and demure. *This could get very interesting.*

"Best of luck," she read the final line aloud, "and we will see you at the ball."

"And cut!" the director called out.

Kelsey was whisked away to an outer room to wait for the others to have their time in front of the camera. She found, however, that her position near an air vent allowed her to overhear the other contestants as they read their cards but only if she listened closely, which she made certain to do.

The third woman to take her turn read the name "Lady Amanda Bartlett." *Bartlett.* That was the last name given to Devon, her pretend fiancé. Kelsey focused all her attention, straining to hear the rest of the description.

"You are the only daughter of the Marquess of Habersham," the woman read. "You are traveling to the Grand Ball in the company of your brother, Lord Devon Bartlett. You are accompanied by your brother's fiancée, Miss Kelsey Grames, of whom your family heartily disapproves, and her brother, Mr. Gregory Grames. Your family has tasked you with determining whether or not Miss Grames will prove a disastrous match for your brother and with persuading Lord Devon to consider his choice very carefully."

The situation was growing more ridiculous by the moment. This historical reenactment was turning into a soap opera.

The contestant who would be portraying her brother took his turn not long afterward. He, according to his card, was just as unsure of Devon and Kelsey's engagement as the Marquess's family was. His card further revealed that the Grames family was in tremendous need of money. He was to encourage the match in any way he could while not giving alarm to Lord Devon or his sister.

Devon must have been the very last contestant to read his card. The small room where all the contestants were being sent was now quite full, and too loud for Kelsey to overhear what his card told him to do and be. The one person in all of this whose motives and goals she wanted most to know she was utterly in the dark about.

Chapter Two

When this competition was over, Devon was going to kill his sister. Right after he took her to England and paid off her medical bills.

He forced himself not to tug at his cravat; that was on the list of things he wasn't supposed to do. How had men 200 years ago made it through the day without stripping everything off? The high, upturned collar poked at his face. The cravat was heavy and hot around his neck. The jacket sat so tight across his shoulders that he could hardly move.

"Read this for the camera," the production assistant said, handing him a thick piece of paper.

"Lord Devon Bartlett, younger son of the Marquess of Habersham." *What is a marquess?* "You are traveling to the Grand Ball in the company of your younger sister, Lady Amanda Bartlett"—was this the Amanda he'd met earlier in the day, the one who talked so fast he could hardly understand her? Three days in a carriage with her . . . Yikes—"as well as your fiancée"—for a moment he couldn't push past that word. Was he really supposed to pretend to be engaged to someone?—"Miss Kelsey Grames"—Kelsey was the one who'd talked to him after plowing into him in the doorway earlier, the one who'd eyed him with unmistakable suspicion.—"and her brother, Mr. Gregory Grames." He'd met Gregory. Nice guy. Funny. That would help make things less miserable. "You have fallen desperately in love with Miss Grames, despite being far above her in rank and position." *So I'm a snob. Great.* "Your task is to convince her brother and your sister, and through them your two families, that yours is a match made in heaven." *I'm in a stupid soap opera.* "As the highest ranking person in your carriage, you are also, by Society's expectations, in charge of your group. Servants, innkeepers, tradesmen and so on will naturally turn to you for instructions. Keep a clear head, and make wise decisions; your companions are counting on you. Good luck, and we will see you at the ball."

He not only had to talk to people but he was also expected to dance? There had to be an easier way to help his sister. He could sell an organ or something.

"Cut," the director called.

The production assistant motioned Devon toward the door. "You're the last of the contestants. Go through this door and join the others. You'll all be taken to the front of the building, where the carriages are waiting. Your carriage has a crest painted on the side because you come from an aristocratic family."

He really, really didn't, though. His parents were both school teachers. He'd grown up in a small house in an old suburb. He currently lived in a one-bedroom apartment and worked as a programmer on the bottom of the ladder at a start-up tech company. He was about as plain and firmly middle class as it was possible to be.

He was going to be terrible at this competition.

He followed the parade of costumes outside. The crested carriage was easy to spot. It not only had a shield with a lion and a crown painted on the side, it also had flags waving from the front corners. It was kind of embarrassing, honestly. Why couldn't this Lord Devon guy be a quiet, keeps to himself kind of lord?

People dressed in historical clothes, but in a plainer more servanty style, stood next to a spread of trunks. They watched the new arrivals as if they were waiting for instructions.

"You are in charge of your group," his card had said. "Servants will naturally turn to you for direction."

He squared his shoulders—as much as the ridiculously tight jacket would allow—and stepped forward. One of the cameras panned to follow him. That was going to take some getting used to. He caught the eye of the servant standing nearest the tricked out carriage.

"What is your name?" He tried to sound confident, but even he wasn't buying it.

"John, m'lord." This actor was good, he even had the accent going for him.

"John, I need you to gather the trunks belonging to myself and my sister"—he suddenly couldn't remember her name—"as well as those for Mr. and Miss Grames." He hoped that was the right last name. "Secure the trunks to the carriage. We want to leave right away."

"Yes, m'lord." John tipped his hat and made a bow. "We'll have you on your way in a trice, m'lord."

The "m'lord" thing was going to get old really fast.

Hopefully that was what he was supposed to do. He'd studied the information the show had sent, but there were too many rules to remember them all. Figuring he was probably expected to leave the servants alone to finish their work, he turned back toward the others. Everyone—literally everyone—was watching him, some surprised, some studying him.

You're a big-time aristocrat, bro. Act like one.

He found Gregory in the crowd. Even in costume, Gregory's red hair made him easy to spot.

"Are you and your sister ready?" Devon asked. "We'll be heading out in a minute."

"Uh . . ." Gregory looked around at the ladies. "Probably?"

The short, blonde, million-mile-a-minute woman he'd met earlier, the one who was supposed to be *his* sister in this game, hurried over to him. "I'm ready, dearest brother. We have such a long journey ahead of us, and I know how much you and Father appreciate an early start. We mustn't keep the horses standing, must we?"

Devon only really understood about half of that. "Standing horses are the worst," he said. He motioned with his head toward the carriage. "Hop in, dearest sister."

She leaned closer and whispered, "A gentleman is supposed to hand a lady up into a carriage. It was in the papers."

He'd forgotten that part. "Thanks for the reminder," he whispered back.

She nodded. "Our carriage is going to win. I'll make sure of it."

"I thought only one of us could win." He was almost sure of it.

She slipped her arm round his and walked with him to their fancy carriage. "I overheard someone on the crew talking about a prize for the carriage with the most total points. If it's true, we're winning it."

"It's a deal," Devon said. They'd reached the carriage, its door already open. "I'm not sure how this part works," he admitted.

"Hold your hand up," she said. "I'll put mine in it as I step up into the carriage. Your hand is like railing on the stairs. It's there for support and to make sure I don't fall on my face."

"Got it."

A moment later, she was inside. She poked her head back out to say, "Make sure you hand up your fiancée as well, even if her brother thinks he's supposed to. You are more important than he is, according to the rules, and you want to make sure he knows it."

It was no wonder the Americans tossed all that British tea into the harbor. They were probably sick of being told who was "more important" all the time.

Gregory rushed over, pulling a woman in a green dress and bonnet behind him. "Found her!"

As Gregory nudged the woman forward, Devon recognized her: Kelsey, who had called him a pushover and had stared at him a little longer than was comfortable. She looked surprisingly hot in her old-fashioned costume.

"This is my sister," Gregory announced. He leaned toward her and said under his breath, "What's your name again?"

"Kelsey," she answered.

"My sister Kelsey."

Devon dipped his head the way the guys always did in the movies that his real sister had made him watch over and over again in the weeks before this competition. That head dip meant "Got it" and "Hello" and "Go away, you're annoying me" and a million other things. It was kind of useful, actually.

The presence of yet another camera moving in close pulled Devon back to the moment and back into his character. "I know your sister," he said. "We are engaged, after all."

"Oh, right." Gregory's mouth twisted up to the side and his eyes took on a snooty look. "Right you are, my good man. Capital! Cheerio! Fish and chips!"

Devon fought back a laugh. Kelsey looked more shocked than anything. Apparently, she hadn't spent much time talking with Gregory that day. He was going to keep them all entertained.

"What a pleasure to see you again, Lord Devon," Kelsey said.

Again with the "lord" stuff. What was it the papers had said about first names? Family could use them. Really good friends. He was pretty sure a fiancé could as well. It wouldn't hurt to suggest it.

"We are going to be married." He felt stupid saying that. He didn't even know her. But he'd agreed to do this, so he would play along. "I think we can be less formal."

Her eyes darted to Gregory, then to the camera, before

settling on Devon once more. "I wouldn't wish to give your family the impression that I am overly forward."

He shook his head. "I'm sure they'll think you're just regularly forward."

She bit her lips closed. Her eyes scrunched at the corners. Devon knew a held back laugh when he saw one.

"I said that wrong, didn't I?"

She nodded. "And kind of insulted me at the same time."

He pushed out a breath. "I hope they're not judging us on how fancy we can talk, because I am going to butcher that part."

"And I hope they *are*. I'll do well with that."

He believed her. She seemed to know a lot about 1815. "I'm pretty sure I read in the packet that it was common way back then for a woman to coach her fiancé in the proper way of speaking."

She gave him a dry, but amused look. "That was in the papers the show sent?"

He nodded firmly. "I am positive it was."

"I guess I had better help you, then."

"And I had better help you." He held out his hand. "Into the carriage, I mean. That is the proper thing for a gentleman, after all."

She laughed lightly. It was a nice laugh, not fake or loud, just . . . nice.

"You're doing pretty good with the 'we're supposed to act like we're flirting' thing," Gregory said. "I don't actually have any sisters, so I'm not sure how my part is supposed to go."

Devon ignored the comment about flirting. "I have a sister. In real life, I mean."

"So, what do I do?" Gregory asked.

"Give her a hard time. But you look out for her, too. You have her back." Even if having her back meant going on a crazy TV show and making a fool of himself in the hope of getting to take her on her dream vacation before ALS took that dream away from her. That's what a brother did: everything he could.

Chapter Three

Kelsey could feel the earliest hints of a headache coming on. Amanda hadn't stopped talking since they'd started down the road. For someone who had only found out her fictional identity less than an hour earlier, she was managing a very detailed retelling of her life. If Kelsey had to guess, based on the backstory that Amanda was weaving, she would say that her traveling companion had read a lot of Regency romance novels. *A lot.*

"And so, I was engaged for every single dance at the Duke and Duchess's ball within only a few minutes of arriving there." Amanda turned her head to look at Kelsey. They, as decorum demanded, had been given the forward facing seats, while the two gentlemen occupied the bench across from them. "Were you at the ball, Miss Grames? I don't recall seeing you there."

The daughter of a lowly vicar likely would not have received an invitation to a ball hosted by a duke and duchess. Kelsey, however, had no intention of admitting the limits of her social standing to a lady charged with undermining her. "I fear that my invitation must have gone astray."

Amanda's expression turned deeply ponderous. "I don't believe I have ever seen you at Almack's, either."

Yes, Amanda was definitely a reader of Regency romances. Kelsey had read quite a few herself, in between textbooks and scholarly writings and first-person historical accounts. She could navigate this web; it was about time all that knowledge was put to good use.

"We must have been there on different nights," Kelsey said. "Which of the patronesses gave you your vouchers? Lady Esterhazy and Lady Jersey both wanted to give me mine, but Lady Castlereagh made the offer first."

Amanda's eyes narrowed. "*Three* of the patronesses sponsored you?"

"My father might be a simple country vicar, but my mother's family is very well connected." Her card hadn't said anything about her character's mother. If Amanda could invent a lavish history, so could she.

"Is that true, Mr. Grames?" Amanda turned her attention to Gregory.

He shot Kelsey a look of near panic. "Yes." He drew the word out, ending the single syllable almost as a question.

"Did you hear that, brother?" Amanda asked. "Their mother is very well connected. Did you know that?"

Devon looked up from his copy of the "Rules and Etiquette" pamphlet. "I did know that. We are engaged, after all. So naturally I have met her mother. She is . . . awesome."

Kelsey shook her head quickly and mouthed the word "lovely."

"She is *lovely*," he amended.

Cameras were mounted in each of the corners of the carriage, recording every moment of their journey. Though he was technically her competition, Kelsey found herself hoping the judges would cut Devon some slack. He was really trying.

"Our mother has not met Miss Grames's mother," Amanda continued. "It seems we do not occupy the same circles in Society."

Kelsey knew this was part of Amanda's assignment, but it was still incredibly annoying. Decorum, propriety, and determination. That was *Kelsey's* assignment. She could manage it.

"It does seem that their paths have not crossed," Kelsey said. "My mother is often occupied with charitable work, doing her duty as a lady in assisting the poor and unfortunate. As a result of those admirable efforts, she sees very little of those ladies who spend their time in other pursuits."

Gregory's eyes pulled wide. "Good burn, Sis."

"Devon." Amanda's shock sounded real. "Are you going to allow her to talk about our mother that way?"

All eyes were on him now. How would he respond? Even if he truly were Lord Devon of the nineteenth century, engaged to a mere Miss Grames, his response might have gone either way.

Without looking up from his pamphlet he said, "Mrs. Grames is exactly what a lady should be, and I'm sure our mother will agree when she meets her. They are both, after all, exactly lovely."

Kelsey couldn't hold back her grin. Devon's answer was perfect. He'd managed to not insult either fictional mother, but did so with an air of confidence that perfectly suited a member of the aristocracy. It was kind of amazing for a guy she firmly suspected was usually shy and quiet.

The carriage came to a jolting and rocking stop.

"Is that it for today?" Gregory asked, looking out the window.

They were supposed to drive for hours each day. Though Kelsey didn't have her phone, she knew they hadn't been in the carriage for that long. Either something had gone wrong with the carriage or they were about to face their first challenge of the competition.

A quick rap against the carriage door was followed by a heavily accented, "Beggin' your pardon, m'lord."

No one moved. Kelsey watched Devon, waiting for him to respond. After a moment, his eyes pulled wide with realization.

He leaned forward and opened the carriage door. Their driver stood on the other side, his hat in his hands.

"Yes, John?" Devon asked.

"It appears there's a country fair up ahead a piece," John said. "I thought I'd tell you so you could ask the ladies if they'd care to wander around for a spell."

"If he thought we would enjoy it," Amanda muttered, "why is he asking Devon to ask us? It's not like we can't hear him."

"Because he is playing his part correctly," Kelsey answered, keeping her voice just as low. "The ladies would not have been directly addressed in this situation."

"Well, maybe more ladies should have said something about it, demanded to be in charge of their own lives."

She eyed Amanda, debating whether or not to push ahead or ignore her. She had heard too many similar conversations in which modern day women harshly judged their historical counterparts without the slightest attempt to understand the very different world in which they lived. Those remembered discussions convinced her to say now what needed to be said.

"For one thing," Kelsey began, "those ladies would have known nothing else. To insist that they were wimps for not demanding something that likely would never had occurred to them is unfair, and it doesn't make sense. For another thing, the most intelligent of ladies would have realized that demanding an immediate, complete change from those customs and rules which rubbed them the wrong way wouldn't have actually helped anything." Kelsey folded her hands on her lap, trying to maintain the demeanor she was supposed to be affecting despite their very modern conversation. "These women were wise and strong enough to know how to work toward change in ways that wouldn't simply make things worse for everyone. They realized that slow and steady really does win the race."

Although her character description had placed Amanda in

opposition to Kelsey, she didn't argue. Indeed, she seemed to really be listening. "I hadn't thought of it that way."

"Most modern women don't. We often assume that women in more oppressive times had all the same privileges that we do. We assume that they had the option of fighting injustice by the same means we do, when that is completely untrue. And when we realize that they didn't have a *modern* world view or didn't speak up for themselves, a relatively new right that we take for granted now, we dismiss them as weak. It's sad really. They were dismissed by the men of their time, and they are dismissed by us now."

Amanda's features pulled in thought. "But I've read lots of books where the women just tell everyone how it's going to be and how oppressive they are, and they just stand up to the rules and live their own life, and it all works out great."

Kelsey couldn't help a little smile. She'd read a few of those as well. "Basically a modern story set against a vaguely historical backdrop, kind of like what we're doing right now. Those can be fun and entertaining, but they're not real. I think that if the women of 200 years ago read those novels they wouldn't recognize the setting as their own time period. And maybe that's okay sometimes. We can enjoy those stories and have fun with them. Reading them makes me appreciate that much more the books that show us how strong the women of that time period *really* were, even if that strength doesn't look the same as our strength now. They were remarkable and that deserves to be recognized."

Amanda nodded enthusiastically. If not for the roles they had to play, they probably would have gotten along well. "I can't always tell which books are accurate and which are just historical*ish*, but I do like when it at least feels like the characters have different worries than we do, and different rules to work with to meet their goals."

"So do I."

"And," Amanda was really warming to her subject, "I love it

when, even if the heroine is going through things that are totally different from anything that I'd ever go through and dealing with restrictions that are completely foreign to me, I can still relate to her and understand what she's feeling. That is amazing. It's a reminder to me that people are people, no matter when or where they lived."

"Exactly." Kelsey turned a bit on the bench to face her, ready to take up the topic with enthusiasm. But out of the corner of her eye, she caught Devon watching her, amusement in his green eyes. She held his gaze with a questioning one of her own.

"I didn't want to interrupt," he said.

She shook her head. "Go ahead." This was about the competition, after all.

"There is a country fair up the road that we have been invited to attend. Gregory says that it sounds like fun. What about you guys—you *ladies*?" he corrected.

She had completely forgotten the discussion that had triggered their tangent. "So long as we have time to still reach our inn this evening." She was certain that the county fair was meant to be their challenge and that they ought to stop, but a lady of sense would always treat the perils of carriage travel at night with the appropriate concern.

"I think we will." Devon glanced at John, who gave a very subtle nod in reply. "If everyone wants to stop, we can."

Kelsey looked at Amanda. "Would you like to, Lady Amanda?"

"I would," she said. "I've read about country fairs. They sound very diverting."

Diverting. Points to Amanda for the historical word choice.

"And you, Miss Grames?" Devon asked. "Would you like to attend the fair?"

She didn't need even another moment to think about. "Lord Devon, I would *love* to."

Chapter Four

The four of them stood at the gate to a fence, behind which was an open field where canopies and temporary shacks had been erected. Kelsey could just make out a pen with livestock to one side. People mulled about, their voices called out, bouncing against each other in indistinguishable echoes. It was exactly the exciting, chaotic mess she'd always imagined at a nineteenth-century country fair, except with cameras on either side of them and a boom mic suspended above their heads.

Devon, who stood beside Kelsey, leaned closer to her and said, "I couldn't find anything in the pamphlet about how to do this part. Do we all have to stay together or just go do our own thing?"

She set her arm through his, as would have been proper for an engaged couple. "The ladies would not be permitted to wander on their own, though gentlemen would."

"That's probably annoying for you," he said.

"Only because I've always had that freedom."

He simply nodded, not needing further explanation or convincing. Either he'd studied more of this era than she thought, or he had a natural understanding of human nature.

"And, do I need to be the one walking around with Amanda, or can that be Gregory?"

That wasn't as easy a question to answer. "The biggest

sticklers would insist that Amanda and Gregory not be paired off without you being in company with them. However, many people would not object if you and I go about on our own and Amanda and Gregory do the same, provided we remain at the fair, and in public."

"So no one can be accused of shenanigans?" His brow pulled low. "Is 'shenanigans' okay to say?"

"Close enough."

He half sighed, half laughed. "Like I said before, I hope they're very understanding on the vocabulary."

Gregory stepped a bit past them. "This looks like a place where a guy could get one of those huge turkey legs."

"There will be plenty of vendors selling food," Kelsey said.

"Which is probably why we were given these." Gregory pulled a small coin purse from his jacket pocket and shook it. Rather than the metallic clanking of coins, the contents made a series of tiny clicks and thuds. His eyes darted about conspiratorially. "I think they're made of plastic," he whispered. "Hopefully, getting thrown in jail for trying to use counterfeit coins isn't one of our 'challenges.'"

Amanda pulled open her reticule, searching through its contents. "I didn't get any coins, counterfeit or otherwise."

"I am certain that your brother will supply you with a few," Kelsey said. "As a gentleman, he would never allow you to be without the things you require." Though it would rub any modern woman the wrong way to have to ask the men in her family for something as simple as spending money, this was the reality that nineteenth-century women had lived every day. She could make the most of it.

"I guess that means I'm supposed to give you a few coins as well," Gregory said. "Or—Or is Devon supposed to do that since he's going to marry you?"

She couldn't help a moment of playfulness. "I wouldn't object if both of you contributed to my county fair funds."

"Well, then, dearest Sister." Gregory strutted a bit as he pulled his coin purse open. "I'm gentleman enough to give my sister a bit of cash." With an absolutely snooty expression, he pulled a few "coins" from his bag. They were plastic and all identical. That would simplify things—no need to learn the many different coins of the era.

Kelsey held out her gloved hand. He dropped four coins there. "I thank you, dearest Brother. And I promise I will absolutely spend them in one place."

Gregory laughed, his eyes crinkling at the corners. "It is a very good thing you're marrying a guy who's swimming in money."

Far from being offended, Devon laughed right along. "That is exactly what I said when I proposed, 'Hey, you should marry me. I'm swimming in money, you know.'"

Gregory clasped his hands and fluttered his eyelashes. In an overly sweet, overly high voice he declared, "'Oh, Lord Devon, you are *so* romantic!'"

Amanda seemed to suddenly remember her part in all of this. "I certainly hope you didn't discuss something as horribly mercenary as money during your courtship and proposal. I would hate to think that money truly was the foundation of this arrangement."

Before Kelsey could respond, Devon put his arm around her and pulled her up beside him. "I wished for her to marry me for no reason except that we love each other. Money had nothing to do with it."

Amanda harrumphed, but with laughter in her eyes. They were all becoming friends, which made their forced rivalry a bit difficult to maintain. "Mr. Grames." Amanda turned to Gregory. "I find myself wishing for a giant turkey leg, would you be so good as to help me find one?"

"You bet." Gregory offered his arm, his very un-Regency

way of speaking contrasting with the period-appropriate gesture. "And maybe they have funnel cakes, too."

"Pray tell," Amanda replied, "what is a 'funnel cake'?"

Gregory laughed as they walked away together.

Devon slipped Kelsey's arm through his once more. "I saw a bunch of guys do this arm thing in the movies Chrissy made me watch."

"Who's Chrissy?"

"My sis—" He stopped short. "Amanda's supposed to be my only sister. Hmm."

Kelsey understood the dilemma. "Perhaps Chrissy is your 'cousin,' who lives in America."

He smiled gratefully. "Yes. That's it." They moved forward, toward the fair. "She had me watch a bunch of . . . 'theater plays' before I came here, to help me get ready for this."

"Ah." Movies set in the nineteenth century. She got it. "Is Chrissy the one who convinced you to do this competition in the first place?"

"Sort of."

They passed a juggler and a knife grinder. A bit further down the path was an apple vendor.

"She heard about this 'road trip' and said how much she would have liked to have done it," Devon said. "But she's not healthy."

He had mentioned his sister's health during their very brief conversation in the doorway. "It is not serious, I hope."

Unmistakable sadness touched his face. "It is."

"Can anything be done?"

He shook his head.

"No wonder you were willing to come and do this for her."

A girl, likely no more than fourteen or fifteen years old, called out to them as they passed. "A pretty posy for your lady, m'lord? Only a coin."

Devon looked to Kelsey.

"It would be customary to buy it," she whispered, knowing that he wasn't as well-versed as she was in these things.

"Though that may be true," he said, "I'd like to know if you *want* one."

"I love flowers," she said.

He nodded firmly and handed the girl a coin in exchange for a small bouquet. "Your flowers, my lady," he said with a flourish.

"I am only a *miss*," she reminded him.

"If Amanda doesn't successfully convince our parents to get rid of you, you'll be Lady Kelsey."

She accepted the offered bouquet. "I will actually become 'Lady Devon Bartlett.'"

"Really?"

"Really. That is the way these courtesy titles work."

"How do you keep it all straight?"

Kelsey spotted a TV camera, barely concealed behind a stack of hay bales they were about to pass. She quickly thought over her answer, rewording it to be period appropriate while still making sense to Devon. "Like any proper young lady, I was raised with my prayer book in one hand and Debrett's *Peerage* in the other."

Devon chuckled quietly. "I have a feeling if Amanda heard you say that, she wouldn't know whether to agree with you or accuse you of having grown up looking for a man with a title." He certainly caught on quickly.

Kelsey raised her flowers to her nose, luxuriating in the sweet smell of them. Her eye caught a slip of white tucked among the stem. On closer examination, she realized it was a piece of twisted paper. She would have simply pulled it out, but thanks to the dictates of Society, the hand not holding her flowers was holding Devon's arm.

"There is something in my flowers," she told him.

He looked for himself, then reached in and pulled the paper out. "Our next challenge, maybe?"

"What does it say?" she asked.

He untwisted it. "It looks like a riddle or a poem.

'You have made it to the fair, now it's time to make a plan.

'Keep your eyes wide open. Spot it if you can.

'Enjoy the day, the 1800s way,

'But you must find the yellow man.'"

Find the yellow man. "That's our challenge? It doesn't say anything else."

"Nothing." He stuffed the paper in his pocket. "Do they mean someone wearing a yellow costume?"

She had no idea. "I suspect they are being vague on purpose. Let's just hope that we'll know him when we see him. In the meantime, let's enjoy the fair. Your 'cousin' would kill you if she thought you wasted this opportunity. I know I would."

"You enjoy this sort of thing, don't you?"

A sigh emanated from deep inside her. "I *love* all of this. I, honestly, love it."

He leaned in a touch closer. "Don't let word of this get out, but I'm kind of enjoying it, too."

"I won't tell a soul," she whispered solemnly.

The afternoon passed as joyously as she could have hoped. They saw performers and tried mince pies and scones. She even had her fortune told, something that would have been a bit questionable in that era, but not entirely unheard of. The fortune-teller had spoken of "sweet success." Kelsey hoped that proved true.

Throughout it all, Devon was a good sport and a lot of fun. He threw himself into the festivities with enthusiasm. She could tell the entire thing was far outside his comfort zone, but he tried it all. He laughed at himself when things didn't go as planned and asked for help on things he wasn't familiar with.

It was a shame they weren't allowed to talk about their actual lives. The more time she spent with Devon, the more she wanted to know him. The *real* him.

Late in the afternoon, they crossed paths with Gregory and Amanda.

"Did you find a turkey leg?" Devon asked.

"Sadly, no. But we did get to watch two puppets slug each other." Gregory seemed to have enjoyed his first experience with Punch & Judy.

Amanda motioned the four of them into a huddle. "Did you get the message in your flowers?"

Kelsey nodded. "But we haven't seen anything that would qualify as a 'yellow man.' No one is wearing a lot of yellow. None of the buildings or canopies are yellow."

"I'm beginning to think that the 'sweet success' you were promised was an empty fortune," Devon said.

Amanda and Gregory exchanged surprised looks.

"The fortune-teller told us the same thing," Amanda said. "And in those same words."

"Maybe it's a clue," Devon said. "'Sweet success.'"

"There are plenty of sweet things being sold by the vendors," Gregory said. "I've spent the day drooling over most of them."

"Anything yellow?" Kelsey asked.

"Yes!" Amanda grabbed Gregory's hand but addressed them all. "Let's go. I'll show you."

They rushed down the paths of the fair, which was not terribly dignified. Kelsey could only hope that they wouldn't be penalized for it. She had seen the other contestants at the fair as well. They were no doubt looking for the same mysterious thing.

They reached a table covered in toffee and candies. The lady selling the goodies eyed them all expectantly.

"There," Amanda said, pointing to a small basket amidst the other offerings. "Yellow candies."

The vendor caught Devon's eye. "Were all of you interested in anything in particular, m'lord?"

The extras had been well trained. Each of them deferred to

Devon, knowing he was the highest ranking member of their group.

"This yellow candy, here." He motioned to Amanda's discovery. "I am not familiar with it."

"A hard taffy out of Ireland," the woman said. "A honey taffy. The people there call it 'yellow man.'"

Gregory let out a shout of triumph.

"How much for the entire basket?" Devon asked. "*All four of us* would like to share it."

"Eight coins, m'lord."

Devon pulled out his coin purse once more. "It might not count if we don't all contribute to buying it," he told the three of them.

Gregory reached into his pocket. Kelsey and Amanda both snagged a couple of coins from their reticules. They each contributed their portion and, in a flash, they had their "yellow man."

"We did it," Amanda whispered anxiously. "For a minute there, I thought you were going to buy it all, Devon, and leave the rest of us out of luck."

He shook his head firmly. "We made a deal this morning, Sister. Our carriage is going to be the winning carriage. Buying it all means the other carriage won't get any."

"Your brother is a sharp competitor," Kelsey said. "I like it."

Devon blushed. Kelsey couldn't remember the last time she'd seen a grown man color up. Oddly enough, she liked that as well.

Oh, yes. This competition was growing better by the moment.

Chapter Five

Devon was actually having a good time. The carriage ride from the fair to the inn, where they were now, had been filled with laughter. Gregory had kept them rolling with his made-up family history. Amanda had matched his creativity with her own stories. Throughout it all, Kelsey continually looked across at Devon, sharing a smile or a laugh, and offering commentary meant specifically for him.

Her company had felt that way at the fair, too. Even with all the distractions there and her obvious excitement at living this dream of hers, she'd made him feel like he was important. She had listened to him, spoken with him, and had seemed to genuinely enjoy his company. Would she have still felt that way if she'd met him outside of this fake life they were living? Would she have even noticed him if he were just the quiet guy in the corner?

"I wonder if the inn has another lamp," Amanda said, glancing around the inn's small parlor where they'd been placed for dinner. "It is very dim in here."

Devon knew what his role was. "I will ask." He rose and crossed to the door. Kelsey had told him earlier that private rooms for dining were reserved exclusively for the fancier travelers. Having a decked-out carriage came with perks, apparently.

The innkeeper spotted Devon in the doorway and stepped up to him, his hat in his hands. The camera in the corner pulled in closer.

"Yes, m'lord?" the innkeeper asked.

"Could we have an additional lamp?" he asked. "The ladies are having difficulty seeing their plates."

The innkeeper dipped his head. "Of course."

Devon had only just returned to the table when the new lamp arrived and was placed within easy distance. The additional light was helpful, though the room was still quite dim. What would people two hundred years ago have thought if they'd seen how bright a modern home was even in the dead of night? And, how were the cameras recording any of this in such a dark room?

"Beggin' your pardon for the interruption, m' lord."

Devon was getting really tired of being called "my lord" instead of his name.

"Cook was thinking of putting together a basket for your party if you'd care to have a picnic tomorrow. She makes excellent scones."

The proposal was made with the same heavy hinting as the carriage driver's question about the fair. The picnic, then, was part of their challenge for tomorrow. Devon knew that he could make this decision on his own if he wanted. Kelsey had explained, when the cameras weren't nearby, that the son of a marquess could do just about anything he wanted to, as long as it was gentlemanly. Marquess, she'd further explained, was a title, like duke or earl.

Still, he decided to pose the question to the rest of the table. "What do all of you think? Should we have a picnic tomorrow?"

Gregory took another dinner roll. "I think we better."

Kelsey nodded her agreement, her eyes dancing with excitement. Amanda wore a similar expression.

Devon addressed the innkeeper again. "We will accept Cook's offer. Tell her thank you."

The man bowed quickly and hurried from the room.

Devon met Kelsey's eye once more. "It is okay to say 'thank you,' isn't it?" he asked quietly.

She scooted her chair a little closer to his. "Oh, yes. In this era, you would not have been the best of friends with a servant, at least not under normal circumstances, but being kind was always acceptable."

"Good. I don't think I could be a jerk to anyone, even if it fit my part."

Her smile turned sweet. "I believe you."

She seemed happy to discover he was a decent person. Maybe she would have noticed him out in the real world. That didn't happen very often.

The next morning, they received another unexpected perk: breakfast in bed. Well, not actually *in bed* but brought to their room on a tray. He and Gregory were roomed together, and Kelsey and Amanda were across the hall.

But their private morning meals meant that, by the time their lunch picnic rolled around, Devon hadn't seen Kelsey all day. It was weird that he missed her even though they'd only met the day before. He wasn't in love, not even close. He simply liked her company. She was fun, and they were becoming friends.

He stood with Gregory in the inn's parlor, waiting for the ladies to come down and join them. Though Devon couldn't find anything in their pamphlet specifically about waiting, there was a section about gentlemen being required to accompany ladies when they were out in public. Based on that, waiting for Amanda and Kelsey seemed like the right thing.

He heard Amanda's steps moving quickly down the stairs just outside of the parlor. She walked as quickly as she talked, and that was saying something. She peeked inside a moment later.

"Is it picnic time?" she asked.

"Right-o. Top o' the picnic time it is," Gregory said. Most of the time, he didn't even try to sound historical. And, when he did attempt it, he was so bad at it that the outcome was hilarious.

Amanda laughed and smiled broadly at Gregory. She crossed to the window seat and knelt, looking outside. Devon returned his attention to the doorway. Kelsey ought to be coming in any minute. Ladies, he was told, didn't walk around inns by themselves in the nineteenth century.

In the next moment, she turned the corner and stepped into the parlor. But the excitement that had been in her eyes the day before was almost gone now. She looked pale and tired.

He stepped up beside her. "Are you okay?"

"I am not feeling particularly well." Her voice wasn't scratchy, like it would have been if she'd caught a cold, but it didn't sound strong either. "I don't know if my bedchamber was overly cold last night or someone at the fair breathed germs on me—"

"Did they have germs in 1815?" Giving his real sister a hard time had always lifted her spirits when her health was poor; he hoped the same approach would work with Kelsey.

Her smile was tiny and seemed a little strained. "Yes, but they didn't know that they did."

"What did they think was making them sick?"

"The climate. A weakness in their bodies. Pretty much anything except microorganisms."

"Sometimes, though, it really is someone's own body that makes them sick."

"Your—" Her eyes darted to the nearby camera. "—*cousin*?"

Playing a part was obnoxious when a person just wanted to have a real conversation with someone. He'd forgotten his role as soon as she'd come in looking sick.

"Yes, my cousin," he said. "She is very ill due to . . . a disease in her own body." He had no idea how to explain something as complicated as ALS in nineteenth-century terms other than "a slow and painful way to die," but he couldn't bring himself to say that either. Months had passed since her diagnosis, and he still had a hard time admitting how it would all end.

"Devon," Kelsey whispered, nudging his arm and subtly motioning toward the open doorway.

The innkeeper stood there, his hat held in his hands. He watched Devon expectantly. But Devon hadn't asked him to come and didn't have anything to say to him.

Kelsey turned enough to be facing away from the cameras and the new arrival but still near enough to whisper to Devon. "He is likely waiting for permission to speak."

"He has to have my permission just to talk?" Devon whispered back.

"It would have been considered both rude and presumptuous for someone of the servant class to speak directly to someone of the upper class without being told that they could."

Devon shook his head at the ridiculousness of that. "And no one thought that was stupid?"

She shrugged. "There are probably a lot of things we do now without a second thought that people two-hundred years from now will think are pretty stupid."

"But I am allowed to be nice to him. You said that yesterday."

Her smile returned once more. "Of course."

He returned his focus to the innkeeper. "Good afternoon," he said.

"And to you, m'lord. Beggin' your pardon, but your picnic is ready whenever it's convenient for you and your party."

Devon nodded. "Thank you, and please thank Cook and everyone who helped put it together."

"I will." He gave a quick bow and left once more.

Devon turned to "his party." Amanda was up off the window seat already, bouncing with excitement, and Gregory was watching Amanda, grinning.

Kelsey was eying those two as well. Her eyes darted to Devon. "That's an interesting development," she whispered.

"What is?" he asked.

She just shook her head. Her next breath sounded more like an exhausted sigh.

"Are you feeling up for the picnic?" he asked.

"If it's in the shade and I don't actually have to eat."

That didn't sound good at all. But Devon had learned early on in Chrissy's disease that questioning a grown woman about the decisions she's made about her own health, as if she wasn't capable of knowing what she was well enough to do or try, was kind of a jerk move.

So he just offered Kelsey his arm and walked with her out of the inn and around to the back, then across the field to where a blanket was spread out underneath a clump of trees. Large cushions had been placed on the blanket. A table was set up nearby with a fancy spread of food, actual plates and utensils, and cloth napkins.

"Is *this* the picnic?" he wondered out loud.

"The upper class never did anything halfway," Kelsey said.

Being upper class back then must have been exhausting. But not half as exhausting as being someone who did all of this for them. When he was done with this competition, Devon was going to eat a microwave burrito on his couch like a regular person.

Kelsey chose the cushion closest to the trunk of the nearest tree. She really didn't look like she felt well at all.

"Does anything on the table look good to you?" he asked her. "Even just a glass of water? I'd be happy to bring you whatever you want." But he stopped up short. "Am I allowed to do that?"

"It would be very gentlemanly of you." She leaned back against the tree trunk. "Some water would be nice."

He ladled water from the punch bowl into a glass, an actual made-out-of-glass glass. *These 1800s rich people really didn't know how to have a laid-back picnic.*

He carefully brought the glass of water back to Kelsey then sat on the cushion next to hers.

"You can get something for yourself," she said between sips. "You don't have to remain here beside me, while your stomach sits empty."

"I will in a second. I just figured you would probably finish off the water quickly in this heat, and then I could take it back with me for a refill."

His prediction was spot-on. A moment later she handed him her empty glass with a thank you and a quiet request for more. And a few moments after that, he returned with a plate of food for himself and more water for her.

Gregory and Amanda sat not very far off. The other carriage team had joined the picnic as well. As far as Devon could tell, no one had been given any kind of challenge. Maybe getting through the picnic without breaking any of the etiquette rules *was* the challenge.

"Tell me about your cousin Chrissy."

"She is amazing." Though he didn't often talk about his sister, more out of heavy worry than anything else, he launched into a rambling discussion of how great she was, the fun things they'd done as children, and how excited she'd been about him doing this show. He also talked about his worry for her, and how hard it was to watch her suffering.

"So, then, this wasn't a matter of you being a pushover," Kelsey said. "You really do love her that much."

"Yeah, I do. And, man, I wish she could have been part of this. She would have loved every single minute."

"She sounds like my kind of person."

He thought about that for just a fraction of a moment. "Actually, I think you two could probably be good friends."

"Maybe—" She hesitated. "Maybe, when this is done, I could meet her sometime. If that's not too weird of a thing to say."

He slipped his hand around hers. "Not weird at all."

Kelsey held to his hand. He assumed that was allowed, since they were supposed to be engaged.

Off in the distance, the inn's servants were setting up some kind of game. Croquet, maybe.

"Looks like that's our next challenge," Gregory said, nodding toward the game.

"Probably," Devon said. "Are you any good at croquet, Kels—"

Her eyes were closed, and her head rested heavily against the tree. She looked even paler than she had a moment earlier. Devon pushed his empty plate aside and scooted over to her.

"Kelsey? Are you okay?" he asked. "Do you need to go back inside?"

Her eyes fluttered a bit but didn't open. "I really don't feel well," she quietly replied.

He settled in beside her, placing his hand in hers again, unsure what he should do. She moved a bit, leaning against him now instead of the tree, her head resting on his shoulder.

"She doesn't look well." Amanda watched with obvious concern. Even Gregory had looked away from the challenge being assembled in the distance.

Devon reached up and touched his hand to her forehead. Either the shade had not been enough protection from the midday sun, or she was running a fever. He tested his own forehead. He was wearing thick layers of clothing and had been sitting outside as long as she had been, but his skin felt much cooler.

"Amanda, will you sit with her?" Devon asked. "I'm going to get some help."

They made the switch quickly. Devon spotted the actor playing the role of innkeeper not far from the table of food. He offered a bow as Devon approached.

"I don't know how to say this in a historical way," Devon said, "and I won't waste time trying to figure it out."

The man's brows shot upward in surprise.

"Kelsey is sick. She's running a fever. We need to send for the set medic and have her looked at, but I don't know who to talk to."

The man dropped his act in an instant. "C'mon. The production assistant is inside the inn."

Chapter Six

Kelsey had no idea how long she had slept, but no light spilled in through the windows of her room at the "inn." She was grateful that the studio had installed some hidden lights. Even with night firmly fallen outside, she wasn't depending on only a few candles to see her surroundings.

The other contestants would likely be at their next destination by now, having dinner and making plans for the final day of their road trip and the ball tomorrow night.

I am going to miss the ball. I've lost the trip to England, lost the money to pay for graduate school, and I don't even get to go the ball.

She was not usually one for feeling sorry for herself, but she couldn't help it this time. This week was supposed to have been her dream come true, and now she was spending it cooped up in a room with "a virus of some kind," according to the medic who had evaluated her. He said she must have caught whatever it was before even arriving on set. Her dream had been doomed before it had even started.

Kelsey turned over onto her side. But this new position wasn't any less uncomfortable than lying on her back had been. Her heart was heavy, her mind spun endlessly over her bad luck, and now her body ached as well. This was not how she'd wanted this week to end.

If she couldn't be the grand prize winner, she hoped the winner turned out to be Devon. He was doing this for his sister, which was pretty amazing, considering how uncomfortable he obviously was with the whole thing. And he had thrown himself into it wholeheartedly.

How had he fared that afternoon without her whispering information to him about expectations and etiquette? She hoped that he'd still managed it. And she hoped that Gregory and Amanda were enjoying themselves as well. The way that Gregory had watched Amanda that afternoon spoke volumes. Maybe something would come of that.

Her heart did an unexpected, almost painful flip inside. *Maybe something would come of that.* Although she hadn't admitted it to herself before, she had kind of hoped something would come of her time with Devon as well. They hardly knew each other, but what she did know about him, she liked. And she liked him enough to want to see if there was something there worth pursuing.

Would the show be willing to give her his contact info? Were they even allowed to? Maybe she could tell the producers that if *he* asked for *her* info they had permission to tell him. But would he? The little hints of interest that she thought she'd seen in him might have been nothing more than the part he was playing.

She was far too sick to sort all of this out at the moment. With a sigh, she closed her eyes and tried to calm her thoughts enough to rest again.

A few minutes later, she heard a quiet knock at her door.

"Come in," she said without opening her eyes.

The door scraped as it opened—a nice touch, since an old roadside inn would likely have had worn-out, noisy doors in 1815. Heavy footsteps drew nearer.

She opened one eye. Then the other flew open. Devon.

"What are you—? I thought—You're supposed to be at your next stop."

He just smiled. "Can I sit?" He pointed at the chair beside her bed.

"Of course." She pushed herself up into a seated position. Why was Devon still here? She couldn't make sense of it.

"You look better than you did this afternoon," he said. "Are you feeling any better?"

"A little less like I'm going to pass out."

He nodded in what looked like relief. "Noah—that's the guy who plays the innkeeper—said he'd assumed that you'd been told to act like you were sick as part of the game. That's why he didn't say anything to the production assistant."

She leaned against the headboard. "I am really glad you didn't think that, too."

"So am I." He hooked an arm over the back of the chair, looking like he didn't plan to go anywhere anytime soon.

"Why aren't you at your next destination on the road trip?"

He didn't hesitate with his answer. "I don't abandon people when they're sick, Kelsey. My sister has never gone to a single doctor's visit alone. She's never spent a single day in the hospital without someone there, most of the time me. How was it that Amanda put it? I'm 'very handy in the sickroom.'"

She wasn't sure if the surge of heat in her face came from his thoughtfulness in staying with her or from a return of her earlier fever.

"I have a little virus," she countered. "Nothing as serious as what your sister endures."

Even that comparison didn't seem to shake him. "Serious or minor, a person shouldn't feel alone when they're sick. That's my take on it."

"But you have to finish the trip to win the grand prize."

He waved that off. "Amanda and Gregory and I had a long, drawn out discussion *directly in front of the cameras* about how a true gentleman would stay with his fiancée until she was well again, and how a true gentleman would not leave his sister in a roadside inn when she was ill. And a lady would stay to offer 'ladylike support,' which, by the way, made me laugh every time Amanda said it. I don't even know why it was so funny. She got frustrated with me, though, especially when Gregory started laughing, too."

"You made a historical argument for not leaving?"

"Yup." His smile slowly turned into a conspiratorial grin. "Amanda helped us figure out how to say it right, but we made our case pretty firmly. The producers said, 'Stay in character.' Remaining at the inn was the only way to do that accurately."

Even in her exhaustion, Kelsey found the strength to return his smile. "Nicely done, Devon. I really, really hope it works."

"It will," he said confidently. "All four of us deserve a fair shot at the grand prize."

"What would you do with it if you won?" There were no cameras in her room, so she felt safe pushing forward with a very *un*historical conversation.

"I'd take my sister to England, while she can still go." Underneath his declaration was a heavy layer of sadness. "It's her dream, and she's running out of time. The money would also pay off some medical bills; ALS is not a cheap way to die."

With that matter-of-fact explanation and the almost hidden catch in his voice, she felt her heart crack a little. "I didn't realize it was ALS."

"I didn't know how to describe it in nineteenth-century words."

They likely didn't have a term for it back then. "It probably would have been described as a 'wasting illness.'"

A shadow crossed over his features. "A 'wasting illness.' That is horribly appropriate. With ALS, the body really does waste away."

She reached across the bed and set her hand in his. "I am so sorry, Devon. I really am."

"You are also feeling warm again." He didn't release her hand, though. He cupped it between his two. "Do you need me to grab the medic again?"

Though it meant that Devon would leave, she could feel the chills growing once more and her head beginning to pound. "That would be helpful, thank you."

He squeezed her hand before standing and stepping out of her room once more. In the silence he left behind, Kelsey's mind and heart began whirling once more: not on her own dashed hopes, but on Devon and his sister and his compassionate heart. How could Kelsey help but feel the smallest beginnings of affection for a man like him?

Soon the medic stepped inside, alone. "I hear you're feeling bad again." He took the seat Devon had occupied.

Kelsey glanced back at the doorway. The empty doorway.

"He'll come back in when I'm done," the medic said with a chuckle. "He's just giving you a little privacy."

"He's a very thoughtful person," she said.

The medic pulled a digital thermometer from his bag. "Yes, he is."

An idea popped into her mind, fully formed and seemingly out of the blue. It grabbed her with such force, in fact, that she knew it would never be shaken until she acted on it. "Do you think, after you've checked to make sure I'm still not dying—" He smiled as she knew he would. "—you could ask the production assistant to come in for a minute? There's something I absolutely have to ask her."

Chapter Eight

Devon had never worn a tuxedo before. Even back in high school, when he'd gone to prom, he'd borrowed a regular suit. But the costume he'd been given for the ball at the end of this history competition was, to his untrained eye, pretty much a tuxedo, only with a big cloth thing instead of a bow tie.

It wasn't comfortable and wasn't something he would have chosen for himself, but it actually wasn't too bad. He stepped out of the carriage feeling less stupid than he'd expected to. And then he looked up.

The "house" where this ball was being held was huge. Columns, at least two stories tall and too thick for him to have wrapped his arms all the way around them, stood every five or six feet all the way across the front. In the wall behind the columns were tall windows, nearly as tall as the columns themselves, and the metal around the edges of the glass looked almost like gold.

Servants in fancy costumes stood along the path to the stone front steps. There were more by the doors, and likely more inside. Even though Devon knew this was only a TV set and that most of the look of it was fake, the enormity of it still made him feel very small.

The son of a marquess would probably think this place was puny. The silent pep talk didn't do much to ease his mind. He was so out of his comfort zone here. If only Kelsey or Chrissy were here with him. They would have known exactly what he was expected to do. Better still, they would love every minute of all of this, and that would have made the whole thing far more fun.

Devon offered his arm to Amanda. At least he knew that part. Gregory walked a pace behind them. Devon had hoped that Kelsey would be well enough to come tonight, but the producers and medic had taken her away from the inn earlier in the day. They were probably sending her home.

He and Gregory and Amanda walked up the wide front steps. Amanda's eager gaze seemed to take in every detail. They stepped inside the door and into an entryway with white marble floors and a large, fancy wooden staircase. On either side of the entryway stood a suit of armor with some kind of flag hanging over it. It was just what he would have expected the entryway of a European castle to look like.

"I am so excited," Amanda whispered.

"It is pretty cool," Gregory responded, looking around as well.

Servants came over and took their hats and Amanda's shawl. Other people wandered about, some dressed like servants, some like the upper class people who would have been invited to something like this. The people in super-old-school tuxedos and fancy dresses were headed through the double doors to the left of the staircase.

That must be where the ball is.

His guess proved right. A small orchestra was set up on a raised platform at the far end of the enormous room. Some chairs had been placed around the edges of the room. People wandered around, chatting. What was he supposed to do now? Wander? Sit? Talk to people? Man, he hoped it wasn't the last one.

He didn't see any guys sitting, only a few women. Those sitting down were older, which made a lot of sense. But a few yards away, was someone younger, who—He did a double take.

Kelsey?

Amanda must have spotted her at the exact same moment. "There's Kelsey. I didn't know they were going to let her come."

All three of them moved in that direction. Kelsey smiled when she looked up and saw them approaching. She was still pale but didn't seem as weak or as exhausted.

He was probably expected to say something like, "How lovely to see you again" or "I trust you are much recovered from your sickness." All he could manage was, "You're here."

"So long as I don't exert myself and I stay near the open windows so I don't get overheated, I have been granted permission to watch the ball. Dancing, I have been told very firmly, is entirely out of the question."

His smile grew on the instant. "You're here."

Amanda laughed lightly. "Gregory, would you be so good as to take a turn about the room with me? I believe our siblings would appreciate a moment's privacy."

Devon didn't bother trying to decide if that was the proper thing. He released Amanda's arm and sat beside Kelsey. "Are you really well enough to be here? I wouldn't want you to grow worse because of this."

"I feel much better this evening than I did yesterday," she said. "And though I know I would start feeling worse again if I tried to dance or doing anything strenuous, I'm just so happy to be here that I don't even mind."

"I don't mind not dancing, either."

She shook her head in obvious amusement. "A sacrifice for you, I'm sure."

He'd liked her sense of humor from the very beginning. It was just one of many things he'd like to know better about her. Before the night was over, he needed to get her phone number or email address or something. He wanted a chance to really meet her without the fake characters and imaginary world. Just the real Kelsey . . . He didn't even know what her actual last name was.

"Begging your pardon, m'lord," a woman said in a heavy accent.

He looked up at the sound.

"Your presence is requested in the entryway," she said. She was probably supposed to be a maid at this fancy house.

"What am I needed for?" Had he forgotten some duty he was supposed to do? He'd studied the section in the pamphlet about balls, and he was pretty sure that escorting his party inside, securing punch for any ladies who requested it, and dancing were his only requirements.

"Your cousin is here, m'lord, and wishes you to accompany her inside."

"My cous—" The words stopped as the pieces fell into place. He'd called Chrissy his *cousin.* "She's here?"

The maid smiled. "That she is, your lordship, and she's so excited, she's near to bursting."

He turned quickly to Kelsey. "I'll be back." With those three words he flew from his seat and rushed back to the entryway.

The sight that met him there stopped him in his tracks. Chrissy was dressed in a beautiful purple dress, just like the fanciest ones he'd seen in the ballroom. Her hair had been fixed up, and she wore what looked like diamonds, though they were likely costume jewelry. Someone had even created a fancy cover for her wheelchair that matched her dress.

But it was the excitement in her eyes that took Devon's breath away. The past few months, as this disease had progressed, had been brutal. She'd been through so much heartache, and so many cycles of grief. Everything she'd imagined her future would be had slowly been taken from her.

She'd kept her chin up, and had kept a positive attitude, but facing a terminal illness doesn't allow a person to ever be the same. In that moment, she looked like the Chrissy he'd known his whole life, eagerly grabbing every exciting opportunity and soaking up every moment.

He took the few remaining steps to reach her. He tried to say something, but the right words didn't come. So he bent down and simply hugged her.

"Isn't this amazing?" she asked, her words slurred and slowed by her disease. She eventually wouldn't be able to talk to him anymore. He tried to keep that fact firmly out of his thoughts for now.

"Why didn't you tell me you were going to be here?" He sat back on his feet.

"I didn't find out until last night. The show called and asked if I could come."

He hadn't heard anything about this. "I didn't say anything to them."

"Someone named Kelsey apparently talked the producers' ears off and eventually convinced them to ask. Since we live kind of close, here I am."

Kelsey. She had made this happen? His mind refused to come up with anything other than *wow*.

"I'd like to meet her," Chrissy said.

Devon jumped into action. "You need to. You'd love her. She's obsessed with this stuff like you are, and she's fun and funny and really kind of awesome."

Chrissy laughed. "You don't sound like the son of a nineteenth-century marquess."

He rolled his eyes. "I've been pretty terrible at this." He grabbed the handles of her wheelchair—she was using her manual one, probably because it was closer to what they would have had two hundred years ago—and pushed her toward the ballroom doors. "Just wait until you see it. Looks a lot like the ballrooms in all those movies. There's even an orchestra."

He took Chrissy right to the middle of the room and turned her wheelchair slowly in a full circle so she could see everything. She commented on things that he hadn't even seen: a chalk drawing of flowers and birds on the ballroom floor, something called "bunting" that had to do with the curtains, and something called "livery" that was related to the servants. Kelsey would have known exactly what she was talking about.

"I think the most important thing for you to see here, though," he said, "is an authentic nineteenth-century history nerd. They are rare, but one has been brought in especially for the ball."

Chrissy gave him a look of amused annoyance.

"I didn't mean *you*, though you probably would qualify." He turned her toward Kelsey. "Over this way."

Kelsey beamed as they approached. She had never met Chrissy, and yet she seemed almost as happy to see her as Devon had been.

The introductions took only a few seconds, and quick as that, the two women were lost in an in-depth conversation about history. Kelsey listened to Chrissy's slow, sometimes muddled words, without a hint of impatience or pity. Devon didn't understand most of what they said, but it was one of his favorite conversations ever.

A lot of Chrissy's friends had drifted away after ALS had complicated her life. Whether those friends were uncomfortable being part of a life that everyone knew would be cut short, or they simply didn't know what to say, or they just didn't care enough to stick around, he and Chrissy didn't know. But it had broken her heart. For this evening, though, she had a true friend, one who was treating her like a whole person.

The musicians began playing a song. Chrissy and Kelsey both looked over at the orchestra with longing. Devon didn't have to read a pamphlet to know what his part was.

He stood and offered a brief bow. "Cousin Chrissy,"—he

almost laughed out loud as he called her that—"I would be honored if you would dance with me."

"Why, Cousin Devon, how very gentlemanly of you." She was clearly loving this.

He turned to Kelsey. "Miss Grames, I would be honored if you would allow me to sit beside you during the next dance while you are sickly and pale and too feeble for dancing."

"How very gentlemanly of you," she said dryly, but with humor dancing in her eyes.

He grabbed the wheelchair handles once more. "C'mon, Chrissy. You're going to dance at a ball."

And she did, over and over again. Gregory danced with her. The guys from the other carriage danced with her. Actors brought in to be part of the crowd danced with her. Devon watched from his chair beside Kelsey as his sister lived a dream they had all given up on.

"Have I thanked you enough for this?" he asked Kelsey.

"Only about a hundred times."

"Then, I'm about a tenth of the way through the number of thank-yous I owe you." He caught and held her gaze. "She will never forget this night. Neither will I. So, thank you."

Kelsey set her gloved hand in his. "This was truly a once-in-a-lifetime opportunity. I knew I simply had to try. I'm glad the producers listened."

"So am I."

Gregory and Amanda were making their way around the outskirts of the room, Gregory pushing Chrissy's chair. Something he said made both women laugh. Chrissy was having the time of her life. It was the greatest sight in the world.

The orchestra played a loud, drawn out chord before stopping abruptly.

"Ladies and gentleman, your attention please." That was the show's host. No one had seen him since the very first day.

"This must be the announcement of the winner," Kelsey said, her voice low.

Gregory, Chrissy, and Amanda joined them in the next instant.

"I hope you win," Chrissy whispered to Devon anxiously.

"So do I." If she could get this much happiness from a single night spent at a reenactment of a historical setting, she would be in heaven actually seeing the places where that history took place.

"We want to begin by thanking all of you for being here. The guests for your enthusiasm and participation. The contestants for your competitive spirit these past few days. The cast and crew."

Applause followed.

"Now, the moment you've been waiting for." The host drew out his pause as he looked them all over. "First, the prize for the carriage with the most total points. We are awarding all four people in that carriage an annual pass to the Antiques Road Trip Theme Park, right here on the soon-to-be-converted set of this television program."

"Awesome," Kelsey said. It was the first time Devon had heard her truly break character.

"The prize goes to the occupants of . . ." The host gave the expected pause for dramatic effect. "The Millard carriage."

Disappointment flooded the faces of all of Devon's teammates. But he was already making plans to come back here with Chrissy. He was sure that a theme park would be wheelchair accessible, even if the show's set hadn't really been. He would get her back here one way or another, so she could go to the country fair, and have a picnic, and eat in the dim front parlor of an inn, and dance at another ball.

"In addition," the host continued after the applause from his previous announcement had died down, "the Bartlett carriage will each be receiving four vouchers for free admission to the theme park."

He'd take it.

"And the grand prize winner of an all-expenses paid trip for two to the British Isles and $100,000 is . . ."

Kelsey held tighter to his hand. He returned the pressure. Though it was selfish of him, he hoped he won. And, if it couldn't be him, he really hoped it would be Kelsey.

Only when the tension in the room had reached painfully uncomfortable levels did the host finally finish his sentence. ". . . Devon Jones, the newly crowned King of the Road."

Shock kept Devon tied to his seat for a moment. Then Kelsey hugged him, and his shock grew even more paralyzing. The temptation to stay in his seat and wrap his arms around her as well nearly kept him there, despite receiving very specific instructions to join the host on the platform.

In the end, he did as he was told. There was a whole flashy ceremony, with flowers and a certificate and picture taking, which felt odd after three days of using no modern technology. Next, the producer and director gave speeches. Then Devon was asked to say something.

He swallowed a few times and took a few deep breaths. "I want to thank Kelsey"—he really needed to learn her last name—"for including my sister tonight. And I want to say to Chrissy, 'We're going to England.'"

The rest of the night felt less like a historical ball and more like the craziness of a TV show. More than an hour had passed before he was able to sit down by Chrissy again and tell her how happy he was to be giving her some of her dreams while she had time to live them.

"You're the best brother in the world," she said. "And I really hope you're the smartest, too." As had so often been true between the two of them, she seemed to know the question he was about to ask before he said a single word. "I hope you're smart enough to get Kelsey's number before the show is over. You don't meet someone like her every century."

He gave her a hug, lingering over it. There'd been too many hard and difficult days lately, and there were many ahead of them. He wanted to remember this one, when everything had been amazing.

By the time Kelsey was allowed to sit back down again, she looked almost ready to drop. This was likely his last chance; he didn't mean to waste it.

"Hey. Do you think, once we're back in the twenty-first century, that I could—? Would you mind if I—?"

As he stumbled over the words, she pulled out a folded bit of paper from the bag hanging on her wrist and handed it to him. "My number," she said. "Once phones have been invented again, I'd really like to get to know modern-day Devon."

"And I'd like to meet modern-day Kelsey."

She smiled. "I'm pretty much just as big of a nerd in the future as I am in the past."

He lowered his voice, as if sharing a secret. "And I'm a way *bigger* nerd."

Her smile tipped higher on one side. "Perfect."

He leaned closer to her, coming within an inch of those tempting lips.

"You might catch my virus," she warned him.

He just grinned. "Worth it."

And he kissed her, something Lord Devon would probably not have been allowed to do.

Oh, yes. modern-day Devon was going to enjoy returning to the twenty-first century and finding modern-day Kelsey there. The future, in fact, had never looked brighter.

About Sarah M. Eden

Sarah M. Eden is the author of multiple historical romances, including the two-time Whitney Award Winner *Longing for Home* and Whitney Award finalists *Seeking Persephone* and *Courting Miss Lancaster*. Combining her obsession with history and affinity for tender love stories, Sarah loves crafting witty characters and heartfelt romances. She has twice served as the Master of Ceremonies for the LDStorymakers Writers Conference and acted as the Writer in Residence at the Northwest Writers Retreat. Sarah is represented by Pam Victorio at D4EO Literary Agency.

Visit Sarah on-line:
Twitter: @SarahMEden
Facebook: Author Sarah M. Eden
Website: sarahmeden.com

Wouldn't It Be Nice

By Raneè S. Clark

Chapter One

For the last two weeks, Jacqueline had held onto the hope that Colin would change his mind about changing his mind—even when the trip had been only days away. Now, as she paced up and down the driveway while the others were loading up the rented van, she still hoped. It was a tiny hope, a mere spark, that this last phone conversation with Colin might do the trick and convince him to come after all.

"You're running away," he said.

Over the phone, she couldn't tell if the edge to his voice came from desperation or from anger at her decision to go on the trip anyway when he thought they needed to work things out. She took a few more steps away from the van, out of the shadows of her parents' house and into the stretch of driveway that the June sun was warming.

"*I'm* going on the trip that we planned together two months ago, the one you bailed out on." She knew what his answer to her next suggestion would be, but she took one more stab at it anyway. "You could still come. It's not too late." It wasn't too late for a lot of things: for Colin to prove that they had a future and that he was willing to make sacrifices for them.

"I saw the group text, Jac. Ivy already found someone to take my place." A keyboard clicked in the background as Colin answered.

Jac clenched her jaw harder with every click. Supposedly, Colin wanted to get back together more than anything. But they couldn't even have a conversation without distractions. He couldn't take a few minutes off work to come here and beg her to stay so that they could work things out? He'd called her instead, and, even then, he hadn't stepped away from his desk or his computer.

"There's still another seat in the van. If you want to make us work, then you need to figure out a way to come on this trip," she said, like an ultimatum.

Colin sighed. The keyboard clicks stopped. So, maybe she would have his full attention for thirty seconds.

"That trip is going to be anything but romantic—us in a minivan with a bunch of other people for two weeks? Stay home. We'll work this out. And, when I finish this story, we'll go do something better. Something more romantic."

"I don't need more romance. I need more *time*. Hours of me and you talking without interruptions." She didn't bother pointing out that when he'd wrapped up this story, another one would take its place. Then their *something better* would turn into a hurried day trip. She'd bet money on it.

"Don't do this, Jac. I can't ditch work for two weeks, but that doesn't mean I'm not committed to you—to us." Colin's voice might sound pleading, but the keyboard clicks had started up again.

So Jac didn't answer. Colin had acted like he could take off a couple weeks when they had all hatched the idea to drive from Montana to Alaska. And Jac had hoped that the time they would spend together on this trip would propel things forward for their relationship. But then he had cancelled on her, something that had happened too often. She screamed inside every time she came in second to his job.

"Bye, Colin." She didn't keep the disappointment out of her voice. She hated that he'd chosen not to come, that he'd let their relationship end, even if he didn't see it that way.

"Don't do this. You know I love you."

She refrained from pointing out all the reasons he'd given her to distrust his words. "I *don't* know," she said instead and then clicked the end button. She pocketed her cell phone and took a deep breath.

Then she turned and scanned the two men and two women standing around the black minivan. They'd all pitched in to rent it for their road trip to Kenai, Alaska, where Ariell's aunt and uncle owned a house. Jac's roommate, Ariell, stood next to her fiancé, Garrett, holding his hand and leaning into him. Jac's sister, Ivy, stood at the back of the minivan, next to a teacher who worked with Ivy at the high school, where she taught English. Liam had flirted with Ivy most of the previous school year—something Ivy had approved of—but neither had made any definite moves yet. Maybe this trip would be the tipping point for them instead of for Jac and Colin.

Jac sighed. She hadn't planned on being the fifth wheel. Hopefully, whomever Ariell had gotten to take Colin's spot would help make this trip less like a couples' road trip. After all, Jac, Ariell, and Ivy had planned it as an escape from their adult responsibilities. Once Ariell and Garrett got married, they might all still hang out, but their friendships would change.

Jac walked slowly toward Ivy, who was helping Liam load the bags into the tiny trunk like she was playing a Tetris game. She glanced up as Jac was making her way back over and gave Jac her condolences with a sympathetic look. Jac didn't have to say a word. That's what being sisters only eighteen months apart did for them—knowing things with a look.

Then a car pulled up in front of Ariell's parents' house next door, parking behind Ariell's red Honda Civic. The driver pushed open the door, stepped out, and leaned his tall, toned form over the door. "Ariell! Where's our tour bus?"

A grin bloomed across Jac's face as she turned toward Ariell.

"Hudson?" Jac cried. "You got Hudson to come?" She almost bounced as she hurried across the connected front yards to meet Ariell's older brother. He grabbed his things from the backseat and met Jac on the sidewalk, where they embraced.

"I can't believe you're coming," she said into his shoulder as her disappointment with Colin settled onto the back burner. Having Hudson there almost completed things.

Ariell really had gone for recreating old times. Jac's family had lived next door to Ariell and Hudson's family for as long as Jac could remember. They had once all been inseparable, rarely spending a night apart if they could help it. The girls' clothes had been scattered between the two closets—some of Ariell's stuff in Jac and Ivy's and some of their stuff in hers. More often than not, Hudson had been their fourth musketeer, even though half the time they'd made him the butler of their tea parties or the dad to all of their dolls.

Hudson let her draw away, but he held her shoulders. "Why isn't Colin coming?"

"Work." She sighed, but the frustration from her conversation with Colin had lightened. "You coming almost makes up for it."

Hudson nudged her as they turned and headed for the minivan. "Only almost?"

Jac laughed and looped her arm through his. Hudson Allen was as much her best friend for life as Ariell. So the trip would be epic. "I thought *you* couldn't come because you had rotations."

"I moved some things around." He drew his arm away to put it over her shoulder and dropped his bag and sleeping bag near the back of the van as they passed.

"You moved some things around?" Jac stared at him in surprise. She might never understand how the laid-back Hudson could ever make it in a high-stress job as a family doctor. But maybe this was exactly it: he knew how to play as well as work. He'd never wavered from his goal since he had first made it at nine years old. Maybe the medical world needed a natural de-stressor like Hudson.

"If any of us needs two weeks of adventure before resigning to adult responsibilities, it's me," he said. "My residency starts in July. And, after that, I'll have no choice but to be boring, on-call Dr. Allen."

She poked him in the ribs. "You will never be boring anything."

Ivy and Ariell joined them, hugging Hudson at the same time and shifting Jac out of the way.

"I told you to pack light," Ivy teased him.

"Couldn't decide which outfits I didn't actually need," he said.

Ivy and Jac laughed at him, but Ariell punched her brother in the arm. She'd been lamenting over that problem herself a few days earlier.

"Hey, Garrett." Hudson left his arm around Ivy's waist as he shook his future brother-in-law's hand and then pulled him in for a quick back-pound hug.

When they pulled apart, Ivy turned toward Liam. "This is Liam. We work together."

"Nice to meet you," Hudson said, shaking Liam's hand.

"Yeah, you too," Liam offered, but his gaze kept darting to where Hudson had kept his arm around Ivy's waist. Hudson glanced over at Jac and Ariell, who both nodded to his unspoken question about Liam.

Ivy rolled her eyes and pulled her arm away from Hudson to reach into her pocket for her phone. "Okay, we're hoping to make it to Edmonton before we stop tonight, and it's already past ten, so let's get going," Ivy said. "I'll drive first."

They all grabbed their things from the driveway and piled into the van, Ivy taking the driver's seat, and, to no one's surprise, Liam claiming shotgun. Jac climbed into the middle seat with Hudson next to her, and Ariell and Garrett settled into the back.

Jac stowed her backpack underneath the seat as much as she could and propped up her pillow on the window. But one look at Hudson's drooping eyes had her ready to change seats with him. "Did you drive all night to get here?" she asked. Hudson went to medical school at the University of Utah in Salt Lake City.

He nodded, yawning to punctuate it. "Finished up a rotation last night."

She unbuckled her seat belt and scooted forward. "Switch me so you can sleep."

He smiled gratefully and slid behind her, resting his head against her pillow. "Mmmm. Lavender, like always."

Jac stepped over his knees, which he had tried to pull up for her, and fell back into his seat. "Tell me that you brought your own pillow. You know there's camping involved in this trip."

"It's with my sleeping bag in the back." Hudson closed his eyes, so Jac refrained from asking him more questions. A few minutes later, he was breathing deeply, his mouth halfway open: the telltale sign he was truly asleep. Jac had always known if he was faking it during a chick flick they'd made him watch or on nights when they'd suspected him of eavesdropping on them in Ariell's room only to find him in his bedroom and appearing to be sound asleep.

Hudson slept all the way to the Canadian border. So Jac kept up conversations with the others to keep her mind from dwelling on Colin and how they'd now truly ended their relationship. At first she hadn't meant to break up with him for good. She'd done it to open his eyes about how their relationship had gone downhill since he'd started his job with the *Billings Gazette* after graduation. And maybe it had been silly to think that doing something dramatic would change his mind. The breakup and the at-least-once-a-day calls from Colin to get back together had proven that he was all talk and no real commitment.

At the border, Ariell took over driving, and Hudson called for the front passenger seat before anyone else could. Although Garrett protested, Ariell mollified him with a kiss, saying, "You don't mind if we catch up, right? I haven't seen my brother in months."

Garrett pulled her into his arms for a long hug. "Of course not," he said, then dropped a kiss on her head before climbing into the backseat.

Normally, Garrett's I'd-do-anything-for-Ariell attitude didn't get to Jac since she was so used to it. But, today, it stung. Why hadn't Colin ever seen the contrast in their relationships? Why couldn't he see what Jac had needed to keep going? She took a seat in the middle row, since she'd left her backpack and pillow there from the first leg of the trip, but she scooted over to take the window seat. The early-summer weather was cooperating beautifully for the road trip—a clear blue sky and a brilliant sun were shining above them.

"So you guys have been neighbors and friends all your lives?" Liam asked from the backseat. Ivy had taken the seat next to Jac in the middle row, forcing him to sit with Garrett.

"Yep," Ariell said. "The Andrews moved in right after Jac was born, and Hudson claimed Jac like the next day." She grinned at her brother.

"Ah, come on, Ariell," Hudson protested, and though he kept his voice casual, red crept up the back of his neck.

Jac leaned forward. "What's this?" she asked. "No way Ariell's actually kept a secret from us about you."

"Because she didn't know about it until this last Christmas," Hudson said.

"Tell us!" Ivy laughed at Hudson's increasing embarrassment.

With a mischievous peek at Hudson and then into the rearview mirror at her passengers, Ariell said, "Every time he saw

Jac, Hudson insisted on holding her and telling everyone she was his baby."

"Awwww!" Ivy and Jac cooed in unison as the men in the back chuckled.

"That's not even the best part of the story," Ariell added, a full-on wicked grin taking over her expression.

"Ariell. Seriously?" Hudson protested, pinching the bridge of his nose.

Ariell's grin vanished at Hudson's irritated tone, and she raised an eyebrow. "You were five, and the story is funny. Why do you care?"

The two siblings shared a look. Then Hudson hesitated before shrugging and leaning back in his seat. "I don't. It's just embarrassing."

Jac shared the confusion that danced clearly through Ariell's expression. Hudson was cool about pretty much everything. Why did one embarrassing story bother him so much?

"Well?" Ivy prodded, and Jac guessed that she'd spoken mostly to clear the awkwardness.

Ariell cast one more glance at Hudson, her little-sister smile returning when he finally rolled his eyes. "When he was five, he used to talk a lot about finding 'his girl' and how he needed to find the right one to marry. My parents would tease him about girls we knew, but he was always so serious about it. Then, one day, he told them that Jac was his girl, that he was so glad he'd found her, and that someday they would get married and the wedding would be 'bootiful.'"

Ivy reached up and shoved Hudson lightly in the shoulder. "I don't know what your deal is. That's the most adorable thing ever."

"Most little boys don't plan their weddings," he said with a sigh and then a laugh.

Jac sat back against her seat with her own laugh. The story

had brought out some possessive feelings for Hudson—not the romantic kind but more nostalgic than anything else. She missed the days when Hudson had been around all the time.

"You're not most boys, Hudson," Jac said, winking at him.

"Ha," he said, the tension melting from his expression as he turned to Jac and Ivy. "I'm sure it was because you guys forced me to play dolls so much."

"*Let you* is more like it." Ivy reached for a grocery sack she'd left between the front seats of the van. "Anybody want something to eat?"

Except for Hudson, they'd all eaten a few hours earlier—lunches that Ivy had basically assigned them to bring. More than once in the planning of the trip, Ariell and Jac had referred to Ivy as *the chaperone* for infusing so much of her teaching persona into things.

They passed around the snacks Ivy had brought, and then the conversation continued. Jac couldn't pay attention like before, though. Her attention wandered as she stared out the window at the flat land surrounding her: farm fields dotting the landscape, and then a small town with its most notable building being a tall, slate gray industrial structure of some kind.

Although she tried to focus only on the scenery around her, it didn't provide enough things to see to keep her thoughts off Colin—especially how quickly he'd lost interest in their road trip after he'd gotten assigned the McNally story at work.

She admired Colin for choosing a field that he was passionate about. Every morning, he was excited to get to work. Jac's job in graphic design excited her too, but she'd still looked forward to two weeks of adventure on the road trip she'd planned with her best friends. Colin had been one of her best friends too. He was supposed to be a part of this.

Of course, if he'd come, Hudson couldn't have, she thought, and Jac didn't like that idea either. They'd barely seen Hudson at

Christmas because he'd only been able to come for a couple days. And that held true for most of his visits since starting medical school.

So, time spent hanging out with him came at a premium. The fact that he'd replaced Colin for this one last fling, before Ariell and Garrett got married at the end of the summer, almost lifted Jac right out of her seat with happiness. Hudson could make things right again.

"What?" Hudson asked, breaking Jac out of her thoughts, and she realized that she'd been staring at him.

"Just glad you're here." She shrugged.

As Hudson grinned back, it struck Jac how much she'd always liked the way his smile reached clear into his cheeks.

"Me too," he said.

Chapter Two

Besides a couple brief bathroom breaks, they didn't stop until they'd reached Calgary. It was after seven, so they'd long forgotten the sandwiches they'd eaten for lunch, and the snacks had gotten old. Dinner was a must, and Ivy navigated them to a Chili's not too far off their route.

"Up for a walk?" Hudson asked Jac as they climbed out of the van in the restaurant's parking lot. He pointed to a walking trail that ran alongside the restaurant and hotel-lined road.

"Of course. Anyone else?" she asked, but Ivy and so, of course, Liam had already strode inside to get a table.

Garrett glanced between Hudson and Jac before he took Ariell's outstretched hand and smirked. "Next time," he said, and they followed the others inside.

As the others disappeared inside the restaurant, Jac and Hudson walked across the grass to the trail. She enjoyed stretching out her legs, loosening her thigh muscles, cramped from sitting so long. When they reached the paved trail, she bounced her knees high to get out the trapped energy.

"Wanna race?" Hudson wiggled his eyebrows.

She pointed to her shoes—flip-flops. "No. For the first time in history, you'd win, and I can't let that happen."

"First time in history?" Hudson scoffed, starting down the walking path.

"Definitely." She settled her stride to the same pace as his, which was faster than she would have walked for a leisurely pace, thanks to his long legs, but it was still comfortable and not too fast. "How's school?"

"Good. It's weird that it's almost over already. Eight years seemed like such a long time when I was eighteen. Now, it seems like it flew by."

"Excited for your residency?" For Jac, talking to Hudson about becoming a doctor would never get old.

He lit up, smiling and swinging his arms more. "Yeah. It'll be nice to be back in Billings again . . . free rent." He bumped Jac with his shoulder.

Would it be like old times? She sure hoped so. Of course, they couldn't act like crazy teenagers anymore, but she still looked forward to having him around again. Adjusting to life without Colin wouldn't hurt as much with Hudson there to distract her. She'd missed his teasing and the way he always made her laugh by turning every situation into something fun. You couldn't help but enjoy life around him.

"Don't you get paid during your residency?" she teased.

"Yeah . . . so?" He kept a straight face long enough for Jac to burst into laughter, then he joined her. "But seriously, I have so much student-loan debt to start paying off—free rent." They walked a minute or so in silence before Hudson asked, "What's up with Colin not coming?"

She sighed, but she was grateful for the chance to talk about it. With Liam and Garrett in the car, she felt uncomfortable unloading to Ariell and Ivy, not that they hadn't heard it before. Even though a tiny part of Jac had hoped she could use their breakup to change Colin's mind about not coming, neither of her best friends had believed he'd come in the first place.

"He changed his mind a few weeks after we started planning the trip," Jac said as she stared at the black, paved trail, focusing on the yellow line that ran down the middle. "His boss assigned him to cover a fatal accident out by the MetraPark after a concert.

At first, it was some routine thing, but it turned suspicious pretty fast. Now, the police think it was a homicide, and so Colin's right in the thick of the story, which could put him on the fast track to—I don't know—bigger stories, a bigger paper, something. He didn't want to leave it."

Hudson rested a hand on her shoulder, warming her even though she didn't need it. Despite being later in the evening, the air around them hadn't cooled much from the higher temperatures of the day.

"And what you hate admitting is that with his job, this probably won't be the last time he bails," Hudson said.

Jac's disappointment reappeared and sank into the pit of her stomach. Why had she expected Colin to change for her? He dreamed about having his byline in big time newspapers, so he would always go after the best, most important story. Had she been wrong not to support him?

"Things have been busy for us since the moment we started dating," Jac continued. "I mean, we had school then new jobs. But things were better before graduation, and I thought we'd have a chance to remember that—to sit back and breathe for a bit together, to talk, to figure us out. He'd even pitched a human-interest story idea on Kenai that his boss had liked. So he could've made this work."

Jac knew that giving up the McNally story would've been a sacrifice for Colin, probably a big one. Maybe it was unfair, career wise, to ask him to do that—but she needed to matter to him too. And, despite all his promises, Colin left her doubting whether she meant more to him than his next big story.

Hudson moved his arm around her, and she leaned into him. "I'm sorry, Jac," he said.

"Thanks."

Another few moments of silence went by as they passed a two-story brick building, a business of some kind, and the area began to look more industrial. They'd only come a few blocks, though, and the warm evening and fresh air still called to Jac, keeping her from turning back toward the restaurant.

So she changed the subject to lighten the mood. "So, how long before you gave up on me being your girl. Six? Seven? Ten?" she teased.

To her surprise, Hudson forced a chuckle and then retracted his arm from around her, shoving both hands into his pockets. "Uh . . ." He tilted his head to study her, biting the inside of his cheek. She read the hesitancy in his expression, but then he nodded to himself. "I don't know," he finally said, turning his gaze to the path in front of them. "Maybe last year, when you were still dating Colin after so long."

Jac didn't realize that she'd stopped walking until Hudson looked over his shoulder at her. Then he came to a halt too, his hands still in his pockets, struggling to keep eye contact with her.

"Are you serious?" she asked. The situation was classic romantic-comedy fodder, but Jac still struggled to wrap her brain around Hudson picturing the idea of *them* all this time.

"It's not a big deal," he hurried to explain. "Not like twenty years of unrequited love or anything. I just . . . I always thought it'd be nice. You and me."

You and me, Jac thought, letting herself picture it too as she continued staring at him. Actual cuddling with Hudson while watching a movie in the Allen's family room and not just during the scary parts. Lunch dates. Dinner dates. Togetherness. It looked a lot like what growing up with Hudson had been like—how the best parts of her life had been, but better.

And with kissing.

Heat rushed into her cheeks as she imagined Hudson coming toward her now, lowering his face to hers—

"Jac? You've been quiet a long time," Hudson said, sounding worried.

She swallowed and blinked, bringing him back into focus. How had she never considered this concept of *them* before? He'd been a constant in her life, a friend who watched out for her—but had she missed the little things? Had she missed Hudson trying to tell her there should be more to their friendship with the way he always took time to help her with homework or to perfect a volleyball skill?

"Sorry. Just . . . wow," she said, sounding like she'd choked on something. "You're right. It would've been nice."

They stared at each other for a few seconds, the possibilities rushing toward Jac and pushing her forward, toward Hudson. She took a step, and he took one too.

Then his phone dinged in his pocket, and the spell was broken. After another second, he reached in and took it out, glancing at the screen.

"Ariell says our table is ready."

Jac nodded but didn't turn to start the short walk back to the restaurant. Hudson held out his hand for hers, and she only studied it a moment before slipping hers inside—not fingers interlocked in a flirty way but with his hand wrapped around hers in the same friendly way he'd held it a hundred times or more.

Yet, everything felt different now, like the last five minutes with Hudson had shifted the way her world spun on its axis.

Chapter Three

The group lingered over their dinners for more than two hours, the conversation never ebbing. When nine o'clock came and they'd just paid the check, they made a unanimous decision to buck Ivy's plan of making it to Edmonton that night. Instead, they booked two rooms at a hotel that shared a parking lot with the restaurant.

Before they separated for the night, neither Jac nor Hudson said anything about their conversation before dinner. Jac wouldn't have minded confiding to him that she and Colin had broken up, but the finality of the end of their relationship hadn't come until that morning.

Besides, her mind still reeled from Hudson's admission. Yesterday, Hudson had been a male version of Ariell, her other best friend. Today . . . today everything she'd thought about her relationship with him had exploded.

Colin called at almost ten, but she didn't bother taking the call outside. Ivy had made a run to a nearby grocery store to replenish the snack stores for the next day's drive, and Jac doubted that she and Colin would say anything that she cared if Ariell overheard. This bothered her for the first time. She and Colin hadn't ever shared anything that she'd kept secret from her best friends. She told Ivy and Ariell everything. And she'd definitely tell them all about the conversation she'd had with Hudson—as soon as she untangled what had happened.

Head Over Heels

But . . . shouldn't there have been plans and pieces of their relationship that were just for her and Colin? Had she shared too much with her friends? Or, was there nothing that had been worth keeping to herself?

"How was the drive?" Colin asked.

"Colin . . . why are you calling me?" She dropped onto the unoccupied queen-size bed. Ariell watched TV from the other one, sparing Jac an understanding look before turning her attention back to the TV, leaving Jac to her conversation.

"Letting this trip break us up is crazy," Colin said. "I'm trying to talk you into your senses."

"It's not just about a trip, and I'm not changing my mind."

"Let's talk about it when you get back."

Guilt crept over Jac as she found herself enjoying the desperation in Colin's voice, like the fact that she was over five hundred miles away—and getting farther away by the day—had finally meant something to him. It felt so symbolic.

"If you have time," she couldn't help saying.

"Jac . . . I'm sorry about the trip, but that doesn't mean—" he began.

"We've gone through this a thousand times. It means something to me. I have to get ready for bed. We ended up stopping in Calgary tonight instead of Edmonton, and Ivy will want to leave early tomorrow to make up for it."

"That's ironic, right? You don't have time to talk to me now."

We broke up! a voice inside her cried in frustration at the unfair way he'd turned it on her. But then she sighed and came up with a friendlier response. After all, Colin was one of Garrett's groomsmen, and she wouldn't make things dramatic.

"Fine. How's the story?" she asked.

"Great. Really great," Colin said, his voice rising with excitement right away. She couldn't express the same enthusiasm that he'd expect from her, though. She'd been tired of this assignment from the day Colin first hinted that he might have to forgo this trip for it. "Of course, I can't say a whole lot over the phone," he said.

Not that he'd say anything about it if I were standing right next to him. She bit her lip. But that wasn't the enthusiastic response he needed, whether Colin should hear it or not. He never trusted her with details about his stories. He held it all back to give her the full experience when she finally read his published article.

If they had stayed together and pursued a future together, what would they have to talk about every day? Too many of their dates for the past year had been rushed lunches and dinners or movie nights where Colin fell asleep because he'd run himself ragged for a story.

In fact, they hadn't had a meaningful conversation in months. She didn't know his dreams, beyond writing big stories or working for a big paper, and he didn't know hers. They hadn't even discussed where they wanted to live or what they expected from marriage or how many kids to have.

"Jac?" Colin said.

"Yeah, sorry . . . I understand." She didn't actually understand, but she'd grown so used to saying it that she couldn't help herself.

"When they break this case open, it's going to be huge. My update today on it already has almost 10,000 hits."

"That's awesome," she said. But then the entire conversation took on a new light—from this side of their breakup—solidifying her decision. He was talking about his job, but only in terms of how many people clicked to his articles from the *Gazette* main site?

"Don't get too excited about it," he said sarcastically.

"I'm sorry, Colin, but it's getting late, and you know how I feel about this story." She rubbed her hand over her forehead, itching to hang up so that she could quit letting Colin drag her trip down.

"This is my job—"

"I know." She hoped he heard all the finality she put into those words. "Good night," she added, but she didn't wait for a reply. She shouldn't have to anymore; they'd broken up. She set her phone on the nightstand and pulled one of the pillows over her head.

"You okay?" Ariell asked.

Jac tossed the pillow aside and sat up. "I am. I didn't realize it, at first, but breaking up with him was the right thing."

"I agree." Ariell waved the remote at her like a queen with her scepter, bestowing her favor, which made Jac laugh.

The door clicked. Ivy came in at the same time that Jac rolled off the bed to stand up. "I'm going to take a shower," Jac said. "What time should I set my alarm for?"

Ivy pressed her lips together and squinted one eye, doing the math in her head. "We should leave by six," she said and then set down the grocery bag she was carrying.

"Yes, ma'am."

Jac rummaged through her duffel bag for something to wear to bed before heading into the bathroom. Since, more than likely, they'd be camping the next night, she enjoyed a long, steamy shower. The other two had turned the TV off by the time she got out.

Within a few minutes, everyone was ready to go to bed. They rock-paper-scissored for who should get a bed to herself. Ariell won, but Jac had spent so many nights in the same bed with either of them that it hardly mattered.

She snuggled down under the light blanket that protected her from the over-air-conditioned chill that Ivy preferred. "I can only take so many layers of clothes off," Ivy always pointed out.

Jac forced all thoughts of Colin out of her head. She'd spent too much time worrying about him. She decided not to risk a thought about Hudson either, and heat rose into her cheeks just thinking about that moment they'd shared on the walking path before Ariell had texted. Jac refused to consider what might have happened if she'd said, "Colin and I broke up."

Not tonight, at least. She had plenty of time ahead of her, over the next couple weeks, to analyze Hudson. Tonight, she'd sleep.

School teacher Ivy had made mini Popsicle sticks with their names on them to draw for driving turns. The next morning, she pulled Hudson's name from where Ariell held them in one hand—minus Ivy's and Ariell's names since they'd already taken a turn driving. Jac hesitated to call shotgun, worrying what Hudson would think, and then Ivy suggested that Liam or Garrett should take it since it had more leg room. So Garrett chose the backseat with Ariell and let Liam have the front passenger seat.

Garrett and Ariell both dozed off right away since everyone had had such an early start that morning. The girls, at least, had risen at five. Ivy leaned forward from her seat in the middle row to speak in low tones with Hudson and Liam. Jac tried sleeping against the window, but restlessness plagued her. So she caught snatches of their conversation—about Hudson's medical schooling, about Ivy and Liam's jobs at a local high school, and about a woman that Hudson had taken out a couple times in Salt Lake. Eventually, Jac gave up on trying to sleep and opened a book instead.

"I'm not stopping for you to puke if you make yourself carsick by reading," Hudson teased, glancing at her in the rearview mirror.

"No big," she replied. "I'm sure Ivy brought a bucket or something. She's like a Boy Scout—always prepared."

Ivy shoved Jac playfully. "I did not bring a bucket," Ivy said as she stole Jac's pillow and rested it against her sister, leaning over and closing her eyes.

"Don't sweat it, Ivy." Jac gave Ivy a pat. "I never get carsick by reading." But Jac laid the book in her lap to talk with Hudson instead. Liam had leaned his seat back, looking like he might take a nap too, so Hudson could probably use the company.

"What book is it?" Hudson asked.

"*To Kill a Mockingbird*. Ivy's teaching it to her sophomore English class, and she had it lying around the apartment. I skipped reading it in high school."

"How do you skip reading *To Kill a Mockingbird* in high school? I thought it was a requirement."

Jac shrugged. "I had Mrs. West. She gave us a choice, and I read something else. Did *you* actually read it?"

"I watched the movie. Does that count?"

"No. Didn't you have to do a report or anything? What'd you get on that?"

"A solid C." Hudson held his hand up to fist bump hers.

She obliged with a laugh. "Here's to hoping that none of your medical textbooks had movies you could have watched instead."

"Don't worry. Just a couple. I'm good."

More laughter bubbled up, and the smile that now wouldn't leave her face made the weight of breaking up with Colin feel much lighter. The answering joy in the sliver of Hudson's expression she caught in the rearview mirror beamed through her. How long ago had she and Colin lost that part of their relationship—the easiness and excitement of spending time together?

Four hours later, Jac drew her turn to drive after they had stopped to top off the gas tank. Hudson called shotgun right off— no hesitation—and this made Jac blush. She ducked her head into her purse, as if searching for something, in order to hide her reaction.

"You've already gotten shotgun once," Ivy protested.

Hudson folded his arms. "I read nothing in your informational brochure about restrictions on calling shotgun."

Ivy huffed at him, shaking her head in good-natured annoyance while the others laughed. "I'm adding it now."

"You can't add it retroactively," Hudson said as he kept a straight face, though no one around him could.

"Fine," Ivy relented.

After Jac had climbed into the driver's seat, her cheeks still burned hot enough that she checked her reflection in the rearview mirror for residual effects. Fortunately, nothing too obvious showed in her pink cheeks.

Once they were on the road, Ivy pulled Catch Phrase from the small bag of games she'd brought. With Ivy and Liam turned halfway in the middle seats, to face the couple in back, Jac almost felt alone with Hudson up front.

He must have felt this too because, after a few minutes of silence, he said in a low voice, "Sorry if I freaked you out last night. I shouldn't have said anything."

"Not freaked out." She shook her head. "Surprised is all. And don't be sorry."

"Okay. I won't be." A slow smile spread across his face as he leaned back against his seat with his head turned to face her.

She wanted to tell him about her and Colin breaking up, but Hudson had said himself that he had just thought that the idea of them was nice. He hadn't exactly declared his love. In fact, he'd told her that he'd given up a year ago.

"Okay," she said. With the cruise control set on the minivan, she drew her knees together and tried to scrunch down in the seat, needing something, anything to cover her embarrassment.

"So . . . Colin and I broke up two weeks ago," she blurted out with her eyes still on the road. She knew how it would sound, her admitting this to Hudson after what he'd said the night before. She had to force herself to turn to glance at him to gauge his response.

"Really?" His surprise seemed to wear off quickly and turn to concern. "What happened?"

His best-friend-like reaction instantly made the conversation feel less awkward, and Jac's nervous, thumping heart thanked him for that. Her heart rate slowed as she spoke again. "This trip happened, I guess. Pretty much anyway. When he backed out, I backed out of our relationship. At first, I thought it would make him see that I was serious about us needing some more time together; I used it as a ploy. But then it was me who got my eyes opened."

"I'm sorry, Jac," Hudson said. The continued concern in his voice made her glance at him again and catch his sincerity in his sympathetic frown and the way his eyebrows drew down. "You guys were together a while."

"Yeah," she said. "But it was a good decision."

"I agree."

Jac's gaze snapped back to Hudson, but he only answered with a chuckle.

"What's your latest project?" he asked.

"Uh . . . my project?" It took Jac a moment to relax, to be thankful that he'd changed the subject. She would have liked to explore what Hudson had meant not only by agreeing that it was a good decision for her and Colin to break up but also by agreeing to not be sorry that he'd said something the night before. But, right now, crowded into a van with four other people, didn't seem like the right place either.

At least, she would have to admit that Colin had been right about the non-romantic atmosphere of the trip—but he'd missed that they didn't need a romantic atmosphere to be happy. She'd enjoyed sitting in this van, chatting with Hudson and the others for most of the day.

"The interior design of a cookbook," she finally answered, ignoring the mischievousness in Hudson's lingering smile at the length of time it had taken her to reply.

"Sounds fun."

"I'm always hungry." She grinned at him. "And it's the type of thing I can do on the road, hence the ability to take two weeks off for a road trip."

"What kind of cookbook?"

"*A Hundred and One Casseroles for Your Crock-Pot.*"

"That's . . . specific." Hudson tilted his seat back as far as it would go, and then closed his eyes against the sunbeams streaming through the window on his side.

Sometimes, as they crossed the Canadian countryside, she half wished they'd chosen to bike this trip—something to enjoy the sunshine, the blue sky, and the clear, clean air.

"We've tried a few of the recipes, of course," she said. "And they're pretty good. There's a homemade mac and cheese recipe with bacon and four different kinds of cheese. Mmmmmm." It'd been excellent comfort food the night they'd tried that. It was something that their mom would have made growing up. And thinking about it now reminded Jac of the many, many dinners where Hudson and Ariell had joined the Andrews for dinner or the other way around.

"Maybe you should make that again in the next couple of days," Hudson said.

"Sorry, I would, but I didn't bring my Crock-Pot. Ivy was strict about how much we could pack."

"The back of this minivan *is* pretty tight."

As Jac's mind lingered on the memories of *family* dinners, which had always included her two best friends, warmth rose with expectation in her chest. "Maybe you'll have time to drop by the apartment for a dinner or two once you start your residency—if you're not too busy playing doctor, anyway."

Hudson rolled his head toward her again, opening his eyes. And she thought she might have seen expectation in his expression too. "Of course. I mentioned the part about me being broke, right? I'll take any free meal I can get—especially home-cooked ones."

"What about the part where you're on call all the time or whatever and never have time for us?" Jac chewed on her lip as that possibility trampled on her hopes of a return to the glory days of hanging out with Hudson again. Then their situation would mirror her disappointments with Colin—never enough time for her. The previously blooming thoughts—of how nice it still might be between her and Hudson, the ones she couldn't quite turn her back on—drooped.

Hudson reached over and laid a hand on her arm. "Then you'll have to bring it by the clinic so we can hang out on my break."

And just like that, one of those pictures of them together popped into her brain. It was something familiar, like her and Hudson sitting at a table, chatting as they ate. But it was different too because their shoulders would touch and, underneath the table, they would tangle their feet together, and he'd interrupt their meal once in a while to reach up and graze his knuckle along her cheek.

"Of course," she said. Hudson's hand lingered on her arm for a moment more before he dropped it. It left tingles of electricity climbing up her arm, going into her heart, and worming their way into her brain.

Their conversation continued like that for the next couple hours as they drove: easy, entertaining, enjoyable, and interspersed with daydreams of the romantic possibilities for how she and Hudson might spend time together in that same old way but much better.

These daydreams left her feeling so antsy that, by the time they stopped for lunch at a fast-food place in Grand Prairie, Alberta, Canada, too much energy threatened to spill out. As they sat and ate, Jac envied the kids in the indoor play area. What she wouldn't give to climb around in the maze of tunnels and nets and slide down the slides to get rid of the jitters in her hands and in her heart.

Once they were back on the road, she and Hudson joined the others in a game of twenty questions, and the rest of her driving shift passed by quickly. For the next leg of the trip, the seating arrangement in the van shuffled again. Liam drew his turn at driving, and, with a mischievous look, Garrett called shotgun immediately after Ivy read Liam's name off the Popsicle stick. The remaining passengers swallowed back laughter at the disappointed way Liam pressed his lips together and then climbed into the driver's seat.

Jac claimed one of the back window seats, ready for an afternoon snooze since she hadn't slept yet that day. She tried not to put much stock in the way Hudson chose to take the seat next to her. Liam had proclaimed that seat to be the best place to sleep and stretch your legs out, besides shotgun. Before long, the others had started a game of Name That Tune, which faded into Jac's subconscious. She fell asleep, listening to Hudson hum some vaguely familiar Taylor Swift song.

Chapter Four

It was after ten before they reached Strawberry Flats, the campground where they'd stay for the night. They hurried to claim a spot before the last light of the day faded with the setting sun. Their tents were simple to put up, and they had it done within ten minutes.

For dinner, they ate sandwiches made from the food stores that Ivy had made sure to replenish before they had left Grand Prairie. Jac took hers and walked to the edge of the lake near their campsite. Shedding her flip-flops, she dunked her feet into the cool water. Then she set her sandwich aside as she leaned back onto her hands and relaxed.

"Mind if I join you?"

At the sound of Hudson's voice, Jac tilted her head back to see him approaching with a paper plate filled with three sandwiches and a pile of chips. No, she didn't mind. She *should* mind far more, considering how upended she'd felt around him since yesterday.

"No, of course not."

He sat next to her, putting his plate down beside him the way she had and ignoring it as he stared at the lake with her. "How are you doing?" he asked.

"I'm . . ." She almost laughed. She wasn't feeling like herself. The ideas that Hudson had planted kept bombarding her mind, flipping her this way and that. "Fine. I'm actually fine," she said.

Hudson turned and studied her, pressing his lips together before letting a smile quirk at the corners. "I'm sorry that I'm not sorry," he said.

"What?" She stifled a giggle at the chagrin in his expression. Again, it struck her how a guy who took so few things seriously in his life had been as successful as he had been so far in medical school, which was intense and hard.

But Hudson had always taken the *important* things seriously. When she hadn't made the volleyball team her freshman year of high school, he'd teased her—as any big brother would. In a way, his teasing had distracted her from the disappointment. But then he'd also left bright orange daises and an enormous almond-toffee candy bar for her in her bedroom that night.

Hudson shifted closer to her, still leaning back on his hands, and the nervous energy she'd been carrying with her all day spiked, zinging through her. Now they sat side by side, his legs stretched out, the closest one touching hers, their arms brushing each others'.

He kept his gaze on her—intense but also playful. "I should be more sorry about you breaking up with Colin. You guys were together for a while, and your heart's probably broken—I'm sorry about that." He moved one hand so that his fingers overlapped hers. "But . . . I'm not sorry that you're not with him anymore."

Too much hope was welling up inside her despite Hudson being right—she and Colin had just split up. And her heart *should* be broken. "But you said that you gave up on me a year ago and that you only thought it would be nice. You and me."

Hudson propped himself on one hand and leaned closer to her, making her catch her breath. "Let me show you how nice I thought it could be." His voice rose at the end in a question. With the hand not holding him up, he cupped her cheek gently, then slid his hand down onto her neck, where his fingers sifted through her hair. In a smooth motion, he adjusted his weight and reached slowly around her with his other arm, pressing his hand gently into her back, guiding her closer it him.

Energy surged through Jac, enough that it could power a thousand light bulbs, and all of them came to life inside her in a blinding, white light kind of way. Stunned by the intensity of emotion he'd caused to erupt inside her, she tried to grip the sandy shore beneath her, hoping to find something to anchor her back to the earth, but it slipped through her fingers, leaving her with only tiny pebbles.

When his lips hovered mere centimeters from hers, he hesitated, his expression asking for her permission. She granted it by leaning into him. As his lips met hers, pressing against them softly, the beauty of his kiss fluttered over her, warming her to the core like sunbeams.

She *could* call this moment nice.

Or, she could call it breathtaking, dazzling, extraordinary.

Sand crunched from somewhere behind them, breaking the fairy-tale-like moment and pulling them reluctantly apart. When Jac turned to look at the approaching figures, it was like trying to see something after staring into the sun. Squinting at them for several seconds, she finally realized that it was Ariell and Garrett.

"Hey, what's up, guys . . .?" Ariell began and then trailed off, murmuring, "Oh, my gosh."

Hudson spoke first. "Hey, Ariell," he greeted her in a hoarse voice. Then he cleared his throat. In the dim light still left after the sunset, Jac caught Garrett's shoulders shaking as though he held back laughter.

"Hey," Jac added politely.

Ariell took another few steps then hesitated. "Can we . . .?"

"Join us? I'd rather you didn't," Hudson said, giving her a glare like a true big brother.

"Mmm-kay. We'll go find someone else." Ariell cast a few

glances over the area and then at Hudson and Jac before sharing a look with Garrett. They turned together and walked back toward the tents, Garrett's shoulders shaking with silent laughter.

Jac couldn't help giggling too. "You'd rather she didn't?"

Hudson leaned back in, and she could feel the smile on his lips as he brushed them against hers again. "Making out with you while my sister watches would be awkward."

She laughed again, then sighed heavily. Kissing Hudson was crazy, exhilarating, far above and beyond nice—but had it been a good idea? As she reached up and ran her fingers along Hudson's jaw, he pulled back a fraction, studying her face.

"What?"

"I don't want you to be my rebound," she whispered.

He wrapped both arms around her again, pulling her toward him gently, but she sensed the strength in his embrace—the need to not ever let go. The same intense emotions welled up inside her, tightening in her chest and threatening an explosion that would engulf them both.

"I won't be," he promised.

"Were you guys *kissing*?" Ariell half whispered, half shouted the second that Jac walked into their tent an hour later. She'd wanted to stay with Hudson longer, but they'd decided to return only because Hudson had pointed out that, with all the group's names back in the pool, one of them might be chosen to drive in the morning.

"That's easy. Yes. Give me another." Jac dropped onto the sleeping bag they'd rolled out for her, a goofy grin stuck on her face.

"You were kissing my brother?" Ariell said, shaking her head.

"Yes," Jac said, glancing over at Ivy, who lay on top of her sleeping bag on her stomach, studying a map on her phone. She looked up and raised her eyebrows at Jac, her expression a mixture of you-go-girl and for-real? The look didn't help with Jac's goofy grin.

So Jac turned back to face Ariell. "Is that a problem? You're the one who told the story about him—and, honestly, that's what started the whole thing—and you talked like it was adorable."

"When he was five and you were three. And, even then, you kept getting mad when he tried to hold your hand." Ariell folded her arms and screwed up her lips. The battery-operated lantern they'd hung at the top of the tent gave just enough light for Jac to see the emotions her friend held back. "You *just* broke up with Colin," Ariell said.

Jac reached over and gripped Ariell's arm. "I promise that this is not some rebound thing, but I will be so careful."

Ariell nodded slowly and took a deep breath. Finally, a smile worked its way into her expression. "I didn't even know he still liked you."

"He didn't." Jac let go of Ariell's arm and fell back onto her pillow. "He thought it would be nice."

Ivy looked up from the map. "Well? Was it?"

Jac closed her eyes and sighed, her body relaxing against the sleeping bag and the rocky ground beneath her, which her thin, inflatable mat barely protected her against. "Yes," she murmured. "So incredibly nice."

The three women dissolved into whispers and quiet giggles—because, of course, Hudson might try to eavesdrop. Life felt so right, so normal, so comfortable despite how topsy-turvy everything his kissing her had left her. When the women had dissected the last few days as though they were high school girls, Jac fell asleep with a wide grin etched into her cheeks.

Chapter Five

Despite being sleepy, from rising early to help the others take down their camp and pack up the van, Jac made sure to stay on her toes when Ivy stuck her hand into her jar to draw the driver for the first shift. If Ivy drew Hudson's name, Jac would shout "shotgun" before anyone else thought to.

But Ivy drew her own name. And, by the speed of Liam's response—a split second ahead of Ariell's mischievous shout of "shotgun"—Jac guessed that he'd concocted the same plan as hers. She chose the backseat, and, of course, Hudson climbed in next to her.

When he stretched his arm across the top of the seat, she leaned into him, resting her head on his chest against the hollow of his neck, breathing in the sporty scent of his deodorant and the smells of the outdoors that lingered on him. He rested his head on top of hers as the passengers in the van settled into their usual morning travel pattern—the passengers in the backseats dozed for a few hours while the driver and copilot spoke in quiet voices.

Jac woke later to sunbeams streaking across her face, warming her, and Hudson's lips on her forehead. The heat that bubbled up inside her from his kiss outdid the heat from the sun's rays. She arched her back to stretch but stayed cuddled against Hudson's side.

"Want something to eat?" he murmured, his lips still against the top of her head. "Ariell's passing out granola bars and fruit. And there's yogurt too."

"Just the fruit." She tilted her head back to stare up at him. Promising Ariell last night that she'd be careful seemed absurd now. Why would she need to be? Every second with Hudson rooted her in happiness more deeply than anything else in her life had in a while. Maybe this had happened quickly, but she couldn't imagine her life without him.

Hudson retrieved a banana for her, and she adjusted her position so she wouldn't squish it against his chest while she ate it. But she stayed close to him, still resting her head back against his shoulder.

"I'm not crowding you, am I?" she asked, realizing that she took up two thirds of the seat thanks to the way she was sitting.

"Never," Hudson said, resting his head on top of hers. She tilted her head back farther to meet his lips. The kiss was quick, thanks to all the company in the van, but still exhilarating. It held all the promise of what would come for them.

The day passed with more games, movie watching, and any other form of entertainment they could think of. The increase in irritated remarks about space and food that day led Jac to believe that the others were getting antsy on their third day straight in the car. But she didn't mind it because she spent it with Hudson.

Since neither of them got drawn to drive that day, they chose to stay wrapped up in each other's company in the backseat. When they wanted it to be, it was like their own world. Jac relished in her time watching miles and miles of pine trees and gorgeous mountain vistas go by from the comfort of Hudson's arms.

They set up camp that night in Tok, Alaska, having crossed back into the United States an hour before arriving in the tiny town. Once they'd set up their tents, Jac and Hudson took advantage of the lingering light of the northern summer and walked down the bicycle path that ran alongside the main highway.

Though she'd enjoyed her day, cuddled up next to him, stretching her legs as they walked felt good too, especially with her hand in his. They passed a few small businesses, some of them looking a lot more worn than others.

After walking for several minutes in silence, Hudson stopped and drew her off the path with him. He circled his arms around her waist, hugging her close, and she leaned into his chest.

After a few seconds of making small circles on her back with his hands, Hudson dropped his arms from her waist and reached down to take her face in his hands, kissing her. He started with the same gentleness—the "niceness"—from the night before, but then his kisses soon grew in intensity, until Jac had to force herself to pull away to avoid getting lost inside the moment. They *were* standing on the side of a highway, after all.

"This is a lot better than nice, isn't it?" he said.

"So much," she said as she leaned back into him, pressing her face into his chest, the softness of his T-shirt caressing her cheek. "I don't want to mess it up."

This time he tilted away, lifting her chin to peer at her with a slight scowl. "Don't worry so much, Jac," he said softly, kissing her nose. "Enjoy this."

She placed her hands on either side of his cheeks, gently pulling him down to her for another kiss, "You're one of my best friends, and I love you." Heat blasted through her cheeks when she realized what she'd just said. But Hudson's smile widened as she rushed on. "What I meant—I don't want to—that sounded scary—"

He stopped her with a kiss of his own. "I know what you meant."

"If I hurt you because I rushed into this headlong, I'd never forgive myself." Although moments before, and all throughout the day, her bliss had overrun every bit of Jac's good judgment, her worries bloomed now anyway.

"Stop worrying so much. I'm a big boy, Jac." He wound his arms back around her, holding her close again.

"But you're a doctor, and, even though you're coming back to Billings . . ." She couldn't say the rest—that it would be just like it had been with Colin. Hudson wouldn't have time for her either.

He studied her face then nodded slowly as it seemed to dawn on him where her worries sprang from. "You know where Whitehall, Montana, is?"

Not sure where he was going with this, she scrunched her nose and pictured the map of Montana. "By Butte?" she guessed.

"Yeah. It's pretty small, less than fifteen hundred people or something like that. There's a small practice there with one family doctor. That's what I picture. I picture Whitehall."

So Jac did too. She pictured Whitehall with Hudson. A small practice like that would keep him busy but not the way that staying in a bigger place like Billings would. He'd have time for her, for *them*. He was saying that he'd make sure of that.

He kissed her again before slipping his arm behind her back and strolling forward with her on the path, enjoying their time alone. They didn't worry tonight about how late it was getting. Tomorrow was a much shorter drive. The drive was only four hours to Fairbanks, where they'd be staying for two days before going on to Kenai. They wouldn't have to get up as early.

When Jac got back to the tent, Ivy and Ariell hadn't waited up for the details. They were sound asleep. But Jac didn't mind too much as she spent the last few minutes before she drifted off imagining Whitehall with Hudson. Picturing her future. Picturing them. And it was so right that she felt it to her core.

Chapter Six

They didn't get to Fairbanks the next day until after three o'clock in the afternoon. Nobody had hurried to get up that morning, and they'd packed up their camp at a leisurely pace. After avoiding it the day before, Hudson was the only one left to drive before all their names got put back in the drawing. Ivy called "shotgun" with a teasing smile, but Jac rolled her eyes and got into the passenger side anyway.

"That's a clear violation of the understood shotgun rules," Hudson had said.

"You're worth the risk," she'd answered, to which the other four passengers groaned.

Ivy had gotten them rooms in Fairbanks at a newer-looking Best Western hotel, and they'd had to skirt around the small city to get there. Like in the hundreds of miles of road before this, pine trees grew here in abundance. Jac watched in wonder as each stretch of dense pine trees passed by her window. Then the trees would be interrupted by a small group of buildings or them stopping at a streetlight. More trees would follow, even right in the middle of town.

Once they got to the hotel and checked in, Ivy claimed the first shower with the excuse that she needed to hit the grocery store across the street for food. Consequently, Ariell made Jac rock-paper-scissor her for the second shower, and Jac lost. By the time she got out, Ivy had returned and was pacing the room, talking on her cell phone.

"No. I don't think that's a good idea . . . You need to call her . . . No, I won't. Call *her*." Ivy pressed her lips together when she saw Jac and then hung up the phone.

"What was that about?" Jac asked, frowning at the way her sister's eyebrows pinched together.

"You'll find out soon enough," Ivy said dryly, nodding toward Jac's phone, which was sitting on the desk in the room. A second later, as if on command from Ivy, the phone rang.

Jac reached over to pick it up, recoiling when Colin's name and a picture of them from several months earlier lit up her screen. "What's going on?" Jac asked Ivy.

"You're going to have to answer that eventually," Ivy said, sitting heavily on the bed. "He's here. In Fairbanks."

Jac stared at Ivy for several moments before saying, "He's *what*?"

"He wanted me to come and get him so he could surprise you tonight at dinner. But I told him that he needed to call you. He's at the airport." Ivy studied Jac right back, her scowl deepening with every word.

Jac dared a glance at Ariell, who met her gaze for a second before turning to look down to her hands. Then Jac's phone dinged, announcing a voice mail. A second later it started ringing again.

The Fairbanks airport was small but busy, Jac noticed as she pulled up in front of one of the two arrivals doors. She'd never answered Colin's call, only texting that she was on her way. She needed enough time to round up her confused thoughts before she spoke to him, but the five-minute drive hadn't allowed that.

Her mind kept replaying the moments when she'd promised

Ariell that she'd be careful with Hudson and when she'd admitted to him how it scared her to think that she might mess things up and hurt him. Hudson had told her to relax and enjoy what was happening between them, and she had. She so had.

But now Colin had shown up. He'd flown over 1800 miles to join her on their trip. What did that mean for her? For them? Or for Hudson?

I'm out front, she texted, drawing in a deep breath. *Black Toyota minivan.*

Less than a minute later, Colin strolled out with his duffel bag, holding a sleeping bag under his arm. He was shorter and stockier than Hudson, a few inches taller than Jac's 5'6". She hadn't realized earlier how much she'd liked Hudson's height, nestling against his chest with his chin resting on her head. Now she remembered how different it was when Colin had held her.

She hit the power sliding door button to open the door on the passenger side, partly for Colin to throw his stuff in, but mostly to help identify her vehicle. Colin grinned at her as he tossed his stuff onto the middle seat, and she managed a wobbly smile back.

Anxiety tightened in her chest. How could she ignore what he'd done? Plane tickets to Alaska didn't come cheap. She, Ivy, and Ariell had checked when they had first started planning the trip. And for him to get one last minute? The knot in her chest tightened.

He pulled open the passenger door, and she punched the button again to close the sliding one.

"Hey," she said as he settled in his seat.

"Hey back," Colin said as he leaned toward her, reaching out to draw her closer. But Jac pulled away, pressing herself into the window. His face fell at her reaction, his brows melting down into a confused scowl. "What's wrong?"

"What's wrong?" Jac let out a short laugh as she jerked the van into gear and eased back onto the street. "We broke up." She should probably stop the car, park it along the curb after the second departures entrance, where it wasn't so busy. Colin deserved a few minutes of her undivided attention to present his case—and, with her driving, she couldn't give that to him.

But the thought of pulling the car over—for them to have a moment alone—made every nerve in her body tighten with anxiety. She had no idea what to do at this point, and so driving felt like the better, easier option, something else to focus on besides Colin.

Colin reached out and took her hand, lacing his fingers through hers, then brought it to his lips to kiss her knuckles. "But I'm here now, like you wanted."

When she'd first broken up with Colin, getting him here had been her endgame. But she had realized that plan had been stupid and Colin would never change.

Was that still true? Maybe he'd finally understood her. She tugged her hand away and gripped the steering wheel. "We're meeting everyone for dinner at a burger place down the street from our hotel. They walked," she added, more to fill the space between them than to inform him. "Hopefully, the other guys won't mind if you stay with them. I mean, there's already three of them anyway, so I don't think they'll have a problem—"

"Jac." Colin reached over to lay his hand on her arm. Before, when she'd ridden in that spot next to Hudson, the space hadn't been an issue. Holding hands, flirting, all of that from the two captain's chairs up front hadn't felt awkward at all. But now, she fumbled over every adjustment, pulling herself inward, though she did let Colin keep his hand there.

"Yeah?" she said. Confusion pressed in on her, filling her throat with emotion as she struggled to get the words past.

"I get it," he said, gripping her arm. "I'm here to show you that I get what you said about me, about us. I came because this trip is important to you."

She'd wanted to hear this for so long. But leaving Billings

without Colin had changed something for her. It wasn't just about Hudson; it was about her realization, about the things she'd seen in Colin once their relationship had ended and the reality of all of it—their true relationship, what their future would be like, how he would always treat her—had hit her square in the face.

"It's not that easy," she finally said.

Colin retracted his arm and leaned his elbow onto the armrest. "Why not?"

Jac didn't speak again until a few minutes later, when they pulled into the crowded parking lot of a strip mall, where the restaurant was located. She cut the engine and pocketed the keys before turning to Colin.

"We broke up, and we've talked about why. Are you telling me that now you're going to make time for our relationship? For me? That we're going to talk about our future?"

But Colin pushed open the door of the van without replying. He strode around to the other side as Jac opened her door. She climbed out too, but Colin blocked her from stepping away from the van. He leaned into her, pressing her against the van with his body, trapping her with his proximity. She gently pushed at his chest as he leaned in toward her, but Colin paid her no heed. He gazed at her intently, his expression pleading with her.

"I'm. Here." He closed the remaining distance and lowered his lips onto hers.

She couldn't help but let him kiss her. There was nowhere she could go to, pressed up against the car door as she was. But she couldn't give in to his expectation that they would get back together automatically. Her reservations remained, however comforting or familiar his kisses were. She pushed against him harder, breaking contact resolutely. She shook her head at him.

"I came here for you," Colin said in a low voice as he straightened and finally stepped away, but Jac's gaze went now to a spot over his shoulder, where a group of people had walked up to the van: Hudson, Liam, Garrett, Ariell, and Ivy.

"Hey, Colin," Garrett said first, awkwardness evident in his voice.

Jac swallowed and looked pleadingly at Hudson. He scrutinized her then turned his gaze away, heading inside the restaurant. She hoped that Ivy and Ariell had explained about Colin showing up unannounced. She also hoped he'd give her a chance to explain . . . everything. Most of all, she hoped that she hadn't just messed everything up between herself and Hudson, exactly as she'd feared she would.

Chapter Seven

Dinner was as awkward as Jac had expected. Everyone there, but Colin, had witnessed her and Hudson's blooming relationship over the past two days, and then everyone had also witnessed Colin's kiss. Neither Ariell nor Hudson would meet Jac's eyes, and she didn't blame them.

But Ivy tried to keep the conversation going with help from Liam and Garrett—and even Colin, whose spirits seemed high. Maybe Garrett's greeting earlier had kept Colin from really seeing the uncertainty in Jac's response after he had kissed her. But how could he continue to miss the way she'd drawn herself in through all of dinner?

After dinner, the group didn't want to waste the summer light, so they drove down to Pioneer Park instead of back to their hotel. Hudson sat in back of the minivan with Garrett and Ariell, so Colin and Jac were left with the middle row. *This won't work*, Jac couldn't help but think, and her biggest concern wasn't even about the tighter squeeze.

The Riverboat Nenana, an old steamship, dominated the view as they walked through the gates of the park. Ivy grabbed Jac's hand and pulled her away from the group as they headed aboard the large boat.

"We're going to the restroom. We'll catch up in a minute," Ivy said as an excuse to the others as she pulled her sister away.

As soon as they had rounded the back end of the boat and

were out of sight of their friends, Ivy didn't bother with the pretense anymore. She stopped and faced Jac, concern filling her expression.

"Let it out," she said.

Jac held up her hands. "I don't know what to think. Colin is here, just like I asked him to be. And he must have spent so much money. Doesn't that mean I should give him another chance?"

"No." Ivy reached over and gripped Jac's upper arms. "Don't let that be a factor here, Jac. You broke up with Colin, so he took the risk by coming here. What do you *want*?"

Hudson. His name crossed Jac's mind in an instant, and she squeezed her eyes shut. It was all so complicated. "That's what I need to figure out."

Ivy pulled her into a hug. "Try not to worry about anything else," she said into Jac's ear. "Not about Colin spending a bunch of money. Not about breaking Hudson's heart. Okay?"

"Yeah. Okay." Jac nodded decisively, grateful that her sister's words had cleared away some of her guilt.

As they returned to the boat, Jac contemplated her options, only halfheartedly involving herself in the tourist activities with her friends. The Nenana had been outfitted with a small history museum about the rivers of Fairbanks and the surrounding areas. As they wandered through, everyone inspecting the dioramas and displays, Colin kept close to Jac. Every time he reached for her hand, she pulled away, and after it happened several times, he finally gave up on pushing things with her.

She needed to tell him that they couldn't pick things right back up as if they'd never broken up, even if he had flown all this way for her. But she needed an opportunity to talk to him—a real, in-depth conversation like they'd had when they were in college. Now that he'd taken this all-important step, would they have an actual future they could discuss?

As they followed the others, Jac found herself glancing at

Colin now and then, remembering the small times when he had come through for her like convincing his editors to use photographs of hers for their stories, or taking the time to set up a video-chat date when he flew out of town suddenly on Valentine's Day. Leaving her on this special holiday had disappointed her back then. Perhaps she hadn't taken the time to consider how much effort that must have taken, much like getting the plane ticket now to join her on the road trip because it was so important to her.

But Jac wanted to talk with Hudson too. Her need to be near Hudson, to reach out to hold his hand, to lean into him for comfort were hard to fight against. It wasn't until they'd left the Nenana and started wandering the "streets" of historical replicas of old Fairbanks that she finally had an opportunity to talk to Hudson. Ivy had gathered in Colin to talk with her and Liam as they had walked ahead, leaving Jac free to fall back and talk to Hudson.

"Hi," she said, bumping into him softly and was rewarded when he smiled back at her.

"Rough day?" he asked, letting his fingers brush hers for a brief second.

"Not until a few hours ago." Here, next to Hudson, the knot in her chest started to shift, loosening, untying itself. They walked in silence, Jac relishing the way everything inside her relaxed. Walking next to Hudson, she didn't have to worry about what might come next. She could just be.

But she knew that she needed to take advantage of this time to talk to him. "*He* kissed me," she said in a low, urgent tone. At the very least, Hudson had to know that.

He stopped and turned so that his back was to the rest of their group, wandering on ahead, his broad shoulders shielding her from their view.

"You don't have to do this, Jac. You don't need to explain to me." He rested his hands on her shoulders, and she stepped toward him automatically. "I said I was a big boy."

She shook her head. "Don't say that, please. It's not like that."

Hudson peered over his shoulder before turning back to her. "You were with Colin for two years, and you've only had two days with me. I'm not going to ask you to make that choice."

Did the rightness of them—their kisses, their friendship, their everything!—not overwhelm him the same way it did her? Did it not spill over onto Hudson at all, even just as they stood there, much farther apart than she would have liked? Did he not realize the way her life had stopped spinning because he had held her grounded?

She hooked her arms to hold on to his. "Thank you. But don't give up on me yet. Please."

He gave her a half smile. "Never."

Taking a breath, she stepped away. "I need some time to think. Can you tell the others I walked back to the hotel . . . *alone*?" she added pointedly, noticing that Colin had stopped on the street ahead of them, while the others moved forward.

"No problem." He winked at her before turning to catch up.

Jac spun around and hurried back toward the entrance, hoping that Hudson could keep Colin from following her. Ever since she'd gotten the phone call from Colin, she hadn't had a chance to stop and ponder on the situation before her. The drive to the airport from the hotel hadn't been long enough, and then Colin and Hudson had both sat near her during dinner, muddling everything inside her.

As she made her way across the large parking lot of Pioneer Park, Jac considered what Hudson had said. He was right. She'd dated Colin and she'd stayed with him for two years for a reason— she loved him. As before, when they had toured the steamship, small things now came back to her. Her relationship with Colin was broken, but had his decision to come here proven that they could fix it? Two days with Hudson didn't change all her feelings for Colin, although it had tilted everything, making it hard for her to grasp at objective truths.

She glanced over her shoulder a few times as she walked back to make sure that Colin didn't follow her. She didn't know how Hudson had kept Colin back, but she was thankful all the same. Her mind continued to spin with possibilities as she walked along the busy street that would take her straight back to her hotel.

Hudson had said that he wouldn't force her to make a choice, but she wanted to explore that option too. With every step along the busy Airport Way, she searched through her brain as she passed businesses, churches, and a Sears store with a mostly empty parking lot.

She admitted that she hadn't felt anything positive about Colin since he had first shown up in Fairbanks, save for the memories she'd conjured up. But was she being unfair? Hudson's declaration about how she'd dated Colin for two years wouldn't leave her mind. She had to consider it.

As she paused to wait for the signal to cross the busy intersection, she took a deep breath, hoping that some clarity would come with it, and took in her surroundings. It was nearly nine o'clock, but the sun still hung high above the trees that lined Airport Way and University Avenue to the west of her.

She tried to shed everything from her mind to just enjoy the moment. When they'd gotten up that morning to drive to Fairbanks, the sun had already risen high in the sky. They'd all watched in wonder at its circular progress around them throughout the day—not the typical rising in the east, setting in the west that she was used to. It was magical. Now, the height of the sun made it feel like midday. *As if my day needed to feel any longer.* But, as she crossed the street and continued on toward her hotel, she found that she didn't mind.

When she reached the hotel, she walked around it, back toward a patch of trees, where she found a picnic table. She sat and watched the sun and the Chena River. To her left, there was a group of cabins for another hotel. Every so often, people walked along the path between them, chatting and enjoying the warm evening.

She turned to stare out at the river. She couldn't just ignore that Colin had hopped onto a plane and had come to Fairbanks for her. It showed he cared enough about her to put his job on hold. Did that mean they could make positive changes in their relationship—like spending more time together and planning their future? If so, then she agreed with Hudson that Colin deserved that chance.

Jac also couldn't deny how her soul flew whenever she kissed Hudson, nor could she ignore the strength that had fortified her when Hudson had taken her by the shoulders at Pioneer Park. But their friendship didn't mean that they could make forever happen, and the fallout of failing to stay together could affect Jac more than she could take. Hudson wouldn't be living far away in Utah anymore either. If things went wrong between them, she'd have to face Hudson on a constant basis. And she couldn't ask Ivy and Ariell to stop spending time with him just because a romance between herself and Hudson hadn't worked out.

And still, a part of Jac itched to take that risk.

"Jac?" a voice called, turning her toward the road that she'd walked on to get around the hotel, where Colin approached her from. "I'm sorry," he said, holding up his hands. "I know that you wanted to think for a while. But I've come a long way . . ."

"No. It's okay." She patted the picnic table bench next to her. "We need to talk."

"In a good way?" he asked, taking the seat next to her cautiously, his brown eyes filled with hesitation.

"Yeah, I think so." She offered him a smile. "It is a pretty big deal that you came, but it doesn't change what I said before."

"Because of Hudson?" Colin's brows came to a slant, and his expression darkened.

Jac tensed but breathed through it. She supposed, considering her interaction with Hudson at Pioneer Park right before she took off, that Colin couldn't help but wonder if her reluctance sprang from her feelings about Hudson.

"Maybe. But I also need to know whether some things are going to change—that your coming here means that you want to work on us, that we'll spend more time together, and that I'll be a priority in your life." She leaned toward Colin, laying a reassuring hand on his leg, hoping that he was as eager to go in this new direction as she was.

"Of course. I've been trying to tell you this all along." He slid his thumb along her cheek then cupped her face to bring her toward him. "I'm here. Doesn't that mean something?"

"Yes, of course. It means so much. But it's not a onetime thing, right? We're not going to go home and let things fall apart again or go back to your work taking priority over our relationship?"

Colin tilted his head at her. "Being a journalist is demanding, babe."

Jac's heart started to sink.

It must have shown in her face because Colin rushed on. "But you're always going to be important. We're going to figure this out." He closed the remaining distance and kissed her.

When they pulled apart, Jac sat back, waiting for feelings of reassurance to wash over her as they had when Hudson had comforted her. But they didn't. Her brain settled on Colin's actual words about his job. *Demanding.*

She tangled her fingers in his, squeezing gently. "But what about next time? What about when we have special plans and you get a big story?"

Colin squeezed her hands back. "That's going to happen. But things will turn out—like they did this time," he added as he tugged her back to him, wrapping his arm around her. "I couldn't believe it, either, when the case broke, and I still had time to come and meet you. Like I said, we'll figure things out and make them work."

His words hit her like a slap and she pulled back from the force of it. "The case broke? What do you mean?"

Colin scowled in confusion. "I mean the police got a tip and solved the case," he explained. "So, as soon as I sent the story off to my editor, I got on a plane to meet you."

She'd convinced herself that Colin had seen the light and had hurried after her. But that hadn't been the case at all. "Nothing's changed," she said as she scooted farther away and then stood.

Colin stood too, moving to come closer, but Jac backed away. "I get it," he said. "You wanted me on this trip, and I made that happen."

She shook her head. "You didn't rush here to fix things. You rushed here because you finished your story—so *now* you have time to fix things with us. That's how it will always be."

"That's unfair. It's my job. I can't take it on the road like you can." He didn't try to come closer anymore.

"That's the thing. You could have come. Your boss liked that Kenai story idea." She folded her arms.

Colin snorted. "The Kenai story wasn't going to get me anywhere."

"It would have gotten you here, on the trip with me." Jac turned to face the river, watching as two kayakers paddled by. How long had she ignored this part of Colin's ambition, asking him to tamp it down for her? The core of the problem hadn't been how Colin had acted. She'd ignored who he really was. Ignored that it wasn't their priorities that didn't match, it was their dreams.

"You're right." She turned around. Colin's shoulders relaxed, and he leaned forward until she put up her hand. "It's okay for you to want the big stories and to chase after them. Someday you'll find someone who's happy to be there, waiting for you, when you're on the other side of one and on your way to making your dreams come true."

Colin caught the hand she held up. "Jac . . ."

But she gently took it away. "I'm not that person, and neither of us deserves to spend the next few years trying to change that."

They stared at each other for a long time before Colin sighed and slumped onto the bench of the picnic table, running his hand over his short hair. "Maybe if I'd listened to you more over the past few months, we could've had this talk in Billings, and then I could have saved myself the cost of the plane ticket."

She stepped forward, laying a hand on his shoulder. "Maybe I should've listened to myself sooner, instead of trying to change you. Let me pay for part of the ticket back."

It took a moment for him to reply, but then he chuckled to himself. "I might take you up on that."

Though Jac would've liked to find Hudson right away, she went back to her own room, since Colin had headed up to the guys' room. According to him, he would stay the night, maybe even a couple of nights here and write something about Fairbanks's midnight sun. The next night would be the summer solstice, and the town would have a 10K run and a lot of other celebrations. This had been the reason Ivy, Ariell, and Jac had planned to arrive in Fairbanks by that day.

"Might as well get something out of this trip," Colin had said to her.

It didn't take long for Jac to explain to Ariell and Ivy what had happened between her and Colin, and they nodded in agreement over everything, except when Jac got to the part about feeling as though Hudson was worth the risk that things might go up in flames.

"Jac . . ." Ariell shook her head, her jaw tightening.

"We're grown-ups, Ariell," Jac said from her perch at the end of one of the beds, where she sat, facing Ivy and Ariell. She leaned forward and planted her hands on Ariell's knees. "And Hudson *is* worth all the risks—but don't worry, a big part of me is sure that this is a safe bet. I've known him all my life. I know exactly who he is, and he knows me."

Ariell let out a sigh. "I suppose you're right."

Jac couldn't wait much longer after that to text Hudson.

Meet me downstairs? I'd like to take an evening stroll and hear you tell me more about Whitehall, Montana.

When she beat Hudson downstairs, Jac worried that, although she'd decided to take the risk, maybe Hudson was having second thoughts. She checked her phone again, confirming what he'd answered: *See you in a few.* She and Hudson had been over twenty years in the making, so a few more minutes wouldn't hurt.

The sun had hidden behind the trees on the opposite side of the riverbank, but it's bright rays still filled the sky. She shook her head in wonder. Past ten o'clock, and to her the sky said it was late afternoon.

"There's an A&W and a Subway and a couple grocery stores, I think."

Jac turned, raising an eyebrow at Hudson as he approached. "What?"

"In Whitehall." He grinned, coming to stand toe to toe with Jac and gazing down at her.

"I love A&W."

Hudson rested his forehead against hers. "So . . . Colin is going home?"

She nodded, feeling reassured by Hudson's gesture. She

reached up to circle her arms around his neck. Then, without waiting a second longer, she tipped her head back, placed her hands on either side of his head and pulled him down to kiss him. As they lost themselves deeper and deeper into the kiss, the bright light of the midnight sun behind her spilled into her.

She continued to hold herself close to Hudson as the kiss slowed and then stopped as they rested against each other, breathing deeply into the moment. "Even though you said that I didn't have to make a choice, I chose you anyway," she said in a low tone.

"Sounds kind of reckless." He moved closer again, his lips smiling against hers.

"Not at all," she said, receiving several more kisses in response before she could argue her point. "I know now what I would be getting myself back into with Colin—if that held a future for us at all. But you? You make Whitehall sound like heaven. Anywhere with you would be."

Epilogue

Hudson leaned forward, reaching out to open the front door of the small, two-bedroom house with the hand under Jac's knees, bumping her hips into the frame of the door. She giggled and tightened her grip around his neck.

"This is ridiculous, Hudson. We've been married almost two years. The time for carrying me over the threshold has passed." But she hung on anyway.

"But this—" he said as he shoved open the worn wooden door to reveal the living room, "this is our first house." He stepped over the threshold and kissed Jac before setting her on her feet. In the dim light, she made out the faded, hunter green carpet.

She tapped a finger to her lips as she studied the room. True, she'd seen it several times, inspecting every inch of it before she and Hudson had agreed to sign the papers, which they had done less than an hour ago—but now it was *theirs*.

"Well, it's no Whitehall," she teased.

Hudson placed his hands on either side of her head and peppered her lips with sweet kisses. Then he said, "Lovell is small too and promises to be just as boring."

She wrapped her arms around him and nestled herself against him. "Good, because you have three years of not-boring to make up for, Dr. Allen."

"You've got it. I'd do anything for my girl."

"Has it been as nice as you pictured?" she asked in a soft voice as she turned to rest her back against his chest, gazing around the room and picturing what kind of furniture she might pick out—after they got new carpet.

He wrapped both arms around her from behind. "Not at all," he teased, and so Jac elbowed him gently in the ribs. He leaned over her shoulder to kiss her cheek then her neck.

"It's been way better. And we're just getting started."

About Raneè S. Clark

Raneè S. Clark and her personal superhero, her husband, live in Alaska where they are raising three future super-villains. When she's not breaking up impromptu UFC fights in her living room or losing to one of her sons at Uno, she loves to read and write. She has a bachelor's degree in history that is probably useless, but she had a lot of fun earning it. She blogs about writing, reading, and editing at http://raneesclark.blogspot.com
    Facebook: Ranee Clark
    Twitter: @RaneeSClark

Head Over Heels

By Annette Lyon

Chapter One

"Who names a girl *Tristan* anyway?" the guy in the Klingon costume asked.

The question, while annoying, wasn't offensive. Tristan got past that reaction sometime around fourth grade, and she'd heard variations a thousand times since. An unoriginal question deserved an unoriginal answer, so she delivered one with a smile. "Turns out my mom and dad named a girl *Tristan*." She added a light giggle to be sure he wouldn't take offense.

She took a surreptitious glance at one end of the room, where a giant timer counted down. Ten seconds left. Then one more round of speed dating to go. Tomorrow would be her last day at Salt Lake Comic Con, and while she looked forward to it, she felt wrung out by all of the excitement, crowds, and celebrities.

She was skipping part of today's convention to have lunch with Alyssa, her best friend from college. After speed dating ended, she'd make a beeline to the media room before heading to the restaurant to write her thoughts and impressions so she wouldn't forget anything. The last hour might have been close to misery, but it had given her plenty to write about—possibly an entire five-day series for her online singles lifestyle magazine, *Single File*.

Klingon guy chuckled, but Tristan could not remember what

they'd been talking about. He tapped his name tag. "You'll have no trouble remembering my name. Plain old Mark. Like in the Bible."

Contrary to his suggestion, the chances of her remembering such a common name were slim to none, but with the timer about to go off, and this mini date having gotten nowhere beyond discussing *Star Trek* trivia and names, she had no desire to keep the conversation going.

The timer buzzed. Tristan breathed a sigh of relief and smiled at the Klingon. Matt? Mark? One of the New Testament Gospels. See, she'd already forgotten. He put his right fist over his heart and bowed in what she guessed was a Klingon gesture. To her, it resembled something from *Galaxy Quest*.

She gave him a slight wave. "Nice to meet you . . ." He'd introduced himself as Worf, so she almost called him that. She checked his name tag. ". . . Mark."

"It was an honor to meet you," Worf/Mark said. "Although . . . I would like to offer a suggestion?"

To her credit, Tristan didn't mention that raising your tone at the end of a phrase didn't actually turn a sentence fragment into a question. Noticing things like that made her a good writer. Pointing them out wouldn't help her love life. Not that actually getting a date from this experience had anything to do with why she'd come to the mecca for adults who played elaborate dress up—*cosplay*, it was called, short for *costume play*.

She'd heard of cosplay before the convention, but the sheer number of people participating and the lengths they'd gone to for authentic-looking costumes blew her away. Some looked store-bought, but others were handmade, with remarkable detail. The convention hosted cosplay panels and how-to workshops—even competitions. So far, her favorite costumes were worn by a twenty-something steampunk couple decked out in cool gears, hats, and coats. The woman wore the coolest corset ever. A close second was a toddler dressed as Gandalf. Attendees constantly stopped cosplayers—total strangers—to get pictures with them. Tristan had caved once, posing with a guy dressed as the David Tennant Dr. Who, mostly because another college roommate, Tara, would fangirl all over it.

Tristan was wearing a thrown-together attempt at cosplay: she'd pulled her hair into three knot-type buns, and crisscrossed thick strips of off-white fabric over her torso, which she'd tied at her waist. A toy light saber on one side finished the look. Most people, to their credit, recognized her as Rey from *The Force Awakens*. But Worf/Mark had made it quite clear he didn't approve. He looked down on all things *Star Wars* because of the prequels, which he called "the George Lucas debacle." Tristan had pointed out that Lucas sold off the franchise before *The Force Awakens* was made, *and* that it wasn't a prequel. The observation garnered her a judgmental eyebrow raise—a reaction that served only as excellent writing material.

"Have a nice day." She looked away, hoping that Worf/Mark would move to the next chair for his next date.

He wasn't so easily deflected. "Do you have a middle name? One that's *feminine*? If so, might I suggest you use that instead?"

"What's wrong with my name?"

"I could be wrong," he said, in a tone that implied he'd never been wrong, "but having a man's name might have something to do with why you're single at your age." He looked to his right, noticed Queen Amidala waiting for him, and sat before her.

"At my age"? What's that supposed to mean? At twenty-five, she wasn't exactly in danger of becoming a crazy cat lady. She could have pointed out to that Worf/Mark might be single at *his* age because of toe-curling halitosis, glasses so big he looked like an insect, or the receding hairline above his plastic Klingon forehead. But truthfully, those things wouldn't have been dealbreakers if he'd been a nice guy. He could have been the hottest

guy on the planet, and she still wouldn't have wanted more than a five-minute date with his arrogance.

Give me a bald head and fly-eye glasses any day, she thought. *Just don't be condescending or rude.*

She glanced between Queen Amidala and Worf and smiled inwardly. Nerd fireworks were the only possible result when a *Star Trek: The Next Generation* character was paired with one from *Star Wars*—a prequel character, no less.

Queen Amidala, whose name tag read *Breanna*, wore full makeup remarkably like that from the movie, and Tristan was impressed with the headpiece. She wouldn't have known where to begin to make something like that. Breanna looked about sixteen but had to be at least eighteen to participate. She smiled coyly at Worf/Mark, making Tristan cringe. He wouldn't be kind to waiflike Breanna, who, in the last hour, had shown herself to be equal parts sweet and smart. She might not have had the features of a supermodel, but neither did 99.99 percent of the planet, but she still deserved kindness and respect, not some arrogant narcissist living in a fantasy—and maybe his parents' basement—who spent their five minutes playing "Let Me Show You How Brilliant I Am," followed by "Here's Where You're Lacking."

The sixty-second window to move to the next date hadn't ended yet. People still shifted about, some standing to stretch, men gradually rotating clockwise on the inside of two concentric circles of chairs. Tristan looked around the room again, as she did between each round. So far, she'd counted four Catwoman costumes, two of Wonder Woman, one from what had to be from *Game of Thrones*, and others she couldn't pinpoint. Somewhere around fifteen thousand people had attended the convention so far, which meant hundreds of women had come dressed as Catwoman alone, and thousands more in costumes ranging from *Once Upon a Time* to *The Flash,* a show she was entirely unfamiliar with.

She jotted down a couple of quick thoughts about Worf into

her notebook, eager to write her report and see her readers' reactions. What had begun as her personal blog to brain dump in had evolved and expanded into a career. Her site had corporate sponsors and advertisers willing to spend big money. She was given prepaid trips to attend events that companies wanted her to review. She'd garnered over four hundred thousand regular readers, and even more who stopped by occasionally. Her most viral post hit eight million views. She wasn't rich, but her website paid the bills.

Right now, however, she was between big accounts, so every penny was getting its life pinched out of it. Much of her success lay in providing consistently fresh, high-quality content, but the longer she kept it up, the harder it became to stand out.

Hence her latest idea: a series focused on the western US that covered different ways singles try to find love. Last week it was a singles bar crawl in San Francisco. This week it was Salt Lake Comic Con. Next week she'd go up to Yellowstone to experience an entirely different kind of singles culture. After that she was scheduled to attend a Beat poet contest for singles in Seattle.

In each city, she made a point of experiencing as much of each location as possible so she could write many future pieces about other topics related to those areas—inexpensive dates, the unique and delicious foods, great hikes, must-see museums and landmarks, and so on. She had a feeling that her readers would eat up a Comic Con report, nerds and non-nerds alike.

Tucking the pen between the covers of her notebook, she sensed more than saw a tall shape of someone approaching her. She looked up and held out a hand to greet her final speed date. She froze, and her heart started to thump triple-time.

Whoa. Loki. Her one big Hollywood crush in the flesh, holding a hand toward her over the back of the chair.

Not Tom Hiddleston, of course. A *very* good thing, because she would have passed out. But this man might as well have been his brother. His costume was perfect—the long black coat, tall black boots, and leather tunic with green and gold accents and layered leather strips that made V's down the front. Even his dark, shoulder-length hair combed back was just like in the Marvel movies.

How had she been in the same room as Loki for almost an hour without noticing him? He must have arrived late; she absolutely *would* have noticed those piercing eyes, mischievous smile . . .

With one leg, he easily stepped over the back of the chair as if it were no taller than a step stool. Sitting, he held his hand out again. She shook it, and he smiled wider, which sent her brain into a bigger scramble. "I'm Mac. Nice to meet you . . ." His voice trailed off as a cue for her to say her name.

What *was* her name again? She stared at their clasped hands and managed to return the shake. "Tristan," she answered, pleased for remembering.

"So, Tristan." He leaned forward and rested his forearms on his thighs, so his face was closer now; he looked even better at this range. She could smell his cologne now, too. "Tell me about yourself."

Her mind went blank. She couldn't have picked her own mother out of a police lineup. She looked down and focused on the funky carpet pattern in hopes of being able to think like the intelligent adult with a college degree she was, but all she could do was play with the curling corners of the notebook and say, "Tell me about yourself. Not about Asgard, of course."

Way to go—you know enough about Loki to make a comment like that. But then she realized that she'd probably been as unoriginal as someone asking who would name their child *Tristan*.

Mac chuckled anyway. It might have been a pity laugh, but she didn't care. She could hear that sound every day of her life and never get tired of it. *Maybe I can manage to record him laughing and use it as a ringtone.* She flushed at the thought. *I am such a dork.*

"I grew up in Southern California," he said. "Pasadena area. You?"

She tried to answer, but her mouth was too dry to make noise without sounding like a frog. Grateful she'd brought along a water bottle, she reached for it, took a drink, then said, "Arizona—Mesa. I went to college in California, though."

"Oh? Where?"

"Berkley." She took another drink, desperately needing to soothe her parched throat again. She hadn't touched her water since entering the room, but Loki's appearance had changed that. After a few more swallows, she set the bottle on the floor again, unable to keep herself from wondering what he'd look like with lighter hair, like Hiddleston's. Had Mac dyed his hair, or was that his natural color? Was it really that long, or was he wearing a good wig like Hiddleston's Loki? Mac's eyes looked green, but maybe the dark hair and green accents in his costume drew out those colors.

Hiddleston's more of a sandy blond. And he's every bit as hot in a business suit. Or a tux . . .

Mac stood, flipped the chair around, and straddled it, resting his arms on the back. "You don't look like a typical con-goer."

"What makes you say that?"

He pointed at her notepad, which she realized she'd been gripping with white knuckles. "Most people come, take in the sights, just have fun. You've been cataloging everything like an archivist."

Tristan raised an eyebrow. "An archivist." How many guys even knew that term?

"Or, you know, something else really smart and intellectual." He grinned.

He's flirting. Actually flirting. And he'd called her smart. In her experience, the few men *not* intimidated by a smart woman had gone the way of the dinosaurs.

"I've been taking notes for work," she said vaguely. Mac continued to study her face. Her cheeks turned warm, and she couldn't look away. Then again, why would she want to? If only *he* would look away, she could admire the view without his piercing gaze staring back in a way that felt as if he could see into her soul.

"So if you're not an archivist, what's your degree in?" Mac asked.

Now it was Tristan's turn to tilt her head in curiosity. "You know I went to Berkley. What makes you think I finished my degree?"

"Call it a hunch."

"Good hunch. I have a bachelor's in English. And before you crack any jokes, let me assure you that it's *not* a 'fluffy' major. Yes, I can use my degree, and I've never asked anyone if they wanted fries with that." She shrugged with all of the nonchalance she could muster, which amounted to less than a thimbleful. She replayed her own words in her head and regretted them.

I probably sound like a defensive spinster, the kind of person Worf thinks I am.

"Duly noted." Mac didn't look at all put off. His smile only broadened, as if he found her even more interesting. "But I have to ask: What would be the punishment if I slip up?"

His teasing tone helped Tristan relax, so she joked back. "Oh, see, then I'd have to kill you. And that would be unfortunate." She held up her fist, pen point facing outward, as if she were ready to stab him. She tilted her head in mock innocence.

Mac raised both hands in surrender. "I wouldn't dare mock your degree."

In spite of herself, she laughed and lowered the pen.

"Honestly," Mac went on, "I've found English majors to be some of the most insightful people I've ever worked with. They see other points of view and know how to communicate it. They bridge teams in a way no one else can. They're the best writers out there, and let's face it, *every* career nowadays requires skill in written communication. So yeah. I think you've probably got a pretty big leg up on most college grads."

In a few seconds, he'd voiced most of her arguments about why her degree was valuable. Of course being able to dissect a William Blake poem wouldn't help anyone design a rocket or advance heart surgery, but the skills she'd learned—analyzing literature, looking at works in different ways, and then arguing and defending an opinion—had served her well. For that matter, the skills she'd learned as an English major—along with her business administration minor—had provided her with the exact strengths she needed to make a successful business as a writer and entrepreneur.

"Besides," Mac added, "I can't exactly mock English majors when my degree is equally mocked."

"Oh?" Laying the notebook in her lap, Tristan leaned forward, intrigued.

He leaned forward too, his eyes narrowed as if facing a challenger and throwing down a gauntlet over who had the most mockworthy major. "Philosophy. With a humanities minor."

In spite of herself, Tristan covered the traitorous smile she couldn't prevent. "No," she said, after trying rather unsuccessfully to restrain her laughter. "You're joking."

"Nope." He sat back, satisfied in his victory of lame majors.

"Talk about a useless degree."

Mac shrugged. "I learned a lot of the same things you did—writing, analysis, communication. Hasn't held me back."

Now *that* was refreshing to hear. "So what do you do for a living?" Tristan asked. "You know, when you're not attending cons or trying to destroy planet Earth." She tapped the cape on his shoulder but then quickly pulled her hand away, painfully aware of having been too forward but really wanting to touch him longer.

Just to see if his muscles are as strong as they look. Even she didn't believe the lie.

"I'm president at a digital marketing—"

The timer buzzed. Tristan looked up, dismayed. That couldn't possibly have been five minutes. The timer confirmed her suspicion—it still showed two and a half minutes to go. The moderator's voice came over the mic.

"Thanks, everyone. We're running a few minutes behind, folks, sorry that we have to cut it short. We need to clear out right away. Feel free to help us set up for the panel coming into this room next: five best-selling authors will be discussing potential pitfalls of stories that involve time travel."

She'd finally found someone she actually wanted to talk to, and their time was up? Too bad she didn't have Hermione's Time-Turner; she'd rewind the last two and a half minutes to relive them—and ask for Mac's number.

"Don't forget your notebook," he said.

They'd both stood, although she didn't remember doing so. She looked down, and sure enough, the notebook had fallen to the floor. "Oh, right," she said in a daze. "Thanks, Lo—I mean, Mac."

He waved as he headed for the door, cape flowing behind him as he walked. Just before reaching the door, he turned and flashed a smile her way. Or had he been looking at someone else? Half a dozen women lined her wall; he could have been looking at any one of them. Her phone buzzed in her pocket, so she pulled it out to see a text from Alyssa, confirming their plans to meet at the Blue Lemon in the City Creek mall across the street. The text ended with the cheerful, *See you in a few!*

When Tristan looked up, Mac was gone. She raced into the hall, but he'd disappeared in the river of people. She leaned against a wall and looked at Alyssa's text again. For a second, Tristan considered canceling lunch so she could track Mac down. But what were the chances of finding him? The corridors were filled with moving people like a giant river. If he'd gone into the giant ballroom or the exhibit hall, he might as well have disappeared through Dr. Who's TARDIS.

Besides, seeing Alyssa happened rarely—maybe once a year since she'd moved to the Rocky Mountains for a position with a regional publisher. This was the only opening in Alyssa's crazy schedule this entire week.

The con went late tonight and continued into tomorrow, but that was no guarantee she'd see Mac again even if he did come the last day. She slipped her notebook into her over-sized purse and returned to the room, where she tracked down the moderator to ask for Mac's contact information.

"He was my last date," Tristan said, realizing that the sentence sounded odd even in context. "And we didn't have time to exchange numbers or anything."

The moderator shrugged, rearranging chairs into a line. "Sorry," he said. "We didn't take down everyone's information."

Mac had arrived late anyway, so they probably had no information on him. She sighed, sent a confirmation to Alyssa, and headed to the media room. *The food at the Blue Lemon had better be excellent to make up for losing Loki.*

Except that she was perpetually single, and her career largely hinged on her remaining that way. So what was the point of trying to find a guy who was hot but who apparently wasn't interested enough to ask for her number? In the media room, she took out her Rey buns and shook out her hair, then unwrapped the tan-colored cloth that was the rest of her costume. After shoving the fabric and light saber into her purse, she typed up a few new notes about Salt Lake Comic Con speed-dating then headed out of the convention center. As she reached the crosswalk, she wanted to find the guy behind Murphy's Law and throttle him.

Life—or perhaps Murphy himself—seemed quite happy to throw delightfully weird things into her path that she could write about, things that added color to her writing, like Worf/Mark with his shiny bald spot. But then, when she least expected it, Murphy mocked her by dangling something in front of her that she might really want, only to snatch it away before she could grab it.

The light changed, and Tristan crossed with a dozen other pedestrians, at least half of whom wore costumes. Tristan raked her fingers through her hair to get rid of any lingering bun head and tried to come up with things to talk about with Alyssa without bringing up the Loki who got away.

Looks like I'll be playing a part, just like all of these superhero fans around me.

Only, I don't need a costume, and I'll be pretending to be a happy version of myself.

Chapter Two

Tristan arrived at the restaurant first, so she sat near the door to wait. Her phone rang with an incoming call, playing the theme song from *Gilmore Girls*. The screen registered an unfamiliar number from Las Vegas. She didn't know anyone from Sin City, but she did regularly get calls from companies and sponsors looking for ad space, product reviews, or other exposure on her website.

"*Single File* magazine, Tristan Spencer speaking."

"Ms. Spencer, hello," a woman's voice said. "This is Pamela Hall, the marketing director of the Venetian-Palazzo Resort."

"Hello. How may I help you?" Tristan was already uncapping a pen and opening her notebook, which she always kept nearby precisely for moments like these. Her notebooks might be low-tech, but they kept her organized and her growing company functional.

"I heard that you're planning a series about singles events across the country."

"That's right," Tristan said. "Mostly the West Coast and the Rockies, although I'd love to do another series featuring other areas of the country."

Read: She'd go to other areas when sponsors based there were willing to foot the bill.

"Have you visited Vegas for your series?" Pamela asked.

"I haven't had the opportunity yet, but I'd love to." No point in saying that she hadn't gone to Vegas because no hotels there had offered to sponsor her. She'd had so much success getting support to go to Idaho, California, Utah, Washington state, and Arizona that she hadn't bothered with Nevada.

"This is awfully last-minute," Pamela said, "but your series was just brought to my attention. And may I say that I'm deeply impressed with your company, and how fast it's grown in such a short period?"

"Thank you so much," Tristan said. She'd given her heart and soul to her start-up, learning more about marketing, social media, click rates, search engine optimization and more over the last year and a half.

"I'm hoping that you or someone on your staff might be available this weekend."

Tristan couldn't help but smile at how Pamela assumed the magazine had a staff of more than one. *Someday*, she thought.

Pamela went on. "We're hosting a singles convention with amazing workshops and keynote addresses, activities at the resort, delicious meals—the works. We believe that *Single File* attracts the exact demographic we're targeting. This year's event has about four hundred people registered, but we're hoping it'll grow to at least twice that size in the next year or two. Having someone like you write about it would be one of the best ways to spread the word."

"What are you picturing?" Tristan asked, a subtle way, she hoped, of asking what the offer consisted of.

"We'll put you up for three nights in one of our suites on the Palazzo side," Pamela said. "Your press pass will give you free admittance to the entire convention, including all activities and meals." It sounded almost too good to be true. "There is a slight catch, however."

Of course there is. Tristan made sure her phone's mic was pointed away so it wouldn't pick up her sigh of disappointment.

"We'd need you here tomorrow morning at about ten o'clock, but I haven't had time to get corporate approval to pay for a plane ticket. I don't suppose there's a way for you to drive here, is there? Where are you now?"

"I'm in Salt Lake." Technically, within driving distance. Tristan chewed the inside of her cheek, trying to come up with a way to make this opportunity work. She'd planned to drive a rental car to Yellowstone on Sunday and stay with Denise, a high school friend. Then Tristan would fly to Seattle and crash on the sofa of Amanda, a cousin who worked for Amazon.

"Not too far, then," Pamela said, sounding excited. "That's great. So can we plan on you?"

"Let me look at my calendar . . ." Tristan said, trying to buy herself some time while frantically thinking through options.

She'd have to see if she could rearrange things so she could fly from Vegas to Idaho. She'd already bought her ticket from Idaho to Seattle; could she afford to buy a second? She'd have to fly; no way could she drive from Vegas to Yellowstone and stick to her schedule. Even if she could, that still left her with the little problem of getting *to* Vegas in the first place. She'd almost certainly need to go by car. Finding a seat on a plane this late would be impossible. So was paying for a third plane ticket. She had only a hundred dollars cash.

In another four weeks when some sponsorships came through, she'd have more wiggle room. Another six months, and she'd have a pretty healthy cash flow. But for now, she had to keep building the business on a shoestring while pretending she had millions. Not for the first time, she thought how glad she was that Alyssa had made a point of saying that she was treating Tristan to lunch. One less drain on her meager funds.

Money would be especially tight until she got paid by a big

name department store. When that check cleared in another week or so, her bank account would stop screaming for mercy. And if she could *get* to Vegas, the resort would put her up and feed her for several days.

"Miss Spencer?" Pamela said. "Are you still there?"

How long have I been thinking in silence? Tristan straightened in her seat and clicked the cap back onto her pen. "Oh, sorry. I'm here. And yes. I'll be there." The words just tumbled out. Now she *had* to find a way to make them true.

"Wonderful!" Pamela said, sounding equal parts excited and relieved—emotions Tristan could only hope to possess again soon. "When you know your schedule, be sure to pass it along, and I'll have the convention information waiting for you on check-in at the reception desk in the Palazzo. You can check in as early as tonight."

"Thanks. And will do," Tristan said. Pamela said good-bye and hung up.

Now what? She stared at her phone screen as if it might provide the answers.

"Why so glum?" someone asked.

Tristan looked up to find Alyssa standing before her. "Hey, you!" Tristan stood, and the two friends hugged. It had been far too long since their last good talk. "When did you get here?"

"Right before you hung up wearing Atlas Face."

That was what they called an expression of worry when you felt as if the weight of the world was on your shoulders. Back in college, they'd worn Atlas Face during finals and after breakups. That was before real life settled in and brought along much bigger concerns, like making enough money to pay for things like food.

"What's wrong?" Alyssa asked.

"Let's order and sit down first, and I'll tell you all about it."

They did, and after settling at a table with their drinks, Tristan explained the situation with as many details as she could bear to give without sounding like a loser. Alyssa had an actual full-time job with medical *and* dental benefits. Even a 401K. Tristan's freelancing, entrepreneurial lifestyle felt juvenile in comparison. For the moment, it didn't matter that more people had read *Single File* than the bestsellers published by Alyssa's employer. By the time Tristan had finished her *Reader's Digest* version of the story, their food had arrived.

"Have you checked craigslist or Buckle Buddies?" Alyssa asked, piercing her salad with a fork.

"I've heard too many scary stories about craigslist," Tristan said, shaking her head. "I've never heard of Buckle Buddies, but it sounds like I could end up stuck in a car full of homicidal Teletubbies. If there's a chance I'll end up with a creeper who will leave my body in the middle of nowhere, I'll pass."

Alyssa chewed thoughtfully. She swallowed and said, "Okay, so craigslist is out. But I've used Buckle Buddies several times. And as you can see, I remained unharmed by furry monster puppets." She held her arms out as if proving her point. "You and the other person decide on the arrangement—how much of the gas you pay for, how many suitcases you can bring along, planned pick-up and drop-off points, all of that. The app has security built into it—it tracks your locations, and if something goes wrong, the authorities can easily find your last known location." Alyssa went on about the benefits of the app, including the ratings and chat features. She even gave tips of which keywords to use and avoid.

"That's a possibility," Tristan said, pocketing her phone. "But first, let's eat and catch up. I need to hear all about your latest boyfriends."

"What about your boyfriends?" Alyssa countered with a raised eyebrow.

Tristan grunted. "If there were any to talk about, you'd already know. The closest thing I've gotten was in the last workshop I went to—Comic Con speed dating."

Alyssa sat back in her seat and laughed. "You didn't."

"Oh, I most certainly did," Tristan said, laughing now too as she picked at her food. "And it was as delightful as it sounds."

"Meet anyone interesting?"

"*Interesting* as in completely weird and therefore perfect material for the magazine? Then yes, I met plenty of interesting men."

"And?" Alyssa pressed.

"And if you mean *interesting* as in potential dating material . . ." Tristan said, avoiding Alyssa's hopeful gaze, "then almost."

Alyssa set her fork down and leaned forward, arms on the table. "What was he like? Light hair? Dark hair?" She waggled her eyebrows. "*Ginger?*"

"Why are you obsessed with redheads?" Tristan said, chuckling. "But I don't know what color his hair is." She dreaded explaining, but there was nothing for it. "This was Comic Con. Everyone in the room had on some kind of costume."

"Even you?"

"Sort of. I did a Rey thing with my hair and stuff." Tristan waved the detail away. "But my last speed date was dressed as Loki. And it was a *really* good costume."

"Oh, swoon." Alyssa meant it, too. They'd both crushed hard on Tom Hiddleston for years. He was even better than her ginger fantasies.

"I don't know if that was his real hair."

"He sounds miles better than the Nameplate Bandit."

They rolled their eyes at the memory of the practical jokester who used to work with Alyssa and drive her crazy, constantly hiding her nameplate in random places. On Halloween, the Bandit came to the office party dressed as Loki, a sight that had almost ruined the very idea of Loki for Alyssa. Of course, Tristan had empathized with every bit of frustration Alyssa had because of her annoying coworker.

"Definitely better than the Bandit," Tristan agreed.

Alyssa took a sip of her Diet Dr. Pepper. "Did you exchange numbers?"

"Didn't get that far. The timer went off early, and next thing I knew, people were rearranging chairs, and he'd disappeared. I was hoping to find him at the con tomorrow, but now I'm supposed to be in Vegas instead. All I know is that he has a degree in philosophy and his first name is Mac."

Alyssa suddenly stilled.

"You okay?" Tristan asked.

"Yeah. Yeah, of course." Alyssa shook her head and returned to stabbing her salad. "Just remembered something for work. Go on."

"We've been talking about me this whole time." Tristan mimed turning a lazy Susan. "Back to you and your love life. New boyfriend?"

"I still want to hear more about you and Loki Boy," Alyssa said. "But . . . I did go out with this really great guy last weekend, and we have another date tonight."

Tristan let out a squeal that even to her sounded a bit like a silly high school girl, but she didn't care. "Spill everything."

After a highly enjoyable lunch, Alyssa paid their tab. "Too bad I have to get back to that whole job thing," she said, standing. "We need a week or two to catch up properly."

"Too bad I have to figure out a way to get to Vegas tonight. I'd much rather stay."

As they tucked their chairs under the table, Alyssa paused. "You know, something just occurred to me. I might know someone you can drive down with."

"Really? Who?"

"MacKenzie Wilson—a fabulous graphic designer who used to work with me. Moved to Vegas last summer for a new job, but came back up for Comic Con this weekend. Some of the others from the office got together for lunch."

"I made you miss lunch with her?"

Alyssa cocked her head. "You trump pretty much anyone, even my mom. But anyway, I happen to know that MacKenzie is driving home tonight."

"Isn't she staying all three days?"

"I don't remember," Alyssa said. "Maybe the three-day passes were all gone? You'd have to ask." They headed for the glass doors and the busy street outside. Alyssa gestured for them to step to the inside of the sidewalk. When they were out of the path of pedestrians, Alyssa pulled out her phone and began typing. "I'm sending the number to you right now so you'll have it. I'll call too, and pass along yours. I doubt Mackenzie has left yet."

"Any idea what she'll charge?"

Alyssa kept typing as she shook her head. "This isn't Uber or Buckle Buddies," she said. "It's a friend of a friend doing a favor. Pitch in some gas money, some snacks for the road, and maybe take a turn driving for a couple of hours, and I'd bet you'll both be happy." She sent the text, and a moment later, Tristan's phone buzzed.

"Thank you so much. I'll send a text right now. What does she look like?"

"Tall, sandy blond hair." Alyssa gestured toward her phone. "Text me when you get to Vegas so I know you didn't end up dumped in a ditch in the middle of nowhere or anything."

"Hey, you said—"

Both of Alyssa's hands went up. "Totally kidding. I'd trust MacKenzie with my life." Her face softened into a more pensive expression—nothing like Atlas Face, and possibly more meaningful. "You deserve to have every bit of happiness and success the world has to offer," she said. "I hope you know that."

"You're the best," Tristan said, hugging her best friend. She had to blink several times to prevent tears from falling. "I'm going to miss you."

As they parted, Alyssa held up her phone. "Keep in touch," she said, walking backward now, in the direction of her office building. "Technology is the next best thing to being in person."

Tristan held up her phone. "Will do."

"Text MacKenzie soon!" Alyssa called. "I'm calling now, so it'll be expected!" She waved good-bye, turned, and walked off, phone to her ear.

Tristan crossed the street to Temple Square, found a bench under a tree, and sent a text to the number Alyssa had sent.

MacKenzie, this is Alyssa Gardner's friend. She probably just called about me. I need to get to Vegas for an event tomorrow morning, and she said you might have room in your car today. I'd be happy to pitch in money for gas and food.

She added a smiley face, tapped send, and reluctantly headed for her hotel. As weird as Comic Con was, she had really enjoyed parts, especially hearing from celebrities who'd starred in shows she grew up watching.

But she had to admit that the best part was Loki. It really was a shame that she wouldn't be able to go back tomorrow to find him.

Chapter Three

As Tristan reached her hotel room, her phone went off with an incoming message: from MacKenzie.

I'd love to have company. I checked out of my room this morning, so I can pick you up as soon as you want to leave. Just say where and when. I was planning to leave at the top of the hour, but I'm flexible.

Tristan went in, let the door close behind her, sat on the bed, and tapped out a reply.

Thank you so much! I can be ready in 15. I'm at the Radisson Hotel. Meet you at the pull through?

As she sent the message, she felt grateful for the hotel comping her room in exchange for a review on her site. Without this room, she would have had to stay in a dingy motel or crash at Alyssa's. While the latter would have been fun, it would also have been entirely unproductive. A hotel room provided the solitude and quiet Tristan needed to work on the road.

One of these days, she'd make enough to simply visit her best friend, and then they could stay up late, talking and laughing and eating ice cream while watching cheesy romantic comedies from the 80s.

Her phone buzzed with another text from MacKenzie. *Sounds great. See you there in a few! Alyssa told me to wear my*

Mickey Mouse baseball hat so you'd recognize me. I drive a red Camry. I'll wear the hat too, but the car might be easier to spot. See you soon.

Everything was turning out better than she could have hoped. She'd prepared herself to arrive in Vegas after midnight, but they'd probably arrive in Vegas around eight or nine, which meant getting a decent dinner and a good night's rest before the singles convention in the morning.

She stared at her phone, trying to decide what to tell MacKenzie to watch for as a way to recognize her. Straight, dishwater blonde hair that came past her shoulders seemed like a pointless description; that description matched half of the local population.

My suitcase is Granny Smith green, and I'm wearing yellow shoes. Her top was nothing more than a fitted V-neck tee—something that had worked under her Rey *costume*—so she didn't bother mentioning the rest of her wardrobe. Her yellow wedge sandals and bright green suitcase would stand out plenty.

A moment later, a reply arrived: *Green suitcase, yellow shoes. Got it.* And then an emoji of a thumbs-up.

She smiled at that. The friendly image gave her the feeling that she'd get along well with Alyssa's friend. Maybe the three of them could hang out one of these days.

With the details of their meeting settled, Tristan started packing. She soon had her suitcase zipped up and the handle extended. She gave the room a final scan to be sure that she hadn't forgotten anything. Too bad it was good for another night; she could have gotten a lot done in a room like this. Maybe she could still get some writing done in the car, using her iPad and Bluetooth keyboard.

If we click as friends, we might end up talking the whole way. She looked forward to the prospect; getting to know one of Alyssa's friends wouldn't be the same as being with Alyssa, but it would certainly be fun. Maybe Tristan could even get MacKenzie to dish some dirt on their mutual friend.

Pulling her suitcase, she left her room and took the elevator to the lobby. By the time she checked out, only eleven minutes had passed since their last text. A sense of satisfaction went through her. The habit of being early helped her avoid problems. She could usually work around things like traffic jams and other obstacles without getting stressed out simply because she'd given herself extra time. Sudden surprises meant stress.

She pulled her suitcase to one of the tall windows flanking the sliding glass doors to wait. The sun was out, but with the approach of autumn, daytime temperatures had dropped. From where she stood, she could keep an eye on the window for a red car without getting goose bumps from waiting outside in the shaded, breezy pull through.

As she waited, Tristan checked the social media accounts for *Single File*. She posted memes she'd created about the single life. Five minutes later, she'd gone through Instagram, Facebook, Twitter, Pinterest, and Snapchat. She glanced up before checking her email and spotted a red Camry pulling in and parking behind a couple of taxis.

Perfect timing.

She pocketed her phone, tilting the suitcase onto its wheels, and headed out the door. Shadows prevented her from seeing much, but when the driver looked down, likely at a phone, sure enough, there was the image of Mickey Mouse. *Definitely MacKenzie.*

The driver got out and straightened into a towering figure well over six feet tall. This was a man. A tall, broad-shouldered man. A *hot* man with dark blond hair poking out from under his hat.

This wasn't MacKenzie, then. Just a man who happened to be driving one of the most common cars on the road. Who coincidentally wore the kind of very hat MacKenzie had said to look for. An odd coincidence, for sure. She stopped by a flower pot and checked her phone as if that was what she'd meant to do all along. A moment later, she sensed more than saw the man walk over and stop a few feet from her. But Tristan kept her eyes glued to the letter tiles of her game, even though she had only vowels.

"Excuse me, Tris—I mean, your name isn't Tristan, is it?"

He knows my name? Her creep-o-meter went to high alert as she slowly raised her face, but seeing him turned the alarm right off. He seemed genuinely confused—and decent.

He eyed the green suitcase and yellow shoes. When he saw her face, his mouth opened slightly in surprise. "You *are* Tristan."

"You . . . can't be MacKenzie, can you?"

"Yup. Alyssa is unbelievable." He chuckled dryly, took off the hat and ran a hand through his slightly overgrown hair before tugging the hat back on. "Should I call her first to tell her she's nuts, or do you want that honor?"

"Um . . ." Tristan said, but then had no idea how to answer. "Hang on." She clicked away from the game and went to her texts to message Alyssa, begging for some kind of clarification—and assurance that her friend didn't really expect her to get into a car with a man big enough to bench-press twice her body weight without breaking a sweat.

Nice to look at was one thing, but there was a reason Tristan had never used a dating app or any other online dating method. And now Alyssa had tried to set her up with a guy without telling her? Not only had Tristan been set up, but for a day-long road trip. She imagined hours and hours of death metal, misogynistic jokes, and body odor.

With his thumb, MacKenzie navigated to a contact on his phone, selected it, then held the phone to his ear. "You don't have to feel obligated," he said to Tristan as it rang. "Really. I'd be happy to have you come along, but I don't expect a woman to go on a trip with a guy she doesn't even know if it would make you uncomfortable in any way."

"Thanks," Tristan managed, still unsure what to do.

You already agreed to go with Alyssa's friend, she reminded herself. *You just assumed the friend was a woman. Would Alyssa really expect you to go with someone she didn't trust?*

She thought back through their conversation and realized that Alyssa hadn't used *she* or *her* when referring to MacKenzie, and she hadn't corrected Tristan when she'd used the same words. With anyone else, Tristan would have chalked it all up to a simple misunderstanding. Tristan might have let it slide as a mistake if it weren't for MacKenzie's clear expectation of meeting a guy named Tristan, only to find a woman instead.

Alyssa was ever the optimistic-matchmaker.

When MacKenzie started talking to Alyssa, he didn't look annoyed or worried—more incredulous. His side of the conversation didn't communicate much, and Alyssa wasn't replying to Tristan's texts . . . likely because Alyssa was on her phone, talking to MacKenzie.

Tomorrow held the potential for taking Tristan's magazine to the next level in readership and prominence. But she had to get to Vegas for that happen, even if it meant being stuck in a car all day with a guy who probably whistled as he drove.

I guess I'm going with him. Please don't let him be a whistler, she thought. *I'd choose even body odor over that.*

"Yeah, right," he said to Alyssa. He listened for a second and then laughed, belying the irritated tone of his words. "Will do. Talk to you later." He hung up and turned to Tristan.

She avoided looking at his face but couldn't avoid the sensation of his very large presence or the pleasant scent of his cologne. Turned out that BO would *not* be a problem. The familiarity of the scent made alarm bells go off in her head. She'd smelled it before. While walking through a department store? No.

Head Over Heels

It brought back feelings of attraction. Maybe an ex-boyfriend had worn it. She quickly eliminated that option too, remembering in a flash the three colognes they'd worn. This one was different—better.

"So, did you actually work with Alyssa?" She needed to know how much of Alyssa's ploy had been a lie. "I mean, you know her—you have her number and everything—but I'm wondering now how much of what she told me about you is true."

"I did work with Alyssa," he said. "I was in the graphics department, mostly designing book covers. Two years ago, a friend decided to start a media agency, so I quit to become his partner, and it's really taken off."

"I assume MacKenzie is your last name—unless she made that up," Tristan said as she narrowed her eyes. "What's your first name?"

"Alyssa's pretty sneaky. I thought running into two Tristans in one day was unusual."

Feeling on edge, she held a hand up. "Wait a minute" Any time she thought she had a mental foothold on things, the rug seemed to be pulled out from under her again.

"Gotta give her credit, though," he said. "She did tell you my real name, even though my Mom is the only person who uses it. To everyone else, my name is the just the first syllable." He stopped speaking and looked at her expectantly.

His words hung in the air as Tristan digested them. The truth seemed just out of reach, but then it dawned on her; she felt as if the sun were glaring in her mind's eye. She knew who she was looking at. "M—Mac?" she ventured, feeling glad that she hadn't slipped and called him *Loki*.

Mac, short for MacKenzie. Duh. Alyssa, you are so dead.

With his lips pressed together and hands in his pockets, he rocked forward onto his toes, back to his heels, and forward again. "Yeah," he said sheepishly.

Tristan gestured up and down his body, which she tried not to pay too much attention to—and failed. "I didn't recognize you without . . ." *How can I put it?*

"The costume's sculpted body armor?" he asked with a teasing tone. "I should really find a way to incorporate that stuff into my daily wardrobe—I'd look so much buffer."

She almost pointed out that his costume hadn't sculpted his arms at all, which looked plenty cut, and that his chest was already nicely shaped—facts easily visible, thanks to the navy T-shirt stretched across his torso. But her brain decided to function enough this time to come up with an equally honest observation that wouldn't make her look too ridiculous.

"I was going to say," she began, "that I didn't recognize you without the hair. That was one really good wig." Her mind spun as she tried to reconcile in her head that the guy before her was the guy she'd drooled over in speed dating. She sat on the edge of one of the hotel's giant flower pots. Her brow furrowed. He came over and sat beside her, saying nothing, as if he knew that she needed a minute to sort through it all.

"So . . . Mac is short for MacKenzie." Hearing herself say the words made them more real.

"Yeah. Guess both sets of our parents had serious issues with naming children."

Looking up, she caught a glint in his eye and couldn't help but laugh with him. For her entire life, people had mentioned that, gee, she had a guy's name, as if they were the first ones to ever notice. Had Mac been teased as a kid for having a girl's name? Probably, seeing as how he went by a masculine nickname.

What a strange and unexpected reason to feel kinship with someone—a guy who looked really, really good with both light and dark hair, short and long. He understood from personal experience what having an androgynous name felt like and they'd both been tricked into this by Alyssa.

Mac thumbed toward his car. "I don't expect you to trust some guy from Comic Con that you met two minutes ago . . . not counting the two and a half from speed dating. I was planning on driving to Vegas on my own anyway. So company would be nice, but I'll also be fine by myself."

"Thanks for understanding," Tristan said, appreciating his insight more than he could possibly know. Being a woman in today's world meant automatically assuming a certain level of danger; a smart woman took precautions. "But Alyssa is my best friend. She said she trusts you. That's good enough for me." She adjusted her purse on her shoulder. Hoping to add a little levity, she added, "I mean, it's not like you'll toss me out of the car in the middle of the desert and drive away or anything."

"Nope," Mac said with a shake of his head. "And I'll be extra careful to say nothing against your English degree so you'll have no reason to abandon me in the desert either." He flashed a cheesy smile, all teeth.

Tristan rolled her eyes and laughed. "Let's get on the road."

He put her suitcase into the trunk as she took the passenger seat and settled her big purse on the floor. The trunk closed with a thunk, and a moment later, Mac got in and buckled up. He tossed the Mickey Mouse cap into the backseat. "Let's do this," he said, starting the car up. He glanced over, noticing that she had her phone out again. "Everything okay?"

"Yep," Tristan said. "Just giving Alyssa a piece of my mind."

"We should pull a prank on her," Mac said as he pulled onto the street. "I'm sure, between the two of us, we can come up with something really good."

She admired his profile as he drove. "I like the way you think," she said as they headed for the freeway on-ramp.

Chapter Four

They reached the freeway in minutes, and with the light traffic of a Saturday afternoon, they flew past one exit after another. With her phone clutched in one hand, Tristan kept eying Mac out of the corner of her eye. Neither of them had said anything for several miles.

Should she break the silence? If so, what should she say? They'd spent only—she checked the clock—six minutes in the car.

Too early to suggest a road-trip game like Slug Bug or the alphabet game. Assuming she'd ever feel comfortable enough to suggest one.

The radio played a song that Tristan recognized vaguely as being from the 80s, and she almost commented on it, but caught herself. What if he didn't like this kind of music like she did? The song ended, and another 80s song came on. Clearly, this was an oldies or classic rock station. She knew this song—Who didn't?—and, its undeniable cheesiness aside, loved it. Her foot even tapped to the music. Feeling self-conscious, she stopped it.

But then Mac's thumb started tapping the steering wheel to the beat. A moment later, his head bobbed too. Tristan smiled to herself and deliberately looked out the window so it wouldn't be obvious that she'd noticed, although she let her foot move to the rhythm of the drums again.

Hey, if Mac has no qualms about enjoying Rick Astley, I won't either. Soon her fingers kept time against the door handle. To her, the silence felt warmer, less strained. She was more comfortable; maybe that's all it was.

She'd never forget her first time seeing the mountains *this close* to cities, where entire neighborhoods climbed the bottom of the mountain. The valley made her feel safe, encircled by mountains on all sides. The sight amazed her every time she visited.

She almost commented on the landscape to Mac, but her cell buzzed, interrupting her train of thought. A quick glance at her phone made Tristan roll her eyes. The text preview showed the whole message: an emoji of a face with a wide grin, as if Alyssa knew full well that she'd gotten away with something.

"Anything important?" Mac glanced at her then focused back on the road.

"Just Alyssa."

"What did she say?"

"Nothing."

Mac raised one eyebrow. "She sent a blank text?"

"She didn't say anything with words," Tristan clarified. "Just sent an emoji."

"Of . . ."

Tristan clicked the screen back on and held it up so he could see it. He let out a single chuckle.

Tristan nodded. "Yep. She thinks her attempt at matchmaking is downright hilarious." She blushed, wishing she could redo the last three seconds. "I mean—"

Matchmaking? She silently groaned. *You seriously said matchmaking. Are you insane?*

Another text came in, making the screen light up again. Tristan knew it would be from Alyssa again and didn't want to look at it, but her eyes were drawn to her phone anyway.

"What did she say this time?" Mac obviously knew Alyssa well enough to assume she'd keep texting.

"Another emoji," Tristan said. "Technically, several."

Bite your tongue, she thought, not wanting to tell Mac about the rows of red hearts and kissy faces Alyssa had sent. Time to put her phone into Do Not Disturb mode. No more interruptions from Alyssa. But before she could type in her pass code, Mac snatched the phone from her hands.

She yelped in surprise. "Hey!" she said, trying to grab it back. "That's illegal, you know."

He'd already held the phone out and quickly looked at it then back at the road. "It's illegal to *manipulate* a phone while driving. I didn't touch the screen."

"But you were reading a text."

"Two lines of identical emojis doesn't really count as *reading*, though, does it?" He grinned and held out the phone for her. She took it and swiped the last message to reply when he spoke up again. "What are you going to say back?"

"Uh . . ." Her brain short-circuited again. Preferably, she could think of something smart and funny to say, then she'd suggest something equally funny to send to Alyssa. Instead, all she came up with were several colorful emoji combinations to send Alyssa—but not when Mac might see them.

Getting tongue-tied wasn't like her. Of course, she typically spent most of her time with her laptop, and many of the people she interacted with were online or over the phone. She rarely had to be within touching distance of a hot guy—forget about spending the rest of her day with one.

"I don't know what to say," Tristan finally said. Boring, but truthful.

"Hmm." He sounded amused, and then he chuckled. Something about it assured her that he was laughing *with* her. The sound was warm and round and inviting. She felt as if she could almost see the cogs turning in his head as he thought.

"What?" she asked, wanting to know what he was concocting.

He changed lanes and set the cruise control. "What do you say we mess with her?"

Tristan adjusted her position to see him better. "What do you have in mind?"

"She thinks she's pulled one on us. What if we go along with it and completely freak her out?" He waggled his eyebrows. As he went on, his voice took on a movie-trailer quality. "Two strangers set up by a devious friend embark on an all-day road trip. But their friend didn't count on the two of them falling head over heels . . . in *love*."

"That would be hilarious," Tristan agreed. "But I'm not that good of an actress."

"You can do it," Mac said confidently. "Practical jokes are the best, especially when you know your mark is going to flip out."

"You do a lot of practical joking, then?"

"You could say it's a part-time hobby. When I worked up here, I pretty much drove Alyssa out of her mind." He nodded with satisfaction. "Good times."

Past conversations with Alyssa returned to Tristan's memory, including the one from today's lunch. "Were *you* the Nameplate Bandit?"

"Hah!" Mac said, obviously delighted. "I didn't know she gave me a name."

"Oh, I know all about you," Tristan said. "How Alyssa had to hunt down her nameplate every day. Did you know she slid it out and took it home with her?"

"Of course," Mac said. "It wasn't hard to steal it during the day. She wasn't *always* at her desk."

"You really do know how to mess with someone. She spent a lot of hours looking for her nameplate."

"More often than not, she gave up in defeat," Mac said. "And I ended up giving it back to her in a way she didn't expect. She had a bunch made up, but eventually I took them all. It was great."

"She's talked about you a lot," Tristan said. "The few times she did find one, she made sure to tell me about it. I felt like I knew you on some level, but I always assumed that you had a huge crush—" She cut herself off awkwardly.

Way to open your mouth and insert your foot.

"Nah, that's not my style," Mac said with a shrug. "Back then, I had a girlfriend. But my job was slowly killing me—searching through thousands of stock photos for eight hours a day, every day will do that to you—and Alyssa was the perfect target."

"The few times she found one, it was a time for celebration. Let's see . . . I remember hearing about her finding the nameplate in various file cabinets, behind a painting, above a ceiling tile—"

"That one might have been my favorite, second only to slipping it three inches deep into the lobby planter. Oh, and maybe inside the diaper changing table in the ladies restroom. Don't ask me how I managed that one."

"Oh, wow," Tristan said. "I hadn't heard about that one. I do remember hearing about the photocopier, the ceiling directly above her chair, *under* her chair . . ."

"Good times," Mac said. "How could I stop, when her reactions were always so big?"

"Even though I felt bad for her," Tristan said, "I have to admit to being impressed—you were tenacious and creative."

"Why, thank you," he said with a faux-solemn nod. "Luckily for me, she never figured out how I took her nameplates and rarely found the hiding places until someone else pointed them out to her. Plus, she never got really mad. Annoyed, sure. But it never lasted long."

"Alyssa's pretty great that way." A pang of missing her friend came over Tristan, along with the renewed realization that it might be months before they saw each other again. But playing along with Mac to pull a prank on Alyssa would help pass the time and ease the ache. She held up her phone. "She pulled one on us, so let's pull one on her."

"That's right—she started it," Mac said, but his tone made it clear that he didn't think he needed any justification.

Tristan navigated to her and Alyssa's texting thread. Thumbs poised to type, she asked Mac, "What should I say? Let's make it good."

Chapter Five

"Tell her how hot you think I am," Mac said offhandedly.

Coming from any other guy—any other *hot* guy, at least—that would have sounded incredibly arrogant, but Mac just sounded mischievous. His eyes crinkled with laughter, as if the very idea of calling him hot were ridiculous.

And that made him even *more* attractive.

Did Mac have the slightest clue about how many girls dreamed of meeting a guy with his classic swimmer's build? From everything she'd seen—and everything she had *not* seen, such as preening in front of windows, smelling of Axe body spray, or using so much product that his hair would crackle when touched—Mac appeared completely oblivious to the fact that becoming a Ralph Lauren model could have been a viable career path for him.

Tristan tore her eyes away from admiring his profile and began composing a text to Alyssa. "It needs to have lots of emojis."

"Definitely," Mac said. "And just enough detail. But it can't be long, or she'll suspect something."

"Trust me," Tristan said, "I know just what to say." She couldn't help but worry one lip with her teeth, the only way to keep herself from blushing like crazy. And she would have done almost anything to avoid showing Mac her obvious attraction. Choosing between those two options, she'd take a bleeding lip if that's what biting on it got her.

She typed a simple sentence: *Well done, my friend.* She followed that with a bunch of smiley faces with hearts for eyes.

"What does it say?" Mac asked. After she told him, he furrowed his brow. "Isn't that a bit vague?"

"It's perfect. Trust me, I know Alyssa—and . . . it's sent." Tristan settled the phone on her knee. A reply arrived quickly. "She says, 'You think so?'"

"What does she mean by that?" Mac asked, sounding confused.

"She wants to know if I really think you're hot."

"But you didn't say anything about me."

"Yes, I did. In BFF-speak."

"So 'Well done, my friend' means . . . 'He's hot'?" Mac asked, trying to understand.

"In this context, yes." She was starting to enjoy herself now that she knew that she could text Alyssa all day *and* tell Mac exactly what she was typing, and he wouldn't know which texts were teasing and which were the truth unless she told him.

They reached a road sign saying they'd entered another county. She hadn't seen a sign showing the miles left to Vegas, but one had to be coming up soon.

"What are you going to say back?" Mac asked.

"I'll read you everything, promise," Tristan said, typing again. She narrated the rest of the exchange as it happened.

He's Loki! And you knew he was, didn't you? Tristan texted.

Duh. Of course. How many guys named Mac have the perfect Loki costume?

You never told me about the Bandit's washboard abs.

Mac burst into laughter at that one. "As if you've seen my abs. Good one!"

How could he not know that his T-shirt left little to the imagination? Suddenly, Tristan really, really wanted to see his abs directly. The thought made her cheeks hot. She took a drink from her water bottle and hoped he didn't notice her blushing.

Alyssa replied. *I guess I was too busy being freaking annoyed at him to notice things like his abs.* Before either Tristan or Mac could come up with a good reply, another text arrived.

Is he driving you completely crazy with trivia about Scandinavian mythology yet? She had added a smiley with a halo above it.

Tristan read the text then added her own interpretation. "She *hopes* that I'm annoyed with you."

"Are you sure she's not worried?" Mac asked. "She might be having regrets. Three months into the Bandit thing, she kind of hated the sight of me."

"I'm sure she still does. That's why she arranged this. She doesn't particularly like you, so she thinks it's hilarious that I'm stuck in a car with Loki."

"About that," he interjected. "How did she know that we met at the speed dating thing?"

Another wave of heat crept up her face. *At this rate, my face is going to catch fire.*

She cleared her throat casually and picked at some nonexistent fluff on her slacks. "I saw her for lunch right after speed dating, and I told her all about it."

"Oh, right."

Phew. He bought that without batting an eye. She couldn't remember if she'd mentioned anyone besides Loki. Had she told Alyssa about Worf/Mark? Tristan doubted it. Ever since meeting Mac, he'd sort of taken up all of her brainpower.

Mac slapped the steering wheel with the palm of one hand. "I've got it. Tell her that you'd love to be stuck with me for a much longer road trip."

"Good one," she said. It was the truth, too—she *did* want a longer trip, even though they'd hardly begun this one. "I'll add that we're thinking about driving through Vegas and on to Disneyland."

"Will she buy that, knowing about your convention thing tomorrow?"

"Hmm. She would if the park were having a singles event. I'll check on that later." Tristan deleted the part about Disneyland. "Okay, I know." As before, she typed the text before reading it to him. "How's this: *We've really hit it off. At this rate, I wouldn't mind if this were a week-long trip.*"

"Excellent."

Tristan tapped the emoji menu. "Adding a purple heart to emphasize the point."

"Ooh," Mac said with an approving nod. "You're good at this."

"Helps to know your best friend really well."

As she was about to send the text, an Air Supply song came on the radio, "Here I Am," in all its 1981 power-ballad glory. Mac began swaying in his seat, wearing a melodramatic expression. From the first word, he sang along as if he meant every word and was passionately in love with her.

She quickly hit the send icon, slipped her phone into her purse, and joined in for the swelling chorus. They belted out the rest of the song at the top of their lungs. The music gradually faded, and the two of them laughed together. The next song, a-ha's "Take on Me", began, and Mac cranked up the volume.

Tristan turned toward him and nodded in the direction of the radio. "I don't come across a lot of guys who listen to 80s pop music—and even fewer who know the lyrics well enough to sing along."

"I could say the same about women I've gone out with—assuming we're talking about our generation."

"Oh, really? Interesting," Tristan said with mock seriousness. "I thought you might be into cougars."

"Just their music," Mac said with a grin. He looked over at her for the first time in several miles—and winked—before focusing on the road again.

Tristan's heart rate seemed to dance along to the quick beat of the music.

"That's not all I listen to," Mac continued. "But there's something special about the 80s."

"There really is," Tristan agreed.

For the next few songs, they sat in a silence filled with energy, until the first piano chords of Chicago's "Glory of Love" came on. Mac held up a hand as if getting ready to cue a choir—but then came in eight counts too soon.

Tristan busted up, then gasped, getting her laughter under control enough to come in with Peter Cetera's high tenor at the right moment. Mac's cheeks had blushed the slightest bit, which sent an excited, wobbly feeling through her chest and into her stomach. She kept singing, and he finally joined in. They danced as well as they could while belted in. When the part came about fighting for the woman's honor, Mac took Tristan's hand dramatically and pretended to be singing to her.

The song faded out, and the DJ came on, introducing, "Hello," by Lionel Richie. Dang, this station played good stuff. Mac didn't let go. Instead, he lowered their clasped hands and rested them on the console between their seats. Neither of them sang, although Tristan had every confidence that Mac knew these lyrics as well as he did the other songs. She didn't sing, either, because that would have broken the spell and ruined the moment.

Their silence continued, and she happily kept her hand nestled in his, in spite of about ten songs coming on in a row that were perfect for singing to. About the time cities disappeared behind them and they entered sagebrush-covered wilderness,

Tristan's eyes grew heavy. The sound of Phil Collins singing "In too Deep" lulled her, making every inch of her aware of how tired she felt.

As she drifted off, she thought she felt Mac's thumb gently stroking the back of her hand. She hoped it wasn't a dream, that it was really the intoxicating sensation of his touch that was carrying her into dreamland.

Chapter Six

The next thing Tristan was aware of, the car door shut, and Mac settled into his seat. He touched her shoulder. "Hey, wake up. We're stopping for dinner."

She blinked several times and looked around, feeling a distinct crick in her neck as she tried to regain her bearings. They were beside a gas pump, which meant that Mac had filled the car. Focusing out the driver side window, she made out the freeway snaking along in the distance.

"Where are we?" she asked.

"Beaver."

"I'm not awake enough to tell if you made that name up."

"It's a real city." He smiled, squeezed her shoulder, and stepped back.

She felt the lack immediately but hid it by rubbing her eyes and reaching for her purse. "I owe you for gas."

"You can pay for the next fill-up."

"But—"

"Let's eat." He nodded toward a nearby building and started up the engine. "If you're hungry enough, their food is excellent."

"What a glowing recommendation," Tristan said, growing more alert. "Although I am starving."

"Then you'll think you've arrived in heaven," Mac said,

maneuvering the car to the restaurant lot. "But I doubt the salad bar would be tempting even if you walked in after being stranded on a deserted island for six months."

"That bad?"

He slid into a parking space and turned off the car. "Bad enough that I'd pay you to get the salad bar just to see you get grossed out by the wilted lettuce."

"I think I'll get fries instead." Tristan got out, slinging her purse over one shoulder.

Mac got out as well and locked the car. "Excellent. I'll give them credit for making really good fry sauce, though."

"You mean like the barbecue-flavored stuff at Red Robin?"

Mac held the door open for her. "Not even close." He followed her in, and they were soon seated in a booth near wallpaper that looked like the aftermath of a tole painting supply store explosion. The server handed them menus and took their drink orders.

After she disappeared into the kitchen, Mac leaned forward against the table. "Utah fry sauce is totally different. It's an acquired taste, but after living in Utah for a few years, I came to love it."

Now that the fog of sleep had left her, Tristan remembered that her phone was still on Do Not Disturb mode. She turned it off and checked for any missed calls or texts. "Oh, wow. Alyssa has been texting and calling me a ton. I have six missed calls and"—she checked the red number by the app—"fifteen texts."

"Excellent," Mac said.

"Care to listen to her voice message?"

He leaned forward as she put it on speaker. As it played, they laughed at Alyssa's clear annoyance over Tristan not replying.

"You're kind of killing me here." Alyssa's voice sounded frustrated. Mac and Tristan both chuckled quietly. "Call or text me back already!"

Her texts were variations of the same theme, with the occasional mention of Tristan's promise to check in so that there would be no worry over her getting abandoned in a ditch.

"She's not really worried," Tristan explained. "It's a joke—and an attempt to get a reply."

"She's genuinely annoyed, though."

"Yeah," Tristan admitted, intending to sound penitent but utterly failing. "I have an idea." She scooted out of her bench and motioned for Mac to scoot in on his side of the booth. She joined him on the other bench. "Selfie," she explained as she held up her phone.

"Genius." Mac put an arm around her shoulders. Tristan happily leaned into the space he'd created for her, and then, with their heads tilted together, she snapped a couple of pictures. She could feel his cheek on her forehead with the slightest hint of a five-o'clock shadow. She'd always liked a little scruff on a man and suddenly wanted to touch his cheek. He shifted positions, so she did too, taking pictures at different angles to make sure they looked convincingly lovey-dovey.

Mac pulled out his phone. "I'll send her a few too." They posed for more pictures, this time with his phone. At one point, Tristan gave in to the urge and leaned in, pretending to kiss his cheek. A split second before she made contact, he turned his head, and their lips met. She nearly gasped and pulled back, her eyes open wide from shock. But he leaned in a little more, still snapping pictures, so she closed her eyes again . . . To make the pictures believable, of course.

That was a mistake. Cutting off her vision only made her a hundred times more aware of every other sense—the smoothness of his lips, the gentle scruff on his chin, his heady cologne. His phone lowered, and instead of taking pictures, he used that arm to draw her closer. Tristan braced herself, pressing her hands against his chest as she sank into his kisses.

The kitchen door banged, and the two of them practically flew apart and pretended to be studying the menu. Tristan touched her lips. Had that just happened? She'd never kissed a guy so soon after meeting him, even as a joke.

But after the first second or two, that kiss sure hadn't felt like a joke. Or maybe she was the only one with a racing pulse. Electricity still coursed through her body. Did he feel the same way?

The waitress smiled knowingly as she approached. She'd obviously seen them kissing—or at least, the end of it. With both of them on the same bench, and Mac's arm around Tristan's shoulders, there was no reason for anyone to think they weren't a real couple.

Why not keep pretending? Tristan pecked Mac's cheek and turned to the waitress, whose name tag read *Judith*. "Could we get some fry sauce? My boyfriend here loves it." She patted his chest with one hand, feeling the muscles under the fabric, and snuggled closer to him, resting a hand on his thigh. She didn't dare look at him; her acting job would crumble if she did.

"Sure thing," Judith said. "I'll be right back with that." Judith looked over the spread she'd laid before them. "Anything else I can get you?"

This time Mac answered. "I think we're good, thanks."

"Holler if you need anything," Judith said then left to get the fry sauce.

Mac didn't speak or move until she was out of earshot, and then he only whispered, "What was that all about?"

"Thought we might as well keep it up. Easier than explaining. And I thought it might be fun." And it *had* been. No, kissing Mac had been more than fun. It had been fireworks-on-the-Fourth-of-July explosive.

"I can keep up the act," Mac said. He flirtatiously nuzzled her ear and kissed along her hairline, making her insides spin like a vortex. He straightened as Judith dropped off the fry sauce, then played with Tristan's hair as he ate fries left-handed.

As for Tristan, it took her twenty minutes to even remember how to eat.

Chapter Seven

They left the restaurant hand in hand. He opened her car door before getting in himself. No one could see them in the now-dark parking lot if they were standing in the brightly lit restaurant, so he didn't need to for the sake of pretense. Not that Tristan was complaining.

Before starting the car, Mac flipped through his pictures and sent one of them kissing to Alyssa—something Tristan had completely forgotten to do herself. His kiss had temporarily turned her brain into mashed potatoes. After reaching cruising speed on the freeway, he reached over and took her hand again. Pleasantly surprised, she threaded her fingers with his and smiled, unsure whether he could make out her face in the darkness.

They quickly picked up where they'd left off, singing along to the radio, with Mac sometimes offering harmonies. They talked easily, telling stories about their families and work—Tristan had some pretty big doozies because of the nature of the Internet. Driving in the dark, his hand in hers, talking easily—it all felt natural, as if she'd known Mac forever and they were catching up.

All too soon, they reached the Strip, and there was the Italy-inspired architecture and bright lights that spelled out *Palazzo*. Dread at having to say good-bye to Mac made Tristan's heart sink to her toes.

"How about I help carry your bags and get you checked in?

No need to pay a bellboy when you've got a young, strapping man like me around." His toothy grin looked remarkably like the silly emoji Alyssa had sent earlier.

"Sounds like a great idea," Tristan said, though she'd packed light and could manage alone.

He parked in the Palazzo's garage, and soon they were heading up an escalator to the lobby. Blocking the check-in desk was an enormous decoration covered in gigantic fake fruit—golden pears and apples four feet tall, several cornucopias, bizarre plastic leaves, and, to top it off, strings of crystals draped like Christmas garlands. The gaudy thing had to be thirty feet across and at least that tall.

"Oh, wow," Mac said as he looked at it. "That's either a terrific practical joke, or someone is about to be fired."

Tristan had just taken a drink of water, and she laughed so hard that it nearly shot out of her nose.

They walked around the monstrosity, weaved through the empty maze of tension ribbon to the registration desk, and got her checked in. After a walk through the smoky casino and a ride up an elevator, they found her room. She hesitated at the door, holding her key card.

Should I invite him in? He might think that means something I'm not offering. But she didn't want to say good-bye yet either.

"Let's grab a bite to eat," Mac said as if he'd read her mind.

"We already had dinner," Tristan said, then mentally slapped herself. He'd handed her the perfect excuse to spend more time with him, and she'd almost declined it. "But I'm totally up for dessert."

"I know a few places in the hotel that you might like," Mac said. "I'll show you around."

"That would be great. I'll just put my bags in my room first." Tristan opened the door.

The room was gorgeous. To her left was a massive bathroom

with a jetted tub, a shower, a double vanity, a toilet room with a door—and a mounted TV so you could watch it from the tub.

Past the bathroom was a king-size bed with drapes on either side of the floor-to-ceiling dark wood headboard, lights shining from above. A couple of carpeted steps led to a sitting area with a sectional, coffee table, entertainment center, and two desks with lamps. She'd never been in such a large suite before.

"How does Häagen-Dazs sound?" Mac asked, settling the suitcase and carry-on near a long dresser, across from the foot of the bed. "The food court on the Venetian side used to have one; we can check to see if it's still there. In the Grand Canal's courtyard, you can almost always find gelato. Or, if you're in the mood for a shake, there's a Johnny Rockets in the food court. We could go across the street to the mall to get something else—I think there's a See's. Oh, and a Walgreens, if you want something really fancy, like Oreos."

"Sure," Tristan said, admiring the view through the sheers of the big windows that covered the far wall. She turned around. "Any of those sound great. Lead the way."

They left her room and returned to the elevator. After reaching the right floor, they headed into the casino area. Her phone buzzed with another text. Tristan paused and held it up so Mac could see and read it over her shoulder. He leaned in to read, bringing his face close enough for her to kiss. Suddenly, Alyssa's text might as well have been written in Sanskrit.

"We so win." Mac held up a fist for a bump.

Tristan blinked and focused on the message.

He sent me a picture of you KISSING. What is going on?!

"We sure fooled her," Tristan said, but her voice sounded wobbly. She held up her fist and managed to bump knuckles with him.

As they continued walking, her eyes stung. She'd stopped pretending hours ago. Granted, she hardly knew Mac, but she'd connected with him on a level she'd never reached with any other guy, even ones she'd known for years. And while she didn't believe she was necessarily walking beside her soul mate, she wanted to explore where things could go with him. But if he'd been pretending all along, then she was the only one feeling a connection.

"The cigarette smoke's getting to my eyes," she said, blinking rapidly and hoping that her excuse would be enough to explain her watery eyes.

Mac reached for her hand and pulled her quickly through the casino. She clung to his hand. At last they reached the Grand Canal, which looked, at first appearance, for all the world like it was outside. Buildings flanked a canal with gondolas, and a dim sky with clouds showed above the buildings.

"The sky always looks like whatever time of day it is outside," Mac said, looking up. "It's pretty trippy."

He led her along the canal, which was basically a glorified mall made to feel like Venice. They passed several luxury stores selling leather, clothing, souvenirs, and jewelry. A number of fine restaurants were scattered among the shops. She even recognized some of the chefs' names from TV.

Mac's step slowed. When she looked up to see why, Tristan found herself looking at a jeweler's shop. His mischievous smile was back as he nodded toward the glittering glass cases. "I know how to reply to Alyssa."

"Oh?" Tristan said casually, but her insides dropped even more—through the floor, maybe. She guessed what he was thinking and reluctantly followed him inside. The long, sparkling cases held necklaces, bracelets, and earrings. One side of the store held row after row of engagement rings.

"Try one on," Mac said, leading her that direction.

Tristan filled in the blanks. "Then we'll take a picture of one on my finger, and we'll make Alyssa think we're eloping . . .

because . . . Vegas." Even to her own ears, her voice sounded lifeless.

Mac gently held her by the shoulders. "Hey, what's wrong?"

If he only knew that his touch makes this whole thing worse . . . But she didn't want him to stop holding her, either.

"I'm . . . just tired," she lied. "Travel wears me out."

His gaze darted to the jewelry cases then back to her. "It was just an idea." After a beat, he let go—to her simultaneous relief and regret—and ran a hand down his face. He stepped closer so he could speak softly without being overheard. His nearness was almost as bad—and as good—as his touch. She could hardly breathe as she kept her eyes trained on a spot on the floor.

"Tristan, I'm sorry I crossed a line earlier. I shouldn't have kissed you like that. I just—"

Even though he didn't finish his thought, she didn't look up. Instead, she pushed her cuticles back to keep her hands busy. She couldn't find a single word to say that wouldn't be either embarrassing—*No, I'm glad you kissed me . . . It was amazing . . . Kiss me again . . .* or a lie—*Oh, it's all good . . . This was all just one big joke anyway.*

Mac's feet shifted uneasily. "Okay, so here's the thing." He swallowed, and his hands raked through his hair before he sighed. "I expected . . . I mean, I was doing a favor for Alyssa and didn't . . ."

She waited for him to finish, her brain feeling ready to burst. "You didn't . . . ?" This time, she managed to look up. Their eyes locked, and she felt the zing between them again. The world dropped away—the jeweler, the canal, the shops, the tourists, the noise. All she noticed or cared about was Mac. Her universe seemed to hang on this moment.

"I didn't expect Alyssa's friend to be smart, funny . . . *and*, well, *hot.*" He shifted his feet, and his neck went red. "I didn't expect to fall for her."

Was the room suddenly spinning? Because she felt light-headed in the best way possible.

"And I didn't expect her friend to be a man," Tristan countered, "a *hot* man who's also smart and funny." Somehow, their hands had found one another, and both sets were clasped between them. "I didn't expect to fall for him, either."

"Really?" He sounded stunned, as if that was the last thing he'd expected to hear.

"Really," she said, stepping closer. "I'm glad you kissed me, even if it was for Alyssa's benefit." Tristan tilted her head one way and then the other as if deliberating. "But, to be honest, I'm going to need a few more kisses for *my* benefit."

"A few?" Worry melted away from his face—a face even better than Loki's.

"Yeah. A few," she said. "A few hundred . . . thousand. I'll let you know when you're off the hook." She gave a one-shouldered shrug.

He laughed and squeezed her hand. They headed for the door without having tried on a single diamond ring. After crossing the threshold, Tristan looked back over her shoulder. "We can always come back later."

Later to play the joke on Alyssa. And perhaps much later still—months or years, maybe—to pick out an actual ring, if her gut could be trusted.

"Yeah," Mac said, as if he understood exactly what she was thinking. Maybe he did.

"Do you like grasshopper shakes?" Tristan asked.

"Any self-respecting man does. Johnny Rockets it is." He led the way out of the canal area to the food court.

Soon they sat side by side at a table with their giant shakes. They already had each other's cell numbers, so they exchanged email and snail mail addresses. They talked about their schedules and when they'd be able to see each other again.

Both mentioned that they could relocate because each of them largely worked online, so the *where* didn't matter much. Maybe they could even travel together for work sometimes.

"Just so we're on the same page," Mac said, scooping a spoonful of his shake, "we're going to give the long-distance relationship thing a try?"

"Absolutely." Tristan cleaned her spoon then waved it as she added, "You owe me about two hundred thousand kisses, after all." She scooped some of his shake and ate it. "So I'm afraid you're kind of stuck with the arrangement." She was being so much bolder than she was used to. She blushed, hoping her teasing had landed.

Mac bobbed his head as if music were playing. "I'm happy to be stuck with you."

Huey Lewis and the News, she thought. *How perfect is he?*

He reached over, scooped some of her shake, and touched her nose with his spoon, leaving a dot of ice cream. She wiped it off with a finger, laughing as his brow furrowed.

"I do see a possible problem," Mac said.

A small worry twisted in Tristan's chest. She licked the melting shake off her fingers. "Oh?"

"Your magazine may have to shift focus if you're not, you know, *single.*"

Tristan shrugged. "I'll either fake it or come up with a new magazine."

He leaned in and kissed her, slow, long, and so deep that her toes curled in her shoes. A flash went off near them. They jumped apart and saw a middle-aged woman with an iPhone, grinning sheepishly.

"Sorry," she said. "You two are adorable. I couldn't resist."

Tristan thought for a moment. "Could you send me that picture?"

"Sure," the woman said. "But you'll have to show me how. I feel really dumb with my new smartphone."

With a few taps, Tristan texted the photo to herself. "Thanks."

"Is that for Alyssa?" Mac asked.

"Nope. Instagram." She returned the phone to the woman and thanked her.

"Don't you have thousands of followers?"

Tristan went on tiptoe and pressed a kiss to his lips. "*Hundreds* of thousands. I want the world to know."

"What about Alyssa?"

"She'll think we're kidding. Then she'll freak out. And *then* she'll claim to have planned this all along and take credit for it." She gazed into his eyes, and the world dropped away again in the way she was coming to love. "I'm oddly okay with that."

He kissed her briefly, making her heart soar. "Let's take a gondola ride."

"When in Rome," Tristan said, referring to the Italian theme throughout the resort. "Or Venice, I guess."

"Or Vegas. Whichever."

As they maneuvered down the corridors through the crowds and entered the Grand Canal, one of Tristan's favorite 80s songs popped into her head. She squeezed Mac's hand and decided to sing, not caring if anyone thought she was weird. This was Vegas, after all.

"Up for a little Tears for Fears?" she asked, eyebrows raised.

"Always," Mac said. She leaned closer, and he put his arm around her shoulders.

She decided to begin the line and let him finish it. "Something happens . . ."

Mac stopped in the middle of the crowded canal, but instead of singing, he looked into her eyes, his gaze intense. Her insides turned to jelly. He reached forward and tucked a piece of hair behind her ear before saying—not singing—the words.

"And I'm head over heels."

About Annette Lyon

Annette Lyon is a Whitney Award winner, a three-time recipient of Utah's Best of State medal for fiction, and a four-time publication award winner from the League of Utah Writers, including the Silver Quill Award in 2013 for *Paige*. She's the author of more than a dozen novels, almost as many novellas, several nonfiction books, and over one hundred twenty magazine articles. Annette is a cum laude graduate from BYU with a degree in English. When she's not writing, knitting, or eating chocolate, she can be found mothering and avoiding the spots on the kitchen floor. Sign up for her newsletter at http://annettelyon.com/contact

Website: http://AnnetteLyon.com
Blog: http://blog.AnnetteLyon.com
Twitter: @AnnetteLyon
Facebook: http://Facebook.com/AnnetteLyon
Pinterest: http://Pinterest.com/AnnetteLyon

Two Dozen Roses

by Heather B. Moore

Chapter One

"Dayna, I'll wait in the car!"

Dayna heard her mom's voice as it carried through the tile-floored condo. Dayna was already regretting promising her brother, David, that she'd drive their mom to his place on the coast of Oregon.

"You work too hard," David had told her. "Mom's always complaining that she never sees you."

Dayna lived two blocks from their mom's Long Beach, California neighborhood, and she stopped by at least once a day, sometimes twice, to check on things. On Saturdays, Dayna took her mom grocery shopping and on any other errands she needed. At sixty-seven, her mom was still a sprightly woman. But losing her driver's license the year before, due to a degenerative eye disease, had been devastating to her.

"I'm on my way," Dayna called back to her mom.

And now, of all things, her mom wanted to rent a convertible. How could Dayna argue when Mom said she'd pay the bill for it? Although, it had meant that Dayna needed to purchase a hat just for the trip. Two, in fact. Dayna didn't quite trust the wind, and she wanted a spare in case her first hat flew off.

Dayna twisted her shoulder-length brown hair into a ponytail, then she secured the baseball cap. It wasn't her favorite look—far from her usual professional attire at the travel agency—but it was practical. And, knowing that she was taking three days off to drive up the California coast until she reached Oregon, Dayna had to hang on to practicality.

Dayna had opened her own travel agency a couple years after college. And now, at the age of thirty-one, she had grown Dream Vacations into one of the top agencies in Long Beach. But she'd put her heart and soul into it. She'd never been away from her company for more than twenty-four hours, and, even then, it had been only once that she could remember. Typically, she'd worked half Saturdays and from home on Sundays.

Double-checking her bag to ensure that she had her laptop, Kindle, and phone and their respective chargers, Dayna turned off the lights in the condo then stepped outside and locked the door. As she did so, her mom tapped the horn on the rented convertible, making Dayna nearly jump out of her skin.

Dayna turned to cast a furious look at her mom, who only laughed in response. "I just wanted to hear what it sounded like," her mom said, "you know, in case we get cut off in traffic."

Dayna shook her head, hiding a smile. She grabbed her bags and loaded them into the trunk. "I think everyone will see us coming well before we would need to honk," she said, eyeing the car's cherry red paint job.

Her mom just grinned, looking like the Cheshire cat, entirely satisfied with herself. She adjusted her sunhat over her neatly curled hair that was the same golden brown as Dayna's. Although her mom's hair color was now the artistic creation of her stylist.

Dayna climbed into the driver's seat and checked the rearview mirror. She'd forgone lipstick today, opting for ChapStick and light makeup instead. It wasn't like she'd be running into anyone she knew, and her overlarge sunglasses would cover up the beginnings of faint lines at the corners of her hazel eyes. Her hazel eyes were once her best feature, according to the men she'd dated in the past. Apparently, it wasn't her entrepreneurial personality that had kept them coming back. As it was, she was completely single now with not even a potential date on the horizon.

"Did you turn off all the lights?" her mom asked as Dayna started the engine.

"Yep," she said.

"What about the hair straightener?"

"Neither of us used it."

"Did you lock the front door?"

"Yes."

"And you're sure that Gwen is okay with picking up my mail?"

"Mom."

"All right. All right. It's just that I'll be gone an entire month."

"I'll be checking on your place as well when I return," Dayna added, trying to keep the exasperation out of her voice. It would be a nice break to have her brother watching out for their mom for a change. Although, Dayna knew that, when it came down to it, she'd miss her mom.

Then her mom's attention was caught by an incoming call on her phone.

Hopefully it is one of her close friends, Dayna thought, *and they'll gab for the next hour.*

"Gwen," her mom said into the phone. "Are you sure you can get my mail while I'm gone?" Gwen said something, and then Mom laughed.

Dayna half listened to the conversation as she drove along the Boulevard until she reached the Pacific Coast Highway, or PCH. David had given their mom the brilliant idea of following a route that a group of PCH enthusiasts had put together. Their map had a list of places to stop, including museums, old-fashioned diners, and bed-and-breakfasts.

When their mom had seen this, she'd been so excited,

pointing out all of the places they could visit between LA and Oregon—thus, the three days of driving, when the trip could have been done in a day and a half.

Their first stop would be lunch at Joe's Diner in about an hour. In the meantime, Dayna was determined to enjoy the perfect September weather. And she told herself, for the hundredth time, that she could rely on her office assistant, Angie, to keep everything running smoothly at work, until Dayna could fly back home.

It wasn't like Dayna would be out of touch either. Hopefully, some of the diners on their route would have Wi-Fi, and Dayna could help with tricky reservations, if needed. Otherwise, she could work off her phone. Not that her mom would be pleased about this. But it was the only compromise that Dayna could come up with.

Her mom continued to chat with Gwen almost the entire drive to Joe's Diner. So Dayna enjoyed the glimpses of the ocean and the slower drives through the coastal towns with their eclectic collections of shops. Maybe, someday, she'd explore shops like that. Someday, when she wasn't so busy. Although Dayna enjoyed booking fabulous vacations for clients, working all day often left her feeling bereft in the evenings by the time she returned to her condo.

"Where are we now?" her mom asked after hanging up with Gwen.

"We're about ten minutes from the diner."

"*Already?*"

Dayna nodded. Her mom was known for losing track of time. This could be a benefit or a detriment, depending on the situation, Dayna decided.

A few minutes later, they pulled into a run-down parking lot. But the diner itself looked charming enough. The large windows reflected the sunlight, and the silver chrome door made a nice backdrop to the bold red lettering on its sign.

Two Dozen Roses

A sleek black BMW pulled in behind them and parked a couple of stalls away. The car caught Dayna's attention because the diner didn't look like a trendy restaurant that would attract the type of people who drove expensive sports cars. When she wasn't in a rented convertible on a road trip with her mom, Dayna drove a silver Honda Accord. Dependable and great on gas mileage, yeah, and perhaps a bit boring. But Dayna didn't have time to drive something that wasn't completely reliable.

As she shut off the engine and collected her phone, purse, and keys, Dayna saw two men climb out of the BMW. If she wasn't mistaken, the men were related. Probably brothers. Both were tall. The driver had dark hair, and the other man had lighter hair that was likely bleached. But their facial structures were similar, and they even had the same gait.

Dayna and her mom climbed out of the convertible as the men strode toward the door of the diner. The lighter-haired man scrolled through his phone, but the darker-haired man glanced over at Dayna. She looked away quickly, but not so quickly that she hadn't noticed his striking features. *Definitely one of those men who probably has a trophy girlfriend. His brother too.* In fact, the light-haired man now stopped, turning to hold the door open for them, having definitely noticed Dayna and her mom the moment before.

Dayna's cheeks warmed as the man's gaze traveled the length of her body. She was being thoroughly checked out, and she didn't like it one bit—not because she wasn't dressed her best but because she prided herself in being an independent woman, free from having to be taken care of by a man. This attitude was probably due to her disastrous short marriage to Paul Leadbetter and to all the subsequent men she'd dated, who had each told her that she had beautiful eyes, but who had then stopped calling her after their second dates.

Dayna had had her fill of men who were just looking for a

pretty thing to hang on their arms and brag about to their friends—women who rearranged their schedules at the smallest request and put their own dreams on hold to follow after the man, not women who had their own schedules and responsibilities to work around.

And it was for this reason that Dayna wanted to slap the pretty-boy face staring at her now. But she averted her eyes and passed the man, saying a polite *thank you* that left no further room for chitchat.

The sign at the front register said, "Seat yourself," so Dayna and her mom found an empty table in the corner of the diner. Glancing around, Dayna noticed that only two other groups of people were seated—an elderly couple, who sat in complete silence as they ate, and a two women, who appeared to be on a business lunch.

Dayna grimaced as the men from the parking lot sat down only a table away from them. She'd be able to hear their conversation and vice versa.

"Those men are good-looking," her mom whispered, leaning toward Dayna. Except, her mom's whispers were never very quiet. "And I don't see any wedding bands on their fingers. They've got to be brothers, don't you think?"

"Shh," Dayna tried to say, but it was too late, for the blonder man had glanced over at them, a smirk on his face and a knowing look in his blue eyes. Dayna wasn't sure if she'd ever felt more self-conscious in her life. *At least the darker-haired man seems to be focused on his menu.* Dayna grabbed her own menu from the holder on the table, wanting to appear absorbed in reading over the selection of hamburgers . . . and more hamburgers. *The sooner we eat and leave, the better.*

Chapter Two

Roman tried to keep the scowl off his face as they drove along the Pacific Coast Highway. But his brother, Garrett, wouldn't stop talking about the woman they had seen in the diner. Normally, this wouldn't have been a huge deal to Roman, but Garrett happened to be practically engaged to another woman. With two divorces behind Garrett now, he obviously didn't have the staying power that other men might. Not that Roman was a relationship expert. The one and only woman he'd ever loved had dumped him after she'd met Garrett. That was marriage number one.

And the woman in the diner, obviously having lunch with her mom, had been one of those girl-next-door types, Roman decided. If his brother had turned on his full charm, she wouldn't have known what hit her, until she was trampled. Roman had thought she was pretty enough, but not like Garrett's usual fare. And Roman would never admit his own interest if Garrett seemed interested as well. Roman had already learned that lesson.

Roman reached for the CD volume knob and turned it up a couple of notches.

"Hint taken," Garrett said in a cheerful voice. Then he started to whistle, and Roman wondered if his brother would ever stop being obnoxious.

The only reason they were on this road trip together was because of their older sister, Denise, who'd died of cancer a few months ago. She'd made them pledge that they'd drive the PCH together, from Los Angeles to San Francisco, just like they all had on family vacations when they were little kids.

Roman knew that this was her attempt to get him and Garrett to reconcile. They hadn't had much of a speaking relationship since Kenzie had chosen Garrett over Roman. And, although the "Kenzie disaster" had been six years ago, it sometimes seemed like only a few weeks ago.

Garrett reached over and turned up the volume of the music, his whistle morphing into a full-blown singalong.

Earbuds, Roman thought. *I should get them out at the next stop.*

Roman might be the youngest sibling of the three, but he often felt like he was the oldest. Denise had been a free spirit and had spent her days working in a hippie jewelry shop and her nights sitting around bonfires on the beach while she breathed in one type of smoke after another.

Roman had blamed this secondhand smoke for her lung cancer, although Denise had always denied it. But Garrett was one of those ambulance-chasing lawyers and had wanted to sue the shop Denise had worked in. For once, the brothers had agreed on something. Denise refused to file a lawsuit, though.

Roman supposed that the world did need lawyers like Garrett. But, did he really need his pearly whites glowing on a freeway billboard?

As for Roman, he was the operations manager at a software firm out in Irvine, which amounted to a lot of traveling and a lot of meetings. He simply didn't have time for this PCH drive. But then he'd decided that he had to honor his sister's last wishes. Ironically, Garrett had taken the road trip request in stride and had even had one of his buxom secretaries print off a PCH tourist guide, which accounted for their decision to stop at the diner.

"Next stop, *Ripley's Believe It or Not! Odditorium,*" Garrett announced, turning his attention from the passenger-side window to the printout in his hand.

"That's not on the PCH," Roman said, glancing over at the map. "We'd have to detour up to Santa Monica Boulevard. Let's just stick with what's along our route."

"This *is* our route," Garrett said, pointing to a red line that zigzagged on the map more than Roman wanted it to. "Denise wanted us to stop at all of these circled sites."

Roman exhaled. "All right." He was a bit curious about the museum anyway. He hadn't been to one since he was a kid and wondered if this one had shrunken heads.

Two work calls came in as he drove there, but he let them both go to voice mail. He didn't relish having Garrett overhear his business conversations, or any other conversations, for that matter. Garrett seemed absorbed now with something on his phone and had, thankfully, stopped singing aloud. So, by the time they had pulled into the Ripley's parking lot, Roman was grateful that his brother had mellowed out.

"Interesting," Garrett said, pointing to a red convertible in the parking lot. "That's the same kind of car Hottie and Paisley Lady were driving."

Roman clenched his teeth, annoyed by Garrett's habit of giving women nicknames, most of them unflattering. "Probably just a coincidence," Roman muttered.

They climbed out of Roman's BMW, the one splurge he'd made with his healthy paycheck before Denise had been diagnosed. Now, he was still paying off Denise's medical bills, for she'd had one of those "emergency" insurances, which basically had covered nothing when she was diagnosed with cancer.

At first, Garrett had contributed a few thousand dollars. But then he'd cried poverty on account of the slow cycle of getting paid only after court cases were won. As it was, according to

Roman's calculations, it would be a good two years before he would be able to pay off all the medical bills.

Garrett breezed into the museum and paid his own way. This left Roman to pay his own way too and create a nice distance between them as Garrett started through the museum first.

Just as Roman was entering the first room, he heard Garrett's voice boom, "What a coincidence. Didn't we just see you lovely ladies at Joe's Diner?"

Roman stopped cold as the two women stared back at them.

"I'm Garrett, and this is my brother, Roman. Although, you won't get more than two words out of him," Garrett said with a chuckle. "He's been mad at me for six years. That guy can sure hold a grudge. Oh yeah." Then he gave the women a huge wink.

It takes a special breed to be an ambulance chaser, Roman thought. *And my brother is perfect for it.*

Garrett was doing his classic I'm-trying-to-be-nonchalant-but-I'm-really-checking-you-out pose as he shoved his hands into his pockets, tipped back on his heels, and flashed a brilliantly white smile.

The older woman smiled back at Garrett. "You're related to one of those too?" she asked. The younger woman's face went still, and her eyes flickered to Roman.

For a second, Roman couldn't move. The sun's rays coming from the front door of the museum had lightened the woman's deep hazel eyes, making them look like flashing gold and green jewels. *This woman might be casually dressed and spending the day with her mom,* Roman thought, *but there is nothing relaxed about her.* Her shoulders looked stiff, her posture erect, and her eyes watchful. Something in her look told Roman that she didn't appreciate the ensuing conversation between her mom and his brother.

Garrett stuck out his hand in her direction. "And you are?" he asked.

"Dayna," she said, her voice formal, reserved. "And this is my mom, Joyce." Again her eyes flitted toward Roman.

He didn't want to come across as obtuse as his brother was claiming him to be, so Roman stepped forward and shook both of the women's hands as well. He thought about saying something like "Nice to meet you," but Garrett was already peppering them with questions, which Joyce was answering quite readily. Apparently, they were also following the same PCH guide.

As the conversation continued, primarily between Garrett and Joyce, Roman couldn't help but steal a glance at Dayna. She was tall and elegant, but there was nothing artificial about her looks. Her nails and hair color and curves all seemed to be quite natural. Roman shook his head. *I shouldn't be analyzing her in this way.* That was something Garrett would do.

And it was plain that Garrett was interested in Dayna, even if it was just to see if he still "had it." Roman decided that he would have no problem now with reminding his brother about his almost fiancée—once they were back in the car. Garrett filled the two women in on their own reasons for doing the PCH route, even making his voice tremble a bit when he spoke of Denise.

The older woman, Joyce, placed a consoling hand on Garrett's arm and said, "You poor dears. What an amazing thing you're doing for your sister."

While Garrett continued to chatter—as if it were the most natural thing in the world to spill his guts about all their family tragedies to two complete strangers—Joyce moved with Garrett through the museum, and Roman followed them. After a few minutes, Roman made a right turn instead of a left and found himself in a room filled with duct tape art. If he were about twenty years younger, he would have liked to experiment himself.

"Six years, huh?" a soft voice said behind him.

He turned to see Dayna, her hazel green eyes peering up at him, her mouth lifted into a smile. "My brother's a lawyer,"

Roman said. "It seems that I've been tried and convicted as the surly younger brother."

Her smile grew. "He *did* mention that he was a lawyer a time or two," she said.

"Only once or twice? I was sure he'd mentioned it at least three times, maybe four."

Dayna laughed, and Roman's heart tripped. *She really is out of Garrett's league,* Roman thought, meaning that he would gladly punch his brother out if he tried anything on her. *No woman this sweet and charming needs a Garrett in her life.*

"He reminds me of my ex," Dayna said, her tone growing serious. "I'm not sure whether to laugh about that or to go dry heave in the bathroom."

Roman just stared at her.

"Sorry, I was probably too frank," she said, shrugging her shoulders. "It can be a turnoff, I know."

Roman couldn't look away, for she'd pretty much said the most perfect thing ever—she was repulsed by Garrett . . . It seemed that they had something in common.

"So, Mr. Software Operations Manager, what do you think about duct tape?" she said, her mouth curving into that sweet smile again.

He released a groan. "What hasn't my brother told you about me?"

She laughed. "I'm sure he's getting an earful about me from my mom right now. She's been trying to set me up with her best friend's son for years."

He couldn't help but smile with her. "You're single now?"

"Divorced," she said as if she'd given this same answer a hundred times.

"Kids?"

"No, the marriage only lasted a few months," Dayna said. "Fortunately, I saw right through him before kids could enter in to the deal. Unfortunately, I'd already gone through the trouble of marrying him."

Roman nodded. Everyone had a story. He only hoped that Dayna's wouldn't become involved with Garrett. But it seemed like she wasn't interested in his brother. For some reason, that fact made Roman feel extremely good.

He looked over at one of the displays. "I didn't know duct tape came in so many colors."

"Oh, it's a *thing* now," Dayna said as she stepped closer to the display, which put her nearer to Roman. Together, they read the plaque that detailed the artist's history. "Nine-year-old girls everywhere are madly making duct tape earrings and bracelets and wallets. I thought about switching over myself, but I didn't want to mess with the grown-up, professional look."

Roman found himself looking at her again—and smiling. "What do you do?"

"I run a travel agency called Dream Vacations."

"Really? I think I've heard of it . . . You own it?"

"I do," she said. Strangely, her voice had sounded a bit hesitant.

"So, this is probably a cliché question, but, do you get to travel to a lot of great places?"

"Hardly," she said, her voice light. "I'm stuck on the computer or phone most of the time, booking other people's vacations. But I hear that *you* travel a lot."

"For business," he said. "Most often on a red-eye then right back, before I can have any downtime or even see the city I'm working in."

She rested her hand briefly on his arm. "You need a new travel agent," she deadpanned.

He didn't know if she was being serious or just teasing. Then her eyes seemed to glow with amusement. So he decided to play along. "I think you're right." He turned back to the duct tape art, his heart still thumping at her casual touch, which had been too brief. "Dream Vacations, huh? Where are you located?"

"Long Beach," she said.

"Do you have a website with contact information?"

"Give me your phone, and I'll add it myself."

He looked over at her. "You're kind of a hustler. I'll bet you've got a great clientele."

She only smiled. So he pulled his cell from his pocket and gladly handed it over.

While she was typing her information into his phone, Roman wished that Garrett would stay in whatever part of the museum he was currently in for a good long while. Roman was actually enjoying himself. This road trip was turning out better than he could have imagined.

Dayna handed back his phone, and they walked to the next duct tape creation, a series of small reptiles.

"Ah, there you two are," Garrett said, his voice cutting across the room.

"I thought you'd gone to the ladies' room," Dayna's mom added.

"I did," Dayna answered, turning toward them. "And then I ended up completely captivated by these duct tape creations. Have you seen them yet, Mom?"

And that was it. Roman watched as Garrett slid in between himself and Dayna, inserting his opinions on the displays, taking over the conversation fully. But this time, Roman wasn't as bothered, for he recognized Dayna's pasted-on smile for what it was. Each time she glanced over at Roman, a shared understanding passed between them. She had seen right through Garrett's charm, and Roman couldn't think of anything better than that.

Chapter Three

They'd agreed to have dinner with the two brothers at the Bella Café, another stop along their PCH route. And Dayna had surprised herself by very much looking forward to it. Or, more specifically, looking forward to spending more time with Roman. She had to play it cool, though, or else her mom would notice her interest, and then there wouldn't be another quiet moment the whole trip.

Right now, her mom was chatting about Garrett as they drove and was repeating some story he'd told her about one of his clients. It seemed like her mom was very impressed with a man who was a personal injury lawyer.

But Dayna wasn't. She was more interested in the lawyer's brother, the quiet, reserved brother, who was witty and intelligent and had been subtly flirting with her at Ripley's. His eyes had been a deeper blue than his brother's, almost gray. Dayna smiled to herself, but her mom took it as Dayna being pleased with her story, and she continued to talk while Dayna's thoughts shifted back to her encounter with Roman.

He'd been wary of her—that, she'd sensed. *Wary and attracted,* she thought. And now she understood why. His brother had come between Roman and the woman that he'd intended to marry. And, even though it had been six years ago, Dayna knew from experience that some types of pain didn't go away. Those pains might fade a little over time, but they always seemed to hover right below the surface.

Dayna's mom asked her to stop at a small beachfront boutique that she had noticed. And, while her mom browsed the trinkets, Dayna checked for e-mail on her phone and sent out some quick replies. So far, Angie seemed to be keeping everything running smoothly. Next, Dayna sent a text to her brother, updating him on their progress. David replied with a thumbs-up symbol, and then her phone chimed with another text.

Test.

It had come from Roman.

Dayna's face flushed, and she turned, moving away from her mom's line of vision. She pretended to be inspecting a rack of magnets. Why had Roman texted her out of the blue? They'd be seeing him in a couple of hours. So, why was he sending her a text now? Dayna's heart thumped as she replied.

Passed.

Are you texting and driving?

Dayna scoffed.

No. At a boutique . . . My mom is buying out the store. And you?

Filling up with gas. Roman texted back. *Garrett's getting some cigarettes.*

He smokes?

Sometimes . . . He just got a nasty voice mail from his girlfriend, Jen. Guess she had concert tickets for this weekend, and he forgot.

Ouch.

Dayna hit send and then paused before typing out another text.

Do you smoke too?

Not since my sister's cancer diagnosis. Doc said it might run in the family.

Sorry about that, but I'm glad you quit.
Me too. Gotta go. See you at dinner.

Dayna didn't know whether she should have been surprised that they'd had a full-on conversation over texting, but she'd liked it. She was usually more of a phone call or email person and had used texting for sending addresses or very quick notes. But she could see the advantages of texting to Roman—neither her mom nor Garrett would know about it.

By the time that they reached Bella's Café, Dayna and Roman had exchanged thirty-seven texts. Not that she was counting. The brothers had gone to some nautical museum, while Dayna had been relegated to two more shops with her mom. Not that Dayna was complaining anymore since this trip was now turning out to be quite interesting. And it was only the first day.

Dayna parked the car, and walked with her mom toward the charming café.

"Good evening, ladies," Garrett said, rising from a chair on the café's outdoor patio. Dayna noticed that the view behind him, overlooking the Pacific, was beautiful. Garrett grasped her mom's hand and kissed the back of it, so Dayna quickly moved past him. Whatever grief that Garrett's girlfriend had given him, he wasn't letting it show one bit.

Then Dayna's eyes locked on the second man who'd risen from the café table. *Roman.* It was strange, seeing this man for the third time in one day. Even though they'd only met a short time ago, Dayna felt that she had gotten to know him. And, strangely, she felt like she knew what Roman might say if Garrett and her mom weren't dominating the conversation. He'd probably joke about the places they'd been "forced" to visit.

Without allowing her mom's input to decide where everyone might sit, Dayna went and sat in the chair next to Roman. She wasn't going to get stuck sitting between her mom and Garrett. If Garrett had noticed, he said nothing, although her mom had definitely sent Dayna a narrow-lidded glance.

Let her speculate. Dayna would never see Roman again after tonight, so a few hours of flirting couldn't hurt.

Garrett started to regale them with a story about one of his clients, who'd caused a nine-car, chain reaction accident. Her mom seemed fascinated and oohed and aahed at the appropriate moments, while Dayna couldn't help but let her gaze stray in Roman's direction.

He met her eyes just as her cell phone buzzed from inside her purse. She pulled it out, only to see a text there from Roman. She was about to ask him why he was texting her when they were sitting right next to each other, when she read what his message said.

Want to go for a walk on the beach after dinner? Just us?

Her heart couldn't help but race, even though Dayna told herself that this would only be a short-lived crush. She looked up at Roman to see that his mouth had curved into a small smile, probably not obvious enough for her mom or Garrett to have noticed.

Yes, she typed back. It was the easiest decision she'd ever made. *But I can't ditch my mom.*

Does she like Italian ice?

She loves it.

Roman glanced at Dayna with a smile then went back to his phone.

Garrett does too. Bring up the subject at the end of the meal, and they can go together.

Leaving us alone?

Yep.

The tingles that were trailing along her skin settled into her stomach.

Ok, she texted back.

The waitress came and left, and Dayna realized that she could barely remember what she'd ordered. She struggled to follow the conversation during the rest of the meal. Every time Roman looked at her, Dayna felt the warmth of his gaze. Every time he laughed or spoke, the sound of his voice seemed to reverberate through her. She had yet to learn more about this man, but there was no denying her attraction to him.

Yet, Dayna knew from her previous experiences that attraction was not enough, not even close. She'd been instantly attracted to her ex. *Roman is different.* She knew this was true, yet it didn't mean that dating Roman would be any safer. But she would go for a walk on the beach with him tonight, she decided. And tomorrow, she'd continue her road trip with her mom— nothing harmed or lost.

At the end of the meal, Roman's advice worked like a charm. And, before she knew it, her mom was heading off with Garrett to get Italian ices, her hand securely linked onto his arm, and they'd planned to meet back up in an hour.

The sun had already set by the time Dayna and Roman stepped onto the boardwalk. The Pacific was mellow today, and the wind seemed barely there—pretty much the perfect setting for a lovers' twilight walk. Although, glancing over at Roman, Dayna suddenly felt an awkwardness seep in. Maybe they were both just expert texting flirts.

"Doesn't your mom drive?" Roman asked.

This question surprised Dayna—that he had even noticed or thought about it. "She lost her license a few months ago. She has macular degeneration."

"Sorry to hear that," Roman said, shoving his hands into his pockets. This natural movement drew Dayna's attention to his tanned forearms. For a software salesman, who probably spent a lot of time indoors, he looked noticeably tanned and fit.

"What about your parents?" she asked, knowing it was probably a sad story since he hadn't mentioned them at all.

"My dad took off when we were young, and my mom's in a care center now."

Dayna was surprised at this. "How old is she?"

"Seventy-one," Roman said. "She has Alzheimer's. Probably the only thing that's been good about it is that she hasn't realized that her daughter has died."

Dayna shook her head. *So much tragedy in one family.* "Life's hard."

Roman stopped and faced her, causing Dayna to stop too. "I didn't mean to make this evening such a downer."

Dayna was about to protest, tell him it was okay, when he reached for her hand, stopping all speech.

"Let's go down to the water," he said.

Dayna let Roman lead her off the boardwalk and onto the sand. He kept hold of her hand as they walked. It felt nice, comfortable, and despite the fact that her heart was racing, she didn't mind it at all. After a moment, she asked him about what his mom was like before she started to forget things.

"She was a lot like Garrett in her own way," Roman said. "Very social, talkative, and she could probably sell you anything. But she was generous too. She worked hard as a single mom—I think that's the one thing I'll never forget about her. She expected her kids to work hard too. We never felt like we lacked anything, and we were never allowed to feel sorry for our situation."

Roman was easy to listen to, easy to talk to, Dayna decided. And, before she knew it, Dayna was telling him about her father, who'd died years before, and about her brother David and his wife and their two kids.

"Is David pretty protective of you, being his only sister?" Roman asked.

"He used to be," Dayna said. "The ironic thing is that he and my ex, Paul, were the best of friends. When things didn't work out for us, I felt like David blamed me. So it put a distance between us for a couple of years, and then he moved to Oregon for a new job. We've never totally gotten back to the way things used to be.

But maybe that's just how it is when siblings grow up and go their separate ways."

"I think you're right." Roman let go of her hand. Dayna felt the loss of his warmth immediately. He bent down to slip off his shoes then looked over at Dayna. "Care to get wet?"

She laughed and took off her own shoes. Then she followed him into the incoming tide until the water was up to her calves. The water felt cool, but refreshing. And, when a larger wave pushed the water higher, Roman grabbed her hand again and drew Dayna back toward the shore.

"I don't think you'll want to get too wet," he said, gazing down at her.

As the wind ruffled Roman's hair, Dayna noticed how his blue eyes matched the deepening shade of the sky, but they were warmer somehow. She didn't know how his old girlfriend could ever have chosen Garrett over Roman. Garrett was good-looking, but Roman was *real* and good-looking.

"I don't mind getting a little wet," she teased, realizing that she was now just as interested in flirting with Roman in person as she had been earlier over texting.

Roman lifted a brow, a half smile on his face.

Uh-oh. "But that doesn't mean . . ." she began to say, trying to tug her hand away from him. Roman held on tight, drawing Dayna toward him slowly.

She knew that she stood no chance against him if he really wanted to get her wet—one of his arms was stronger than her entire body. But, as he pulled her even closer, his gaze seemed to change from teasing to serious. Dayna wished that she could read Roman's thoughts. Then she decided that she was too scared to.

His other hand wrapped around her waist, and she could practically feel his body pressing against hers, even though they weren't fully touching yet.

"Dayna . . ." Roman said in a low voice.

She knew that look—the look of a man who intended to kiss her—and she didn't back away. Instead, she moved closer to Roman and ran her free hand across his shoulder and behind his neck. He smelled good, faintly of cologne and something else, something definitely masculine.

She didn't know what he might be wanting to say, but she'd be fine with finding out later. Right now, the only thing Dayna could think about was kissing Roman. Crazy, she knew, and she'd probably regret her impulse later. For now, she could only focus on this one thing.

She raised up on her toes at the same moment that Roman leaned down. And it would have been the perfect kiss, the type of kiss from a romantic movie, when something knocked against her legs, causing Dayna to nearly lose her balance.

"Ouch!" Dayna said, staggering backward, as Roman grasped at her to hold her upright.

Bouncing away from them was a soccer ball, and coming toward them were a couple of kids around ten years old. One of them apologized as he raced past.

Roman laughed, but Dayna only felt disappointment. Then she shook those thoughts away. *I've been saved from doing something impulsive,* she told herself, for she'd practically thrown herself at Roman, and they'd only met a few hours ago. *Ridiculous.*

She took a deep breath then cast a smile at Roman, who was now standing with his hands in his pockets, watching the kids fetch their ball right before it got caught in the surf.

Back to reality, Dayna thought. *And it's probably a good thing.*

Chapter Four

Roman stared at the hotel room's ceiling as it lightened with the rising sun. It was still early, but he hadn't slept much last night. The good-bye with Dayna had been much more formal than he'd wanted, and he'd spent half the night debating whether or not he should call her—or even text her.

He'd done neither, deciding to let the night pass without entering into an awkward conversation about what had almost happened on the beach or what it might mean. He'd only just met Dayna, but he was feeling drawn to her more than he thought possible. And he'd almost blown it by being too forward too fast. It wasn't typical of him to try to kiss a woman on the first date, and the walk on the beach last night hadn't really been a date.

Even worse, while driving back to the hotel, Garrett had told him that things were really rocky with his girlfriend, Jen, and that he might be breaking up with her after the trip, but that he wasn't too sad because he'd been really impressed with Dayna and would probably ask her out after the road trip. That's why he had decided to get to know Dayna's mom more, Garrett had explained, because he wanted to "do it right" this time around.

Roman didn't even try to guess all that was going on inside Garrett's convoluted thoughts. It had made Roman sick to his stomach as he listened to his brother talk about Dayna as if they were already moving forward in their friendship. Apparently,

Garrett had been oblivious to the attention that Dayna had been giving to Roman, and their private walk on the beach hadn't raised any red flags in Garrett's mind either.

Roman debated about whether he should tell Garrett that he had almost kissed Dayna and that she was interested in *him*, not Garrett. Instead, Roman decided to let his brother ramble. And, when they had checked into their hotel rooms, Roman had been more than glad to call it a night.

But now, with the morning's arrival, Roman still felt unsettled. What if Garrett did break up with his girlfriend and started calling Dayna? Would she go out with him?

The only hope that Roman could hold on to was that Dayna had told him she wasn't interested in Garrett. Yet, when Roman had first started dating Kenzie, he never imagined that Garrett would come between them. Sometimes, Roman still missed Kenzie, her easy laughter, her spontaneity. Dayna was more reserved, more serious, but he could tell that she had a big heart. She'd been hurt too, and she'd been through a lot. They were also both in a caretaker position with their moms.

This morning, they were all meeting in Monterey Bay at the aquarium, as arranged last night by Garrett and Joyce. The place would likely be full of tourists and school groups, too public to have a private conversation with Dayna. So Roman reached for his phone.

He hadn't silenced it last night so that he would know if Dayna tried to call or text. He shouldn't have been surprised to see that she hadn't sent him anything. But he was surprised at the disappointment that he felt.

By the time he'd dressed and checked out of the hotel, Garrett was just coming out of the doors to join him in the car.

"Sleep well?" Garrett asked, plunging on before waiting for Roman's answer. "I slept with a smile on my face all night. Today will be fantastic. I only wish I could thank our sister for her brilliant plan."

Brilliant, all right, Roman thought. If only he had been on this trip without Garrett and didn't have to worry about Garrett's interest in Dayna.

"Did you talk to Jen last night to get things worked out?" Roman asked, pulling out of the hotel parking lot and onto the main road.

Garrett puffed out a breath of air. "This trip has been good for us, I decided. Put a little distance between us to figure things out."

"What do you mean?" Roman asked in a sharp voice. But he couldn't help his tone. His brother was already getting under his skin, and it was only 8:00 in the morning.

"Just that I'm going to have a great day today and not worry about anything," Garrett said in his best lawyer voice. "I'm on vacation and, in a few hours, will be spending time with a beautiful woman and her charming mother at a fantastic aquarium. There are always other fish in the sea." He barked out a laugh at his own joke.

Roman clenched his jaw and almost ran a red light. He slammed on the brakes just in time.

"Hey, watch it," Garrett said, throwing him a glance. "I can drive if you want."

Roman shook his head; he didn't trust himself to speak. He continued along the PCH, hardly listening to Garrett's prattle about a work client. When Garrett started talking about Dayna again and about what she'd said at dinner the night before that had captured his interest, Roman couldn't stand it anymore. Whether or not he would ever end up dating Dayna, Roman was sick of the way his brother thought that he could have any woman he wanted.

"Back off of Dayna," Roman said, cutting off Garrett's one-sided conversation.

Garrett laughed. "You serious?"

"Dead serious."

Garrett went silent for a moment, and Roman kept his focus on the road. It was better that they have this conversation now, before they were with Dayna again. Roman couldn't explain why he felt so defensive and so protective of her. But, after a sleepless night, Roman knew that his interest in Dayna wasn't something that was going to blow over quickly. And, whether or not she returned his feelings, Roman didn't want to see her get hurt by his idiot brother.

"You like her," Garrett stated. Then he chuckled. "You really like her, don't you?" He lightly punched Roman in the shoulder.

"I guess I do," Roman said, stealing a glance at Garrett's grinning face.

"So, you want to arm wrestle over her or something?" Garrett asked. "Make a bet; who can get the chick the fastest?"

"You're a piece of work," Roman said, not bothering to hide the disgust in his voice. "I don't know how any woman can stand your mouth."

"Whoa," Garret said, holding up his hands. "Where's all this coming from?"

Roman was glad that he was driving because, if he wasn't, he might be in a long overdue fistfight with his brother. "You're cocky and treat women like objects. The only reason you're nice to Joyce is because of Dayna. You don't really care about her mom, do you?"

Garrett shrugged. "She's a nice lady and has an interesting daughter. What's wrong with being friendly?"

"You're practically engaged to Jen," Roman said. "You're emotionally cheating on her."

"*Emotionally cheating?* Whatever, man," Garrett said as he pulled out his phone and scrolled through it. "Check this out. Texts from Dayna. Read 'em and weep."

Roman felt his heart rise in his throat. He grabbed the phone and read the texts as he stopped at the next light. Garrett was definitely trying to flirt with Dayna, but her responses were short. Polite, but short.

Roman didn't know if he should be relieved that Dayna didn't seem to be flirting back or bothered that she'd been texting Garrett last night and this morning, while Roman had received nothing but silence from her.

He handed the phone back to Garrett, his thoughts tumbling. "She said that you reminded her of her ex-husband."

"Paul?"

Roman assumed that Joyce must have told Garrett the guy's name.

"That's not such a bad thing . . ." Garrett said. "I mean, she *did* marry him, right?"

The light turned green, and Roman accelerated. He decided to go all-in with this conversation. Whatever the outcome, it would be better than watching Garrett flirt outrageously with Dayna at the aquarium.

"She said that her ex . . . Paul . . . was a cheater and that she should have known it from the beginning. He was too sure of himself, cocky, and wasn't afraid to check out other women when she was with him."

"Ouch," Garrett said.

For a moment, Roman thought he might have actually gotten through to his brother.

"Well, they just weren't meant to last," Garrett said, the confidence firm in his voice. "I'm a loyal guy—to the right woman, that is." He laughed to himself. "The only couples who worry about commitment are the ones not meant to be together."

This conversation could take a number of wrong turns, Roman realized, and it had already gotten off track. But he refused to bring up Kenzie to rehash the fact that he was still angry at Garrett, angry that, after all that happened with Kenzie leaving him for Garrett, Garrett had thrown it back in both of their faces by divorcing her in the end.

As Roman drove in silence, Garrett continued to talk about what Dayna's hang-ups about relationships might be after divorcing Paul and how she and Garrett had a lot in common—both being divorced—and how he was just going to keep an open mind and see what happened.

"If you two end up together, then great," Garrett concluded. "I'm not about to call you out in some sort of duel."

But Roman felt the opposite. In fact, if it were 1815, he would be seriously considering dueling his own brother.

By the time they pulled up to the aquarium, the two brothers had dropped the subject of Dayna, and the music on the radio was the only sound between them. Roman saw two women, standing by the entrance to the aquarium, looking at brochures. The tall woman, with golden brown hair grazing her shoulders, turned toward them as Roman and Garrett climbed out of the car. His heart thumped at the sight of Dayna watching him walk toward her and at the smile that had bloomed on her face. He was a goner, and he couldn't deny it.

Chapter Five

As Dayna watched the BMW pull into the aquarium parking lot, she tried not to let the fact that Roman hadn't called or texted her since their near kiss on the beach bother her. If that soccer ball hadn't been kicked at them... She wondered what might have happened and whether she'd be regretting it now. But she would never know.

She couldn't say that she was too surprised that Garrett had texted her several times about the mundane details of meeting up at the aquarium. But the fact that it was Garrett, and not Roman, who'd reached out to her had made her wonder if she was more interested in Roman than he was in her.

Yet, as she unabashedly watched Roman get out of the car and stride toward her, with Garrett a couple of steps behind, Dayna saw the look of intent in his eyes. Perhaps Roman hadn't been ignoring her in the way she'd thought. In fact, he had probably been wrestling with his emotions all night like she had.

It was a lot to assume. But Dayna had learned to identify and to trust her instincts after leaving her ex and entering the dating world again. It was why she hadn't lasted more than one or two dates with other men and probably why they each had stopped calling her. She wasn't going to waste her time with someone who didn't seem capable of completely investing in her.

"Hi," Roman said, stopping in front of her and capturing her gaze with his own.

Her breath caught, which was totally a teenage reaction, and she felt her face heat up. "Hi. How was your drive?" she managed to say.

Even though she'd had little sleep and had been stressing about this meeting, once she'd spoken to him, it seemed like no time had passed and nothing was awkward.

"Great!" Garrett said, joining them. He leaned over and kissed her mom's cheek then made a move to do so with Dayna.

But she shifted back and said, "A large school group just left, so our timing is perfect."

"Sounds . . . *perfect*," Garrett said, winking at her.

His flirting was so obvious that Dayna found herself looking at Roman to see what he thought. Was this how it had started with his ex-girlfriend Kenzie? Garrett taking over everything? But instead of finding what she thought might be an irritated Roman, he simply stood there, hands in his pockets, a slight smile on his face as he met her gaze.

What? she wanted to ask him. *What's going on here?*

"Ladies first," Garrett said, and her mom moved forward, a big smile on her face as she started to chat with Garrett. Then he motioned for Dayna to walk in front of him. Since Roman hadn't said anything after his initial hello, she followed her mom toward the ticket window. As she passed Garrett, he said in a not-to-be-missed loud whisper, "You look stunning today."

Dayna mumbled a thank you but kept walking, unsure of how to react. Roman had to have heard this. Garrett was being way too forward. Wasn't Roman going to do anything about his brother?

"It's our treat," Garrett said as they reached the window. He made a show of pulling out a hundred dollar bill from his wallet and sliding it across the counter.

"We can pay for ourselves," Dayna protested at the same time that her mom said, "Oh, thank you!" Her mom turned and said, "Let them be gentlemen, dear."

Two Dozen Roses

Dayna tried not to roll her eyes in response.

Garrett looked over at Dayna and gave her a triumphant smile, as if he'd just won something. *And, perhaps he had.* A thought started to form in Dayna's mind that she at first dismissed, but then she couldn't ignore. It was like Garrett was goading Roman on—flirting with Dayna openly in order to get Roman to . . . do what?

Dayna wasn't entirely sure. But the way Garrett was trying to flirt with her seemed over the top, even for what little she knew about him. As a group, they entered the building and turned first to the section with the octopus tank and touch pools. Dayna glanced back at the two men. They were definitely not speaking to each other, so maybe they weren't in cahoots.

Had Roman given up on her and decided to let Garrett step in? Maybe she'd completely misread both men. But, what about Garrett's supposed girlfriend then? As they reached the octopus tank, her mom and Garrett oohed and aahed over the majestic creatures, while Roman moved over to one of the touch pools. These were crowded with little kids, dipping their hands into the salty water.

"So, if I were to book an exotic trip, where would you recommend?" Garrett asked Dayna.

She'd been asked this question many times before, usually when a guy found out what she did for a living. She replied with her standard answer, "Where's your dream place to visit?"

Garrett folded his arms and acted as if he were truly considering her counter question. "I guess the clichéd answer would be Hawaii, but I *would* like to go there. Have you been?"

"A couple of times," Dayna said, not mentioning that the first time was right after college with a group of girlfriends that she no longer kept in touch with and that the second time had been for her honeymoon.

"Ah, so you could act as a tour guide as well?" Garrett said, giving her a wink.

Dayna felt like she was being suffocated. Garrett's flirting or teasing or whatever it was rubbed her completely the wrong way. The brother she *was* interested in wasn't even paying her any attention, and she was becoming more confused by the minute about Roman. Frustrated, she wholeheartedly blamed herself for developing a silly crush in the first place.

"This road trip is about the extent of any vacation experience that I have," she said in a lighthearted voice, as if his questions hadn't been thoroughly grating on her nerves.

"Do you ever get someone who changes their mind after booking a reservation?" Garrett asked.

"Not often, but it's happened a few times," she said. She really didn't want to discuss the details of her day-to-day operations right now. Not when she was feeling just plain irritated.

She turned toward her mom before Garrett could ask her another question and told her that she'd catch up with them in a little bit.

Before her mom could ask any questions, Dayna left the room and walked across the bridge to the special exhibit. There, she slowly walked along the aquariums of jellyfish, watching their graceful, flowing movements. Despite the questions tumbling in her mind about Roman and Garrett, the beauty of the ocean life felt peaceful.

As she wandered along the massive glass wall standing between her and the jellies, Dayna lost track of time. When someone spoke her name, it startled her out of her reverie.

Roman came to stand next to her, and she cast him a sideways glance. "Did my mom send you to find me?" she asked.

"No, I've been here a while," Roman said. "I wanted to come talk to you, but you seemed so enraptured by the jellies."

"They're strange and fascinating at the same time," Dayna said in a casual voice, although she was curious about what Roman had followed her in here to talk about.

"I agree," Roman said in a low voice. "Hey, I want to apologize for my brother."

"Do you do that a lot?"

He chuckled. "I do, in fact."

Dayna finally met his gaze. His eyes were as dark blue as the water the jellies swam in. "He's pretty persistent," she said.

Roman nodded and leaned forward. "I told him that I like you, and he's decided to call my bluff."

She stared at him. "Meaning?"

"Meaning . . ." Roman started, his gaze holding hers, "that he's decided you're a woman worth knowing and dating, and that he's even thinking of breaking up with his girlfriend now."

Hot and cold rushed through Dayna at the same time. She supposed she should be flattered, but she was mortified. "I'd never date a man like him."

As the edges of Roman's mouth curved upward, Dayna started to feel like they were the only ones in the aquarium. "What about a man like me?" he asked.

The breath left her for a moment, and when Dayna could speak again, she said, "You don't seem too eager to compete with your brother. He's been doing all the talking and texting."

Roman didn't seem fazed by her gentle reprimand. He took a step closer, invading her personal space, but she found she didn't mind in the least.

"If we hadn't been interrupted on the beach," he said, "I don't think you'd be saying that."

"Maybe it was just good timing," Dayna said, "stopping us from making a mistake."

But Roman didn't agree with her this time. "I was kept awake enough last night to know that nothing with you could ever be a mistake."

Dayna shook her head, if only to clear away the light-headedness that was growing stronger by the moment. "Look, Roman, I like you. But this trip feels sort of surreal, not like my regular life. I don't know what's going to happen when I'm back home, back to working, and back to living my life."

Roman shoved his hands in his pockets. "I understand, and I'm not a pushy person."

"I've noticed," Dayna said in a dry tone.

He lifted his brows and then laughed. "Let me rephrase. I'm not normally a pushy person, but I'm not going to let Garrett bulldoze you into dating him either. Whatever does or doesn't happen between us, you're much too good for my brother."

"So, are you going to start flirting with me incessantly too?"

"If that's what it takes," Roman said. He slipped his hand into hers, intertwining their fingers. When he'd held her hand at the beach, that had been warm and comfortable. But now, this felt like something more . . . *intimate*.

"I'll let you know when you need to ratchet up the flirting," she said in a half whisper.

"Deal," Roman said. "Now, let's go see the tide pools. They were always my sister's favorite."

Chapter Six

Roman rubbed the back of his neck as he stood outside the café, waiting for Dayna. Joyce was reading aloud from a brochure about Fort Bragg, the area they were now in. They'd had a late lunch near Glass Beach, north of San Francisco. Garrett hadn't let up on the flirting; in fact, he seemed to be getting worse. Last night, Garrett had told his girlfriend, Jen, that he was thinking about taking a break from their relationship. When Jen agreed, this was essentially a green light, in his mind, to pursue Dayna.

Roman had called Dayna last night, after she'd had time to settle in at her hotel. She'd said that she didn't want to create friction between the two brothers, so she wanted to be the one to talk to Garrett. Roman could tell that she'd already said something to her mom, and it had made a nice difference, for Joyce was paying more attention to Roman now, rather than hanging on every word from Garrett.

Dayna had texted to Roman during lunch that she wanted to talk to Garrett alone, to set him straight once and for all. So Roman and Joyce had left the table and were now waiting outside.

"Let's walk along Glass Beach," Joyce said, pulling Roman from his thoughts. "The pictures in the brochure don't do it justice." She gave a quick shake of her head. "I can't believe that people used to toss their trash over the cliffs, into the ocean."

Roman was about to agree, when Dayna came out of the restaurant alone.

"Where's Garrett?" Joyce asked her daughter. "Did everything go all right?"

That was a loaded question, and by the look on Dayna's face, Roman wasn't sure of the answer.

"He's making a phone call," Dayna said. "At least, that's what I told him to do if he wants to be a smart man."

Roman lifted his brows. "What happened? What did you say?"

"Well," Dayna said, slipping her hand into his and smiling.

Roman took this as a good sign.

"He's calling Jen to apologize and, hopefully, to get things back on track. And, as for you and I . . ." She shrugged. "I guess we'll see what happens."

Joyce clapped her hands. "Wonderful!" she said as she looked at Roman. "You and your brother are both great men, and I'm glad to see that my daughter's at least interested in one of you. She hasn't been dating enough."

"Mom," Dayna said, her face turning pink. But the reprimand was more of a tease.

Joyce looped her arm through Roman's then peered over at her daughter. "We're going to Glass Beach. You've got to read about it." She handed over the brochure, and Dayna took it.

Then Roman felt Dayna's fingers tightened around his own, and so he squeezed back. He couldn't wait to hear Garrett's take on the conversation with Dayna.

As they neared the beach, bright colored sea glass intermixed with the sand, creating a stunning visage.

"How beautiful," Joyce said, pointing to the rainbow of colors. "I'm going to walk toward the water and give you two time to talk. Alone."

"That's fairly obvious, Mom," Dayna said with a laugh.

Her mom only smiled and released Roman's arm. Then she set off on her own.

Two Dozen Roses

After she was out of earshot, he said, "So, how did you convince my brother to become a standup man?"

"I told him that even if he changed his name to Roman and dyed his hair brown that he would only be half the man that his brother is," Dayna said.

"Wow." Roman didn't know if he should feel extremely flattered or sorry for Garrett. He slowed to a stop and faced Dayna. "What did he say to that?"

"He laughed, actually," Dayna said. "But, when he realized I was dead serious, he apologized for making me feel uncomfortable."

An apology from Garrett to a woman? This had to be a first for him. "He wasn't angry or offended?" Roman asked.

"I think that he knew he was already beaten, so he just had to admit it to himself," Dayna said, smiling up at him. The wind was stronger on the beach, and she smoothed her blowing hair back from her face.

"*Has* he been beaten?" Roman teased, keeping his tone light, although his pulse was pounding like mad.

"What do you think?" she asked in a soft voice.

Roman wanted to kiss her there and then. But he wasn't sure if he wanted Dayna's mom to witness their first kiss. He glanced at the shoreline and saw that Joyce was a ways down the beach. Other tourists milled about, but at least they were strangers, ignoring them. He turned again toward Dayna and smoothed back the hair blowing against her face.

"So, tomorrow we head back home, and you keep driving to Oregon. And I was thinking . . ." He lost his train of thought. *Maybe I could just give her a brief kiss.*

"You were thinking . . . what?" Dayna asked, stepping closer until she brushed against him.

He grasped her other hand in his, their fingers linking together. "That I could call you in a couple of days, when you're back, and we could, maybe, go to dinner or something?"

"Hmm," Dayna said, a smile lifting the sides of her mouth. "That would be fine, as long as you don't bring Garrett."

"Don't worry about that. Garrett won't even know."

Dayna laughed, and Roman realized that he couldn't help himself anymore. He released her hands and cradled her face. Then, as he pressed his mouth against hers, Dayna moved into his embrace easily, and it was like he'd always held her in his arms. As they kissed, the blowing wind and the tourists on the beach didn't seem to bother Dayna, and Roman stopped noticing anything that wasn't Dayna.

Chapter Seven

Two days later, Dayna hugged her mom and her brother good-bye on the doorstep of David's house. She'd stayed there overnight. As great as it had been to see David, his wife, and their kids, Dayna had been away from the office too long as it was. Even though her mom had asked, Dayna refused to change her morning flight time.

Her assistant, Angie, had been fabulous in Dayna's absence, but a couple of new issues had cropped up last night that she felt better about handling herself. And . . . if she were to be completely honest with herself, she wanted to see Roman again. As soon as possible.

Their kiss on the beach had made Dayna believe that there may be something to those romance novels she'd read as a teen. Sure, she'd fallen in love with Paul, marrying him with rose-colored glasses on. But her year-long relationship with Paul wasn't nearly as real as her three-day acquaintance with Roman felt. These two men existed in completely different spheres.

"There's the taxi, Mom," Dayna said, picking up her bag. "Have a great time, and I'll see you in a few weeks."

"You'll be there to pick me up at the airport?" her mom asked again.

"Of course," Dayna said. It was the third time this morning that her mom had brought it up. Dayna looked over at David, silently asking for help.

"Dayna will be there," David said. "After you fly out, I'll call her to make sure she's on her way to the airport."

"I've got my own flight to catch now," Dayna said. "Love you guys."

David nodded, and her mom gave Dayna another clinging hug. If Dayna didn't hurry, the taxi would cost her twice as much as expected. So she hurried off the porch and climbed into the taxi, sighing with relief as the car pulled away from the curb, leaving her brother's suburban house behind.

Things had been tense between Dayna and David at first, and her mom's constant chatter about the trip had been the only saving grace. Until she brought up Roman. Then the questions set in. Dayna tried to be as nonchalant as possible about Roman. She knew that her brother still held out some hope that she and Paul would reconcile, for Dayna had suspected that David still kept in touch with Paul. But her brother would just have to get over it.

The taxi ride passed swiftly, and soon Dayna was checking in at the airport counter and then heading toward the gate. Once she was in her seat on the airplane, she sent a text to Roman. They'd been texting a lot during the past two days and even had a couple of phone calls.

Plane taking off soon, she typed. His reply took only moments to come in.

Can't wait to see you.

Her face flushed, and her heart thumped. Was this really happening? Was she really crushing on a man that she'd met on a road trip?

"You must love flying," a woman said, settling in next to Dayna.

"Oh, just looking forward to going home." And Dayna was. More than she ever would have thought possible.

Thankfully, the woman pulled out a Kindle and started to read, leaving Dayna to her own thoughts. She had no idea how things would end up with Roman, but she told herself to enjoy this moment and, hopefully, the many more.

By the end of the flight, her stomach had tied itself into nervous knots. She and Roman had planned to go out tonight. And, while it was still hours away, Dayna's mind was racing through all that she needed to do beforehand. She'd need to catch a taxi home, then drive her car to the office, where she'd help Angie lock down some corporate event bookings. Then she'd head home again to get ready.

Dayna hadn't even decided what to wear yet and wished that she had a free hour to browse the boutiques. But there wouldn't be time for that, especially if she wanted to shower and wash her hair.

Once the plane pulled up to the terminal, Dayna hurried off the plane, grateful that she didn't have to go to baggage claim. She made her way to the exit with the waiting taxis. As she stepped outside into the warm air, she stopped dead.

A man who looked almost exactly like Roman was standing near the curb. He wore a light blue shirt and tie and was standing with one hand in the pants pocket of his dress slacks. Then he turned, and there was no doubt that it was him. Dayna also saw that he was carrying a bouquet of pink roses.

"Roman," she said, her stomach starting to do somersaults as he walked toward her. She hadn't forgotten how tall he was or how much she loved his blue eyes and his smile, but seeing him here at the airport was a very nice reminder.

"What are you doing here?" she asked.

"Surprising you," he said with laughter in his voice. Then he leaned down and kissed her cheek. "Do you like the roses?"

"Um, yes!" she said, taking them from him. Then she wrapped her arm around his neck, tugging him closer. She kissed him on the mouth, making their second kiss just as public as their first kiss had been.

But Roman seemed to have no problem with sliding his arm around her waist and pulling her in for another kiss. When he broke away, he said, "I was hoping you'd be glad to see me."

She smiled at him, feeling nervous and elated all at once. "I can't believe you came to the airport."

"I thought I could drive you home or to work or wherever you needed to go."

Dayna raised her brows. "Couldn't wait until tonight?"

"Nope," he said softly, and Dayna realized that he was still close enough to kiss. But, with the way her heart was pounding and her skin was heating up, she decided that she needed to breathe a little.

She reluctantly stepped away from him, grasping the roses and reaching for her bag.

"I'll carry your bag," Roman offered, easily lifting the bag. "I'm just a few spaces down."

"You took quite a risk, parking in the taxi zone," Dayna teased.

"It would have been a greater risk if I'd missed you coming out of the airport," Roman countered.

"Why's that?" she asked.

"Because then the roses would have wilted, and I would've had to stalk you at your office or something."

She laughed. "Is that what you're doing? *Stalking* me?"

Roman smiled, but then his expression sobered. "I never thought that going a couple of days without seeing you would turn me into a stalker." As they reached his car, he opened the passenger door to let her in.

"Hmm," she said, slipping her hand into his, holding onto Roman's warmth for a moment. "I think you're the best looking stalker I've ever had."

His brows furrowed in response. "You've had others?"

"A woman can't tell all her secrets, can she?"

He just grinned. "Where to?"

"You can drop me off at my condo," she said. "I need to take my car into work. Speaking of work, do you have the day off or something?"

"Taking a long lunch." As he held her gaze, Dayna realized that she was holding her breath. Roman released her hand and stepped away, saying, "We've got company."

Dayna looked behind her to see a ticket cop striding toward them.

"Get in, and I'll talk to him," Roman said. Then he shut the door after her.

From inside the car, Dayna turned in her seat to get a good look at Roman as he talked to the cop. There was a lot of hand waving and then a disapproving frown from the cop, but Roman got inside the car without a ticket in hand.

"He let you off?"

Roman winked at her, and for a second, he reminded her of Garrett. But Roman was so not Garrett, and for that, she was grateful.

"He was a softy after all," Roman said.

"It's nice to know there's still some compassion in the world."

Roman laughed and pulled out into the slow traffic, steering the car around the long line of taxis waiting at the curb. Then he reached over and linked his fingers with hers. "How was your flight?"

"Smooth and short," Dayna said, looking over at him. Had he really taken half the day off work to drive to the airport and taxi her around? "I hope you don't mind that I have to work this afternoon."

"Nope, I'm still planning on dinner, though," he said as he looked over at her, hope evident in his eyes.

"Yes, but now I can't surprise you."

"With what?"

"With looking better than I do now—after getting up early and being cramped in an airline seat."

"Hmm," Roman said, meeting her gaze for a couple of seconds then looking back at the road. "I was going to mention something, but I thought better of it. Being a gentleman and all."

"Really?" Dayna deadpanned.

Roman chuckled. Then his cell rang from where it sat on the middle console, causing Dayna to glance down at its screen. *Kenzie.*

Dayna felt her heart about stop. Roman released her hand, glancing at the phone too, then silenced the call. He linked their fingers again, but Dayna had frozen. What were the chances that he knew two Kenzies? An ex-girlfriend and maybe someone from work? But Dayna had been on enough first and second dates to know that she wasn't about to waste her time with a man who was seeing someone else.

"Is that your Kenzie?" she asked.

"She was never mine," Roman said in a careful voice. "I'm not sure what she wants. She started calling me yesterday. Left a pretty cryptic message."

"That's strange," Dayna mumbled, but her mind was racing in a dozen different directions.

"Look, don't worry about it," Roman said, his tone sounding more casual now. "She's probably trying to track down Garrett or something, but he's being a real class act and ignoring her."

The brothers did seem to have something in common—screening Kenzie's calls. In Roman's case, Dayna wasn't too sad, though. "Well, she did used to be your sister-in-law."

"Yeah," Roman said.

Silence descended between them as Roman merged onto the freeway.

"You should call her back," Dayna said, even though it sent

her heart racing to suggest such a thing. "She obviously needs to talk to you."

Roman cast her a surprised look.

"What are you afraid of?" Dayna asked. "Unless you aren't really over her."

"Ouch," Roman said. "Is that what you think is going on?"

Dayna gave a shrug. She liked Roman, she really did, but she'd never play the fool again. "I don't know what's going on, and I'm not sure you will either, unless you call Kenzie and ask. And if she does want to get back together with you, then you have a decision to make."

"She doesn't want to get back together," he said. "I mean, it's been years."

But Dayna heard the uncertainty in his voice—not hope but just enough of a question that she knew she'd done the right thing to press him.

"Exit at the next off-ramp," she said.

Roman exited, and while she directed him the rest of the way to her condo, Dayna wondered if they'd really be going out tonight after all.

After he pulled up to her place, he removed her bag out of the trunk and carried it to her front door.

"Thanks for everything," she said, unlocking her door.

"Dayna . . ."

When his voice trailed off, she turned to look at him. "I think you owe it to yourself to at least find out why Kenzie is calling. It won't hurt my feelings. I'm a big girl."

Roman blew out a breath of frustration, matching her inner feelings with his own. But she wasn't about to let him know it. As he kissed her on the cheek and then left without another word, Dayna wondered if she'd ever see the man again.

Walking into the dimness of her empty condo, Dayna knew that she would truly miss him.

Chapter Eight

Roman drummed his fingers on the steering wheel as he sat in his car, parked in a grocery store parking lot. Dayna had told him to call Kenzie back, but he hadn't told Dayna all of the history between them—at least, not all of the history since Garrett and Kenzie's divorce.

Kenzie had started calling Roman a couple of months after the divorce. At first, he had talked to her, and they'd fallen into a sort of odd friendship again. Mostly, this was Roman comforting her and encouraging her to date again. When Kenzie said that she wanted to start meeting him for lunch, Roman had been wary. But then she'd backed off, and they'd resumed having just the phone calls.

Whenever she started dating someone new, Roman wouldn't hear from her for a while. Then the phone calls would start up again. He'd never told anyone about this, not even Garrett.

Then, when Denise had died, Kenzie came to her funeral. Roman hung in the background as Kenzie had offered her condolences to Garrett, but he could feel her watching him throughout the services. When she called the following day, he'd ignored her call. After a half dozen calls and a few unreturned messages, she finally gave up.

Yesterday, she'd left him a message, a tearful one, full of apologies and her long list of regrets . . . about *them*. And that's what had scared Roman—hearing Kenzie's apologies had tugged at a long-forgotten part of his heart.

Roman slammed his palm against the steering wheel. Dayna hadn't known how right she was—Kenzie really did want to get back together again. Well, her exact words had been, "Can you ever forgive me? Can you ever give us another chance?"

It was for this reason that Roman had wanted to see Dayna as soon as possible. He needed to see her. Watching her walk out of the airport, he'd felt that pull again that he'd had since their initial conversation in the Ripley's museum. He was excited about Dayna like he hadn't been about any other woman for years.

He wanted to get to know Dayna better and to see where their relationship might lead. Kenzie's timing couldn't be worse.

Roman picked up his phone and squeezed his eyes shut for a moment. He'd told Kenzie all those years ago that he loved her, and he had. But did he still? Was that why, after six years, he still felt the pain of her betrayal? If their breakup had been a regular one, one not involving marrying his own brother, would Roman be over Kenzie by now?

Dayna might have said courageous words, but he'd seen the hurt in her eyes. That should be comforting to him, to know that she really liked him too, but it only made him feel like an idiot. He knew that talking to Kenzie over the years and letting her continually bring up their past had kept his heart exposed. He'd been the one *letting* her stay in his life, not the other way around.

Roman knew now that he had to cut her off completely. This was the only way if he was ever going to move on. He didn't know where Dayna and he would end up, but he did know that Dayna deserved the best. And if he allowed Kenzie to keep one finger on the pulse of his heart, it wouldn't be fair to Dayna or to himself. He just hoped that he wouldn't hurt Kenzie too much by doing what he knew he must.

Roman also knew that it was ironic—him dreading telling Kenzie something that might offend or hurt her—when she had been the one who'd broken his heart by marrying his brother. The juxtaposition wasn't lost on him. It seemed clear that meeting someone like Dayna had finally opened his eyes and had given Roman the motivation to do what he should have done years ago.

So he selected Kenzie's phone number and pressed *Call*. It rang only twice before she answered.

"Roman, how are you?" she said immediately, using her low, sultry voice.

"I'm fine. What's up?" he asked, cutting her off from making further small talk.

"Oh, you're not fine," she said in a purring tone that he'd once found sexy. But he was surprised to realize that he just felt irritated by it now. "Tell me what's wrong. Is it work? Is Garrett being a jerk again? Are you missing Denise?"

With each question, his irritation grew progressively worse. "Why are you calling, Kenzie?" Roman asked, wishing that he didn't have to be so sharp with her, but she wasn't going to let up.

"Oh, sorry. If this isn't a good time, I can call tonight," she said, her tone coming across as pouting.

Roman knew Kenzie well enough to know that she wanted him to backtrack. But he wouldn't do that this time. "Don't call me tonight. I'm returning your call now, so tell me why you called."

"Well." She puffed out an audible breath. "If you're going to talk to me like that, I'm not sure that I should tell you why I called."

Roman shook his head even though she couldn't see it. Had Kenzie always played these kinds of games with him, and he just hadn't realized it until now? "Do you need me to get Garrett to sign some sort of legal form?" he asked. When she didn't reply, he knew she was in full pout mode now. "No? Then is it something else? Your health? Or, are you looking for a new job, and you need a business reference or something?"

"No," she said, her voice sharp and annoyed. "You got my messages. You know what I want."

Roman exhaled and let the silence grow between them. "Do I?" he finally said in a quiet voice. "There was a time when I thought I knew what *you* wanted, and that was *me*. But I was dead wrong, Kenzie. It's been six years now; I need to move on."

She let out a small gasp. "What are you talking about? Are you seeing someone else?"

"Someone *else*?" Roman asked, the heat of anger spreading across his neck. "I haven't been seeing *you* since you *married my brother*," he spat out. It wasn't like he hadn't said these words to Kenzie before, but now Roman knew that when he hung up with her, he wouldn't ever be speaking to her or seeing her again.

She sniffled, and Roman knew she was crying. Normally, he would have felt horrible. But then he thought of Dayna, who was probably feeling horrible right now as well. He didn't owe Kenzie anything, and he hadn't for a long time. It was time that he allowed himself to move on, to stop wishing there was some way he could change the past.

"I hope you find the perfect man someday, Kenzie," he said. "But we're not good together. You just realized it sooner than I did, and I took a lot longer to accept it all and move on."

"So, what are you saying?" Kenzie asked in trembling voice. "You've moved on?"

"Actually, I have," Roman said. "I'm dating someone, and I don't know where things will go or how they'll end up, but that doesn't matter. What I do know is that I won't be giving us a second chance. *We* were over a long time ago, whether I wanted to believe it or not."

Kenzie was surprisingly quiet, so quiet that, after a moment, Roman said, "Are you still there?"

"I am." She paused then said, "This is really good-bye, isn't it?"

"Yes," Roman said.

"There's something different in your voice now," she said in a thoughtful tone. "Who is this woman you're dating? Has she met Garrett?" This question might have hurt him on a deep level if Roman hadn't already written off Kenzie and removed her from his heart.

"She has." He took a deep breath. "And she chose me. Good-bye, Kenzie."

After another beat, Kenzie said, "Good-bye, Roman."

He pulled the phone away from his ear and clicked *End*. He didn't know whether Kenzie was about to say something more, but he'd said his good-byes, and she'd been given the chance to say hers. He pulled up her contact file on his phone and blocked the number. Then he erased the file completely.

He sat in his car for a while longer, just soaking up the fact that Kenzie was really out of his life for good now. *Completely.* Roman only hoped that Dayna wouldn't be too upset about how distracted he had become when Kenzie had called.

He picked up his phone again and called Dayna's number. After a couple of rings, it went to voice mail. So he ended the call before leaving a message. She was probably in her office by now, he decided. Pulling up the browser on his phone, he did a Google search for Dream Vacations. The location was only a few miles away, and Roman hoped that Dayna wouldn't mind having a visitor.

Chapter Nine

"You can go home," Dayna told Angie after she stepped into the office. It felt good to be back, and Dayna could feel the stress draining as she sat at her desk and logged onto the computer.

Angie was wearing red-rimmed glasses today. She had about a dozen pairs and liked to match them with her outfits. "Are you sure, hon?"

"Yeah," Dayna said with a laugh. "You've put in enough overtime. You've been amazing, by the way. Thank you for holding down the fort."

"Well," Angie said, stretching her fingers over her computer's keyboard. "It is Friday, and I do have a date."

"With Jack?"

"The very one," Angie said, and then she flashed a white smile. "How about you? Any Friday-night plans or just the usual? Working."

Dayna winced at this comment, but she didn't let it show. "Actually, I have dinner plans with a man I met on my road trip." At least she hoped so. And she hoped it wasn't the type of dinner where Roman was going to tell her that he wanted to start dating Kenzie again. Without looking at Angie, Dayna knew that the woman's mouth had dropped open.

"Say that again?" Angie said.

Dayna looked up and smiled at Angie's shocked expression. "It's only a date, Angie. You go on them, like, every night."

"*I* go on them," Angie said and pointed one of her long, red painted nails at Dayna. "*You* don't."

Dayna started to regret that she'd said anything to Angie because what if the dinner date didn't happen tonight? What if the phone call between Roman and Kenzie had made them both realize that they belonged together after all?

"So," Angie said, perching on Dayna's desk. "Tell me every detail."

Dayna looked at her glowing computer screen. "I really need to catch up so that I'm not stuck here *all* night."

"Then give me the five-minute version," Angie said, clasping her hands together as if she were about to beg.

"All right," Dayna agreed and told her the basics, not stopping when Angie scowled at Garrett's interference. But, when Dayna told Angie about the phone call from Kenzie, Angie placed a hand over her heart.

"You told him to call her *back*?"

"I did," Dayna said.

Angie narrowed her eyes for a moment. "Are you trying to torture yourself?"

"I'm trying to stay sane here and not date a guy whose heart isn't available."

Angie nodded, but she didn't look wholly convinced. Then her eyes widened as she looked past Dayna toward the windows. "Who is *that*?"

Dayna turned to see who Angie was staring at. A man was crossing the street, heading straight for their office, a bouquet of red roses in hand. Dayna felt her own eyes widen.

"Roman. It's Roman," she said. What was he doing at her work, and why was he carrying roses?

"That's the guy you met on you road trip?" Angie asked.

Dayna could only nod.

"I don't think he's here to break your date. You know what red roses mean, don't you?"

Two Dozen Roses

"But he already gave me roses today, at the airport," Dayna said, mostly to herself. "Pink ones."

"Well, honey, he's back," Angie said. "And he's carrying red this time."

Dayna stood, joining Angie in gaping at Roman as he stepped onto the sidewalk, glanced at the office sign in the window, and then crossed to the door.

As he tugged the door open and walked in, Dayna thought her heart might stop. The second his gaze met hers, she knew. Somehow, she knew.

"Hi," he said. "I hope you don't mind me stopping in."

"She doesn't mind," Angie said, "and neither do I."

Dayna laughed, although it was mostly a nervous laugh. "Roman, this is Angie. Angie, this is Roman."

In that moment, with Roman standing in her office, the top button of his shirt undone, his tie gone, and his sleeves rolled up, carrying another bouquet of roses, Dayna realized that she had been hoping with all her heart that nothing in Roman's past would come between them.

"Nice to meet you, Road Trip Guy," Angie said, crossing to him and sticking out her manicured hand.

Roman shook her hand, raising his eyebrows. "I see that you know our story."

Our story. Dayna had to admit that this had a nice sound to it.

"I've gotta run," Angie said, looking back at Dayna then miming holding a phone to her ear. *Call me,* she mouthed.

Dayna nodded but hardly noticed the rest of Angie's departure since Roman was walking toward her now.

"This office is in a great location," he said.

"When its lease came up, I snatched it," she said. "More roses? Are we flirting again?" She leaned against her desk for support as Roman continued to walk toward her.

But he stopped just short of her and placed the roses on her desk. "I was hoping we're past flirting," he said.

"Hmmm," Dayna said, feeling a bit breathless now. "So, then why two bouquets of roses in one day?"

"Because . . ." Roman moved even closer, placing a hand on her waist. "The first one was because I missed you; the second, because I owe you an apology."

The warmth of his hand on her waist heated the skin beneath the layers of her clothing. "For what?" she practically whispered.

"You were right," he said. "Kenzie did want to get back together. But I told her that she was a part of my past."

"Really?" Dayna found herself starting to breathe again. "How did she take it?"

"Better than I thought she would. But that doesn't matter," he said, "because whatever she thinks or doesn't think no longer concerns me."

"And I get roses for that?"

Roman smiled, wrapping his other hand around her waist.

Dayna placed her arms about his neck, if for nothing else, to stay balanced. She felt like an electrical current was shooting through her from her head to her toes.

"The roses are because I'm hoping you'll be part of my future." He leaned down and pressed a light kiss on her mouth.

When he lifted his head, Dayna wouldn't let the rest of him pull away. "Did I ever tell you that I love roses?"

Roman grinned. And, when he leaned in to kiss her again, Dayna made sure that this kiss would be one he wouldn't soon forget.

About Heather B. Moore

Heather B. Moore is a *USA Today* bestselling author. She writes historical thrillers under the pen name H.B. Moore; her latest are *Slave Queen* and *The Killing Curse*. Under the name Heather B. Moore, she writes romance and women's fiction. She's one of the coauthors of The Newport Ladies Book Club series. Other works include *Heart of the Ocean, The Fortune Café, The Boardwalk Antiques Shop,* the Aliso Creek series, and the Amazon bestselling series A Timeless Romance Anthology.

    For book updates, sign up for Heather's email list: hbmoore.com/contact
Website: HBMoore.com
Facebook: Fans of H. B. Moore
Blog: MyWritersLair.blogspot.com
Twitter: @HeatherBMoore

Try, Try Again

By Aubrey Mace

Prologue

Six Months Ago

I was scrubbing over and over a stubborn, sticky spot on one of the tables in the bookstore's café where I worked. I don't know what the spot was from, but as long as I'd been working at removing it . . . it wasn't going anywhere. I would have normally given up long ago and left it for someone else to worry about, but it also gave me the opportunity watch Justin, my coworker, who was currently sitting at a less sticky table on the other side of the café, staring out the window.

That particular table was usually inhabited by his girlfriend, Julia, who was blonde, slim, and looked like she had stepped straight out of an Anthropologie catalog—eclectic, rustic, modern—everything that I wasn't. Despite having previously come to visit Justin during nearly every shift for as long as I'd worked here, Julia had now been absent for three days.

Justin hadn't mentioned the reason for this turn of events, and I didn't like to ask. It wasn't any of my business, no matter how much I wished that Justin's affairs and mine might someday intersect. However, I was starting to worry that Justin wouldn't be here at all for much longer if he didn't do something more productive than stare out the window. I still didn't want to disturb him, but I didn't want him to get fired either. So I took a deep breath and walked over to his table with my dishrag.

"Justin," I hissed, as I started scrubbing at his table purposefully to cover his lack of initiative.

His head spun around like he'd forgotten where he was temporarily. "What?"

"If you're going to zone out, you should at least do it in the bookshelves, where you're less likely to be spotted."

He smiled. "That's why I like you, Sarah—you're always looking out for me."

"Somebody's got to."

"I thought . . ." he said, then trailed off.

"You thought what?" I asked as I moved to the table next to him, keeping up the illusion of busyness, even though I'd cleaned this table already.

"I thought if I sat here long enough, you might come over here and ask me what was wrong," he said, ducking his face down into his shoulder before lifting his eyes to look at me. It was adorable, and I would have given a week's salary for him to be pining over me like that.

I glanced in the direction of the register, but our boss was nowhere to be seen. I was obviously going to run out of things to clean before Justin could tell me what had happened. It was thirty minutes from closing, but the store was empty, and I'd polished everything at least three times. Curiosity was killing me, and I was ready to take my chances. So I slid into the chair across from him.

"You win. What's wrong?" I said, smiling in a way that I hoped was encouraging.

"Julia and I broke up."

"I'm so sorry," my lips said obediently. But I wasn't sorry. These were, I confess, the very words I'd been hoping to hear.

I felt guilty for being pleased for two reasons: First, Justin and I were friends, and he was completely smitten with Julia and must therefore be miserable now. And, second, Julia had always been incredibly nice to me, even though it must have been obvious

Try, Try Again

to her that I had a crush on her boyfriend. Anyone who came into the store could probably see it all over my face, anyone but Justin himself, who only had eyes for Julia. So, this had made it impossible for me to hate her, no matter how much I envied her for having everything that I wanted.

"Thanks," Justin said.

"What happened? Or, is that too personal?"

Justin and I were very good friends. We both liked *The Night Circus* and *The Blacklist* and MUSE and caffeine. But we were not the kind of friends who had discussed relationships.

He sighed. "You know how, sometimes, you have the sudden epiphany that you've met the person you want to be with forever?"

I couldn't help smiling. "Does this happen to you often?" I asked. Other than my Justin worshipping from afar, I hadn't been in a serious relationship for two years. So I had nothing to contribute to this conversation: I liked Justin a lot, but I was by no means sure that I wanted to spend the rest of my life with him. And *forever* was something that my finite mind had trouble even considering. But, since he'd just been dumped by the person he had thought was his soul mate, I decided that my feelings on the subject didn't really matter.

"You know what I mean," Justin continued. "You're talking to someone, and you have so much in common, and she's so pretty, and suddenly you realize . . . she's the one."

"If you change the pronouns to masculine ones, I think I can imagine what you're talking about."

"Right," he said, rewarding me with a small laugh. This was going so well. We'd always been on roughly the same wavelength, but this was different—him telling me about his girlfriend troubles. I felt like a psychologist, so thoroughly did I have him figured out.

"So that's what happened? You told Julia she was the one, and she didn't have the same epiphany?" I said sympathetically.

Instead of the understanding I was expecting to see, his face went completely blank. What had I said wrong?

"Julia wasn't *the one*. That's why I broke up with her," he said slowly.

"I thought that she broke up with you," I said.

"Why would you think that?"

"Because you've been sitting here, at Julia's table, looking morose all night."

"*Morose?*" he asked, playfully mocking me with his eyes.

"Look it up—there will be a picture of you in the dictionary."

"I know what it means. Maybe I was just pretending to be *morose* so that I could lure you over here," he suggested.

I shook my head, wanting nothing more than to get back to where we were a minute ago. "I'm sorry. I'm confused. If Julia wasn't the one you realized that you want to be with forever, who was?"

"You," he said.

Chapter One

The Final Countdown

I tapped my finger on the arrow key repeatedly, running quickly through the columns, until I saw something that registered: Chester Calvin Vaughn; 1936–2016. My breath caught in my throat, but Lottie didn't even notice.

My eyes were swimming over the screen now as Lottie continued to drone on in the background. Not that I didn't love Lottie, but I had bigger concerns at the moment. I scanned through the rest of the obituary, until I got to the part where it listed the surviving family members—wife, children, a brother, grandchildren . . . *Bingo*.

"I mean, I've only got four weeks left," Lottie said.

I finally lifted my eyes from the screen, feeling guilty that I'd been ignoring her. "That sounds pretty morbid. You're not dying—you're pregnant."

"Eighteen years to life with no chance of parole—that's what I'm looking at. And trust you to come to that conclusion; you're obsessed with death."

"I'm not obsessed with death," I huffed, angling the computer away from her so that she couldn't see that I was looking at the obituaries.

"Whatever. This is the last chance I will have to do anything fun for ages."

"Not necessarily. Lots of women go over their due dates, especially with the first baby." I knew this fact because I worked at an ob-gyn, not because I had any experience with having children myself.

"You're not making me feel any better, Cooper," Lottie said.

Lottie had a habit of referring to me by my last name, Cooper, instead of my first, Sarah. I think she's just jealous of anyone who has a plain name. We'd been best friends ever since we were thrown together as roommates in college. And the first thing she had told me was how much she hated her name. Apparently, all her brothers and sisters have names from a previous century. She's the oldest child, so she got her mother's name. In fact, her mother and her grandmother are both named Lottie, which seems like it would be confusing if you hung out together much. Once Lottie had found out that she was having a girl, I asked her if she'd be continuing the tradition. She snorted, so I had taken that as a no.

"Seriously, we should go somewhere or do something. This is my last chance."

"You said that already," I said, my eyes back on the screen again.

"I know, but you weren't listening then. I could tell."

"I was listening," I said as I read that the funeral was Saturday, and the viewing was Friday night. I wasn't close enough to Justin to go to the funeral. But, going to the viewing is what a supportive friend would do. I hadn't seen him lately, but I had hoped we were still friends. I still harbored the distant thought that, one day, we might be more than friends, but I was afraid that I might have missed that chance.

"Lottie, what would you say if I promised to take you on a super fun road trip and you would only have to do one thing for me in return?" I asked in my sweetest voice.

Chapter Two

We Put the *Fun* in Funeral

"I'm not going to like this trade-off, am I?" Lottie asked.

"It's nothing," I said. "It'll take ten minutes."

She sighed. "What is it?"

I turned my laptop around so that she could see it.

"A funeral? You want me to go to a funeral? I rest my case—you're obsessed with death."

"Only to the viewing. I didn't know him well enough to go to the funeral."

Lottie slowly smiled. "You didn't know *him* at all, did you?"

"Of course I did. I wouldn't go to a stranger's viewing for kicks, would I?"

"You would if you knew that Justin was going to be there. Or, is it only a coincidence that they have the same last name?"

"Maybe," I said guiltily.

"I knew it. You only want to go so you can stalk him."

"I haven't seen him in a while, and this is a good opportunity. Besides, he's probably really upset, so this is what a good friend would do—comfort him during this difficult time."

She shook her head. "You want to ogle him."

"I do not!"

Lottie squinted at the screen. "The funeral is in Boise!"

"Hence the super fun road trip."

"I don't want to go to Boise. I want to go to Cali and plant myself in the sunny sand like a beached whale."

"Then we'd be going the wrong way—the funeral is in Idaho."

"So, where does the fun part come in, exactly?"

"After the viewing. I promise you the super funnest road trip you've ever been on."

She hesitated, her hand resting on her ballooning belly. "I'm a giant pregnant woman, so I have nothing to wear to a viewing."

"I saw you in a black dress two weeks ago."

"It's too tight now."

I stared at her in disbelief.

"I'm serious. And, before you judge me, you try growing an entire person. I gain weight just *looking at* food now."

"You can squeeze into it. Come on, it'll be great," I said.

"I guess it's either this or stay home and watch nonstop basketball with my husband . . ." she said, then trailed off.

"Well?" I said finally.

"I'm thinking."

I rolled my eyes.

Then she shrugged. "All right, I'll go."

"Thank you, thank you, thank you!"

"But the post-viewing festivities better be spectacular."

Chapter Three

Driving Miss Lottie

Lottie sighed loudly.

"What? What is it?" I said quickly.

"Nothing. I'm fine."

"It doesn't sound like you're fine." We'd been in the car for two hours now, and she had kept shifting around in her seat. I'm sure it was hard to get comfortable in her condition, and I was wondering now if this trip was such a great idea.

"You've got to stop panicking every time I make a noise. You're making me nervous," she said, trying to adjust the seat belt so that it wasn't cutting her in half.

"You're making *me* nervous. You're the one who's about to pop. I can't believe your husband even let you go."

She barked out a mirthless laugh. "It's March Madness, and he's got Pizza Hut on speed dial. He won't even notice that I'm gone."

"Are you guys okay?"

"We're fine. But I do like him better when he's not under the influence of basketball twenty-four seven."

"I'm beginning to think this was a mistake. What if you have the baby early?"

"I thought that you said I was going to go over my due date," Lottie said, looking mildly amused.

"What if you start having contractions?" I argued. "What if there's a storm, and we get stuck in a snowdrift, and you have the baby in the car, and I have to deliver it? Just because I answer the phone at an ob-gyn office doesn't mean that I know anything about the birth part!" My tone of voice was rising, and my heart was suddenly pounding.

"Trust me, the idea of having you as my midwife is as scary to me as it is to you. Honestly, you can think of more things to worry about than anyone else I know. Is it even supposed to snow?"

"I don't know. I should have checked that before we left."

Lottie craned her head around, checking all the windows. "It's blue sky as far as the eye can see. You want to worry about something? Worry about what you're going to say to Justin."

"Have I ever mentioned that you have such a knack for making people feel better?" I was quiet for a moment while I contemplated all the ways that this could go wrong. I couldn't believe we were actually going to the viewing. It was the kind of thing I usually would only have considered doing. I might even have gotten into the car, telling myself I was going. But then I would have chickened out after an hour and turned around. Only now, I had Lottie with me, and she'd make me follow through, if for no other reason than because it was her last chance to ever have fun again.

"What are you thinking about?" Lottie asked.

"You already know what I'm thinking about. You told me to think about it, and now I can't help myself."

"Right. What I don't get is why you never told him you liked him."

"It's . . . complicated," I hedged. Lottie was one of those people who said what they wanted and usually got it, whereas I was the opposite. I usually waited and hoped that the universe would magically sense what I wanted and send it to me with little or no effort on my part. And then, in the rare instance when the universe actually came through for me, I panicked.

"It's only complicated because you made it complicated. He liked you."

"I have no idea what his feelings toward me were, liking or otherwise." How I managed to tell her a lie this momentous with a straight face I'll never know.

"He liked you," she repeated. "I could tell."

"You never even met him! Anyway, if he had, it's *liked*, past tense now."

"Not necessarily. I guess we'll see soon enough," she said, grinning wickedly.

At least one of us is having a good time, I thought.

She closed her eyes and leaned back against the seat. Lottie had always had a habit of falling asleep with little warning, but pregnant Lottie had been known to doze off even in the middle of a sentence. So she must have finally gotten comfortable because she was out in thirty seconds.

But the more I thought about Justin, the more I was convinced that this was a bad idea. I considered turning around and heading for home. We might even be able to get there by the time she woke up. Maybe I could convince her that I drove to Idaho, went to the viewing, and then drove home while she had slept through the whole thing.

I was quickly heading into full-on panic mode. So I took the next exit and pulled over into the parking lot of the nearest gas station. I leaned against the steering wheel and allowed my eyes to drift shut, remembering the one kiss I'd shared with Justin Vaughn.

Lottie was right when she had said that I'd never had the guts to tell Justin that I liked him. But, what she didn't know was that one night, what seemed like ages ago, he had tried to tell me.

Chapter Four

Six Months Ago

"Me?" I squeaked in a voice that didn't sound like mine.

"You seem surprised," Justin said.

"I couldn't be more surprised."

"Why?"

"Well, for starters, you broke up with your girlfriend like five minutes ago!"

He smiled as if he was humoring a small child who'd said something cute but ridiculous. "It wasn't five minutes."

"Close enough."

"But we're friends, right?"

"Well, yeah."

"Good friends?" he pressed.

"Sure. But being good friends and being soul mates are pretty far apart on the relationship spectrum, don't you think?"

"Are you sure?" he asked. Then he reached across the table and put his hand over mine, and my heart felt like it might collapse. This was exactly what I had wanted. So, why was I responding this way? I'd had no idea that this was coming, and I suddenly knew that I couldn't have this conversation right now. I needed some time to think.

Try, Try Again

I practically exploded out of my chair, saying, "I have to do something."

Justin looked confused. "What do you have to do?"

"I . . . forgot to pull a book for someone who called to reserve it earlier," I lied. Really, I had to get away so that I could organize my thoughts without my secret crush—who'd abruptly announced that he liked me—staring me down.

"Sarah, you don't have to run away," Justin said, sighing loudly.

"I'm not running away! I'm doing my job, unlike some people I know." I had meant this to sound teasing, but I was so flustered that it probably came off as accusatory instead. Not knowing how to fix it, I wandered off to find a book for the imaginary person who'd supposedly called earlier.

But Justin followed me, saying, "Sarah . . ."

There were a million books in the store, but I had no idea what I was looking for. Since no one had really called, all I had to do was pick one and slap a reserve ticket on it. Then I could put it away later. So I darted down the self-improvement aisle, which happened to be the closest one.

What was Justin thinking? He'd never given me any signs that he might be interested in something more than a friendship. Maybe he was one of those guys who couldn't be alone, and he'd simply gravitated toward me because we were already friends and it would be easy, which would almost make sense if she'd broken up with him. I didn't want to immediately fall into a relationship with someone who'd just broken up with someone so recently. Julia was probably still curled up with a tube of chocolate chip cookie dough, wondering where it all had gone wrong.

As Justin rounded the corner, I pretended to be searching for something specific.

"Sarah," he repeated.

"What?" I replied. In desperation, I pulled out a copy of *Men*

Are from Mars, Women Are from Venus, using it as a shield. I'd hoped that he would have taken the hint from my obviously made-up errand that we weren't exactly in the same place right now.

He grabbed my upper arms and swooped in to kiss me. *So much for taking a hint.* If I'd thought I was surprised by his revelation before, I now realized that had been nothing, compared to this new feeling: a combination of euphoria and panic. *I'm glad he has good aim,* I thought. For, if he'd missed my lips in his sudden voracity, both of our noses would have certainly been broken.

I dropped the book onto the floor and surrendered as he pressed me into the bookshelf, obviously trying to convince me with his lips, where his words had failed before.

Then Justin started kissing my neck, and this felt so nice that I tried not to think about how inappropriate this was for work behavior and how, if our boss happened to come looking for a diet book, we'd both certainly be fired. Finally, my brain rebooted, the panic won out, and I pulled away.

Justin's face was red, as if he'd finally realized what a reckless thing he'd done. "I'm sorry," he said.

"No, I'm sorry," I said. "I wasn't expecting this. You should take some time to decide what you really want."

"You mean that *you* need some time," he said, not unkindly.

"Maybe we both do. You just broke up with Julia. We're good friends, and I like you." I tried to straighten my hair, which was probably now a testament to exactly how much I liked Justin. "We have fun together. But you have to admit, this is a pretty big shift."

As I tried to beg him with my eyes to understand, he smiled, but it seemed cool—like four o'clock in the afternoon, when you know the sun is still there, but the light feels different. Not so warm and farther away.

"I didn't mean to go too fast," he said. "Take all the time you need."

Chapter Five

Car Talk

A nd that was it.
I had assumed that Justin would renew his pursuit after a decent interval, but he never did. Later, he got a new job, and then I didn't see him for a while. Eventually, he started coming to the bookstore again, and he was nice to me—friendly, like before he had tried to kiss me—but that was all: just friends.

And then I got a new job. I had still gone into the bookstore at least once a week, but I never did see him. Often, I stayed awake at night, trying to figure out what might have happened. Was he fickle? I would wonder. Was I too cold?

My memories of that night now had a sort of haze hanging over them. And, when I replayed it now, I wasn't sure how much of it was real and how much was colored by regret. Maybe I should have been more spontaneous and let it happen: worry about the consequences later. But I'd never been much for spontaneity.

"Why are we stopped?" Lottie said suddenly.

My head popped up in surprise. "I thought you'd sleep for hours."

She yawned. "I'm more of a catnapper these days. Shouldn't we be halfway to Boise by now?"

"We are halfway to Boise."

"Are you sleepy? Because I could drive," she offered.

"I'm not sleepy."

"You could have fooled me. There's an imprint of the steering wheel on your forehead."

"I was . . . resting."

"Why can't you admit that you were tired?"

"I wasn't tired! I only got off at this exit because the car was making a funny noise."

"Really? What kind of noise?" Lottie was one of those people who actually knew something about cars; I couldn't even put air in my tires. I should have considered this when I was creating my excuse. What would be the least worrisome noise for a car to make? I wondered.

"A sort of thumping noise?" I tried.

Her face wrinkled. "Oooh. That could be bad."

"It was a very soft thump. It was probably nothing."

"Maybe I should look at it," Lottie said, unbuckling her seat belt.

"You're practically ready to deliver. You're not climbing under my car."

"I might as well take a look," she said. "I have to use the bathroom anyway."

"You have to go again? We stopped just thirty minutes ago."

"Cooper, I'm like ten months pregnant. I pretty much have to go all the time," she said. "Are you coming?"

"I'm coming. I want to get a Coke. But you're not fixing the car. If we hear the noise again once we get on the road, we'll take the next exit and find a mechanic."

She snorted. "Then you'll pay a fortune, when I could fix it for nothing."

"I don't care. Your husband would never forgive me if you

got stuck under my car and ended up having the baby in a gas station parking lot."

"You worry too much."

"One of us has to," I said. "You never worry about anything."

Chapter Six

GPS Meltdown

"I don't hear anything," Lottie said.

"See, I told you it was nothing."

As she shushed me and cocked her head, continuing to listen, I rolled my eyes and took a sip of my drink. *It would have been easier to just say I was sleepy,* I told myself.

"When did you hear it?" Lottie asked. "Were you braking?"

"No, I only heard it once. Maybe I hit a rabbit or something."

She narrowed her eyes. "Why do I get the feeling that you made up this mysterious thumping sound?"

"Why would I make up something like that?"

"Maybe so that you didn't have to explain why you really had pulled over."

"We should be getting close now," I said, ignoring her perceptive comment.

"Yeah, you should take that exit."

"We're not *that* close."

"The GPS on my phone says you should exit here," she argued as we drove past it.

"I printed off directions before we left. Besides, your GPS is not to be trusted."

"My GPS is fine!"

"Remember the time it told us that there was a Sonic Drive-In in that housing development?"

"One time," Lottie said. "One time my GPS is wrong, and now you think it wants to destroy your life. We're going the wrong way, anyway."

I frowned. "No, we're not."

"We are," she insisted. "The sun is the other way. I'm pregnant, and the baby needs sun."

"Patience, we'll get there."

"Not going this direction." She sighed deeply.

"What? What's wrong?" I asked.

"You're not going to start that again, are you?"

"See that sign?" I said, pointing triumphantly. "It says *Boise: 27 miles*."

Lottie sniffed. "I'm sure my exit would have gotten us there too."

"If we didn't have to be somewhere at a specific time, I'd go back just to prove you wrong."

"So, you're sure you still want to go?"

"Of course I am," I said, my voice sounding much more sure of this choice than I felt. But I had made my decision. I had no idea whether Justin would still be interested or whether he ever really had been. But, for once in my life, I was going to swallow my fear and ask for something that I wanted.

"Well, you better find a place for us to change our clothes," she said.

"We have a hotel room. We can change there."

"Okay, but I'm warning you: if we check in at the hotel, I'm not leaving again. Once I take these shoes off and put my puffy feet up, I'm in for the night."

I thought about that for a minute. "We'll change at the next gas station," I said.

"Wise choice."

Chapter Seven

Pit Stop

"Why are there so many people here?" Lottie asked. The lot's parking spots were all filled, and additional cars lined the curbs. "Is the world ending, and we missed the memo?"

"I'm not sure," I said as we pulled up to one of the gas pumps and I got out to fill up. Lottie managed to extract herself from the car and then stretched. I'd swear that her belly had gotten bigger in the last few hours.

When the tank was full, we took our dresses and headed inside. Suddenly, I remembered. "I know why this place is so packed," I said. "It's the Powerball. It's over a billion dollars now, and they're announcing the numbers tomorrow."

"Riiiight," Lottie said.

"Do you think we should get some tickets?" I asked.

"That depends. Do you have any money you'd like to throw away? Because, I'd be happy to take it."

"You can't win if you don't play," I said.

"You sound like a lottery spokesperson."

The line for tickets snaked around inside the store and ended outside the door, where the sun was making a valiant effort for mid-March. And, if I wasn't with a hugely pregnant lottery hater,

I probably would have bought a few tickets. For I'm one of those people who genuinely believes that I have a chance at winning. I understand that this is statistically ridiculous, but I think it's worth a few bucks to imagine for a couple of hours that I have a chance to become a billionaire, no matter how small that chance is.

We squeezed through the crowd of people, made our way to the bathroom, and changed. I did my best not to laugh when I saw Lottie standing in front of the tiny gas station mirror, pulling on her too short black shirt. She was attempting to make it long enough to meet the accompanying black skirt while frowning at her reflection. Obviously, she hadn't been joking when she had said that it didn't fit anymore. But I kept a straight face, mainly because I didn't want the next viewing we attended to be mine.

"You want to buy tickets, don't you?" she asked as she applied her lip gloss.

"We don't have time to wait in that line."

"But, you do want to buy them," she repeated.

I shrugged. "It's exciting. There's something in the air here. Can't you feel it?"

"The only thing I feel in the air here is mass desperation."

I smiled. "Not a gambler at heart, then?"

She snorted. "I'll hold on to the little money I have, thank you."

"But think about what a great story it would make—baby Lottie could be set for life."

"We're not naming her Lottie."

"Baby Sarah?"

"Don't press your luck, Cooper."

As we made our way back through the organized lines of people, we got some very interesting looks. One of the women in line, who was filling out her Powerball slips, did a double take when she saw us.

"You girls are a little overdressed," she said. "In fact, you look like you might be on your way to a . . ."

"Funeral," Lottie finished. "Yup. That's where we're going," she said, still tugging on her shirt.

The woman's face fell. "Oh, I'm so sorry. Family?"

"A friend," I said.

"That's too bad," she said. She was wearing two long strands of pearls: one with huge black globes, like caviar, and another in pastel shades, like fat jelly beans. She touched them absently, and I noticed how shiny they were, probably from being compulsively rubbed all day. I wondered if she even realized that she was doing it. But she kept staring at Lottie's stomach. "Do you mind if I touch your belly?" she said finally.

Lottie shrank back. "Why?"

"You know—for luck," she said.

Lottie hesitated. "That's . . . strange. And unlikely. But, I guess it couldn't hurt anything."

The woman patted Lottie's belly tentatively. "What are you having? No—let me guess. It's twins, isn't it?"

"Nope, just one."

"A boy, right?"

"It's a girl, actually," Lottie said. Despite her initial annoyance, I could tell that she was trying to keep a straight face at this point.

The woman looked disappointed. "Hmmm. Maybe this isn't my lucky day. I coulda sworn it was a boy."

"Well, ultrasounds have been wrong before," Lottie said. I wondered why she was bothering to humor the woman so much. I mean, Lottie had done some incredibly kind things for me over the years, but she wasn't exactly known for her patience.

The woman gave her a little smile. "Yeah, I guess it could still be a boy. You never know. What's your due date?"

"April 7."

"And what's your birthday?" the woman asked.

"November 22," Lottie said, looking mystified.

Try, Try Again

"What about you?" the woman asked, pointing to me.

"January 31," I said, noticing that the woman had used those numbers—1, 4, 7, 11, 22, and 31—to color in the little bubbles on one of her Powerball tickets.

"That one's a winner," she said as she began furiously rubbing the pearls again.

"Well, we better be going," I said.

"Good luck with your cards," Lottie told her.

"Good luck with your funeral," the woman said.

"She'll probably win," I said as we were getting into the car. "Then you'll wish we'd bought a ticket."

"If she wins, I'll show up on her doorstep with my newborn to demand my share," Lottie said.

Chapter Eight

Funeral Crashers

I glanced at the clock again. 4:35. The viewing would be over at 5:00, and we were still sitting in the car in the mortuary's parking lot.

"I hope that I didn't put on this outfit, which is slowly strangling me and my unborn child, for nothing," Lottie said, breaking the silence in the car.

"We're going in," I assured her. "I didn't want to be too early or look too eager." Even as these words were leaving my mouth, I realized how ridiculous they sounded.

"There's only twenty minutes left, Cooper. I think you've passed the *fashionably late* threshold an hour ago. But hey, it took you longer to back out of this plan than I had thought it would. You made it all the way to the parking lot."

"I'm not backing out," I said.

"Well, unless this guy is psychic and he somehow senses that you're out here, you're going to have to actually walk inside."

I glared at her. "I'm ready to go in any time. I was waiting for you."

"Waiting for me to what—go into labor? Because, at the rate we're going, my daughter will be speaking in full sentences before we get in there!"

Try, Try Again

"Come on," I said, opening the door to show Lottie I was serious. She raised her eyebrows and got out of the car.

As we entered the mortuary, I saw that it was small with only a tiny lobby and two viewing rooms. Tonight, only one of the viewing rooms was in use. *This is it,* I told myself. *No turning back now.* So I squared my shoulders and started walking toward the door. But Lottie didn't follow.

"Are you coming?" I whispered.

"Uh, no," she said.

"What? Why not?"

"I didn't even know him!" she said. "I'm here strictly for moral support. Plus . . ."

"Plus, what?" I demanded.

"I hate viewings," she confessed.

"I don't think anyone really enjoys them."

She squirmed a little. "I'm going to tell you a secret: I'm genuinely afraid of dead bodies."

For as long as I'd known Lottie, she had always been the brave one. Nothing ever scared her. So, for her to admit this, she must have been terrified.

"Well, I guess you never really know everything about a person, no matter how long you've been friends."

"Don't hate me," she begged, and I felt bad. Lottie had never begged for anything.

"It's totally fine. I'll go talk to Justin, and you stay out here," I said, steering her toward a plush looking chair. As she sat down and sort of sunk into it, I wondered if I'd ever get her out again without assistance.

"I gotta say that you're braver than I thought, Cooper."

"Bodies don't bother me."

"That's not what I meant."

I forced myself to smile before turning toward the door to face my fate. "Well, we're about to find out," I said under my breath.

Chapter Nine

Hello Again

There were more flowers in the viewing room than people. Some were funeral arrangements that you might order from a florist, but others were large potted plants. I didn't know much about greenery, but I did recognize the showy orchids in colors that I couldn't believe were natural. There was even a flat of plants sitting on a table that looked like early starts of tomatoes. So I took comfort in the fact that, if I chickened out once I got inside, all I needed to do was find a flower or plant cluster to hide behind until it was safe to bolt for the door.

As I entered the room, I spotted Justin right away. He was standing by an elderly woman, who must have been his grandmother. He was wearing a dark suit that looked new, his hair was shorter than I'd ever seen it, and his eyes were red. His grandmother put her hand on his arm and leaned closer to say something. Whatever she had said made him smile, and my heart melted. I'd missed that smile. Then a man walked up to Justin, and they shook hands, followed by an awkward hug.

Suddenly, I was struck by how terribly intimate this all was. I felt like an intruder and decided that I shouldn't be here. Of course, this was the moment that he turned in my direction and noticed me, so it was too late now to do anything about it. His eyes widened briefly, and he excused himself from the conversation and started toward me.

What am I going to say? I wondered. And, why hadn't I planned this out on the drive up here? All I could do now was take my cues from his behavior and hope that he didn't think it was inappropriate for me to be here as well.

"Sarah, I'm so . . . surprised to see you," he said, his voice halting.

That was inconclusive, I thought. *Surprised in a good way? Or surprised in a bad way? I am going to have to wing it.* "I noticed your last name in the obituaries online because I read the obituaries sometimes, well, at least once a week, so I guess it was luck that I happened to notice your last name, and I thought you might be related because Vaughn isn't such a common name, and I learned that I was right—it was your grandfather—so I thought I'd stop in and see how you were doing," I said in what might have been the longest run-on sentence in history.

"You could have come to see me next week, when I was five minutes away instead of five hours," he said.

He's annoyed that I'm here. I shouldn't have come, a voice in my head chided. "I'm sorry. I was going to be in Idaho anyway," I babbled, which *technically* could have been true, if Lottie's fondest dream for her last days of freedom was to travel to the potato state.

"I should go . . ." I began to say.

"Wait, I didn't mean to sound ungrateful," Justin said. "I'm glad you came. You just caught me off guard, that's all." He smiled, and the room seemed a little less threatening.

"It seemed like a good idea until I got in here, and then I realized how private it was. I've never had anyone close to me die, I guess."

"Really? You're lucky."

"Yeah, I guess I am. Well, I should go," I said again.

"Hey, this is almost over," Justin said. "Then we could talk, if you wouldn't mind waiting a few minutes."

"Sure. I'll be over there," I said, pointing to a few padded folding chairs lining the edge of the room.

"Okay," he said.

I sat down in one of the chairs and watched as Justin walked back to the man he had been talking to before. Together, the two of them went to the casket and looked inside while continuing their conversation. Then the woman who I'd assumed was Justin's grandmother came over and sat next to me.

"Thank you so much for coming. I haven't seen you in years," she said.

I smiled. "I don't think we've met before."

"We have, but you were probably too young to remember."

"I think you may have mistaken me for someone else," I said gently.

"Aren't you Kathy's daughter?" she asked, her brow wrinkling in confusion.

"I'm no relation. I'm Sarah—one of Justin's friends. I came here to see how he was doing," I explained.

She laughed. "Isn't that nice? You look just like Kathy, though. But I guess she was here a while ago, and her daughter too, now that I think about it. So she wouldn't be back again, would she?"

"Probably not," I said.

"I'm Justin's grandmother, but maybe you already guessed that. And that's my husband, Chester," she said, pointing to the coffin as though he might sit up any moment to shake my hand.

"It's very nice to meet you."

"You're sure you're not Kathy's daughter?" she asked again.

I started to wonder if we might still be having this conversation for the rest of my life or, at least, the rest of hers.

"I'm pretty sure. What beautiful flowers you have," I said, trying to change the subject.

"Those are Chester's flowers."

"He liked to garden?" I asked.

She nodded. "Those tulips came up in the yard a couple of days ago. In a week or two, there'll be millions of them, but these were the first. Everything else we brought in from the greenhouse."

"The orchids are amazing."

"Do you know about flowers?"

"Very little," I admitted.

"I only know a few of their names. To Chester, they were like family. He spent so many hours alone with his orchids and vegetables in the greenhouse that I wondered sometimes if he liked them better than he liked me. That's why we brought them all in—so he could say good-bye."

This idea, of bringing someone's plants to a viewing as guests instead of as props, made me teary-eyed. Luckily, this was the moment that Justin chose to reappear, before I started full-on blubbering.

"Justy, I want you to meet someone. This is Sarah," she said.

"I know, Gram. Sarah's my friend."

"That's right, she said that. Don't ever get old, dear," she said, patting my hand. "The mind is the first thing to go."

"Your mind is in great shape, Gram. You've just had a long day," Justin said.

"Maybe you're right. Would you like some tomatoes, Sarah?" she asked.

It took me a minute to figure out that she meant the plants I'd spotted earlier.

"She probably doesn't have a place to grow them . . ." Justin began to say.

"I'd love some tomatoes," I said.

She beamed, standing up more quickly than I'd have thought she could. "Let me get them for you," she said. "I'll be right back."

Justin gave me an amused look. "Tomatoes? Really?"

"Yes, *Justy,* tomatoes," I said teasingly.

His cheeks went pinkish. "She's always called me that, even though no one else ever has. You don't have to take them, you know."

"How do you say no to a woman who's just offered you the tomato plants that her deceased husband grew?"

"She's been giving away plants all night," he said. "You should have seen this room when we started. It was like a jungle."

This conversation felt a little more normal, like a chat we might have had in the bookstore. Then Justin's grandma returned with an entire flat of tomato starts, which I took awkwardly.

"Thank you so much," I said.

"My mom's going to take you home. Are you ready?" Justin asked her.

"I think so. But I need to tell your Grandpa good night first. It was lovely meeting you," she said, shaking my hand.

"Nice to meet you too," I said. Then she shuffled back toward the casket, and I watched as she proceeded to have a conversation with dearly departed Chester. Out of the corner of my eye, I noticed Justin watching me.

"That's sweet, isn't it?" I remarked.

"They've been married for fifty-five years. I don't know what she'll do without him around." Justin's voice sounded sad. "Let me tell my parents that I'm leaving, and then we can go," he said.

"I'll be in the lobby," I said.

Chapter Ten

Time Out

I found Lottie in the chair that I'd left her in, trying unsuccessfully to play a game on her phone without being too obvious. She finally glanced up and gave me a strange look.

"What?" I asked.

She nodded at my flat of tomatoes.

"Oh, these—they're a present from Justin's grandma," I said.

"I noticed other people walking out with plants. But I guess I'm not up on my funeral etiquette. Is that a thing now?"

"I doubt it. She thought I was someone else. But I think she liked me," I whispered excitedly.

"What about Justin? Does *he* like you?" she whispered back.

"I hope so. He says he wants to talk."

"What have you been doing in there all this time—braiding each other's hair?"

I rolled my eyes. "There were other people that he needed to visit with. And he was waiting for the viewing to be over. But he'll be out here any minute."

"That's awesome. I'm thrilled for you," she said. "I've only got one question."

"Yeah?"

"What am I supposed to do while you guys are getting reacquainted?"

Crap. I was going to have to alter my original plan. I couldn't exactly leave Lottie in this chair for the rest of the night while I flirted with Justin. (Just mild flirting, of course; the man was grieving, after all.)

Then Justin came out and smiled at Lottie. "Hey, did you find a friend?"

"This is Lottie, my best friend from college. She came with me on this little adventure," I explained. "I thought that maybe we could all go to dinner, if you're up for it," I said to Justin. *Please be up for it.*

"That sounds great," he said, and he even sounded sincere. I was grateful, given that I had sort of sprung it on him that he would be getting a two-for-one deal.

"You guys should go," Lottie said.

"Come on, it'll be fun," I said.

"No, really, I'm so tired, and my back hurts, and my feet hurt, and I'm so pregnant that I could cry," she said.

"You're pregnant?" Justin deadpanned.

Lottie laughed. "He's funny. I like him."

"Are you sure you don't want to go?" he asked Lottie. "I feel like I'm crashing your party."

"Believe me, the only party I'm attending tonight is the one in our hotel room in my pajamas," she said. "Just buy me a Big Mac on the way."

"You've got it," I said.

"But now, I'm going to need some help getting out of this chair," she said.

"May I?" Justin said, reaching for her arm.

"Thank you," she said. I took her other arm, and we both lifted Lottie to a standing position.

"That's much better. Ten more minutes, and I'm afraid that this chair would have swallowed me whole," she said, tugging on her shirt yet again.

"I like her. She's funny," Justin said. He held the door open for us, and we walked out into the rapidly chilling evening. "So, I'll follow you?" he added.

"We'll get checked in, and then I'll be ready to go," I said.

"It was nice to meet you, Lottie," he said.

"Very nice to meet you too. I'm sorry about your grandpa," she said.

He nodded. "Thanks. See you in a minute."

As we got into the car, I let out a huge sigh. "Thank you. You're the best," I said.

She wrestled the seat belt down over her huge belly, saying, "You owe me, Cooper."

"I do. I totally do."

"You'd better marry this guy," she added, "or, at least, bring me back something decent for dessert."

Chapter Eleven

Table for Two

"So, where should we go?" Justin asked as I was climbing into his car.

"I'm good with whatever. We don't even have to go out if you don't feel like it. I'm sure you've had a long day."

"I am tired," he admitted. "But I'm also starving."

"Okay, you pick."

"You can pick."

"You're the hungriest."

"But you drove all this way," he argued.

"Just choose something!"

Justin laughed. "Did you know that where to eat is the thing that couples fight about the most?"

"I thought couples fought about money the most."

"No, choosing a restaurant. I read a survey."

"We're not a couple, though."

He looked right into my eyes without flinching and said, "We could have been."

I couldn't meet his gaze, and I felt the heat rising in my face. I had expected this topic, but not two minutes after we started talking. "Let's go to Costa Vida," I said, pointing to a sign in the distance.

"See, now I know how to get you to choose where to eat—bring up something that you don't want to talk about," he said. He seemed to be joking, but his eyes were kind.

"You're the one who's starving. Eating first, talking later."

"Fair enough," he said.

It was quiet as we pulled into the restaurant and parked the car. Maybe Justin had taken me literally and wasn't going to attempt to speak to me again until there was food in front of us. As he held the door for me, I was greeted with the comforting smells of Mexican food.

I was probably crazy to have shown up at the viewing. But I'd always regretted how we had parted and had thought about what might have happened if, after he'd kissed me that night in the bookstore, I hadn't pushed him away. This was what I'd wanted for months—to finally know if I'd made a mistake, to get closure . . . or, perhaps, to start something entirely different. Still, I couldn't help but be a little jealous of Lottie, who was snug in bed in our hotel room, eating McDonald's and watching cable TV.

We ordered and then took our food on trays to a table.

"So . . ." Justin said.

"So." Was he really going to launch immediately into an interrogation again?

"That's a huge burrito," he said, pointing to the overflowing pan in front of me.

It was all that I could do to not sigh out loud in relief. "Those nachos of yours aren't exactly tiny either."

"This is funny."

"What's funny?"

"Us, having dinner together four hundred miles away from home when I haven't even really talked to you lately. If someone had asked me this morning what I thought I'd be doing tonight after the viewing, this would have been the last thing that I could have imagined." As he scooped up a pile of sour cream with one of his chips and ate it quickly, I tried to think of something to say.

"Why are you here, Sarah?" he asked.

I'd forgotten how direct Justin could be until now. But I should have known that he wasn't going to settle for polite chitchat. *I am not going to make the same mistake as I did in the bookstore six months ago, though,* I thought. I didn't know if he still felt the same way about me, but I'd had plenty of time now to consider my own feelings. And I wasn't going to let him hijack the conversation again.

"Tell me about your grandpa," I said.

He paused, staring at me for a minute. His face was blank, and I wondered if he was about to drop another bombshell on me. I knew that he still wanted to talk about why I was here and what had changed my mind. But, in the end, he must have decided to humor me and roll with it.

Chapter Twelve

Chester Vaughn, We Hardly Knew Ye

"What do you want to know?" Justin asked.

"What was special about him?" I asked, taking a bite of my giant burrito. I knew that ignoring his question about why I was really here, at least for the present, might end up okay or might backfire spectacularly. I could only hope that I knew what I was doing.

He stopped eating, and his face crunched up for a minute. I was afraid that he was going to cry. Suddenly, talking about our non-relationship seemed infinitely less frightening. But he quickly recovered his composure, distracting himself by distributing salsa onto the mountain of nachos before him.

"He was a great guy: funny—much funnier when he wasn't trying to be. He knew a million corny jokes that you couldn't help but laugh at, even though they were terrible. He loved gardening, and he loved gambling."

"You didn't mention Grandma in that list," I said.

"He loved her too, but she was farther down the list, I think. He usually spent all day in the yard when it was warm enough and several hours in the greenhouse when it wasn't. He'd bet on anything. And, when there wasn't something to bet on, he'd make things up: which plant would come up first, what Grandma would cook for dinner, whether my sister was having a boy or a girl . . ."

I laughed. "He sounds like a character."

"He was. The gambling used to drive my grandma crazy. Back when slot machines ran on coins, I remember that there was always a big plastic cup, full of nickels from one of the casinos, in their kitchen. This was before they moved to Idaho—they used to live five minutes away from my house when I was growing up. He went to Wendover whenever he got a chance, but the level of the coins never seemed to change. He always used to say that he was the luckiest gambler in the world."

"Because he won a lot?" I asked.

Justin shook his head. "Because he never lost and never won; he always broke even. He said that all the time. I told Grandma that she should have had *that* engraved on his tombstone. Everyone else thought it was funny, but she didn't laugh."

"Did she mind?" I asked. "Not being first in his life, I mean."

"If she did, she never said so. She seemed happy just to take care of him. He loved his plants, and she loved him, I guess." Justin stopped for a minute, as if remembering something. Then he laughed.

"What?" I asked.

It took a minute before he could stop laughing enough to tell me. "I drove him to Wendover once—I was barely legal, I think. By then, hardly any of the casinos had machines that took coins anymore. But he sat in the passenger seat with his big cup of coins in his lap all the way there. He said that he had to bring them for luck. When we got there, he lugged his coins inside, gave me twenty dollars, and told me to have a good time. I added that to the twenty bucks I had brought with me. And, in an hour, I was broke."

"Oh no. What did you do?"

He kept laughing. "Nothing. I didn't even have enough for

the buffet, which would have at least killed a couple of hours. So I bought a bag of chips and a soda and found somewhere to hang out until he was ready to go."

"How long was that?"

"Hours. All day. I was bored to death. When he finally found me, he was still lugging around the same cup of coins, and he couldn't understand why I wasn't having fun."

"That's a great story," I said. "You must have some wonderful memories of him."

"I do. Thank you for reminding me. I wish I could tell him one more time how great he was."

Justin's nachos were gone by now, and he was looking teary-eyed again. But I was losing ground with the giant burrito.

"Well, I don't think I'd be able to finish this if we sat here all night," I said. "And I don't want to keep you out too late. You've got another long day tomorrow, and I'm sure that you will want to get some sleep."

"But we were going to talk about why you're here, remember?"

"I was worried about you," I said. "I wanted to make sure you were okay. We used to be good friends, and I miss that."

"Is that all you want to be?" he asked. "Friends?"

Still not feeling ready for this conversation, I said, "I just had the best idea."

He rolled his eyes. "You're really going to keep dodging this, aren't you?"

"No. Listen, you said that you wished you could tell your grandpa one more time how much he means to you. Well, I just thought of a great way for you to remember him."

He looked curious as he asked, "How?"

I stood up and said, "Follow me."

Chapter Thirteen

Lottery Tickets

"Turn in here," I instructed.

"Uh, what are we doing at the gas station?" Justin asked.

"Did you know that the Powerball jackpot is over a billion dollars right now? It's a record amount, and they're drawing it tomorrow."

Recognition seemed to dawn on his face. "Lottery tickets! What a great idea. You're right—Grandpa would love that."

"It's a long line, though," I said. The crowd of people had now spread from the sidewalk in front of the store into the parking lot.

Justin smiled. "I don't mind if you don't."

"My friend and I stopped here to change our clothes on our way into town, and I actually had wanted to buy some tickets then. But it was getting late, and Lottie gave me a hard time about what a waste of money it was."

"But that's the fun part!" Justin said. "I don't really think I'm going to win, but imagining what I'd do with the money if I did is the best."

"EXACTLY! I tried to explain that to her, but she takes practicality to a new extreme."

Try, Try Again

"I'm really glad that you came, Sarah," Justin said. "If you weren't here, I'd probably be at my grandma's house, moping."

"I'm glad that I came too," I said. And I was, even if I still wasn't sure what I'd do about our unfinished conversation.

"Shall we?" he asked.

As he stuck his hand out, I tentatively took it, and the warmth spread from his fingers into my own, traveling up through my arm, making me feel pleasantly buzzed. I told myself that just because I now held his hand, this didn't mean that we were betrothed or anything. There was plenty of time to figure all that out later.

So we joined the line at the back. Down the line, people were passing slips to fill out numbers on, and there was almost a party atmosphere. It had been a warmish day, but now that the sun was down, the temperature was dropping rapidly. I was wearing a jacket, but I now wished I had a heavy coat instead.

I noticed a man by the door with some kind of animal, but we were still far enough away that it was impossible to tell what it was.

"What is that?" I said, pointing toward the ball of fur.

Justin squinted. "I can't tell, but I think it's on a leash. Dog, I guess."

As the line moved slowly forward, Justin told me how his grandfather used to take him to the gas station and let him fill a fountain drink, mixing all the flavors together. I wrinkled my nose up. "That sounds disgusting," I commented.

"It was disgusting," he said laughing. "But that was part of the appeal as a kid, I think. I felt like a mad scientist."

When we got close enough, I could see that the animal by the door had a striped tail.

"Is that a raccoon?" I asked.

"What? No. It couldn't be. Who keeps a raccoon on a leash?"

"Well, what kind of a dog has a striped tail?"

As the line moved forward again, it became apparent I was

right. There, sitting by the door, looking bored, was the biggest raccoon I'd ever seen. Well, the only raccoon I'd ever seen, in person anyway. But it was huge.

"Pardon me, but is that a raccoon?" I asked the man holding the leash.

"Yep," the man said.

"He's so cute! I've never seen a raccoon on a leash before. Is he friendly?" I asked.

"Sometimes," the man said.

"Can I pet him?" I asked, my hand already halfway extended.

"I wouldn't," the man quickly said.

Justin made a sound that was halfway between a laugh and a cough as I shrank back.

"Okay. Sorry," I said, turning back to face Justin.

"He likes hot dogs," the man offered.

"Does he?" I said politely back, noticing that Justin was suppressing further laughter.

"They have hot dogs in there," the man continued.

"Good to know," I replied. I was beginning to wish I'd never commented on the raccoon in the first place.

"I like hot dogs too," the man persisted.

"Well, who doesn't?" I finally said. At this point, I was afraid that Justin was going to hurt himself by trying so hard not to laugh. "Well, I guess we'll . . . see you later," I said to the man.

He brightened a little. "Okay. We'll be here."

Once we got inside, Justin howled with laughter. "I think you made a new friend," he said when he could finally talk again.

"Who? The man or the raccoon?" I asked dryly.

This set him off laughing again.

"How many tickets do you want?" I asked him.

"How many hot dogs do you want?" he asked.

Now I was the one who couldn't stop laughing, and every time that I thought I had it under control and that it was safe to look at Justin again, he'd bust up, and then I'd start laughing all over again too.

"Okay," I sputtered. "At this rate, we're never going to have these slips ready."

"I know, I know," he said.

"How many are you getting?"

"Maybe five? That's ten bucks, right?" he asked.

"Yeah. I think I'll get five too."

Except for the old country music and the surrounding chatter in the background, it seemed quiet for a minute while we filled in the number bubbles on our cards. The quantity of people crowding together in the small gas station made it feel uncomfortably warm, so I took off my jacket and tied it around my waist.

"If you win, what would you buy?" I said when I had finished choosing my numbers.

"What would I buy with a billion dollars?" Justin said, half laughing.

"Yes! This is the fun part, remember?"

"Hmmm. Okay. Well, first, I'd pay off the house for my grandmother. She isn't planning on staying there because she can't keep up with the yard and she doesn't want to see it get run-down. But, if I had a billion dollars, I could hire a maid and a groundskeeper for her. Then she wouldn't have to lift a finger."

"That's very generous."

"Thank you," he said.

"What else?"

"Uh, I'd pay off my parents' mortgage and send them on a nice trip for putting up with me all these years."

I laughed. "What else?"

"I'd make sure that my niece had enough money to go to college wherever she wanted."

"I'm pretty sure that you don't have a niece that's college age."

"She's two," he admitted with a smile. "But it's never too early to start saving. And I'd buy my sister a big, shiny black truck—she always wanted one."

"Very good choices," I said. "But someone is missing on that list."

"Oh, I'm sorry—what did you want?"

I smacked him playfully in the arm. "Not me, silly! You. What would you buy for yourself?"

He shrugged. "If I'm getting a billion dollars, I'm sure there would be plenty left over for me once I've taken care of my family."

"You don't really get a billion dollars, you know. Lots of it goes straight to taxes, so it's really only like eight hundred million," I said.

"Well, that changes my wish list drastically," he joked. "I'm going to have to cut back on some of the grander dreams."

"Yes. You can't have it all, even when you win the jackpot. But you have to tell me at least one thing that you want for yourself," I said.

"A purebred sheepdog," he said.

"Because you're worried about your sheep wandering off?"

He laughed. "Because they're loyal."

"That makes sense."

"What about you? What's on your list?" he asked.

"The first thing I would buy is a home for that raccoon."

"What makes you think he doesn't have a home already?"

"No, his *own* home: With the deed in his name. And a refrigerator full of hot dogs."

"He's going to be one lucky raccoon."

"But I won't win . . ." I began to say.

"Ssssh, don't say it," Justin said, putting his finger on my lips.

As he did so, I jumped. I hadn't meant to, but this action was just so unexpected. It was still plenty warm in the gas station, but goose bumps spread now across my arms.

"I'm sorry," he said, moving his hand quickly away.

"Don't be. Your hands are cold; that's all," I lied.

"Grandpa always said, 'Whether you think good things will happen to you or they won't, the universe will somehow sense this and make it happen,'" Justin said.

"Okay, then, I guess we're going to win." Our place in line had reached the hot dog station, and I started loading one up with relish and mustard and onions.

"Are you hungry *again*?" Justin asked, grinning.

"Ha ha. This is for my new friend."

"I'm not sure if raccoons like all that stuff," he said.

"This one is for the guy holding the leash," I said, then put another hot dog into a bun, placing it in a red checkered paper tray, leaving it naked. "That one's for the raccoon."

Chapter Fourteen

Raccoon Man

"You're still here!" I said happily as we went back outside.

"I told you we would be," the man said. The raccoon said nothing, of course, but I'd like to think that I saw a hint of recognition on his face.

"These are for you," I said, handing him the two paper trays while Justin watched in amusement.

"That was awfully kind of you," the man said. "He's going to be so excited; he loves relish." He put the loaded hot dog down on the ground in front of the raccoon and then took a big bite of the plain one. "Look, Calvin—dinnertime."

"Your raccoon's name is Calvin?" Justin asked.

"Yep."

The raccoon picked up one end of the hot dog daintily with his little gloved paws and nibbled at it. But the tray kept moving, and he was having a hard time staying on top of his meal. So I crouched down, thinking that I could try to hold it still for him. I got within inches of the tray, when he suddenly growled loudly at me. I jumped back, and Justin grabbed my arm, pulling me away.

"He roars like a lion," I said, my heart hammering in my chest as I imagined just how close I'd come to spending the night in the ER, getting rabies shots.

Try, Try Again

"He didn't mean anything by it," the man said. "Hot dogs are just his favorite thing. He wouldn't have hurt you unless you had tried to take it away. Really, he's a big teddy bear," the man whispered, as though he were worried that the raccoon might overhear and become offended at the loss of his tough-guy reputation.

"Sure he is," I said. Now that the immediate threat was gone, the raccoon had gone back to his treat, licking the relish methodically from his paws. I probably could have enjoyed watching him eat it all night, but I was beginning to feel like we were interrupting their meal.

"Well, we've gotta get going," I said. "Good night."

"Thanks so much for the hot dogs," the man mumbled. "Sorry Calvin scared you."

"No problem," I said.

We walked out and got into Justin's truck. I'd bought Lottie a pint of Chocolate Fudge Brownie Ben & Jerry's, but I'd been holding it in line for a while, so it was starting to feel soft already. There was a cup holder between us, so I wedged the pint into it.

"Did you see the way that guy was wolfing down that hot dog? I should have bought him more," I said. "But I didn't want it to seem patronizing. Do you think he's homeless?"

"Maybe they just like hanging out at the gas station, bumming hot dogs, and scaring innocent bystanders," Justin said.

I laughed. "I hope so."

Justin was quiet for a minute as he drove me back toward my hotel. Then he said, "My grandfather's middle name was Calvin."

I gasped. "That's right! I saw it in the obituary. Do you believe in reincarnation?"

Justin snorted. "No, I don't think so. I mean, I think there's something after this life, but not *that*."

"But maybe it's a sign—your grandfather wanting you to know that everything is okay and that he's happy," I persisted.

Justin smiled, but his eyes seemed sad. "It's quite a coincidence, but I'm not sure I'd say it was a sign."

I smiled back at him.

"Anyway, my grandfather hated hot dogs," he continued, and I laughed. And then things seemed better again.

Chapter Fifteen

A Perfect Kiss

"Well, thank you for dinner. It was a great night, and I'm really glad I came," I said. We were sitting in his truck in the hotel parking lot, and despite being exceptionally brave all day, I had now reached the point where I was all out of bravery.

Justin stared back at me in disbelief. "Oh, no. You've been putting me off all night, and now you have to tell me the truth."

"All right, you win," I said. "The truth is that if I win the Powerball, I'd buy a massage chair for myself. Don't judge me."

He glared back at me, undeterred.

"I'm sorry. When I get nervous, I make jokes," I said.

"I know that. I know you better than you think," he said, his face softening. "And you don't have to be nervous; I'm not the IRS. I just want to know why."

"Why what?"

"You know exactly what I mean," he said. "I went out on a major limb and told you that I'd decided you were perfect for me, and all you could do was back away as if I'd admitted I liked dressing up as a clown in my spare time."

"You'd barely broken up with Julia," I said. "So it was terrible timing, and I didn't want to be your rebound girl when you couldn't possibly have known yet what you wanted."

"That's *why* I broke up with Julia in the first place—she was great, and I liked her a lot, but something was missing—she wasn't you," he said simply.

I shook my head as I realized my mistake. My plans for getting closure or a second chance were all unraveling. "No. See, this isn't a good time for you to be making decisions either: You're upset about your grandpa. And I promise that I meant well, but I shouldn't have come. I'm sorry," I said and got out of the truck with my melting pint of ice cream and headed toward the hotel lobby door. Then I heard the other truck door open and then close behind me as Justin ran after me. Suddenly, his hand was on my shoulder, spinning me around.

"No, not this time," he said. "I told myself that if I ever had another chance, I would try harder to convince you. I won't let you go without telling you everything."

I was going to cry now, I could tell, which was stupid, given that I wasn't the one dealing with a loss. "I'm sorry," I repeated.

"Why? What are you sorry for? For coming? For playing with me when you obviously had no intention of following through?"

"I don't know," I said too loudly.

"That's the first honest thing you've said to me about this all night. You don't know what you want. You didn't know before, and you still don't know now. I thought, when I saw you walk into the viewing today, that *maybe* you'd finally figured it out. But I guess I was wrong." He took a step back and then another.

"I came because I was worried about you."

"Not good enough," he said, turning to walk back to his truck.

"I came because it was a good excuse to see you again," I called after him.

"Why did you want to see me?" he asked, turning back to face me.

"Because we're friends . . . and I missed you when you quit the bookstore."

"I had to quit," he said, taking a step forward and lowering his voice. "I couldn't stay there and see you every day, knowing that you weren't interested."

"But I *was* interested. You kissed me out of nowhere and caught me completely off guard. I thought that you would give it some time—I thought it would be good for both of us . . . Why didn't you ever ask me again?" I finally said. There were tears on my face now, and I felt guilty about that. I wished that I could have waited to cry until later because now it just felt like one more way that I was manipulating Justin.

"Because every time I looked at you, you seemed wary—like an animal in a trap."

"It must have been my desperation you saw. I wanted you to ask me again, but I didn't know how to tell you . . . Then I thought you'd changed your mind," I said lamely, looking down at my hands.

Justin stepped closer, lifting my chin to look into my eyes. "And I was sure that you hadn't changed your mind. So, why bother asking? I guess communication isn't our strongpoint," he said, smiling bitterly, placing his hands on my shoulders. "I thought we were getting past that. But here we are, right back where we started."

"Well, I'm the one who jumped in with both feet this time. But I didn't think it through, and it isn't the right time," I said.

"There will never be a *right time*, Sarah. Sometimes you have to take a chance."

I felt like I'd done this all wrong now. But, here he was, still interested.

"Is that why you came today?" he asked. "Are you ready to take a chance?"

"You're not ready," I said.

But he shook his head. "I was ready six months ago. You're the one who's been dragging your feet."

"I probably shouldn't have come. It wasn't fair to you."

"Don't you get it? I was thrilled when I saw you. That is the part that isn't fair."

I was doing it again. Justin probably understood why I panicked before, but this was different. I had initiated this. But I had the feeling that if I stepped back now, he'd never trust me again. How could I make him understand what I'd been thinking all this time?

I sighed. "I was so jealous of Julia," I admitted. "So, when you broke up with her and wanted us to be a couple, I should have been ecstatic. Instead, I panicked because I believed that good things couldn't happen to me. But I'm tired of letting go of good things in my life because I don't believe they're possible. I'm tired of being afraid of happiness."

"What are you saying?" Justin asked hoarsely.

I took a deep breath. "I'm saying, I choose you."

He was stone-faced for one terrible moment before breaking into an impossibly sunny grin. "I chose you first," he said playfully.

So I leaned in and pecked his lips quickly before he could argue his point further.

"Hey, I was supposed to do that," he said.

"I know. But I'm making up for lost opportunities."

Justin was still smiling as he leaned in, pressing his lips against mine. As he kissed me, I closed my eyes. I could smell what was left of his cologne, and my brain wanted to catalog it forever, so I breathed in more deeply. Then he wrapped his arms around me, his fingers gently caressing the back of my neck. I shivered in response, although I wasn't sure whether to blame this on the kiss or on the increasingly cold night.

But he rubbed my arms, asking, "Are you cold?"

I smiled shyly. "Maybe. Or maybe you're just a good kisser."

"I could try again if you're not sure," he teased.

He leaned in again, pressing his lips against mine, pulling me closer to him, and our kisses deepened, until everything around us fell away. There was nothing but his lips and my lips; I was beginning to feel fuzzy on why I'd ever pushed Justin away in the first place.

"I should go inside," I said, pulling away reluctantly. "You need to get some sleep."

"Come tomorrow," he suggested, "to the funeral."

"I can't. I promised Lottie a super fun road trip, and she's been such a good sport about letting me hang out with you instead. Besides, I'm afraid she's going to have her baby any minute now."

Justin laughed.

"Anyway, you're going to be so busy with your family tomorrow, you won't even miss me."

"Wanna bet?"

"But, as soon as you get home, I'd love to see you," I said.

"Well, let's see. Which night are you available?"

"All the nights."

"This sounds promising."

"*Promising* is the perfect word for it. I can't guarantee anything, but I do like you a lot," I said and ran my thumb across the scruff on his chin. "I know I'm late to this party. But, you know how sometimes you have the epiphany that you've met the person you want to be with forever?"

Justin smiled and then made a face like he was thinking hard. "It's strange, but I feel like I've heard those words somewhere before."

"I heard someone wise say that once, and it stuck with me."

"But that sounds like something that would only happen to a really lucky person."

"Maybe my luck is changing," I said.

He brushed the hair back from my face and then said, "Sometimes we make our own luck."

I wasn't sure I believed that, but I knew I wanted to and I was done second-guessing this. I stood on tiptoes and started to kiss him slowly, deliberately. I wanted him to know that I meant this, and I felt myself melting into his embrace. Justin didn't seem like he was in a rush either, as he had six months ago in the bookstore. This kiss was the kind that felt like it might be building to something more permanent.

I began to think to myself that things actually seemed to be going rather well this time. Then he suddenly began to laugh.

I frowned and pulled away slightly. "What?"

"You know, everyone is going to think I've lost my mind tomorrow," Justin said.

"Why?"

"I'm so happy, and it's not really cool to be walking around at a funeral with a silly grin on your face."

"I'm sure you'll be plenty sad tomorrow."

"Yeah, you're right. But, if anyone had told me yesterday that today would end up being a great day, I'd probably have punched them."

"I still feel like I sort of put you on the spot," I said.

"And I'm grateful you did."

"But . . ." I began to say.

But Justin planted his lips on mine again, this time to keep me from arguing. As he ran his fingers through my hair, I shivered again.

He pulled back again and pointed to the ice cream. "You're probably freezing, and I'm sure that holding this doesn't help. You better get inside so that your friend can eat it before she needs a straw."

I shook the pint tentatively, and it sloshed around. "I'm afraid it's too late."

Chapter Sixteen

Next Stop . . .

I used the key card to let myself into the hotel room, hoping that Lottie would already be asleep.

But she wasn't. Between the pillows on her bed and the ones she'd brought with her and the ones she'd stolen from my bed, she'd made herself a sort of nest. The blue light from the television in the dark room gave her an eerie glow.

"You look . . . comfy," I commented.

"It's almost eleven, Cooper. I was getting ready to call the police and report you missing."

"I'm sorry that I left you alone all night. I feel like a bad friend."

"I'm a big girl, I can handle it," she said, but she shot me an evil grin. "I'm guessing that it went well."

I ignored her comment and said, "I brought you something."

She took this bait, my possible new romance being temporarily forgotten. "I hope it's edible."

"Of course," I said, handing her the soggy pint of ice cream.

She frowned. "It looks like ice cream but it feels . . . wrong."

I ducked my head guiltily. "I think it's melted. But I meant well!"

She rolled her eyes. "Did you get distracted by something shiny?"

"No."

Lottie gave me a look.

"Maybe," I admitted. "We talked for a long time."

"*Just* talking?"

"There may have been some other stuff."

"I knew it," she crowed. "I knew that he liked you. Tell me everything."

"You better eat that first," I said.

"Why? It's not like it's going to get more melted." But she carefully took off the lid and drank the liquid part. Then she attacked what was semi-solid in the middle with a plastic spoon while I told her about my evening with Justin.

"Of course you went back to buy Powerball tickets. I knew you would," she said when I had finished.

"You did not know. I didn't plan it—it's because he told me about how his grandpa loved to gamble!" I explained. "Were the Powerball tickets really what stood out most to you in that story?"

"What? You mean the kissing?" she said while scraping the bottom of the pint with her spoon.

"How can you sound so casual about it? I guess kissing isn't any big deal for married people who know they have someone to smooch any time they want."

"Yes, my life could be a romance novel," Lottie said sarcastically. "I didn't mean that it wasn't worth mentioning but that it's not like you haven't kissed him before."

I froze. I had never admitted to Lottie, or to anyone else, the way that Justin and I had kissed inside the bookstore.

"What are you talking about?" I asked.

Lottie set the empty carton on the nightstand and then folded her arms across her chest. "This isn't the first time you've kissed Justin, is it?"

"Why would you say that?"

"I can tell," she said.

"How can you tell?"

"I can tell just by looking at two people whether they've ever kissed before," she said. "The minute I saw you two together at the mortuary, I knew."

"How could you possibly know that? What are you—some kind of sorceress?" I demanded.

She smirked. "No. But your answers confirm my suspicions."

"Why do I always fall into these traps with you?"

"I am your kryptonite," she said. "So, you really like him, don't you?"

"Yeah, I think so."

"So why did you stop kissing him until now?"

"We had only kissed once before," I admitted. "He'd just broken up with someone. It's a long story."

Lottie settled back into her pillow nest. "Good, you can tell me tomorrow on the long drive to whatever super fun location we're headed to."

Maybe now wasn't the best time to tell her that there were no concrete plans for the rest of the weekend. "Lottie . . ." I began to say.

"It's okay," she said, interrupting me. "I already know where we're going. But I didn't want to ruin your surprise."

Her eyes were closed, and I smiled. "Where do you think we're going?"

"Hawaii."

I laughed. "I can't *drive* you to Hawaii."

"Then we'll fly. You owe me, Cooper."

"You're too pregnant to fly," I said. "They'd take one look at you and laugh you off the plane."

She sighed, her eyes still closed. "You're probably right. But, once I have this baby, you're taking me to Hawaii."

"Don't you think your husband might object to you taking off and leaving him with a newborn?"

"He's the reason I'm in this predicament in the first place," she said. "He owes me too."

"Okay, I'll start saving up."

"So, tomorrow, while we have our giant breakfast . . ." she started.

"We're having a giant breakfast?" I asked, interrupting her.

"No good driving on an empty stomach," she said. "Besides, the best road trips involve giant breakfasts. And, while we're stuffing ourselves, you can tell me all about Justin and about where you're going to find some sun to plant me in."

I hesitated for a moment.

"There isn't anything fun planned tomorrow, is there?" she said. "You only said that to get me into the car. Do you think this was how I wanted to spend my last days as a free woman—trapped in a tiny car for hours so that you could . . . drool over a boy?" she demanded, but her voice was much less angry than I'd expected.

"Of course there's something planned tomorrow!" I said quickly.

Luckily she'd fallen asleep, buying me some time. So I plugged my phone in to charge and started searching for a nearby location with something to make a hormonal pregnant woman happy.

Chapter Seventeen

One Week Later

"So, did Lottie have her baby yet?" Justin asked, caressing the back of my hand with his fingertips.

I shook my head and smiled. "She's still got about three weeks left."

"Seriously? I thought she was two weeks overdue."

I laughed. "I won't tell her you said that." I couldn't believe that we were sitting in the bookstore at the table by the window on our first official date.

"And, what did you end up doing for the rest of your super fun road trip?" he asked, taking a sip of his mocha.

"Lottie wanted to go to the beach and get some sun, so we drove to Portland," I said.

Justin nearly spat out his drink. "Uh, there isn't exactly *beach* weather in Portland right now."

"I know. So we walked on the sand with our jackets and an umbrella that was too small, and it rained the whole time. But at least she can't say that it wasn't memorable."

"You're a good friend," he said, giving my hand a gentle squeeze.

"Don't tell Lottie that. She still hasn't forgiven me."

Justin looked from side to side before speaking in a low,

conspiratorial voice. "You know, I always wanted to kiss you in here." He brushed my hair back from my face.

"You did kiss me in here," I said, smiling. As I met his gaze, I felt the heat rising in my face. "Should I be worried about your memory?"

"I meant that I wanted to kiss you here when you would be happy about it."

"I was happy about it the first time," I said, slipping my hand into his, intertwining our fingers.

"I'm pretty sure that you weren't," he protested playfully.

"I learned that *you* had broken up with Julia, and then, ten minutes later, you were kissing me. I felt a little overwhelmed."

"The way you brushed me off, I thought that I'd blown it with you for sure," Justin shook his head wistfully.

"I didn't brush you off," I assured him. "I had only wanted you to take a minute to think about if I was really what you wanted."

"I knew you were what I wanted as soon as I met you. It just took me a while to decide to make it happen."

"Not as long as it took me," I said with a smile.

"I won't argue with you there," he said playfully, finishing his drink. "But at least you came around." Then, as he fixed his intent gaze on me again, his tone became more serious. "No matter what happens, Sarah, I'll remember that forever—you, showing up at the viewing. I think the last time I was *that* happy to see someone was when I was in second grade and my mom was an hour late to pick me up one day."

"That happened to me once," I said, remembering. "My dad was all apologies when he showed up. But I wasn't happy to see him—I was angry," I admitted.

"Really?" Justin asked, his concern evident.

"Yeah, my parents got divorced when I was five," I explained, looking down at our hands. "I think that, for a while, I was mad about everything."

"I never knew that about you."

"There's probably lots of things we don't know about each other," I said, meeting his gaze again. "But, I do know something about you now," I added mischievously to change the subject back to us.

"What?" he asked, smiling.

"You like kissing girls in bookstores."

"Not *girls*—plural—just you."

"Oh, good," I said, in a mock relieved tone. But really, I was relieved. As I gazed into his eyes, I thought about how I wanted to be the only girl that Justin would be kissing for the foreseeable future.

Then Justin leaned over, whispering against my neck, "Does that sound like something you might be interested in doing again?"

Goose bumps spread across my arms. "Here's what's going to happen," I whispered back playfully. "Give me a one-minute head start, and I'll hide somewhere. When you find me, kiss me breathless. I promise to be very happy about it this time. Deal?"

"Deal," he said. He looked so excited at the prospect, it was almost comical.

So I stood quickly and wandered off to find a good hiding place—but not too good—after all, I wanted to be found this time.

About Aubrey Mace

Aubrey Mace lives in Sandy, Utah. She attended LDS Business College and Utah State University. Aubrey has three published novels: *Spare Change,* which won a Whitney Award for Best Romance, *My Fairy Grandmother,* and *Santa Maybe*, which was nominated for a Whitney Award for Best Romance.

When she isn't at her day job or writing, Aubrey enjoys cooking, gardening, traveling, and spending time with her family. She likes dark chocolate, birds, and British comedy; the order of preference changes, depending on the day.

Website: www.AubreyMace.com
Twitter: @AubreyMace
Facebook: Aubrey Mace

More Timeless Romance Anthologies

For the latest updates on our anthologies, visit our blog:
TimelessRomanceAnthologies.blogspot.com

www.ingramcontent.com/pod-product-compliance
Lightning Source LLC
LaVergne TN
LVHW021756060526
838201LV00058B/3123